GIRL UNDER GLASS

MONICA ENDERLE PIERCE

GOLDEN FLOWER

STORIES THAT STAY WITH YOU

Text Copyright © 2012 Monica Enderle Pierce
Cover Illustration Copyright © 2017 Qistina Khalidah
Copy Editor Jim Thomsen
Cover Design by Scott Pierce
Book Design by Monica Enderle Pierce
Created with Vellum
ISBN-10: 098597611X
ISBN-13: 978-0985976118

"Amazing Grace" lyrics by John Newton, 1779 (public domain)

Description: Equal parts science fiction, suspense, and romance, Girl Under Glass moves from a post-apocalyptic wilderness in the American Pacific Northwest to a high-tech world aboard an alien starship furnished with all the stolen comforts of Earth. Readers meet Rachel Pryne, whose parents' lifelong and life-ending connection to the Ohnenrai has set her upon a path she never wanted to travel. And they're introduced to Ehtishem, an Ohnenrai soldier who exists to save his dying people, but who faces enemies inside and outside of his own military.
The only possible solution to the Ohnenrai's extinction lies within Rachel, but all she wants to do is protect her daughter and see Earth's alien conquerors go straight to hell.

To Scott for teaching me to think, "How can I?" instead of "I can't."
To Emeline for being my precious pearl.
To Mom for believing in me.
To Dad for never accepting my excuses.
And to Kevin and Brian for challenging me.

GIRL UNDER GLASS

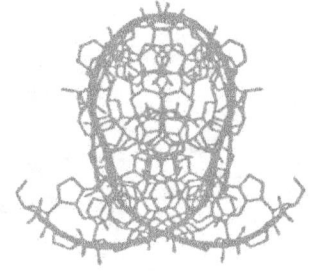

PART ONE
CELL

ONE

THE DOGS GROWLED.

I glanced to where they sat beside the fireplace with their heads lifted and ears perked. "Jack, Audie, what is it?" Listening, I heard only rain drumming on our metal roof, so I shrugged and turned back to the stove. I plucked a scalpel from the boiling water with tongs, placed it in a sterile box, and blinked steam from my eyes as I chased a needle around the pot. "Dang. C'mon."

I stopped when the dogs lunged toward the door.

Pearl stiffened at the table, her doll's clothes forgotten. Wide-eyed and watching me, my seven-year-old daughter knew better than to make a sound as Jack and Audie growled and paced.

I wiped my hands and grabbed the shotgun from the kitchen wall mount. At the door, I pulled up the peephole rag and scanned the yard.

A man stood by our fence. A towering, dark man.

"Oh, Christ. There's a Stranger inside the gate. Stay here. Stay quiet."

Pearl nodded. She scrambled into the kitchen and retrieved the scalpel. I chambered a round and said, "Heel, dogs," as I opened the

3

door. They flanked me, all hackles and teeth and threats, as I crossed the porch and strode through the rain and mud, the shotgun wedged against my shoulder.

He wore the gray-and-green fatigues of an Ohnenrai field tech.

"Don't you move." I leveled the gun at his chest as I came across the yard.

He raised his arms and his gaze traveled from the gun to Jack and Audie. "I'm not here to hurt you. I need a comtab," the soldier said in English. His fatigues were torn and muddy. A large gash, encrusted with blue blood, stretched from his temple to his cheek and cut across his nose. His left eye was swollen, and blood caked the edges of his nostrils. His hands were bloodied and bruised.

The dogs snarled, their hair raised and their ears flat.

The towering pines creaked and whooshed, and water droplets showered us as I stopped and tightened the gun against my shoulder. "No comtabs here, Ohnenran. Not even a phone. You're in Suffer."

I wasn't sure why I didn't fear him. Maybe it was because the dogs crouched between us, maybe because Pearl stood behind the closed cottage door. Or maybe because fear was so familiar that I'd developed a calloused heart.

He shot me a dark look then his expression smoothed in the automatic way of his people. "I know where I am." He shifted and a grimace flitted across his face.

"Then you know you don't belong." I'd never seen an Ohnenran look bedraggled.

"May I put my arms down? Your dogs will shred me before I ever get close to you." He added in a monotone, "Not that I'm any threat, ma'am."

My palms were sweaty, but I didn't dare wipe them. I tightened my grip on the gun. Maybe I wasn't as fearless as I'd hoped. "What're you doing here?"

He lowered his arms. Jack stepped forward and Audie snarled.

The man's hands shot back up. "Last night's storm caught me on the Upper Ribbon Trail." He grimaced and shifted. I glanced at his right leg. Mud and blood caked his fatigues from the knee down. It'd thundered and blustered all night and I didn't envy this man being caught in the storm. "I'm not here to harm you," he said. "You have my word."

"Which isn't worth shit."

"You don't know me, yet you threaten my life?"

"You're Ohnenrai." The name twisted from my lips like a curse. He was the first Stranger I'd spoken to in the twelve years since my parents had died in Ohnenrai custody.

Jack and Audie rumbled their agreement.

"You'd shoot me because I was born on another planet?" It sounded unreasonable, but I wouldn't back down, not from one of Earth's conquerors. "I can't undo my birth, can I?" he added.

I raised the gun to point at his head. "I can."

His chin lifted as he folded his arms and looked down at me, his face a blank canvas. I didn't doubt that the Ohnenrai people's emotional detachment had made it easy to kill billions of Terrans. The dogs advanced, baring and gnashing their teeth. The man eyed my protectors. "Varet!" The word boomed from him even as he remained expressionless.

I started at his power and the dogs ceased their threats. I looked at the outsider with newfound respect. I didn't know Strangers raised their voices; I'd heard that even in battle, with death snapping their souls from their bodies, they stayed cool. *Maybe that's not true.*

He watched Jack and Audie resume their slow, threatening advance but didn't flinch.

Instead, he looked back to me, his eyes hard. "Well?"

I studied his wounded face and held his gaze, debating, deciding. "Jack. Audie. Heel." The dogs stopped. Their snarls subsided to grumbles. They looked from the man to me then retreated to my side. "Show me your leg," I ordered.

The Ohnenran lifted his pant leg to reveal a swollen gash running the length of his shin. His calf bulged over the rim of his boot and the flesh was purple and black. How he'd managed to hobble around on that thing, I couldn't imagine.

As he straightened I said, "Remove your jacket, lift your shirt, empty your pockets, turn around." He did. There was nothing but dirt and lint and bruises. I lowered the gun but didn't put the safety back on. "Pearl?"

Behind me the cottage door creaked. "Yes, Momma?"

"Set the cot by the hearth and get my medical bag. We've got a customer."

I pumped the shotgun and handed it to Pearl. "Shoot him if he looks at you funny." I'd left the soldier in the rain and returned to the house to gather my medical supplies. He'd crossed our porch but had stopped at the threshold of our dark, tiny home.

"My name is Ehtishem Zain." He proffered his hand but dropped it as I stared.

"Leave your jacket on the porch and come in." I pointed at the cot beside the fireplace. "I need to reset that ankle."

"How do you know it's broken?"

"Any fool can see that."

Jack and Audie grumbled and paced.

"Audie, with Pearl." The brindle dog took his place at her side and faced the Stranger. "Jack, heel." The large black hound followed me into the kitchen. He also watched the man, who more than filled the doorway.

The soldier's aloofness made my shoulders hunch. The

emotional detachment of the Ohnenrai had led to the Suffern nickname for them—they were strange, strangers to us, and strangers to each other, or so I'd been told. They didn't marry, didn't pair. Their children were raised in groups without parents.

I exhaled slowly, quietly, and flattened my palms on the counter, willing my hands to stop shaking. Then I got morphine tablets from a cupboard and lifted the pot of hot, sterile water from the stove. Ignoring the man, who'd remained in the doorway, chin to chest with his hands relaxed at his sides, I left the water on a table beside the fireplace and popped open the cot. I took the oil lamp from atop the hearth and hung it on a wall hook then turned to him.

His short-shorn black hair topped the doorframe and his green pants looked like the heavy canvas type I'd seen on the Ohnenrai soldiers who sometimes air-dropped supplies. Ehtishem Zain towered over our men.

I gestured toward the cot. "I need to cut off that boot." He hobbled across the room and sat.

Beside me, Jack growled.

I pulled a stool between us, draped one of the towels across my knee, and rested the Stranger's foot on my leg. I pulled heavy shears from my brown leather bag then cut his pant leg up to the knee and away. I unlaced the boot and eased it back from his swollen ankle. And was relieved to see that he didn't have a compound fracture.

Pearl, accompanied by Audie, scuttled across the room.

"Don't run with that weapon."

"Sorry." She eased back to the bedroom doorway, the gun in her arms, muzzle down.

Ehtishem Zain watched her. "Isn't she young for a firearm?"

"She's seven and not too young to know how to defend herself." I gestured at the floor. "Remove your shirt and drop it here. Do you have any allergies?" He shook his head as he took off his long-sleeved, gray, thermal shirt.

I didn't know much about the Ohnenrai, but I knew they were human or close to it. I knew their blue blood bound oxygen with copper, as well as iron. I knew their secondary heart acted like a sump pump. I knew their black bones contained melanin. My mother had taught me to heal them; my father had told me to kill them. I pulled a stethoscope from the medical bag. "Do you have any abdominal or chest pain? Any difficulty breathing? Have you coughed up blood?"

"No."

I listened to his lungs and palpated his abdomen. The man was so solid he'd probably crushed whatever he'd landed on. Still, a slow bleed could hide from me and he was bruised front and back. "Ever had morphine?" I uncapped the bottle.

"I don't want it."

I paused. "You don't realize how painful this will be, soldier."

"I can handle pain."

I shrugged, capped the bottle, and picked up the scissors. He lay back on the cot and closed his eyes. He didn't flinch as I cut through the heavy leather of his boot, eased it off, and pressed my fingers into his flesh. Finally, I straightened with a sigh. "Well, there's no way of knowing what's under all that swelling."

The Ohnenran sat up and nodded. His ankle and foot were banded—blue to purple to black—from the blood and fluid that had rushed to the injury. "What do you advise?" He eyed his distorted ankle, his reaction no stronger than if I'd I told him that leaves grow on trees.

"Rest and elevation. The swelling should reduce over the next few days. Once I can feel the break, I'll know whether to cast or operate." I scrutinized his face for any reaction, but his features remained serene. "I'll splint it; don't put any weight on it. Clear?"

"I understand."

"Cleaning your wounds will take time and be painful. I'll start with that cut across your face before getting to your leg." I retrieved his shirt. "Put that on."

Ehtishem Zain did so, folded his hands in his lap, and closed his hazel eyes. I studied him and set to work. "Tell me if you feel pain."

"Do what's necessary."

The gash was deepest across his high right cheekbone and tapered to a scratch as it crossed his broad nose to end low on his jaw. I cleaned dirt and grit from the wound. "I'm putting a few stitches below your eye." His self-control was disconcerting. He said nothing, didn't even twitch, as I punctured his brown flesh again and again with the needle. Finished, I said, "All right. You'll have scars; nothing I can do about that. You can relax."

Once again, he settled back.

Pearl brought clean water and towels.

I examined his leg and was surprised to find little debris inside the wound, though it was deep enough to expose black bone in some places. "You cleaned this?"

"As best I could in running water." Sleep slurred his words.

"A creek?"

He nodded.

My jaw clenched. Creek water was full of bacteria. No wonder there was an infection. I flushed and debrided the wound then packed the gash with clean, damp gauze. "This is a wet dressing. It'll remove infected tissue as it dries."

"He's sleeping, Momma."

I stared at his relaxed face. *How could he sleep through that?* I didn't know any Terran man who could take that much pain using only self-control. The clank of Goat-Goat's bell carried across the yard and through my thoughts. "Did you bed down the animals?"

"Oh, sorry." Pearl straightened. "I forgot." She handed me the gun then scurried out the door. "C'mon, goat, the chickens already beat you to bed."

I watched her for a moment before turning back to tending the sleeping Stranger's leg. Pearl and I looked so alike with our dark, wavy hair, long limbs, and heart-shaped faces. But gazing upon her brought a terrible, weighty feeling that we would never escape Suffer or Elder Cyrus—the man who tormented me. She and I had green eyes, but where mine were dark like the sea, hers were ice-green. Pearl had Cyrus's eyes, and sometimes I had to look away from them.

Audie barked. I glanced out the open door to see him circle and nip at our poor dairy goat. She stamped and snorted, tossed her head in protest, then scuttled into her rickety little shelter. Audie lunged and hopped and pranced around Pearl as she closed Goat-Goat's pen, peered into the hen house to count the chickens, then crossed the yard to lock the gate. A few moments later, she thumped up to the porch and peered through the doorway. "Momma." Her gaze darted from the man's closed eyes to me. "Come see what I found."

"Hold on." I clipped a needle free from stitches on the Stranger's left palm. He was battered from head to toe, evidence of quite a fall. I'd have to watch his pulse throughout the night; that would reveal any internal bleeding I might have missed.

What does it matter if he dies? I sighed, wiped my hands, and trailed Pearl. It would matter to the Ohnenrai when they came looking for him. I pushed away thoughts of armored troops and blazing gunships. *Heal him and get him out of Suffer. Fast.*

Pearl ran across the yard and stopped outside the gate. When I reached her, I saw a military pack at her feet. It was almost as big as Jack. She said, "He musta left it, Momma. Can we open it?"

I studied the muddy, green bag and checked the fasteners. "It's locked." I straightened and glanced toward the house as I sucked air through my teeth. "Hmm. He left it where he couldn't easily reach it." I grabbed the shoulder straps and hefted. "Oh Lord in Heaven." I sagged beneath its weight.

Pearl caught the other end and we staggered back through the rain to the house and left the pack on the porch. I retrieved his jacket and went through the pockets, but they were empty, so I brought it into the house. I'd expected a weapon, a broken comtab, tools, something. Why had he tried so hard to appear non-threatening?

Pearl and I lay in bed. "I thought they didn't carry packs." Her breath tickled my neck.

"Infantry don't. He must be a scout or a technician, someone in the field for long periods. He's not wearing a bio-suit." That meant no outer armor, though he was big enough to handle an Ohnenrai mech-suit.

"But he's a soldier."

"What makes you so certain?"

Audie groaned, stretched, and stuck his nose in Jack's ear. The dogs always slept on a salvaged mattress and blankets beside our bed. Pearl yawned and shrugged. "I dunno. Just am." She sighed and snuggled Holly Dolly's headless, ragamuffin body to her. Her muscles went lax as she dropped into sleep.

I envied her. More often than not sleep eluded me. And when I did find it, nightmare visions of drowning, bindings, violation filled my mind and I awoke afraid, panicked, nauseated. Nightmares and flashbacks were the stuff of my days and nights.

The bedroom door bore no lock; the dogs were all the early warning we needed. The shotgun leaned in its rack beside the bed, always loaded and within reach. The plink of rain on our street sign roof lulled me to sleep.

I awoke with a scream strangling me and stared into the dark fighting to block the too-familiar face of my enemy. After Pearl's birth I'd learned to wake from most nightmares without moving or crying out. Pearl had learned to give half-conscious comfort when I failed.

I slipped from the bed, tucked the blankets around her, and embraced the chilly room. The cold air made me shake and pushed back my panic. I lit the oil lamp, retrieved the gun, and eased through the door.

The Ohnenran's breathing was deep, even, reassuring. I retrieved a thick wool blanket from the bedroom and threw it over him, then bent and checked his heart rate. *Unchanged.* My gaze traveled over his face. The long scratch and swelling around his eye didn't detract from his exotic handsomeness. The Ohnenrai were an attractive people—all long-limbed, powerful grace and dark eyes, dark skin, dark hair. And this man stood out from those I'd seen.

Reluctance to return to my nightmares made me hover and stare. Ehtishem Zain's face and physique, an example of God's artistry and irony, drew me toward him, made me yearn. Where others ran from his kind, frightened by such unearthly perfection, I tilted toward the Ohnenrai as my mother had, as my father had. Always.

"Someone will come for you." Twelve years had passed since my mother had said that. Twelve years had gone since my father had told me I was a double-edged sword. *"Strike when you need to."* Twelve years since their deaths. And that was long enough to stop waiting, to give up hope, to believe those were the delusions of a traumatized fourteen-year-old.

TWO

AS USUAL, Pearl and I awoke to the rooster crowing. We snuggled in bed, loath to face a cold house and a damp day. Jack and Audie curled tail-to-nose beside the bed. They, too, seemed reluctant to embrace the frigid morning.

"Okay, baby girl, the chickens won't let themselves out." I traded kisses with Pearl and sat up. "And I need to check the Stranger's leg."

The dogs rose and stretched and wagged their skinny tails. Pearl sat up, swung her legs over the bed, and disappeared beneath sloppy dog kisses. She giggled as the dogs snuffled and whined their love.

I stood and stretched, arching my back and spreading my arms out then collapsing back into myself. "Jack, heel." I slapped my thigh and the dog came to my side with his floppy ears lifted and his keen eyes expectant. I rubbed his face, enjoying the simplicity of his affection, then went to the small bathroom. I used the toilet, splashed my face and rinsed my mouth, then layered on pants, a long skirt, and two long-sleeved tops. Pearl followed suit, picked up the shotgun, and followed me into the main room.

Ehtishem Zain rose to his elbows and watched us. Dark circles rimmed his eyes and his face was flushed.

The dogs circled us, their attention always on the Stranger. I cracked an egg for each of them and Pearl began breakfast as I went to the hearth and unbanked the fire. Jack joined me, slurping egg from his muzzle.

My breath left a thin cloud and I was glad I'd thrown the extra blanket over my patient. I met his tired eyes. "You didn't sleep well."

He shook his head. "I woke a few hours ago and couldn't get comfortable." He was breathing rapidly.

I pulled the stool to his cot then pressed my hand to his temple. "You have a fever; I'm not surprised." I turned down the blanket, removed the splint, and undressed his leg. An angry dark line clawed from his calf to his knee and halfway up his thigh. Green pus oozed from the wound and the edges were purple and swollen, the skin stretched and shiny.

The thick, warm scent of fried eggs and toast filled the room. Ehtishem Zain covered his nose.

"Nausea?" He nodded. "You're fighting a blood infection." I went to the kitchen and fixed a cup of tea then returned to the Stranger and helped him sit up. "It's ginger. It'll settle your stomach." I then filled a pot with hot water and measured in salt. While the water cooled, Pearl and I ate at our small table. Afterward, she went out to free the chickens and steal their eggs.

I carried the pot to the hearth, retrieved several clean towels, and returned to the cramped kitchen. I considered my cache of Amoxicillin but decided against it. What I had wouldn't stop sepsis from killing him. And if I cured his infection with a poultice it meant that the medication would be available for Sufferns. No one knew when the next supply drop would happen. "How's your pain?"

"Tolerable." He sipped his tea and watched me.

"If you need morphine, tell me."

"I don't."

I bit back a reply as I settled on the stool and spread a towel beneath his leg.

"How bad is the wound?" Ehtishem Zain asked.

"If the infection continues to spread, you'll die. I don't have the right antibiotics to stop it. But you're healthy and strong." I shrugged and set to abrading the wound with salt water and a towel. "You can try prayer, but I find it's ineffective."

He didn't react—to my words or the procedure.

Pearl returned with Audie and the eggs. "Eight, Momma." She wore a big smile. "My new rooster's keeping the girls happy."

I laughed. "Indeed." Her brunette braid swung across her back as she cleaned and stored the eggs and started on the dishes. "When you're done, please run to Judith's. Take her four eggs and a head of the cabbage you pulled yesterday. I need slippery elm and more fenugreek. Do we need flax seed too?" She checked the herb pots and shook her head. "Good. Take Audie and come right back. I need to poultice this leg."

"Yes, Momma." She put the frying pan up to dry and left with Audie. The gate clacked behind them.

Beside me, Jack settled his chin across his paws and continued his watch. The Stranger put down his tea. "She's helpful."

"She's none of your goddamned business."

"No need for defensiveness. I think you're fortunate to have a useful girl. But if you don't want me to compliment her, or you, I won't."

I sat back and studied him wondering if he was full of shit. "I can't read you people. I don't know what you're thinking, what you mean by the things you say. So maybe it's best if you say little or nothing at all." I thought I saw a twitch at the corner of his mouth, a furrow of his brow, but I blinked and his face was impassive.

He nodded, settled into the pillows, and closed his eyes. Soon enough his breathing deepened and he slept.

Deciding his self-control was as effective as morphine, I cleaned the wound with abandon, but the swelling of his ankle prevented me from feeling the bones. *A few more days, then I'll know. If he lives that long.* The gate banged. "Damn it. I have *got* to fix that gate," I muttered.

"Momma, I— Oh, sorry." Pearl tiptoed to the kitchen and pulled the herbs from her bag.

I joined her. "Judith was generous." I emptied the herbs into their pots, set the kettle to boil, and pulled a piece of muslin from a drawer.

Pearl peered around me at the Stranger. "How long will he be here?"

I squatted to her eye level. "Until he's well enough to leave on his own two feet or is carried out. Does he scare you?"

She cocked her head to the side and her brow furrowed as she considered the question. "Not really." She grinned and threw her arms around my neck. "It's not like he can run or anything."

I smiled and hugged her small body. "No, I'm pretty sure you can outrun him, Pearly Girly. But don't lose your caution." I stood and gave her a little swat. "Thank you for getting these. Now off to your chores." Pearl stuck out her tongue and headed to the yard, undisturbed by the world. Audie followed her.

I prepared a poultice with the herbs and applied it to the man's leg. As I wrapped a fresh towel around his calf, the gate banged and the clear tenor of Judith's husband, Lot, carried across the yard.

"I see your mother has yet to fix the gate."

"Hi, Lot." Pearl's voice held the only sunshine of the day.

Jack pricked his ears and his tail thump-thumped the wood floor. "Go on, dog." I gestured to the door. He rose but didn't leave my side. "You're a good boy, Jack." I rubbed his chin and sighed. *Here we go.*

The door creaked and Lot stepped into the house shaking rain from his blond hair. He stood many inches shorter than Ehtishem Zain. Strange, he'd never seemed short before.

"Word travels fast," I said.

"Yes." He came to me and looked down at the sleeping Stranger. "The Elders want to know how long he'll stay." Jack stuck his muzzle in Lot's hand and whined. His plea was met with pats and scratches and, "Hey, dog."

"Until he walks out on his own two feet or they decide to carry him to the nearest Gate." I glanced up to see Lot's reaction. At one time we'd been friends; before Joshua's death, before Pearl's birth, before I was hated.

Lot's mouth twisted and he ran his hand through his hair. "How bad is the leg, Rachel?"

The Elders weren't happy.

"His ankle's broken. How bad I can't tell until the swelling eases. That'll take a few days. If he's lucky I'll be able to reset and cast it without surgery. The wound is another story. There's a nasty infection brewing and he's feverish." I gestured toward Ehtishem Zain's face where a red flush tinted his cheeks. The only good news was the lessened swelling around his now-greenish bruised eye.

"So this isn't a quick fix."

"No. Unless he dies."

Lot glanced around the dark, cramped room. "How'd he get here?"

I shrugged. "Said he got caught in the storm night before last. He was hiking the Upper Ribbon."

"Alone? Well, we know he's an idiot. That's something to report." I snorted. Lot toed the Stranger's jacket and added, "Looks like military."

I nodded. "Looks like it. Seems unlikely, though."

"Why?"

"You said it yourself; he's an idiot. And he would've been missed by now. More likely a Gate tech."

"No bio-suit?"

"Nope."

He grunted then glanced out the window as Pearl's laughter and the protests of Goat-Goat carried into the house.

My stomach tightened as I braced for the coming discussion.

"She shouldn't be here, Rachel." Lot looked down at the Ohnenran. "Not with him in the house. It's not safe."

"No? Huh. I can see how this feverish, crippled man poses a threat to Pearl—after he gets past Audie and Jack, and disarms me. Please, Lot, you and Judith know I'm not stupid. I won't endanger Pearl. Ever."

"Be reasonable."

Heat flushed my face. I took a breath, held it, and let it go. I wrapped the towel around the Stranger's leg then stood to face my dead husband's best friend. "I know where the real danger lies for Pearl and it's *not* in this cot."

"Rachel—"

"Six weeks, Lot. I have six more weeks. I won't give up a single day with her. You tell the Elders they won't get her one minute before her eighth birthday. Not one goddamned minute early."

"Watch you mouth, woman." He crossed himself and anger set his jaw.

But I didn't care. So what if I blasphemed the damned Elders and their bastard god and their friggin' laws? It wasn't the first time; it wouldn't be the last. "Pearl stays with me. Or, so help me, I will shoot anyone who tries to take her."

"Don't be hysterical."

"Do you have anything useful to say?"

He looked at me with hard eyes. "I'm done. I've seen and heard enough. I'll tell the Elders he'll be here for a while. And Pearl is safe —for now." Lot left the house, planted a kiss atop Pearl's head, then banged through the gate and disappeared among the pines and maples.

"An idiot?"

I stiffened and turned expecting to see accusation in the Stranger's eyes. "Yes." Instead, I thought I saw a hint of glee tighten the corners before neutrality returned. I gathered the dirty towels and stood. "My mother had a saying for people who go into dangerous places unprepared."

"Oh?"

"A fool and his flesh are soon parted." I dropped the towels beside the front door.

"Hmm. A wise woman."

I returned to get the filthy water. "I'm sorry we woke you."

"You didn't. My churning gut did. I need a latrine."

I nodded and went to the door. "Pearl? Come in." She dropped Goat-Goat's fresh straw, brushed her hands on her apron, and scurried to the cottage. I pointed to the shotgun. "Chamber a round and shoot him if he threatens us. Our visitor needs the bathroom."

Pearl did as I instructed while I pulled crutches from beneath our bed then returned and picked up the splint. I slid it onto Ehtishem Zain's leg—careful to keep the poultice in place—then helped him stand. "Between the infection and the fever I don't trust your balance." I tucked a crutch beneath his right arm. "I'll keep you steady. Don't put any weight on that foot. Try anything funny and Pearl will shoot you in the ass."

The Stranger hesitated. I lifted his left arm across my shoulders and put my right arm around his broad back. "C'mon, I don't want you crapping on my floor."

He grunted and we set off. The twelve-foot journey felt interminable and my muscles trembled by the time we reached the toilet. Again, the Stranger hesitated.

"I have seen many asses and peckers in my time, Ehtishem Zain." I huffed exasperation. "I've been the only medic in Suffer since I was fourteen and I trained with my mother from the age of three. You don't have anything I haven't seen."

He nodded, dropped his pants, and allowed me to help him sit. I closed the door. "Call me when you're ready."

I pulled clean blankets from the crate in the corner of our bedroom then followed Pearl into the main room where I pulled the covers from the cot. I piled them with the dirty towels and the Stranger's canvas jacket beside the door. "We'll do the wash later."

The return trip with Ehtishem Zain was more arduous than the first and he collapsed on the cot, sweaty and shaky. He closed his eyes and his breathing had deepened before I got the splint off. Satisfied that the infection had slowed, I replaced the poultice with a fresh one.

I joined Pearl in the yard to help clean the animals' bedding. We tended the garden and came away with more cabbage and a handful of potatoes each. Then we tackled the laundry.

Ehtishem Zain slept while I pushed worry away. Judith would be angry at my attitude with Lot, but her husband had no business in this matter. I paused to watch Pearl play tug 'o war with the dogs. *Her welfare is no one's business but mine.*

THREE

PEARL and I strolled the gray, beaten path to Hub Road. It wound downward through thick, old forest, each side so overgrown with dark gray and green that we couldn't see more than a dozen feet into the woods. Ferns sprouted from the trunks of lichen-encrusted trees like fur and feathers. Moss coated rocks, rotten logs, and droopy branches. The dense growth of trees and bushes muted light and sound.

The path to and from our home felt like a cathedral. This was where I found holiness, not in the bluster and bombast of Elder Cyrus's lunatic ravings.

Audie and Jack zigzagged across the track, disappeared into the forest to investigate smells and sounds, and chased squirrels and rabbits. They reappeared ahead or behind us, loped through the heart-shaped wild violets, and waggled around us.

Our destination was Judith's house at the far end of Main Street. Pearl studied mathematics, botany, and history under her tutelage. After lessons she and Judith's boys, Mark and Matthew, would play while I checked the progress of Judith's pregnancy.

This was her seventh child. She'd miscarried her first two, and the third child had died within hours of birth. Then Matthew and Mark had arrived, followed by another late-term miscarriage, and now this baby. All her losses were girls.

I've buried so many babies, so many little girls.

Few children were born in Suffer; even fewer were female. *None for Joshua.* I'd conceived only once with him and the baby had died in utero at six months. A girl.

I stroked Pearl's dark curls and smiled as she looked up. "I love you, Pearly Girly."

"I love you too." She wrapped her arms around my hips and we bumped along the path, crossing steps and laughing.

"You promised to tell me about Monopoly."

Pearl and I were sitting with Judith on her back porch. Today's lesson focused on history.

"Monopoly? Oh, right. World War Two and POWs." Judith nodded and rubbed her belly. "So you remember how the Monopoly game we borrowed from Luis didn't have the original tokens?"

Pearl nodded. "You said the game should've had a hat and a dog and a car."

"Yes. And houses and hotels. Well, during World War Two, Germany held a lot of British and American soldiers in prison camps."

"Like Suffer is a camp?"

"Kinda. None of us were soldiers and we have more freedom than the Germans gave the Allied soldiers. The Germans didn't treat them well, so they wanted to escape. But the soldiers needed maps and money and tools for getting away."

"What did the Germans do?"

"Do?"

"To the soldiers. You said the Germans didn't treat them nicely."

"Oh." Judith peered at me over her glasses.

I met her gaze. "They starved the soldiers and tortured them." I continued sewing a tear in one of Pearl's yellow skirts.

"Oh. That's mean." Pearl screwed up her face.

"Yes," Judith said. "Very mean. Anyway, the British government asked the company that made Monopoly to print maps of Germany on silk and hide tools and money in the game sets. Then an organization called the Red Cross took the games to the prisoners when they visited the camps."

"What's silk?"

"A type of very smooth fabric. They used it instead of paper because they could fold the maps really small and silk doesn't make noise when it's unfolded."

Pearl cocked her head. "What's the Red Cross?"

Judith stretched her back. "An organization that assisted people during wartime. They took food, medicine, and other aid into areas where civilians were affected by war. They were a neutral party, so the Germans never suspected them."

"How come they haven't come to Suffer?"

Judith sighed. "Because they don't exist anymore."

"Oh."

I sewed while Pearl learned. Judith often remarked on what a quick study she was. "She works to comprehend things, not just give the right answers," she once told me. "I wish the boys would follow her example."

Matthew and Mark took after their father in preferring construction, destruction, and mechanics. Scrap wood, wire, pipes, and conduits littered Judith's backyard. A treehouse— perched precariously within the arms of a large, old maple in the middle of their yard—underwent continuous renovations. A bucket and pulley and patchwork linoleum flooring were its most recent upgrades. The boys were working on adding power next.

Pearl's adventures in home improvement with Matthew and Mark were a great source of pride and I didn't discourage her from keeping up with them. The more she learned the better she'd live.

Her history lesson ended and we retired to Judith's sunny, yellow kitchen to share bread, cheese, hard-boiled eggs, apples, and pickled beets. I envied Judith's electric stove. All of Suffer had solar-sourced electricity, which meant hot water, warm rooms, light, and refrigeration. Pearl and I used hydrogen batteries, sparingly, for winter heating and our small refrigerator only. I was lucky to have a working toilet and clean well water.

"Doesn't it frighten you to have an Ohnenran in your house, Pearl?" Judith asked. I looked up from slicing bread.

Pearl shrugged. "No. He's sick and his ankle is broken. Besides, the dogs would get him before he came close to Momma or me." She chomped on an apple. Judith watched her thoughtfully. Pearl added, "He seems nice."

We stared at her.

"Why do you say that?" Judith looked at me.

Pearl shrugged again. "I dunno. He just does."

Matthew and Mark appeared in the doorway, spied Pearl, and gestured for her to join them. Happy to have the older boys' interest, she looked to me for permission and hopped out the door at my nod. I was grateful to Judith for openly allowing her boys to play with her; most of the children in Suffer were told to avoid Pearl.

The children's voices carried into the warm kitchen from the porch. "You have an Ohnenrai soldier in your house?"

"Is his blood really blue?"

"Yup, it's blue." Pearl's attempt at nonchalance was clear. "But we don't know if he's a soldier or a Gate tech. He broke his ankle."

I watched them through the open door.

"Wow." Matthew stared at Pearl. "I hear they're huge. Is he as big as a bear?"

When the Ohnenrai brought supplies, Suffer's children were kept safely tucked away. Few of them had ever seen a soldier.

Pearl laughed. "Not a grizzly, I don't think." Her tone lowered. "He does have to duck to get through the door, though."

"Tall, then." Mark, the eldest, nodded.

Pearl added, "Yeah. He's a lot taller even than your dad."

Matthew's tone dropped. "Is he scary?"

Pearl laughed. "No. Just serious." She paused and I heard her chomping on the apple. "I'll tell you one thing that's amazing."

"Yeah?"

"He can take *a lot* of pain."

"What do you mean?" Mark asked.

"He didn't want morphine or anything. He had a really high fever and a bad infection, and when Momma palpated his broken ankle he didn't move or react at all."

Judith and I washed and listened.

"What's palpated?"

Mark snorted. "It means she poked and prodded and moved his ankle around to figure out where it was broken, right, Pearl?"

"Right."

"Wow," Matthew repeated. "I remember when I broke my left pinkie toe. It hurt so much."

"Yeah, you cried."

"You'd've cried, too, Mark!"

"Would not."

Pearl said, "Yeah, you would've. I've seen grown-ups cry 'cause of broken bones."

"So he's tough," Mark said.

They moved into the backyard and their voices faded.

25

Judith set her knife down and turned to me. "She doesn't fear the Stranger at all, Rachel. Don't you see this is dangerous?"

I sighed. "She doesn't fear him because he's no threat. He has a broken ankle, a high fever, and a blood infection. I have two big dogs and a loaded shotgun."

"But his *presence.*" She shook her head and looked away from my gaze. "Who knows what he's thinking? They don't think like us, Rachel. They aren't human. I mean they are, but they don't value the same things we do. They don't value life. They don't fear God. They don't even *believe* in God. If you can't see his threat to you, can you at least admit he's a danger to Pearl?"

I threw the towel into the sink and turned to her, hands on my hips. "Why does everyone think I would endanger Pearl? What do I gain from having this man in my house? Nothing! Nothing but scrutiny and criticism. Nothing but threats to take Pearl." My voice tightened and tears welled in my eyes, dampened the corners, and threatened to spill. "I would send him away if I could." My words were low. "But I cannot refuse him treatment, Ohnenrai or not. Fate delivered this Stranger into my hands. I am a medic; I will do as my mother did." I sure as hell wasn't going to add that I'd been told someone would come for me. Especially since I didn't know if that someone was *him.*

"Yes and look where that got her. And you. He'll have no gratitude for what you've done, Rachel. He cannot move now. But when he can? Do you think the dogs will stop him? He doesn't feel pain—"

"Of course he feels pain. He's not a monster, Judith. And I can defend myself."

"Oh? You may be taller than all the women and most of the men in Suffer, but you're no match for an Ohnenrai soldier. Having him in your home is stupid."

The tears spilled their banks. "I didn't ask for this, any of it. You know that, Judith. Please. Don't you judge me too. I took an oath to humanity. I swore to heal and to do so blindly."

She reached up and brushed the tears from my cheeks. "I don't know what you've done to invite such testing from God. But he gives us what we need and no more than we can handle. This terrifies me, Rachel. Yet, there must be a reason for this man's presence, though I can't see what it is." Her hug was awkward, separated as we were by her enormous belly.

I nodded and sniffled. "I know." I glanced down at her stomach. "You've dropped. Any contractions?"

She smiled and placed her hands over her womb. "Nothing much. A rumble here or there. He's head-down today but keeps doing somersaults." She shook her head. "As active as his brothers."

I smiled. "Willing to keep up with them before he's even drawn a breath." I retrieved the towel and folded it. "I'll do a quick exam before I leave. I doubt much has happened. You have a month, I'd guess."

I looked around her kitchen. Lot was handy; he'd scrounged a window for the ceiling and yellow paint. He and one of the other men kept the community's power up and running year-round. I envied Judith's bright, sunny home. My dark stone cottage only received early morning light through the tiny kitchen window. Cheer, light, and laughter always filled her house.

She gestured toward her unborn son. "Of course not. He'll sit just like this and make me waddle for five more weeks, like his brothers did."

I nodded, draped the towel over the sink edge, and shook water from the blue plastic colander. I ran my hands around its ragged rim. "How much for this?"

Judith grinned. "You may not have it." She jabbed her knife toward the children playing chicken chase in the yard. "I'd give up one of those rotten boys before I'd give up my precious colander. It's an antique, you know."

We laughed. The item was a piece of junk from a landfill.

"Pearl?"

She poked her head through the treehouse window. "Yes, Momma?"

"I'm going now. Lot will bring you home after dinner. Do you know where Jack is?"

"He followed Mark to Honorius's."

Honorius butchered the animals that John, Abel, and Joseph brought in. Judith had told me they'd returned with a bull moose that morning. Honorius would have the carcass allotted by now.

"All right. Bring the dogs home with you."

"Okay, Momma." She disappeared from view.

"Bye, Pearly."

Her muffled voice carried down to me. "Bye!"

Judith stood in the kitchen doorway wiping flour from her hands with an orange-and-white checkered towel. "Maybe you should go get Jack."

"I'm fine." I didn't mean to sound terse, but I didn't want to release the worry I'd worked all morning to control. "Thank you for feeding Pearl. And for caring. Please don't worry, Judith. It's not good for the baby."

Her hands went to her belly. She nodded. "Lot will get her home before dark."

I cut through the yard, passed beneath the clematis-draped arbor, and headed for home. "Just keep Cyrus away today, God. Please? You know I don't ask for much." I wasn't carrying my shotgun; the Elders didn't permit weapons in Suffer. Only the hunters carried arms.

I passed Isaac and Rebecca, my former neighbors. They averted their eyes. I ignored them back. Most Sufferns were in lessons with the Elders or working, so I had a quiet climb beneath the trees.

I thought of Pearl's opinion of our patient. He did seem nice. And I knew Judith was right to find that acceptance terrifying. Yet the man was nothing but polite. He showed respect to me and to Pearl. He obeyed my medical directives to the letter. I'd taken him to and from the toilet, sat beside him armed only with scissors, turned my back on him again and again. Not once had Ehtishem Zain threatened us.

"In a choice between him and Elder Cyrus, I'd take the Ohnenran in a heartbeat." But was that what he wanted?

I thought of my father translating for the Ohnenrai and the U.S. military; my mother shoulder-to-shoulder with their med techs, treating Terrans and Ohnenrai injured during the Hundred Days. Things had gone bad so quickly and no one had seemed to know why. My parents' hurried last words had come as we'd hid from Ohnenrai soldiers in the woods behind my uncle's house.

I started as a deer bound across my path and into the trees, her tail flashing white. "Oh, you scared me." I put my hand to my thumping heart. "More than I scared you, I think." I looked past the spot where she'd emerged and spied my little wood-and-stone hunters' cabin. Green- and brown- and rust-hued moss crept up the walls, covered the roof, and overran the river rock chimney. The porch steps and slats were more rot than wood.

But when the Children of Divine Suffering had labeled me a sinner and turned their backs on me as I stumbled away from the Scaffold, my stomach swelling with a baby not my husband's, a baby forcibly conceived, this little cabin had offered shelter. It had given me its secrets—the shotgun and shells to keep predators at bay. It had housed Audie and Jack, two orphaned pups. It, alone, had witnessed Pearl's birth. *Dark and cold and dank you may be, but you're home.*

Cyrus had never caught me in the cabin. Elsewhere he'd cornered me. More than once along the trail when, like today, I'd left the dogs with Pearl and taken a chance. After Friday Prayers when he'd permitted Pearl to dine with the congregation while he offered me private counsel. As I left patients at night having sent Pearl home with the dogs before it grew dark.

I reached my yard and gazed upon the structure. What little paint showed was flaked and dingy white. A weathered plywood board covered what once was a large front window. *You keep me safe, little house.* It was stupid to believe that the rotting old structure protected me, but I knew it did somehow. And if the Ohnenran could be within its confines, maybe he meant Pearl and me no harm.

The gate creaked a protest as it opened and thwacked its discontent as it closed, and the roses growing along the fence shuddered in agreement. The gate had been painted soft green when I found it, and I'd carved vines and roses into it. Now its paint was long-gone. Rain and snow, sun and wind had silvered the wood. It showed the creep of time and rot and the only green left was bright moss growing from the bottom up. Yellow and peach roses mounded around its posts and twined across the fence.

"I remember when you didn't complain so much," I told the gate as I paused and studied my enclosure, a barrier to keep the animals in ... and out.

Neither elegant nor well built, its length consisted of scrounged boards and scrapped signs from the freeway barricade. One listed cities that no longer existed—Seattle, Bellingham, Vancouver. Others bore business names—The Home Depot, Circuit City, The Woods Coffee. Few in Suffer thought about these places, though their skeletons decayed within reach of the detention colony.

I tried to push away thoughts of the Hundred Days. It was a

time when every nation had drowned in wave after wave of terrorist attacks, a flood of fear and violence. I didn't want to remember my father as the Ohnenrai mouthpiece, defending them as they destroyed everything to save us from our own terrorism.

My gaze traveled over one white sign. Its large, purple block letters proclaimed: *The Ohnenrai Bring Help*. Someone had used red spray-paint to turn *Help* into *Hell*.

I still heard thunderous Ohnenrai troopships and gunships and felt massive, bone-rattling explosions. If I closed my eyes I could see them dispersing mech-suited soldiers. I could see them leveling London, New York, Buenos Aires, Istanbul, Beijing, city after city. The White House burning, mosques crumbling, Canada afire from British Columbia to Nova Scotia. I could see the towering smoke plumes that had blackened the sky as oil wells burned on every continent and at sea. And I could see the blue-white flash of their orbital bombs and feel the heartbeat of utter silence before hell arrived.

But even worse were my memories of my father's voice breaking as he told my mother that the Ohnenrai had betrayed us. *"They lied, Ellie."* He'd dragged us into the woods as my mother had sobbed and I'd clung to her, crying. *"They'll destroy everything 'to save us from ourselves.' Those lying, murdering bastards!"*

The clank of Goat-Goat's bell cut through my reverie and I looked up to see her weeding the perimeter of the fence. Dandelions grew there, as big as Pearl's hand. Some days they were the only sunshine in our gray lives. The chickens clucked and burred and scratched in the straw, their black-and-white feathers fluffed against the cold, damp day.

I shook my head as my speckled nanny goat looked up. A yellow bloom bobbed between her lips and her bell joined the steady patter of rain, the sound of the chickens, and the long low creak of swaying pines. My stomach rumbled. "Goat cheese and apple. I have dried apple in the pantry, Goat-Goat. Whaddya think?"

"Sounds delightful."

I gasped and jerked around as Elder Cyrus emerged from behind the maple tree in Goat-Goat's pen. He'd been hiding between the tree, the fence, and the ragtag stable. Cold seized my chest and my breath quickened. The chill rose to my scalp and crept down my arms. I ducked my head and hurried toward the house. I wanted distance between us. Always.

Cyrus stepped from Goat-Goat's pen. He reached for me, trailing his fingers through my dark curls as I passed. The hair on the back of my neck stood and acid crept up my throat. I kept my gaze on the door to my sanctuary. *Get inside. Get the shotgun. Why the hell didn't I get Jack?*

I almost made it past him. But he seized my upper arm with his spidery fingers and yanked me back. "No greeting, Rachel? How inhospitable and unlike you." Cyrus was thin, almost gaunt, but not weak.

His breath warmed my cheek. I looked at the taut muscles of his forearm to avoid his gaze. Snake-like, they wove over his bones and beneath his flesh, creating hollows that moved with every twist of his wrist. He was pale skin and blue veins, salt-and-pepper hair, and hard ice-green eyes. At thirty-six, he was only ten years older than me, but authority and madness made him seem primeval.

"Hurrying to that Ohnenran's side?"

"He's my patient, Elder. Ohnenran or not, God delivered him into my hands."

"Humph." He released me with a shove toward the door. "Introduce me."

I rubbed the pain from my arm. Cyrus pressed flesh against bone, and the ache held on. I scuttled across the yard and porch and pulled open the cottage door wishing I could shut him out of my world.

Ehtishem Zain sat on the edge of the cot, his leg propped on the stool, my shotgun across his lap. My breath caught and my stomach plunged to my knees. *Jesus H. Christ, I'm caught between Death and the Devil.* Our eyes met and the Ohnenran shook his head with the slightest of movements. He swung his legs back to the cot, placed the shotgun beside them, and twitched the blue blanket to hide the weapon.

Cyrus thudded up the porch steps.

I hesitated and hid my indecision by removing my muddy shoes. *What's worse—the enemy I know too well or the one whose motives are unknown?* I chose to trust the unknown and crossed the room to touch Ehtishem Zain's forehead. "You're still feverish." I turned and gestured toward my old enemy. "This is Elder Cyrus. Ehtishem Zain, Elder." Then I focused on the Stranger's leg.

While I changed the dressing and steadied my shaking hands, the Ohnenran and the Elder regarded each other.

"How did you get here?"

"I hobbled."

"When are you leaving?"

Before my patient could answer I straightened. "He'll leave when he can walk without crutches and pain." Irritation and distrust honed my tongue.

Cyrus strode across the room. He loomed over me and glared down at the Stranger. "Not soon enough." He clamped his sharp fingers on my shoulder. "I will speak with you, Rachel. Outside."

I glanced at Ehtishem Zain, but he wore the inscrutable Ohnenran expression I hated so much. As I rose, Cyrus's hand traveled down my arm to my elbow. He steered me back to the door. Once on the porch, I pulled away from his grasp.

"Pearl should not be here. I will recommend her removal to my house."

I glared at him as my hands curled into fists and my fear curled into anger. "He's no danger to her. He's fighting infection and fever. He can't walk. You know Jack and Audie will shred him if he goes anywhere near her, Cyrus. Don't think you can take Pearl from me. Don't you try."

Quick as an asp he grabbed my hair and yanked me against him. "I will take what I wish. You will not stop me, Rachel. I am nested within your heart and beneath her skin." Cyrus's words slithered into my soul as his left hand slid around my waist and brushed my breast.

"Let us go."

He grinned like a mad dog and pulled me closer. I closed my eyes and clamped my mouth shut as he flicked his tongue over my lips.

"Medic?" The Ohnenran's deep voice came from within the house and broke Cyrus's spell. My tormentor shoved me away. "Tomorrow I'll recommend Pearl's removal to the Elders."

He stalked across the yard and banged through the gate. A shower of yellow and peach petals littered the ground in his wake. I held still, fighting panic, then doubled and vomited into the pink azaleas that edged my house.

"Kar-va jaidhyantai aiwiyo?" Ehtishem Zain asked if I needed water.

I whirled around and almost stumbled off the porch. "Nava," I answered without thinking.

He filled the doorway, a crutch tucked beneath his right arm, the shotgun in his left hand. A flicker of something, some emotion, crossed his face as I wiped my mouth with my sleeve.

Shit. I cleared my throat. "You shouldn't be up. Go lay down and raise that ankle." I tried not to look at the gun as I drew a slow breath and stepped toward him.

He did as I ordered, placing the shotgun on the table. He hesitated before turning toward the cot and grabbed the table edge. I ducked beneath his left arm and steadied him against my side feeling the tremor of his muscles. "Let me help you."

He nodded.

Once he was settled, I poured two glasses of water and sat beside the cot as he gulped his down. He drank one more glassful before I finished sipping mine, then he lay back and closed his eyes while I stared at the shotgun and wondered.

FOUR

EHTISHEM ZAIN'S fever eased as his leg healed. After two days the swelling had lessened but not enough to palpate for the break. "Everything looks good." I cleansed his skin, careful around the jagged line of stitches I'd just sewn up the length of his shin. The angry dark line that had reached for his heart no longer existed.

"May I get off this cot for more than bathroom breaks?"

I cocked my head to the side and regarded the ragged bandage in my hand. "Haven't you already?"

He didn't respond. I glanced at him from the corner of my eyes. He was propped up on his elbows watching me, his expression inscrutable. "That was necessary and brief. I want to go outside."

I bit my lip and returned my attention to winding the bandage over and under and around his leg. "All right. You can go to the porch. But use crutches and elevate your ankle."

"Agreed." He lay back and closed his eyes. I gathered the dirty bandages, cloths, and water and went to the kitchen.

"Do all Sufferns speak Ohnenrai?"

I paused. "So you noticed that."

He was propped up again and there was no accusation in his tone or expression as he nodded and replied, "Zant."

I shook my head. "Only Pearl and I, and we only speak it at home."

"How did you learn?"

"My father was an interpreter." I turned to the sink. "Do you think Terrans are too stupid to learn Ohnenrai?"

"Of course not."

I left the bandages to soak then joined Pearl on our rickety front porch to sew until The Cross bell summoned us to Friday Service. *Was that a test? Should I ask if he was sent for me?* I glanced at Pearl. *Will we go with him if he was?*

"Momma?"

"Mmm-hmm?"

"Do we have to go to service tonight?"

I looked up from darning a sock. "Why do you ask? Do you feel all right?" She nodded without meeting my gaze. "Did you have a fight with one of the other children?"

"No."

"Well, then?"

Pearl tightened the knot on a button she had reattached to her pale blue blouse. She wound the thread twice around the button and jerked her hand to snap the thread. "It's just that ... I don't believe in God, Momma." She looked up as her words rushed forth. Her eyes flashed a challenge even as she bit her lower lip.

A wave of sadness carried a lump to my throat. I bent over my darning to hide tears that threatened like a sudden summer storm. I nodded and swallowed. "I know, baby. But it's our only regular contact with the colony. It's important to show them that we haven't given up." I met her gaze. "To show them we're not broken."

She sighed, folded the mended shirt, and added it to the "finished" pile. "If God exists, he's mean. I don't want to follow a mean god."

I pulled the sock tight over the smooth river stone I used as a darning egg. "Me neither, Pearly." I started on the next row of stitches.

After mending three pairs of socks and two aprons and letting the hem out on one of Pearl's dresses, I sent her to wash up while I checked the Ohnenran. His fever had broken and sweat beaded his forehead and dampened his shirt. His presence made me think of my parents, something I hated to do. They'd often argued after the Strangers had revealed themselves. My mother, like so many others, had feared the turmoil their arrival brought.

"*Maybe we're too eager to trust them, Joe.*"

"*Ellie, you and I know them better than most. Have they ever hurt us?*"

"*No, but—*"

"*Most people just want to do what's right and I don't think the Ohnenrai are any different. We should give them a fair chance; they're struggling, just like the rest of us.*"

"*But what if we're wrong? We need to think of Rachel.*"

"*I am thinking of her. They're her future.*"

The Ohnenrai had been a part of my life long before they'd impacted most Terrans. My parents had been abductees from childhood on. As adults, they'd met through an online support group. My mother was an endocrinologist; my father was an air force pilot and a linguist.

"*But that's what scares me, Joe. I don't want them taking her too.*"

"*If that's all they wanted, they'd have taken her long ago. We'd be dead already, hon, if their intentions were bad. This is our chance to help so many people, El.*"

We left Ehtishem Zain with bread, cheese, and water on a crate beside the cot as the sound of the bell—an empty oil drum with a hammer suspended inside—carried faintly through the trees.

While Pearl made a game of kicking pinecones for the dogs, I marveled at her devil-may-care temperament. But I couldn't muster one of my own. My beautiful, laughing daughter was a constant reminder of Cyrus's predation, Joshua's death, and the colony's rejection. I forever stood accused of sin, weakness, and mental infirmity. Sometimes I wondered if they were right, if I'd hallucinated the rapes, especially when Cyrus was solicitous. But he always faltered and showed his true colors and proved that everyone had wronged us.

Still, my old friend Guilt was waiting when we reached Hub Road and all the neat little houses of Suffer came into view beyond the compound gates. They weren't perfect, but they had electricity and heat and weeded yards. Guilt pointed out the smiling children without patchwork, ill-fitting clothes, ragged haircuts, and headless dolls. Guilt directed my attention to the fathers hugging their wives and children and giving out kisses and smiles.

We reached Suffer's chain link fence and I peered up at the rusty razor wire that protected the compound.

Adam smiled and opened the gate. "Hi, Rachel. Hi, Pearl. I was wondering if you were gonna make it tonight." He was fourteen and had gate duty every Friday.

I returned his broad smile as did Pearl. "Of course. We can't miss one of Elder Cyrus's rousing sermons."

Adam laughed. Elder Mary's youngest son was an easygoing boy who, away from his peers and elders, readily spoke to me. "He'd probably insist on a private service and take up half your day, right?"

His comment was innocent, but I cringed and turned away. "Jack. Audie. To me." They left off sniffing the fence perimeter.

"C'mon, Momma, I wanna see who's at The Cross." Pearl

caught my hand. "See you, Adam." She pulled me forward and waved back at him.

The Cross was an open square where Hub Road and Main Street met at the center of Suffer. The community lived within a fenced compound that had once housed all of us as children. Before the Hundred Days, the camp had been a refuge for Terran abductees and their families. Afterward, the Ohnenrai had removed the adults and had added one hundred thirty-two Terran orphans to the handful of children who'd been left behind.

A twelve-foot fence and four guard towers separated civilization from wasteland. Two long, low buildings occupied the east and north perimeters, and a two-story hall and administration building—God's House—sat at the southwest corner of The Cross. There was a brick schoolhouse on Hub Road and little one- and two-bedroom houses marched up each side of Main Street.

Beyond the colony's gates were broken streets and barren cement foundations, burned-out cars and toppled telephone poles. But alders and pines, blackberry vines, horsetails and dandelions were reclaiming the land and softening the vicious scars that war had left behind.

Earth's captors had worked with Cyrus, Mary, and Jonah—the eldest children—to establish a governing and administrative system for the camp. Eleven months later they'd unlocked the gates and left. The children hadn't devolved into chaos. They'd kept order and sent scouting parties north, east, and south; west was the Pacific Ocean. All reported back weeks later having encountered no other Terrans or Ohnenrai, only impenetrable border fences to separate Suffer from the rest of the world.

Supply drops were infrequent and irregular, and on one of those runs the Ohnenrai had dropped me. I was fourteen.

The Cross was already astir with people when we reached it. Pearl and I spread our blanket at the back of the congregation and settled with the dogs. No one greeted us. When service was held outside, The Cross became God's House and Pearl (for being my child) and I were sinners. We were not to be addressed within the boundaries of The Cross. I was tolerated because Suffer needed a medic. But no one likes a sacrificial lamb.

Standing atop the Scaffold, Elder Cyrus chatted with Paul and John Benjamin who remained below. He nodded, looked up, and caught my gaze before I could avert my eyes. I looked away as he summoned the congregation to order. "Welcome to God's House. All are welcome—both sinner and saved."

When I'd become pregnant with Pearl, I'd hidden it as long as possible, afraid of what would happen when the evidence of Cyrus's predation became obvious. But, in the end, it hadn't mattered that Pearl was his child not Joshua's. The Sufferns had been relieved to have Cyrus brutalize one person, rather than torture the whole community. And I was sure they were thinking, *Better Rachel than me*. But that didn't mean they wanted to see Pearl and me every day. I wasn't a pleasant reminder. So they'd branded me the evildoer and had run me out of town. It was easier to tell themselves that I'd lied than accept the guilt that accompanied the truth.

Cyrus held his Bible aloft and paced the length of the twelve-foot Scaffold. "In the *Book of Mark* it is written: *And these signs shall follow them that believe: In my name shall they cast out devils. They shall speak with new tongues. They shall take up serpents. And if they drink any deadly thing, it shall not hurt them. They shall lay hands on the sick, and they shall recover.*"

Judging from the glazed eyes around me, we were well into the third hour of the Cyrus Show, and he was getting to the spectacle. The box and the bottle at the front of the Scaffold told the congregation that Elder Cyrus meant business tonight. But it also meant he was close to wrapping up.

He slammed the Bible on the podium and the crowd jumped. He swept his gaze over our heads and resumed pacing. "I tell the Four Horse-me-en, God is not dead. I speak the name Je-su-us. He soon shall rise."

Cyrus droned, his rhythmic rise-and-fall pattern almost mesmerizing. "And the Bible say-ays, He soon shall rise. And the Bible say-ays, the meek shall rise. And the Bible say-ays, our time shall come." The first half of each sentence rose up on the last doubled syllable, was followed by a monotone second half, and ended with a downward slur. The result was a sound wave that could go on for four, five, even six hours.

"It's time to ride ou-out, to speak the Word of God. I told the Four Horseme-en, it's time to ride out."

The adults and teens, with the exception of the pregnant women, stood throughout.

Children under thirteen sat and, eventually, lay on blankets at the adults' feet.

"And the Bible say-ays, these signs shall come. And the Bible say-ays, Je-sus shall come."

An old apple tree sheltered the Scaffold. Someone had built the platform around the tree, showing enough respect for nature to let it live. But that very year the tree had stopped bearing fruit. It leafed and bloomed, but it produced no apples.

"And the Bible say-ays, these are the signs. And the Bible say-ays, cast the Devil out."

I peered past the tree's branches. The massive bulk of a patrolling Ohnenrai warship blocked the starry night sky. Its jewel lights winked at us.

"Do you know how I cast the Devil out?"

Diamonds, rubies, sapphires, emeralds. Wasn't there a song about a woman in the sky with diamonds?

"By the pow-er of Je-sus Christ. Hal-lelu-jah!"

My mother had called the Ohnenrai mothership a colossal cruise ship in the sky: *"As if someone tied every ship on Earth side-by-side and end-to-end. All lights and portals and spires. And inside, Rachel, like nothing you've ever seen, a city teeming with people. A city in the sky."*

But all I saw was menace when I looked at their ships.

"And the Bible say-ays, speak the ho-ly tongue."

I grimaced, shifted, and pulled my brown shawl tighter as a cold breeze stung my cheeks.

"Do you know how I speak the ho-ly tongue? By the pow-er of Je-sus Christ. And the Bible say-ays, healest thou the sick."

Pearl dozed at my feet with Audie and Jack. I was supposed to wake her for the sermon. "Do you know how I healest the sick? By the pow-er of Je-sus Christ. And they shall li-ive!"

The damn fool couldn't heal a paper cut.

"And the Bible say-ays, take the Ser-pent up." Cyrus crossed the stage and retrieved the wooden box. He set it upon the podium, lifted the lid, and extracted a very sleepy rattlesnake. "Do you know how I take the Ser-pent up? By the pow-er of Je-sus Christ." He strode from one end of the Scaffold to the other, the snake held aloft. "And I shall li-ive. Hal-lelu-jah!"

The snake slowly coiled around his arm, docile in the cold air. Its tongue flicked up and down, in and out, but it seemed as unimpressed by Cyrus's act as I was.

"I want you to take heed of what the Bible says. I want you to take heed of what the Bible says."

I looked around The Cross and saw some heads nodding—whether in agreement or sleep I couldn't tell. The teenagers were hanging on Cyrus's performance; they loved his jump-shake-kiss-a-snake shows. He only pulled them out for special occasions. No doubt this one was inspired by my patient's unwelcome presence.

"We know the Bible i-is, the Word of God." Cyrus crossed the stage and returned the snake to its bed. "And the Bible say-ays, drink the poi-son." He mopped sweat from his temples and took a drink from a mug then retrieved the bottle that sat beside the snake box. I knew it contained strychnine, though I didn't know how he obtained it. "Do you know how I drink the poison? By the pow-er of Je-sus Christ."

And the power of hypocrisy. I also knew his mug contained activated charcoal mixed with water. It would absorb the poison before it reached his bloodstream.

"And I shall li-ive." Cyrus poured the strychnine into the bottle's small cap, downed the poison, and chased it with a healthy swig from his mug. "Hal-lelu-jah!"

He proceeded to stomp and rant for another half hour, his body and brain agitated by the small amount of strychnine that did make it into circulation.

"And the Bible say-ays, Hal-lelu-jah! And the Bible say-ays, Hal-lelu-jah!" Cyrus ended with enough Bible thumping to wake the dead. "Chil-dren! Hal-lelu-jah!"

Every time his book smacked the podium, the congregation jumped. "Hal-lelu-jah! Chil-dren! A-men!"

Every jump pushed him further into frenzy until those in the front row wore his sweat and spittle.

Thank God we're banished to the back.

"Praise the Lord! A-men! God be prai-aised! A-men!" Finally, he stretched his arms forward and grasped the front of his podium. He leaned toward the congregation and said, "Children of Divine Suffering, once again, the Devil is at our gate. He has come to poison our children with words from his forked tongue. Be wary. Praise God that we have each other." His gaze landed squarely upon me as he reached out toward me. "Extend your hand to guide those who believe they do right by aiding him. They do not know he walks in disguise. Pray for those whose judgment is clouded by the Devil. Pray for them and yourselves."

I glared at Cyrus and ignored the attention that turned my way from all directions.

He lowered his hand. "Come eat with me, Children. In the name of God. A-men."

Too bad the snake didn't get him this time. I always rooted for the snakes even though it meant I had to attend Cyrus. He milked them, but their bites brought pain nonetheless. And his suffering eased mine, if only a little. My thoughts were ungodly. But God had abandoned me first; he was a bastard in my book, just like Elder Cyrus.

The worst part of Friday Prayers now came. The Children of Divine Suffering staggered about on stiff legs and sore feet setting up tables and makeshift stools from stumps, barrels, and crates. Everyone brought food for a potluck meal. All except Pearl and I. We weren't permitted to break bread with the community.

We sat on the edge of the Scaffold and shared food brought from home—bread, cheese, a hard-boiled egg, and a small, mealy apple. When the rest of the Children sat to eat, we could leave. I'd chosen a spot that put us upwind from the roasting spits. Still the scent of smoked venison made our stomachs rumble. Normally, I brought a little meat to share, but with another mouth to feed in the house that couldn't be spared.

Pearl waved at Anna Maria Rodriguez. At thirteen, Anna Maria was the girl closest to Pearl's age in Suffer. She trailed her parents—Luis and Patricia—as well as Elder Cyrus and Elder Jonah. The group stopped within earshot.

"What about Tobias?" Luis stood several inches shorter than the Elders. He was a smart man and was kind to Pearl and me. He'd plumbed the entire Suffern community and had replaced the rust-frozen pump that brought well water into our remote cabin. I hadn't asked, and I was certain he would have been instructed not to had he sought the Elders' permission.

"Possibly. Though they're closer in age than I like. Tobias still has some growing; I'm not sure he's ready for the responsibilities of family." Jonah studied the people coming and going from the tables. He and his wife, Beatrice, mentored Anna Maria.

Suffer's few girls became community property at age eight, and the Elders chose mentors—male and female—to prepare them for marriage and adulthood. They were married at thirteen.

I was fortunate that Joshua had claimed me the day I'd entered Suffer. He'd stepped forward before the Elders even had presented me to the community. "I claim the girl for my wife." I'd been terrified, but he was a good man. He hadn't touched me until I'd said I was ready. Joshua was nine years older than me, but I was his first wife. He'd never appreciated the community's pressure to put him to stud.

Cyrus was watching me. The bread in my mouth grew too thick to swallow. I choked it down with goat milk. My appetite soured, so I split the rest between the dogs.

"Has Michael shown any willingness to take a second wife? Mary's not young and it seems unlikely she'll produce any more viable offspring after this one." Patricia spoke of the Children of Divine Suffering's only female Elder like she was a brood mare ready for the glue factory.

My stomach churned.

"That's true, Patty." Luis nodded and glanced at Anna Maria. "Anna should produce some good, strong babies for him. She has my mother's wide birthing hips."

Pearl and Anna Maria made silly, cross-eyed faces at each other until Patricia pinched the girl's arm. Then she looked down.

"Too bad Joshua is gone. Anna Maria is weak-willed. A trait he would have found appealing." Cyrus's words cut through the crowd's laughter and chatter.

Don't look. But I glanced at the group anyway. Our eyes met, and I dropped my gaze. I knew Cyrus took great pleasure in knowing I'd heard his suggestion.

"Joshua? True, Anna would be a good option for him, but he's dead. I suspect you'd've been hard-pressed to persuade him to remarry anyway; shame that it is. I doubt he'd've wished to chance the humiliation he suffered with the last one." Jonah stood with his back to me, but I was certain he knew I'd overheard.

Luis turned toward Anna Maria and our eyes met. He dropped his gaze and shifted from foot to foot. "Ah, well, there's no point in wondering what the dead would do." He crossed himself. "Not that I would give her to a man who won't trust a woman, good reason or no." Patricia nodded and ignored me.

"C'mon, Pearl." I picked up our ragged basket.

"But, Momma, they haven't sat."

The tired edge in her voice plucked my last nerve. I swallowed a rebuke. "We're leaving now." I caught her hand. "I don't want an argument. We have a patient to attend."

As we cut between the old brick school and Mary and Michael's cheerful blue house, Judith's eldest son, Mark, hopped off the school's narrow side stairs and trotted to Pearl. He glanced toward The Cross as he shoved a bundled cloth into her hands. "From Mom." He scurried between the buildings. Pearl shoved the parcel into our basket. It held food pilfered from the community potluck. Judith often put her boys up to the task of sharing with us. There was nothing I wouldn't do for her, though she took risks I didn't approve of. And I was grateful, especially in light of my confrontation with Lot and her disapproval of the Stranger in our house.

People strolled the street bringing blankets, lanterns, drinks, and food. They smiled and chatted and directed their gazes away from

Pearl and me. They crossed the road and themselves at our approach.

As we reached Hub Road, Jack and Audie stopped and pricked up their ears, then charged through the schoolyard and disappeared around the far end of the building. I inhaled to call them, but a voice chilled me and I turned.

"Why, Rachel, taking Pearl home so soon?" Cyrus strode toward us. He smiled and nodded to other Children as they thanked him for his *enlightening* sermon. "You'll miss the music." He spoke with a voice reserved for me—a sharp tone that cut not deep but shallow, like paper slides through skin and nerves. It was a slice that remained open from dread, a cut he salted again and again.

I cringed. "Yes, Elder, we must go. Other duties await our attention." Pearl eased behind me as I shifted to protect her. She trusted Cyrus no further than she could throw him. It was a sentiment I encouraged.

"Of course." He nodded at Lot and Judith as they passed, Matthew between them holding their hands. "When will we meet that new baby, Judith?"

"Soon enough, Elder. Soon enough." She returned his smile, though her face was tight, like plastic. I wondered if that was for my sake.

Cyrus turned back to me before Judith finished answering. "If you wish, Pearl may stay. I will see her home."

"Momma, I'm tired." This time I was grateful for the whine in Pearl's voice.

"Thank you, Elder, but the added duties in our household are exhausting her. I want her in bed early tonight."

"Yes, a wise notion." The words came from Elder Mary, and I jumped at her voice. I hadn't seen her turn from Main Street.

Cyrus squinted as she waddled toward us, then he smiled and nodded. "Of course. Mother knows best."

Had she noticed the sibilance of his last word? Probably. Mary was no fool, and she'd known him for twenty-three years. More than once she'd intervened on my behalf. She seemed unruffled by the friction that doing so created and I suspected she enjoyed his irritation.

Suffern Law was the one advantage I had over Cyrus. The three members of the Elder Council had to agree upon decisions that affected the community's girls and women. I was certain that Mary had blocked Cyrus's many attempts to take Pearl.

She stopped beside us, one hand on her back and the other on her very pregnant belly. "Elder, a word with you about the stock-rooms?" She turned to Pearl and me. "I hope you don't mind if I take Elder Cyrus from you, Rachel."

"Of course not, Elder Mary. Goodnight to you. God bless you."

"God bless you both."

Mary turned, but Cyrus clasped his hands before his chest and murmured, "I shall pray for you and Pearl this evening, Rachel. I do so worry about you, alone, with that soldier."

Jack and Audie reappeared. Cyrus stepped back as they circled. They'd treed him once and I'd let him spend a long, cold night on a pine bough. Ever since he'd been more careful and more vicious, but I didn't regret it. "Don't concern yourself with our safety, Elder. Audie and Jack are quite enough protection." I grabbed Pearl's hand and headed for the gate before Cyrus escaped Mary.

But as we climbed through the forest, the wind rose and so did my anxiety. Two days of Cyrus was too much. Rain fell, first pattering through the trees, then drumming harder until the leaves bucked and slashed and did little to shelter us from the sudden thunderstorm. I threw the blanket around Pearl and we ran for the house, its dim oil lamp a beacon guiding us. But I was fighting to stay focused, to remain grounded in myself, as my surroundings and my mind grew hazy, and the emotions of my past threatened to drown me again.

Our gate banged shut behind us as the first flash of lightning lit the night.

I stopped.

Pearl jerked around and seized my hand. "Momma, you're in our yard. Tell me what you see. What's around you? Tell me."

I blinked and tried to concentrate on her words. "What?"

"You're fighting a flashback, Momma. What do you see? Look around."

A flashback. I'd taught her how to help me when they seized my brain and thrust the emotions of my past into my present. I hated coming out to find her huddled and crying with the dogs, terrified by my terror and her helplessness. "I see you. You're Pearl. You're my daughter. I see Jack. He's a black dog. I see—"

Thunder boomed and rumbled. I shrank back. The haziness grew. I felt disconnected from my body.

"No, Momma. Tell me." She tugged on my hand. "Jack, Audie. Speak!" On her command both dogs began barking.

My mind balanced between *now* and *then*, and I tried to focus on the dogs, on my child, on keeping my memories and emotions at bay. "I see ... a ... um."

"Rachel. You see me."

My head jerked up as the powerful baritone carried across the yard and I tumbled back into the present. I swallowed and nodded. "Yes. I ... do." I squeezed Pearl's hand. "I'm all right." We ran to the porch as Ehtishem Zain disappeared back into the house.

FIVE

I ROLLED over and immediately awoke.

Pearl was gone.

I jerked upright and inhaled to call her, but her high, sweet laugh stopped me. She laughed again, the sound like a bell. *When a baby first laughs an angel is born.* Where had I heard that? *Or does it get its wings?* I shook my head. *Heaven must be crowded. No wonder they didn't notice the shit that's going on down here.*

"But how do you do that?" she asked.

I held my breath and strained to hear Ehtishem Zain's warm voice.

"Patience. Practice. Allow yourself to make mistakes. Learn from them and make them work for you. Some of the greatest discoveries come from mistakes, you know."

I used the bathroom, dressed, and went into the front room. Their voices carried from the porch and I peeked through the open front doorway.

Ehtishem Zain sat on a crate. Pearl was perched beside him. She leaned forward and watched as he did something. Jack and Audie were sprawled on the porch, snoozing in a pool of sunlight.

"There." The Ohnenran held something in his palm. "Try it."

Pearl picked it up. "What is it?"

"A spinner. You've never seen one?" A note of surprise lifted his voice. He took the object back. "I'll show you." He balanced it on the rotting, wood porch rail, twisted his fingers, and let it spin.

"Oooh, it dances." Pearl's low voice was full of wonder.

The top rotated on a short point beneath a flat disk. A longer post rose above the disk. It twirled and hopped across the uneven surface, then wobbled and bobbled as it lost speed.

"Catch it before it hops into the bushes."

Pearl snatched it off the rail just as it tipped. "May I try?"

"Of course. I made it for you."

I peered through the trees at a clear blue sky. "After we do the wash."

"Oh, Momma, did you see what Ehtishem made?" She skipped over and held the little top up for inspection.

"Yes. I see. Did you thank him?"

She turned. "Ferahi-va."

He bowed his head. "Va kanikar."

"It's a spinner. It dances, Momma. I'll show you."

I touched her cheek. "Wash. Chores. Lessons. Then you may play."

Pearl blinked. "But, Momma, I wanna play with this."

"Pearl." I didn't want a scene before the Ohnenran, and I didn't like her lack of caution.

"Just a few minutes, then I'll do my chores." She turned away.

"Pearl Ellenore Pryne. What did I say?" My patience stretched. I was tired, exhausted by the flashback, the soldier's presence, my existence. I tried to be patient and trust Pearl to want to help me; she usually did. Maybe that's what made me snap.

"Just a few minutes, Momma."

"Inside the house, Pearl. I want to speak with you privately.

Please." I avoided the Ohnenran's gaze as I turned and went to the kitchen. *One, two, three, four...*

Pearl followed, her lower lip trembling. "Momma, please."

Five, six, seven... I closed my eyes and drew a deep breath, *Eight, nine, ten,* and released it. *Keep it together, Rachel.* "We have wash to do. You know how rare a sunny day is. You may play when we're done."

"But I want to play with this *now*. Just for a few minutes."

The whine in her voice cracked my self-control. "Child, you are pushing my buttons and I'm on the brink of losing my patience. Please put the spinner on the counter. It will be there when we're finished."

"But—"

"Put it *here*." I smacked the chipped tile counter. "Now. Please."

She jumped. Her face twisted and tears spilled down her cheeks. "Mom-ma."

I leaned over her. I was being a bully now, but my restraint was in jeopardy. "Don't make me take the spinner from you, Pearl. I don't want to do that. Please just *work* with me."

She swallowed her sobs and mopped her tears with her sleeve. "O-kay." She put the top on the counter.

We took blankets and towels down to the creek and set to work. A wide, low waterfall created our bathing hole. Fallen logs and large gray boulders, their faces worn smooth by water and time, interrupted the creek to create pools, some shallow and some deep. This was where I came to shiver and cry and scrub Cyrus from my skin.

Silence stretched and tightened between us as we washed clothes, towels, and blankets. I hated the tension. We only had each other and we rarely fought. I hated bullying her, hated losing my patience, hated that I couldn't let her play and be seven. "Pearl?"

She looked up. We stood beside the cold creek and twisted the water from a tattered green blanket. Once again, Audie and Jack lounged in a patch of sunlight.

"I'm sorry, baby. I was as mad at myself as I was with you."

She nodded. "I'm sorry too, Momma. I just wanted to play."

"I know. I wish I could just let you play." She took the blanket, and I plunged my hands into the icy creek water. I kept them there until my joints ached. My skin was red when I straightened, but the pain calmed me. Jack and Audie, apparently inspired by me, waded into the creek for a drink.

As Pearl and I gathered the wash and followed the trail up from the creek to our house, I said, "I want you to keep your guard up around Ehtishem Zain."

"But—"

"I know he seems nice, but he's an Ohnenrai soldier. You can't trust him. Don't forget, Pearl." She sighed and nodded, her lips pursed.

The strain between us persisted as we returned to the house and hung the wash over lines, bushes, and fencing in the yard. Then the chicken coop and Goat-Goat's pen needed cleaning. It was hard work and not something I expected Pearl to do alone. I took advantage of the mindless work to give her lessons. "What are the signs of shock, Pearl?"

By the time we'd finished, the sunlight was fading and she had forgiven me. We collected and folded the wash then retrieved a handful of feathers she'd gathered to make something fancy for Holly Dolly. The trees cast deep shadows across the yard as we headed for the house. Pearl sighed. "I wish she wasn't headless, so I could make her a new hat."

"I know. Poor Holly Dolly." My great grandmother's doll had started life as a stylish lady with a delicate calico gown and matching bonnet to shade her strawberry curls.

We'd seen no sign of the Stranger as we worked and now found him asleep. I'd left lunch and our few books piled beside his cot before we went to the creek. *Lord of the Flies* was open and face down on the floor. I decided not to wake him.

Pearl and I shared a quiet meal and took turns spinning the wooden top across the table. She picked crumbs from her plate with her finger, mashed them into a little ball, and popped it into her mouth.

"We need to make more cheese. And bread." I inspected the intricate lattice design that the Stranger had carved into the top's disk. "Tomorrow morning, Pearly." I stabbed the last bite of boiled potato onto my fork and held it out for her.

She shook her head. "I'm full."

I finished it and sipped tea as I considered the problem of clothes and shoes for Ehtishem Zain. *No Suffern man comes close to his size.* I stood a head taller than all the community's women and made what few clothes I owned, but access to cloth always stymied me. I did my best to mend holes and scrounge fabric scraps. Pearl's clothes were castoffs from Judith and Mary's boys. I could stitch his pants, but his boot was beyond my skill and no one in Suffer would fix it for him. I sighed.

"What's wrong?" Pearl looked up from teaching Holly Dolly how to use the spinner.

"Nothing really. I just don't know where we'll find shoes for him." I lifted my chin in the Stranger's direction.

"Oh. I do." Pearl left Holly on the table and went to the man's military pack. We'd scraped off the mud and left it beside the hearth.

"Pearl."

She opened the bag, yanked out a pair of enormous, worn boots, and clunked them on the floor. Grinning like a pixie she shoved her feet into them and shuffled toward me, the loose metal fasteners clanking.

"What are you up to?" The Ohnenran's deep voice made us jump.

Heat flushed my cheeks and ears. "Pearl, put them back."

She giggled and turned around, her movements exaggerated, her arms wide for balance. The Stranger chuckled, three short laughs. "I don't think they make Ohnenrai service boots for babies," he said.

"Baby?" Pearl faced him, hands on her hips, outrage lifting her tone.

"Toddler? Isn't that what you call the next age group?" He looked at me for confirmation.

"I'm not a baby or a toddler!" Pearl tried to stomp her foot, but it popped out of the boot and she fell over. She lay where she'd landed and giggled as Audie and Jack covered her with slobber.

A laugh bubbled up from my belly and I felt my face relax, until I glanced up to find the Stranger watching me. I swallowed the amusement and snapped, "Pearl. Put those back and get ready for bed."

She pushed the dogs away, returned the boots with a mumbled, "I'm sorry," and retreated to the bedroom without a glance at me.

My tone had been sharper than I'd intended, but her ease with the Ohnenran disturbed me.

And it was infectious.

"I'm not offended. Ohnenrai children rarely display such cheer. She's a joy; you're fortunate."

The chair screeched as I pushed back from the table. I went to the bedroom door, paused, and turned to him. "I know where my only joy lies, Ohnenran. I don't need you or anyone else telling me. And I won't lose her—to your people or mine."

Despite Ehtishem Zain's excursions, the swelling in his ankle had lessened after four days. Pearl sat beside me and watched my exam. "I need to palpate for the break," I said to him. "Do you want morphine? This will hurt. A lot."

He shook his head and lay back. He drew and released a slow, deep breath, then relaxed.

I inhaled as well and pressed fingers to flesh hard, harder, until I found the break low and angled to the inside across his fibula. "Here it is. Without x-rays, you'll just have to learn what feels abnormal, Pearl." She nodded.

"She may feel the break." The Ohnenran's offer surprised me.

"I, ah, all right. Thank you. That's generous." I guided Pearl's small fingers.

"I feel it." She nodded and looked at me. "I thought it would be bigger."

"So did I. This is a surprisingly simple fracture." I closed my eyes, bent over his ankle, and continued pressing and pushing, but nothing else felt broken or out of place. The level of swelling compared to the actual injury surprised me, and I wondered if it was an adaptation of Ehtishem Zain's body or common to all Ohnenrai. I straightened and looked at him. "Well, all that swelling did you a service; it held the bones in place. There's no need for surgery, and if you agree to stay off this foot I'll continue with the splint instead of a cast."

The Ohnenran propped up on his elbows. He regarded his ankle and us. A fine sheen of sweat beaded his hairline, the only proof of his agony. "I will obey my doctor's orders."

A month had passed. *Two weeks, goddamn it, only two weeks until Pearl's eighth birthday.*

Jack trotted beside me, his saddlebags bulging with greens,

pickled artichokes, dried beans, and flour. I'd traded two jars of pickles, a dozen potatoes, a tooth extraction, and our playing cards for the food. Ehtishem Zain ate more per meal than Pearl and I did in a single day. The playing cards were a sacrifice, but I hadn't aided the man so we could starve for the rest of the winter after he had healed and left, a departure that loomed on the horizon. And even if we went with him, we'd need more food.

Pearl had stayed behind to help Judith clean her house. The baby was low and head-down in her pelvis, and she found chores uncomfortable and exhausting. The boys were in lessons much of the day now.

We could follow him. He must know a way through the Gates. And he owes us. We saved his life. I lifted the gate rope over its post and opened the gate. It moved without protest, without shaking the length of the dilapidated fence. I stared. Metal hinges, dull and scratched but rust free, supported the gate. It no longer leaned askew like a tired old gypsy. I opened and closed it again and again. No complaints. No clatter. No bang.

Did Luis? I shook my head and looked to the porch. Ehtishem Zain leaned on his crutches in the doorway. "You fixed the gate?"

The slightest smile tugged up the corner of his lips as he nodded, then he looked down and shifted his weight.

The chickens scurried around my feet as I crossed the yard toward him. "I ... ah ... you shouldn't be on your feet, you know."

He brushed his hands on the sides of his pants leaving dirt and rust streaks. "I sat." Again, he looked away. "I knew you'd say that."

I reached the porch steps. When he looked back at me I said, "Thank you. I'm grateful. Really."

Ehtishem Zain retreated into the house. "I know it bothered you."

Jack stood beside me his tail wagging like a clock pendulum. I scratched his left ear and followed the soldier into the cabin. The dog stood as I emptied the pack and lifted it from his back, then he trotted over to my patient for attention.

A strange silence hung between us. *Why did he fix the gate?* I knew how to be resentful, but ever since the encounter with Cyrus I'd felt a sense of gratitude toward Ehtishem Zain and didn't know how to handle it. How could I feel gratitude after all his people had done? Yet I did. We'd never spoken of it, but I didn't doubt the Ohnenran would have shot my tormentor had the Elder not backed down. What I didn't understand was why. *Why would he kill Cyrus? To protect Pearl and me?*

He'd said nothing about being sent for me. I'd said nothing about being wanted—or was it needed?—by the Ohnenrai. And if I *was* a double-edged sword, it seemed a mistake to let him under my skin. But there he was. *Jesus Christ.*

I retreated to the yard, unable to swallow the tension between us any longer. I brushed Jack until his coat shined. It was unnecessary; Pearl diligently tended the dogs' coats daily. Then I sang as I weeded the garden.

"Amazing Grace, how sweet the sound that saved a wretch like me." Between Mary and Judith's pregnancies and Ehtishem Zain's care, the weeds had gotten a strong hold. "I once was lost, but now I am found. Was blind, but now I see." Dandelions, clover, and bindweed flew over the chicken wire as I yanked them without mercy. Goat-Goat waggled her tail and filled her bottomless gut.

"Twas grace that taught my heart to fear and grace my fears relieved. How precious did that grace appear the hour I first believed." I dug out a dandelion root thicker than my thumb. "Through many dangers, toils, and snares we have already come." I untangled bindweed from its chokehold on the strawberries.

"Tis grace hath brought me safe thus far and grace will lead me home." Pearl's high, sweet voice soared around mine as she and Audie entered the yard. "The Lord has promised good to me. His word my hope secures. He will my shield and portion be as long as life endures."

She knelt beside me, and I kissed her cheek. "Yes, when this flesh and heart shall fail and mortal life shall cease, I shall possess within the veil a life of joy and peace." I looked past her to find the Stranger leaning on his crutches on the bottom porch step.

Our eyes met.

Pearl and I finished the song. "The earth shall soon dissolve like snow, the sun forbear to shine. But God who called me here below will be forever mine."

Ehtishem Zain looked up at the sky then turned back into the small, dark house.

SIX

"THE FIRST PERSON I saw die was my Uncle John." I closed my eyes and his wide-eyed, startled face emerged from memory. "I remember how surprised he looked as he stared down at the hole in his chest." I wiped the wet plate Pearl had handed me and put it in the rack above the counter. Ehtishem Zain remained at the table. Pearl said nothing. She knew my horror stories. "I was younger than Pearl the first time I helped amputate a man's leg. It took so long. I'm still amazed he survived." I dried the iron skillet and returned it to the stovetop. Pearl pulled the sink plug and wiped down the basin's scratched enamel sides as I wiped the counters and stove. I reached for her damp towel. "Did you put out fresh bedding?"

Pearl sighed. "I'll do it now."

I kissed her temple. "Then we'll go to Judith's."

Her scowl disappeared. "C'mon, dogs."

I draped the towels over the sink and crossed the room to gaze out the door at her. The Ohnenran settled across the cot, his back against the wall and his foot upon a stool. I joined him, pulling up the other stool and removing his splint. I rested his foot across my thigh. "Tell me your pain on a scale of one to ten, one being mildest."

He nodded.

I stretched and flexed, turned and twisted his ankle.

"Two," with a twist to the inside. "One," as the heel pushed down. "Hmm, one, maybe two," from a twist to the outside.

I ran my fingers around the ankle, probing the tendons. "Anything?"

"No. It's fine."

Pearl's laughter and the dogs' barks carried into the house as I pulled a rolled bandage from my bag and wound it around his foot and ankle. "As long as you're careful and pay attention to any discomfort I'll keep off the splint and you can give up the crutches."

"That's sooner than you expected."

I nodded and wound the stretchy fabric over and under and around. It was amazing that the bandage, stained and frayed as it was, still stretched after so many years of abuse. "You don't have to elevate it unless there's swelling. A little won't be a problem, but if we see a lot I'll put on the splint."

"I'll be careful."

I looked up and our eyes met. His pupils dilated. I dropped my gaze and swallowed. "You've been a good patient."

He leaned forward and touched the back of my left hand with his index finger. I stared at his hand. It was so much larger than my own. "Ferahi-va—thank you. Rachel." The inflection in his tone made me look up. There was a slight curve to his lips—a smile. "For fixing, rather than shooting, me."

I released his foot to the floor and retrieved the splint and the used bandages. "You gave me no reason to shoot you."

"Even though I was born on another planet?"

His teasing stunned me and, blushing at the memory of my rudeness, I stood and stepped away. "I'm sorry. I was unkind that night. You surprised me."

Neutrality returned to his voice. "Have I offended you?"

I shook my head and bit my lower lip. "Ferahi-va."

"For what? You and Pearl have been helping and sacrificing for me. You owe me no thanks."

"Yes. I do." I met his gaze again. "You would've shot Cyrus." I twisted a bandage around my hand and looked down at the discolored fabric.

"Ah. Yes. I believe in rashnu."

"Justice?" I garroted my hand with the bandage. "I've known these people half my life, and they'd rather swallow lies than give Pearl and me justice."

He leaned forward. "What happened here?"

His quiet question and expression made me want to tell him about Cyrus and Joshua and the Children turning their backs on me. It made me want to tell him about my parents' cryptic messages. But I bit my tongue. "All the adults now in Suffer were children when your people interned them. Many came from religious sects that had joined together to protest the occupation." I took the bandages to the kitchen. "Few know what happened to their families. Maybe they're in other colonies or behind other Gates." I plugged the sink and ran some water to soak the bandages. "I'm one of the lucky ones who never has to wonder. I know my parents are dead."

"Rachel." He paused and I looked at him. "We knew our presence would provoke fanaticism. We didn't expect your people to turn that into a religious war against each other."

I shook my head. "Religion isn't terrorism."

"We know that. I know that. But one hundred days of worldwide terrorist attacks was, in my opinion, one hundred too many. The Ohnenrai should have stepped in sooner. We stood by too long while fanatics murdered innocent people."

"No, they didn't *stand by* for long. Your people jumped right into the fray and showed the fanatics how it's done. The Ohnenrai had no business being here, period, Ehtishem Zain. Don't blame Terrans for reacting with fear and anger. At least we *feel*."

He studied me. "You think we don't feel?"

"No."

"No, you don't think that or no, we don't?"

"No, you don't feel. You don't have emotions. Not the way Terrans do."

Ehtishem Zain shook his head, and I thought I saw a glimpse of sadness in his eyes. "We feel, Rachel. Fear most of all."

I snorted and turned my back.

"Why do you think we work so hard to contain our emotions?"

The drop in his tone and tightness of his voice caught my attention more than his words. I paused in washing the bandages. Soap bubbles popped in the sink, and wind whistled between the eaves and the wall above my head. I shivered and turned.

Ehtishem Zain was staring at me. He ran his hand over his close-cropped, black hair as his jaw tightened and a furrow appeared between his eyebrows. "What could be worse than losing yourself to your emotions?"

"Not feeling. That's worse I think. Much worse."

His expression smoothed. "Oh? All those uncontrolled emotions brought your people to their knees. Brought death. Destruction. Your internment."

I began to respond, but Pearl staggered through the cottage door, the laundry in her arms. "It's raining."

"Goddamn it. The blankets." I dashed out the door relieved to escape the weight of his unexpressed emotions, and mine.

The delicacy and complexity of Ehtishem Zain's carvings astonished me.

I returned from Sunday Afternoon Sermon the next rainy evening, exhausted from standing through one of Cyrus's marathon six-hour rants. Pearl, equally tired, had needed to be carried home. I staggered into the house, paying little attention to the Ohnenran, who sat on the front porch.

Once Pearl was settled, Jack and Audie trailed me to the kitchen. Too tired to eat, I gave the dogs water, poured a cup for myself, and leaned against the counter, eyes closed, trying to muster the energy to put Goat-Goat and the chickens to bed.

"Do you need help with the animals?"

Not for the first time, I noticed the resonant timbre of his voice. *Is there anything flawed about him? Besides his birth, of course.* I looked to where Ehtishem Zain filled the doorway. "How's your ankle?"

"Good enough to lead a goat into her pen."

"But not good enough to chase chickens around a muddy yard." I shook my head. "As tempting as the offer is, I want you to stay off that foot."

"But—"

"You agreed to heed your doctor's orders." I pushed away from the counter and slapped my thigh for Jack as Audie assumed his usual guard post in the bedroom. Ehtishem Zain eyed me from the doorway. I saw tightness in his jaw and mouth. "You disagree?" I said.

"You don't realize I'm much stronger than your usual patients."

Exhaustion lowered my self-censure and irritation bubbled to the surface. "*You* don't realize how many people make that same assumption and delay their recovery, soldier." I shooed him out of my path. "Since I'd like to get rid of you before there's no food left for the winter, I'd appreciate your continued cooperation."

He stepped back to the porch as I moved through the door. He now walked without crutches, although a limp slowed him as he went to the seating crates, picked up two things, and turned.

I froze, my gaze fixed upon the short, sharp knife in his right hand. I thought of the shotgun in its holder on the bedroom wall, safely out of reach. Pearl asleep in bed. The dog snuffling around the yard, oblivious to anything but the smells on the air. I knew the Stranger whittled and, of course, that meant a knife. I didn't know why I reacted.

Ehtishem Zain looked from me to the knife. His brows furrowed and stayed drawn down for a long moment. "I will never harm you or Pearl." He folded it and went into the house. "You've suffered enough, Rachel."

As he passed I saw the other object he held—a small piece of pine carved into an open rose. I looked down; wood shavings littered the porch. I wanted to follow him, to apologize, to ask what he meant. Instead, I stumbled off the steps and slogged through the mucky yard, pulled Goat-Goat into her pen, and exhorted Jack to help me chase the chickens.

When I returned to the house—muddy, exhausted, and chagrinned—the banked fire glowed within its coals and Ehtishem Zain lay on his cot facing the wall. Jack trotted to the bedroom and curled up with Audie while I wandered into our tiny kitchen. I stared at the beans soaking on the stove then poured another cup of water, sighed, and slumped at the table.

"Where is your food?"

I spilled water down my dress as I looked up.

The Stranger sat up. Tightness still showed around his mouth.

"Are you hungry?" I asked.

He swung his feet to the floor, stood, and hobbled across the room. He sat opposite me. "No, I'm fine. Where is the food that is allocated to you and Pearl?"

I almost laughed, would've if I hadn't been so damned tired. "No food is allocated to me. And the Sufferns barely provide for Pearl. Mostly, we eat what we grow, find, or catch. Or what is bartered for medical services." Wondering if I was facing some kind of trouble, I added, "I'm sorry for my earlier remark. Of course I expected to feed you, and I'll make do this winter. I've done some bartering and there are plenty of stray cats, squirrels, and rabbits to trap." I shrugged. Going without meals so Pearl had enough was nothing new to me. "We've been through lean times before. I'll go without..." His expression halted my thoughts. A dark hardness had settled over his face, and once again I wished for the shotgun.

His hand, resting upon the table, closed into a fist. "Intolerable."

I'd never considered that word terrifying until it slipped from his lips. His manner—cold and still as concrete—contained a weighty anger like a dam holding back a river. One crack and rage would pour down upon those who dared his wrath. I swallowed dry fear and leaned away. "Honestly, there's little food allocated to us."

I flinched as the Ohnenran slammed his fist on the table. But his voice remained calm as he replied, "Yes, Rachel, there is. Every colony has precise rations. You and Pearl are included in those calculations for Suffer. Your Elders receive a detailed delivery manifest that indicates how much is to be distributed *per individual*." He looked toward the bedroom then turned his gaze to me. "This is worse than I imagined."

He's not angry with me.

As if reading my thoughts, Ehtishem Zain leaned forward and his expression softened. "I'm not angry with you. Your earlier remark was justified. You should not struggle because you gave up food for me."

"But why would they withhold rations?" I asked the question more to myself than to the Ohnenran. Of course I knew the answer. *That goddamned bastard.* Cyrus wanted me weak.

SEVEN

AUDIE'S RUMBLE was the first sign of trouble. Jack joined him and set to growling and pacing. The gate banged and the chickens squawked and fluttered away from rapid footfalls crunching the gravel.

"It's Adam." Pearl dropped the peephole rag and opened the door as Mary's son reached the porch.

"Rachel, come quick. Mother's in labor and it's bad."

I'd grabbed my bag the moment Pearl had identified him. Now I threw my brown wrap over my hair as I crossed the room. "C'mon, Pearl. I'll need your help." That Mary's delivery wasn't going well didn't surprise me. The baby was big. I'd warned her to send for me the moment she went into labor, warned her that the baby might have to be cut out whether Michael, her husband, approved or not.

Adam's gaze jerked between the Ohnenran and me. I turned to my patient. "Stay off that foot."

Mary and the baby were beyond my help when we arrived. Michael glared at me as I entered the bedroom. She lay cold and gray, naked and exposed. "Adam, tell the Elders what's happened.

Pearl, go tell the women." I turned as I rolled up my sleeves. "I need to be certain the baby is gone, Michael."

He stared at me as I washed my hands. "Do what you must." He turned away but paused and added, "If the baby is dead, leave it in her. I'll bury them together. I guess it's how she'd want it."

I tried to force the baby back up, but it was so deeply lodged in Mary's birth canal I'd have to break her pelvis to remove him. My only option was to cut through her belly. "Oh, Mary, this shouldn't have happened." I was glad Michael had left the room. I didn't doubt he'd blocked her c-section. He'd never wanted her to have one and we'd argued about it. I'd called him an old fool and had told him he'd kill her if he prevented it. I hated being right.

A slap and harsh words told me Michael was taking his rage out on Adam. Mary's youngest son had defied his father in fetching me. He'd pay a harsh penalty for it, but I couldn't interfere.

The placenta had ruptured. Mary's belly was full of cooling blood. It spilled out over her pale body, staining the sheets, the bed, the floor. I didn't care. *Let him see what he's done.* I found the umbilical cord and the infant's chest—both still. I closed my eyes and felt the baby's body. Another boy; another big, strong boy whose struggles to escape had cost his life and his mother's. I stitched Mary's womb and skin, cleansed the gore from her body, and covered her with a clean blanket. I washed her life from my hands and instruments, packed my medical bag, then went to tend Adam's fresh wounds.

Michael glowered at me as I entered the living room. "Well?"

I went to the corner where Adam stood facing the wall. "I'm sorry, Michael. They were in God's hands before I got here."

"Weak. Old and weak." He turned around the room like a caged animal.

A wise woman would keep quiet.

"I shoulda taken a younger wife years ago."

Blood dripped from Adam's nose. I grabbed a stool. "Sit." I yanked gauze and scissors from the bag and tried to ignore the misogynist pacing the room.

"How old are you, boy?"

Adam winced, whether at his father's question or my ministering I didn't know. "Fourteen, sir."

Stay out of this.

"Fourteen? Already? I wasted fourteen years on that woman? Think of how many children I could have. And now she goes and dies on me and takes the baby with her."

I straightened. "Enough! I told you the baby was big. If I'd been called here when labor began they'd be alive now. Her life and the baby's were in your hands, Michael. *You* let them die."

His hands curled into stony fists as he stomped across the room. "You'll pay for those words, harlot."

Adam began to stand, but I shoved down on his shoulder as I stepped around him, scissors in hand, ready to make the boy an orphan.

Our fight ended before it began as the door opened to Pearl, Cyrus, and Jonah. The men engaged Michael as Pearl and I tended Adam. When David and John, Michael's older sons, arrived with their wives, Pearl and I made a hasty retreat.

She spoke as we passed Suffer's perfect little homes. "Momma?"

"Yes?" I really didn't want to talk. Too much grief and anger polluted my mind.

"Why didn't Michael send Adam sooner?"

Because he's an evil, misogynistic bastard who deserves to have his testicles diced. "I don't know, Pearl. I really don't know."

"Didn't he love her?"

We passed through Suffer's gate and I shivered. I'd forgotten my wrap in Mary's room. "No, I don't think he did."

"But they were married."

"A lot of people marry without love, Pearl. Especially in Suffer."

Then there was only the soft sound of our skirts and the tap-tap-tap of a flicker looking for dinner high up on a dead tree.

"Did he do that to Adam?"

"Yes." I looked down at her. "Honey, don't ask any more questions tonight. I don't have any happy answers."

The dogs seemingly sensed our dark mood and stayed close, forgoing their usual wildlife safari as we followed the winding path up into the forest.

The lowering sun set the sky afire as we reached our yard. "I'll get the chickens and Goat-Goat, Momma."

I nodded and thumped up the porch, the brown leather bag gaining weight with each step. I glanced at Ehtishem Zain, who sat on one of the porch crates. "Did you eat?"

"Are you all right?"

I wasn't sure what startled me more, the depth of concern in his voice or the look of it on his face. I stared at him then looked down. Blood covered my light gray dress. I nodded. "Mary and the baby died."

He remained silent. I looked up to find him watching Pearl and the dogs. He whispered something too low for my ears then touched two fingers to his heart, to his forehead, and raised them upward as if releasing something to heaven. "They are a loss that should not be."

I dropped the bag, crossed the yard to snatch a clean dress from the wash line, and headed for the gate. "Leave the animals, Pearl. I need to bathe. Jack! Audie!"

Chickens squawked and scattered as my daughter and dogs loped after me.

His gesture says he believes. In what? A higher power? Questions had occupied my mind from the moment I saw the Ohnenran's gesture. *Was it a show?* The questions and fear of nightmares kept me awake into the night. *What higher power can the Ohnenrai embrace beyond their own? I've never seen any sign they're religious or believe in anything other than their own might.* I pulled a blanket around my shoulders and left Pearl asleep.

Ehtishem Zain lay on his cot reading by firelight, but he looked up as I entered the room. "Will there be an inquest?"

I shrugged as I poured a cup of water and ignored my empty stomach's complaints. "Likely. Because she was an Elder." I watched him over the rim of the cup as I sipped, then I lowered it. "She's not the first Suffern woman to die in childbirth. Death and birth, birth and death; we walk such a fine line."

"There is great power in women."

"Is there? Tell me where. I'd like to find some."

He closed the book and sat up. "You survive, Rachel, despite denial of food, proper shelter, aid. Why do you persist? Why not give up?"

His emotionless words triggered pride, rage, and a concrete certainty that I must protect my child. "Pearl."

He nodded. "That is something we lack."

"Children?"

He made a little noise in his throat. "No, a connection to them, a drive to protect them as individuals. When they are very young, they're strangers. Once they're old enough to leave the Nest, they're enemies or allies."

"You view your children as enemies?" I crossed to the fireplace and settled on the warm hearth. "How sad."

"Hmm. Sad. I never thought of it that way."

"Do you have any children?"

"Offspring, yes." He looked down at the floor. "Children, no."

"What does that mean?"

He met my gaze again. "We don't raise our own children, Rachel. They're conceived according to formula, raised in groups, trained for occupations as determined by caste. The Ohnenrai rarely foster long-term relationships."

How awful.

"Most Ohnenrai connections are about competition. Only the Elite families marry, and those bonds are for power and privilege."

I tilted my head and studied him. "Why are you strangers to each other?" The coals settled, sending a small whoosh of embers up the chimney.

"We never know when someone will die." He sat back. "The people in the two ships orbiting your planet are all that's left of a billion Ohnenrai."

"What happened to your world?"

He looked up at the ceiling as if seeing through it. "Orbiting Terra is a mother ship large enough to hold eight million people. In a matter of minutes that ship bridged a distance that light needs over five hundred years to cross." His gaze returned to me. "That kind of power demands sacrifices."

His neutral expression seemed a strange accompaniment to his sad story. "How is that possible?"

"What?"

"Covering that distance? Destroying so many people? What technology permits such a thing?"

"We bend space."

I must have looked confused because he explained, or tried to. "We harness stars to open wormholes. But the technology is stolen and its owners are a vengeful people. They destroyed Ohnenrah as my people watched. And we're still feeling their wrath in the genetic degradation they began. They've slowly destroyed us from the inside out, and we've been helpless to reverse their vengeance. There are fewer and fewer Ohnenrai children to raise."

I couldn't imagine his people helpless. *What kind of enemy have they made?* The destructive technology he implied stopped my breath.

An owl whoo-whoo'd and the wood on the fire sighed.

"Yet you do to us what was done to you. How can you live with yourselves?" I watched the grotesque shadows that lurked within the fireplace then looked at him. "How can you face me?"

His eyes reflected the banked fire's faint red glow; the rest of him was lost to darkness. "It shouldn't be like this. But we lost our way when we lost our planet. And it continues unabated—the death and destruction. I'm not sure my people know how to stop."

I turned away. "The Ohnenrai must be very desperate."

"Why do you say that?"

"Because only desperate people would bring their suffering to others."

"We weren't always this way. But, yes, now we're broken and desperate." Ehtishem Zain lay back on the cot, his hands behind his head, and stared at the ceiling. "Desperation spawns mistakes."

I folded my knees to my chest, rested my cheek on them, and watched the slow pulse of the glowing coals.

I opened my eyes to the gray light of early morning and Pearl's steady breathing. I didn't remember coming to bed.

Today we faced a funeral, maybe an inquest. Certainly questions, accusations, judgment. Mary's and the baby's deaths focused attention on me.

I gazed at Pearl's beautiful face; so like my own—her bow lips curved in a slight smile, her thick, black eyelashes, her long, heart-shaped face and narrow nose. *My perfect Pearl.* Only her ice-green eyes weren't mine. She stirred and opened those eyes, and I had to look away.

I sat up and spied the blanket neatly folded across the foot of the bed. Then I realized the dogs were gone. I reached for the shotgun but stayed my hand as I heard a short, sharp whistle and the dogs yipping. The porch creaked and the dogs' nails clicked across the wood.

"Something smells good." Pearl hopped out of bed and cracked the bedroom door. "Oh. Momma, look." She began to open the door.

"Pearl Pryne, get dressed." She slammed the door shut and scuttled to the washroom. I followed her to the doorway, and she faced me with flushed cheeks and a trembling jaw. "Where's your caution, child? You seem to forget he's our enemy."

"I'm sorry. It's just that he's so ... nice."

I swallowed a lump of fear and chagrin. I knew she felt that way. *So do I.* "He is dangerous, Pearl. And in a few days I will send him away. Then we will be left to fend for ourselves as we always have. You. Can't. Trust. *Anyone.*" The words were as much for me as for her.

Pearl nodded. "I-I just want to be friendly, Momma."

I sighed. "I believe in good manners and civility, you know that. I just don't want you getting comfortable. I don't want either of us doing that." *The folded blanket. Christ, Rachel, heed your own advice.* I hugged her and wiped her tears.

We dressed and joined Ehtishem Zain at the table.

Though the meal was no different than what Pearl and I cooked, somehow eggs and toast, honey and yogurt tasted better because someone else had prepared them. And Pearl's delight only grew when she learned the Ohnenran had completed most of her morning chores.

"I couldn't milk Goat-Goat. I've never done it and didn't think she would appreciate my efforts."

Pearl offered to teach him.

"Another time." I cleared the dishes from the table. "We have a funeral today. No dawdling please."

She nodded, thanked Ehtishem Zain, and skipped out the door. The world was right again for her.

"You disapprove."

I glanced at him. "Of the meal? No. I didn't lie when I said it was delicious and a pleasant surprise. Thank you."

He turned a small wood object in his hands, one of his carvings. "Not the meal, her relaxed caution. You think she should trust me less."

"I think Pearl should trust no one." I added kindling to the stove and water to the wash pot. "Trusting others makes you weak."

"No. Trusting blindly does, but you must teach her to choose who to trust."

"Don't you lecture *me* about teaching trust, Ohnenran. My parents trusted your people. That earned them each a death sentence. I trusted my Elders. That got me raped and pregnant and rejected!"

The words hung between us, defying gravity, defying privacy, defying my will to retrieve them. I swallowed and pushed past him. "I have a funeral to attend."

Snatches of conversation swirled around Pearl and me.

"Ohnenran..."

"...terrible sin..."

"Who fathered the girl..."

I wanted to walk away, run from the innuendo and rumors. The pressure of judgment flattened me. Their continuous dissection made me feel transparent. But I wouldn't disrespect Mary and her baby. So I endured the murmurs and the sly and not-so-sly glances.

Cyrus was droning. "A mother's love is tainted by the sins of Eve, yet in heaven shall it be cleansed and purified in the glory of God. And so our sister rises up to be with her maker, to be made as pure and perfect in heaven as she was impure and tainted on earth."

I wanted to punch him in the mouth. *Bastard.* Pearl and I stood apart from the Sufferns but not far enough to miss the shift in their attitude and glances. Their gazes now traveled over me, over Pearl, then beyond. After the fourth such look I turned to the trees and saw him.

Ehtishem Zain stood at attention at the edge of the woods.

"In the *Book of Revelation* it is said: *He will wipe away every tear from their eyes and death shall be no more, neither shall there be mourning nor crying nor pain anymore, for the former things have passed away.* And so we shall not mourn our departed sister and the child we will never know. They are with God. There is no pain for them. There is no fear. There is only His glory and the glory of a mother's sacrifice."

What the hell is he doing? I knew the Ohnenran was paying respect, but I wondered if he had any fear, or sense.

"No. Do not fear for those who have gone ahead to heaven, Children. Rather, fear for yourselves. God's test is yet to come, but already the Devil lurks among us. He grows fat on our weakness, lulls us into false security, and tempts us to trust. Do not forget the sacrifice of those who go before you unto that veil. They walk ahead of you in the valley of the shadow of death that you may have no fear."

I was torn between slapping the Ohnenran for his audacity and hugging him for his respect. Instead, I stood and endured, as always. I endured a eulogy that strayed from a dead wife and child toward an attack upon my daughter and me. I endured blatant stares and former friends shifting further away. I endured Pearl's questioning look as she noticed the growing gulf between *us* and *them*.

"Thou preparest a table before me in the presence of mine enemies. Thou anointest my head with oil; my cup runneth over. Surely goodness and mercy shall follow me all the days of my life, and I will dwell in the house of the Lord forever. A-men."

Never had I been so grateful for Cyrus to shut up. I caught Pearl's hand. "Let's go home."

"But what about Judith?"

Damn. She'd had mild contractions for several days, but Lot had caught me as we'd arrived for the funeral. Her contractions had changed that morning.

"A word, Rachel."

I stiffened. Cyrus stood behind me, his hand pressing my elbow.

"There will be an inquest this evening. A matter of procedure, I assure you. No one doubts you did your best. You always perform admirably, especially under pressure." He caressed my arm.

I swallowed and nodded but didn't turn to him. "Of course, Elder."

"Let's see ... Adam will be punished for defiance after the wake. You'll tend his wounds, of course. Then we have some procedural matters. So you'll return to God's House before sunset. Thank you." His hand slid down my arm, over my wrist, then away.

I inhaled against panic and focused on the hollow thud of dirt hitting Mary's pine box. I didn't fear the inquest; I'd been through plenty of them. The facts were plain and irrefutable. The baby's head had been too large to pass through the birth canal and he'd become lodged. The infant's struggles had torn the placenta away from the uterine wall. Mary had bled to death and the baby had drowned inside the womb. I'd warned Mary, Michael, and the Council of this possibility. I'd maintained that she might need a caesarean section and that a vaginal delivery could kill them both.

Bile burned my throat. I feared scrutiny. I feared anything that brought attention to Pearl and me, anything that Cyrus could twist into an excuse to remove her from my protection.

I will kill Pearl and myself before I let that bastard touch her.

I looked toward the trees, but Ehtishem Zain was gone.

When dirt filled the grave, and Mary and child were no more than worm food, the colony moved to the day's next event—the flaying of skin from her youngest child's back. His crime was defying his father in attempting to save his mother and unborn brother. His crime was seeking help.

Judith turned from the Scaffold, her advanced pregnancy an excuse to avoid communal cruelty. "Pearl, go with Judith. I'll come by after the inquest. If her status changes significantly send one of the boys for me."

"Okay. Should I take Audie?"

"Take both dogs."

Pearl ran to catch Judith, taking her arm as the dogs circled.

Adam, stoic as his mother, endured the whipping with few tears. I wished he would cry. After, as I applied arnica and antibiotic ointment to his welts, he let silent tears flow. Rebecca, his oldest brother's wife, held him. I gave her instructions for changing his bandages then headed home to eat and speak with Ehtishem Zain, if he had returned.

As I threaded through the woods wishing I had Jack with me, I thought about the Ohnenran's departure. Pearl's birthday loomed and I had no idea how to keep Cyrus from taking her.

Someone will come for you. I still heard my mother's whispered words.

I thought of Audie and Jack. *The dogs trust him. And he knows it. But so what?* I couldn't see why he would want Pearl and me. What would the Ohnenrai want with two castoffs of a castoff society? Maybe my parents were wrong. Maybe I was just a dull-edged nothing. Maybe the Ohnenran really had just broken his ankle and needed help. Maybe my memories were nothing more than delusions. *Nothing more. Nothing special. And it doesn't matter. He's leaving soon, then we'll pick up our lives.*

The thought of dealing with Cyrus again tightened my chest. I inhaled against panic, and then again. The soldier's presence had deterred my predator. *He could've—should've—left weeks ago.* But having a protector, deliberately attained or not, had brought a relief I hadn't realized I'd needed. And the thought of losing that buffer made my guts churn. *When he leaves, we'll go right after him. Maybe we can follow his trail. Maybe there's a way through the Gate.* "Maybe."

Cyrus stepped into my path. "Maybe, what, Rachel?"

My mind and body went cold and my breath caught.

"Maybe you should return to your followers and leave this woman and her child alone."

I jerked around at Ehtishem Zain's voice. Once again, I stood between Scylla and Charibdis. Only this time I knew which was the worse monster.

"Maybe you should consider the damage you've done to her already tenuous reputation, Ohnenran."

I turned back. "What *he's* done? How dare you call the kettle black? The only thing he's done, Elder, is obeyed orders to remain off his feet until his ankle heals. He's been an ideal patient and a gentleman. A word I would never use to describe *you*."

"Well, Rachel, the Gate Patrol is quite interested in your *gentleman*." Cyrus looked past me. "They found his presence in Suffer rather surprising. Criminals usually avoid detention colonies."

I looked at Ehtishem Zain. Of course his expression remained unreadable. I looked back to Cyrus's dark sneer and began to laugh. Perhaps it was exhaustion, perhaps fear, likely both. "You're an idiot if you think I'll believe that. Why would the Ohnenrai care what you have to say?"

Cyrus's sneer twisted into a snarl, but Ehtishem Zain closed the space between us and the Elder stepped back. Cyrus spat at the soldier's feet then stomped past me. "Enjoy your laugh, woman. I'll see you at the inquest." He looked over his shoulder at the Ohnenran. "You know I'm right. Your days in Suffer are numbered, hu."

"Ahzish," the Ohnenran muttered as Cyrus retreated.

"He's worse than a snake," I responded to Ehtishem's curse.

"And I am worse than a pig."

"Don't say that." The words came from somewhere deep inside me. A part of me that wanted to believe Cyrus had lied, that knew I shouldn't trust Ehtishem Zain but did anyway.

I continued down the path, but stopped at the gate and surveyed my home. I'd been so enmeshed in my own struggles that I hadn't seen reality. The dilapidated cabin's roof failed to block the elements —rain in the spring, mosquitoes in the summer, wind in the fall, snow in the winter. The yard consisted of mud and dung and weeds. The fence sagged and bowed, held up and yanked down by blackberry vines.

The Ohnenran stood beside me, his hand on the gate and his gaze on me.

Cruelty, threats, innuendo. So many vile words and deeds filled my mind. Mary's avoidable death, Michael's rage and misogyny, whispered accusations and judgment from all quarters for so many years, my husband's death, Cyrus's cruelty and his covetous eyes on Pearl. Cyrus. Pearl. *My precious Pearl.*

"I can't do this anymore." I stared at the horrible, dilapidated shit-hole where I'd birthed and raised my daughter. A crack in my defenses widened. A trickle of despair threatened to become a deluge. "I cannot."

The Stranger touched my elbow. "Walk with me."

He led me to the place in the river where I bathed, the place where I'd washed away so much fear and sin. At the shoreline a red-winged blackbird balanced atop a cattail, tick-tick-ticking to companions among the reeds. The water flowed swift and cold, runoff from melting snow swelling the river. The lowering sun turned the water gray, the sky orange and purple.

We reached the shallow rapids and Ehtishem Zain turned to me. "There is an underground settlement, Haven, several weeks' south of here by foot. I can take you and Pearl there, Rachel. You only have to ask. You only have to trust." He looked down at his large hands and nodded. "I know that's asking a lot, and you have every reason not to. I have nothing to offer but my word." He reached toward me, his palm open and inviting. "For what little it is worth in your mind, you have my promise to do everything I can to get you away from Suffer and protect Pearl and you."

I stared at his raised hand, scarred palm outward, hovering as if to touch my cheek. I didn't respond. *Ask him what Cyrus meant. I shook my head. No. What does it matter?*

He lowered his hand but leaned toward me, his knees bent and head ducked to look into my face at my eye level. "I'm offering my help." His brow drew down and his voice deepened. "Take it."

"I'm sorry. I don't know how to trust." I stepped back. "Anyone." I turned for the house.

"I'm supposed to be dead, Rachel."

I stopped but didn't turn. "Are you a criminal?"

"No, but—"

"That's all I want to know. You're leaving, so keep the rest to yourself, Ehtishem Zain."

EIGHT

"YOU'LL PAY for those words, harlot." Michael's threat repeated like a litany in my mind as I sat alone in the judgment room on a wooden bench facing the three members of the Elders Council. The next eldest member of the Children of Divine Suffering, Michael now held his deceased wife's seat. Without Mary's support, I was sunk.

I didn't bend to your will seven years ago, and I won't start now.

Jonah, the ostensible head of the council, rapped a gavel on the table. The sharp sound reverberated through the empty room. "We have reviewed the circumstances of our colleague's and her unborn child's deaths and find no fault in your actions, Rachel Pryne. The circumstances were, in this council's opinion, unfortunate and unforeseeable. We see no grounds for punishment."

Unforeseeable? I bit my tongue until I winced and nodded silent acceptance of their stupidity.

"Have you any words on this matter?" I shook my head and rose. "Remain seated. There is another matter this council wishes to address."

Michael pinned me with a malevolent, half-lidded gaze, and I braced for his lies as I sat. No doubt I'd pay with my hide for my disrespect. Well, they'd find out just how much pain I could endure. Adam had nothing on me when it came to stoicism.

But it was Cyrus, not Michael, who spoke. "The Ohnenran does not belong here. Today he demonstrated his ability to travel. This council can see that he lingers for no good reason and endangers your daughter with his presence and influence."

I stood and the bench tipped back striking the floor with a sharp *bang*. "His influence? What sway can an Ohnenran soldier hold over my daughter? How stupid do you think Pearl is?" I did nothing to disguise the contempt in my voice. "How reckless do you think I am?"

"You will watch your words and your tone, woman. And sit. This council speaks the will of God." Jonah rapped the gavel.

"And I speak the will of her mother."

"You are long compromised, woman. This council decides the girl's path."

"As her mother, I have no right to determine what is best for her?"

"Sit." Jonah's voice filled the cold room.

"I won't. And I won't be silent. I don't trust the judgment of this council. Let the community decide what will happen to us, like they did before."

"Enough."

"Let the Ohnenran speak for himself. Let him give his reasons for staying. Or do you prefer lies and innuendo? Pearl and I will stand on the Scaffold again and face the Children. I have the right to request community judgment for her."

"You have no rights. Your child is the property of this council. Our decision is final. The girl will go to Elder Cyrus tomorrow morning. You may leave, Rachel Pryne."

With those words, my world shuddered. The pieces fell away

and a new one coalesced, a world where Earth's enemy became my ally. I stared at Jonah, stunned by his order, by the hard finality in his voice. I opened my mouth then snapped it shut, turned, and rushed from the room. There was no point in arguing and no time for fighting. My only advantage was their assumption that fear of the unknown would stop me from leaving Suffer. I ran through The Cross, past the Scaffold—its whipping post stained with Adam's blood—and toward the gate.

"Momma! Wait!" Pearl ran down Hub Road behind me, her long braids bouncing across her shoulders and her skirt rustling. "Momma, Judith's laboring. Her water just broke." She huffed several deep breaths as she grabbed my hand and tugged me back toward my only friend's home. Jack and Audie snuffled and waggled around us. I held back, my feet and mind wanting only to flee Suffer. "Momma?"

I glanced across the square and saw Cyrus watching us. My stomach rolled and bile crept up my throat. I swallowed and felt the acid burn of fear in its wake. *Judith's laboring.* I turned away from his oily smile. "All right. Do I have time to get my bag?"

Pearl nodded. "I think so. Lot's with her and she said she doesn't feel like pushing yet."

"Let's go back to the house." We set off at a jog, the dogs circling and venturing in and out of the dense, green forest. Their passage rustled ferns and they yipped as they chased black squirrels. An indignant blue jay, his charcoal crest flashing, called harsh criticism of their enthusiasm. Pearl laughed.

We entered the house and I went for my bag beside the cot. "I need clean towels from the medical cabinet, clamps and scissors from the sterile box." Pearl fetched them.

Both dogs nuzzled and whined as the Ohnenran scratched their ears and chins and watched us. He sat on the cot, his back against the wall, and a book in his lap.

Our eyes met.

I'm offering my help. Take it.

I swung my gaze to Pearl then back to the Stranger. He put the book aside and shifted to the edge of the cot. He mirrored my glance at Pearl, and then returned his gaze to mine.

Someone will come for you.

"Will you keep your promise?" I asked.

Ehtishem rose. "Yes. You have my word." The dogs calmed and pricked up their ears.

"Help us. Please. They mean to take her from me."

"Momma?" Pearl's voice was high and tight. She ran to me.

"When?" he asked.

"Tomorrow morning."

He nodded once. "What is happening now?" The calm neutrality that settled over him soothed the fear knotting my guts.

"Judith is delivering her baby."

"You must attend her." It wasn't a question. "How long?"

"A few hours."

Pearl tugged my hand. "What's wrong?"

I looked at her but couldn't stop the tears that ran down her cheeks; there was no time and it was best she shed her fear now. "The Elders want to take you tomorrow. I won't allow it. We're leaving Suffer when I return." I turned back to the Stranger. "Ehtishem promised to help us reach another community. He will keep us safe."

He nodded. "Go to your friend, Rachel. Can Pearl remain here? With Audie?"

"Yes."

"Good. We'll pack for quick travel. The dogs will come. We can't take Goat-Goat; we'll release her and the chickens. Be prepared to leave when you return."

I knelt before Pearl. "Do as he instructs. I'll be back as soon as possible. I'll get you away from Cyrus."

"But, Momma—"

"No. Cry now, Pearl. There won't be time later."

I took the towels and instruments and left. As I trotted back to Judith's house, Jack at my side, I squashed any fear of the looming unknown, any fear of the madness in trusting an Ohnenran with Pearl's safety. I had no choice.

———

Judith's delivery had been slower than I'd expected, and I'd left her and her new son sleeping only a few hours before dawn.

"Bring me the screwdriver, Pearl." Back in the cabin, I pulled aside the crate beside our bed as she scurried from the room and back. The tool's flat head fit into a groove in a floorboard and I popped up the wood piece. I pulled it out and removed its neighbor then fished a plastic bag from the hollow. Within were two boxes of shotgun shells.

The dogs' nails clicked across the floor as they turned and trotted into the main room, both rumbling deep in their chests. Male voices carried across the yard. I checked the gun's chamber. It held three rounds. *Jesus Christ, I don't want to kill anyone.* I stuffed the ammunition into my bag and followed the dogs. "Stay behind me." I touched Pearl's shoulder.

"Quiet, dogs." Ehtishem spoke evenly. The floorboards creaked as he crossed the room and went out to meet our now-mutual enemy.

I stepped to the door, the gun resting in my arms. They knew I had it; hopefully the sight would be enough. I shivered in the predawn cold and glanced up through the trees. Stars still winked, their glow growing fainter as dawn awakened the world to a rosy gold morning.

"Step aside, Ohnenran. You've sped this matter, but it's not your place to speak." Jonah's distinct nasal voice came through the shadows as the group emerged from the trees. He opened my gate.

Four men had come for Pearl—Jonah, Lot, Cyrus, and Luis. I hated seeing Lot and Luis there. No doubt they'd been included as voices of reason and reassurance. They were the closest I had to male allies in Suffer. *It won't work. I have a new ally now—a real ally.*

"If my presence provoked this situation, it is my business." Ehtishem took one long stride to the edge of the porch and stopped, looking down upon the men. His hands and arms hung loose at his sides, but the sheer size of him would have turned back three Suffern men. A group of four, however, showed that they'd anticipated trouble, and they approached with sure strides and lifted chins.

"Rachel, we don't want a fight. This is about what's best for Pearl. You know that."

I glared at the speaker. His tired face showed the only weakness of the group. "Lot Jones, you don't belong here. You should be at home caring for your wife and newborn son, rather than taking my child from my arms." He flinched as my sharp words sliced right to the heart of the matter.

"Rachel, be reasonable." Luis stepped forward and raised his hand, palm outward. "You know this is about Pearl's well-being and education. We want what's best for her. And you." He ignored Ehtishem.

"You bald-faced liar. You'll put her into the hands of the Devil himself."

"That's enough, woman!" The chickens rustled and squawked at the booming anger behind Jonah's words. "I'll not have you blaspheme a good man. Elder Cyrus offers to care for and educate your bastard child, and you show not one lick of gratitude. You're not fit to mother the girl. That's been quite clear for some time. But we've held off taking her because no one saw your instability as a threat to her welfare. Until now." His gaze slid to Ehtishem then snapped back to me.

I stared at him, at them, at the satisfaction that wrinkled the edges of Cyrus's watery green eyes. My hands shook and I thumbed the gun's safety, struggling not to shoot him right between those eyes.

Cyrus gripped Jonah's shoulder. "Calm, please, Elder. There's no need to cut the poor woman down. We know she came to us traumatized by childhood horrors. Let's not add to her woes." He looked at Ehtishem. "Stranger, this business does not involve your opinion, and there's no reason for you to stand between us and the girl. The men of this colony care for our women in accordance with your people's laws as those laws abide by the will of God. I assure you I will treat Pearl as I do all other girls and women of this colony. She will be housed, fed, and educated. Her mother's fears are unfounded and caused by underlying infirmities that we wish to heal with God's help."

I saw Cyrus squeeze Jonah's shoulder and both men stepped forward.

Ehtishem angled his body and shifted toward them, but he still seemed relaxed. His voice, however, held cold steel. "I'm quite aware of how this colony's men treat the women, and if you follow Ohnenrai law some of you deserve death for your crimes against them. As for your claims of instability, in the six weeks I've been with Rachel and Pearl I've seen no sign of infirmity or danger in their relationship. I am prepared to leave Suffer. I am not prepared to leave this woman and child in your hands."

The four men stared at him.

The chickens burred and clucked and Goat-Goat shuffled her straw. Pearl's breath rasped. The dogs growled.

Cyrus spoke. "This is not Ohnenrai business. You've stayed out of our affairs this long, Stranger. Why involve yourself now?"

"Because I asked him to protect us." My finger tapped the shotgun's trigger guard.

"Are you insane, Rachel?" Lot's hands curled into whiteknuckled fists and the other men glared at me.

Hatred curled around us, waiting to strike. Luis and Lot exchanged glances as they flanked the two Elders and the group approached the porch. Ehtishem stepped back and shifted into a lower, defensive stance. I still had to stand on my toes to see past his hulking frame.

The men lunged. The dogs snarled behind me and Pearl whimpered. Ehtishem blocked the attacks, turning aside hands and twisting away from strikes. As he moved forward, I saw that all four assailants held knives. Luis circled, but Ehtishem blocked his arm and struck fast and hard, knocking him flat—a bear swatting a wasp. The other three men swarmed the Ohnenran.

Jonah landed on the ground and Ehtishem now held his knife. Lot and Cyrus stepped back, but so did the Stranger. He pivoted, slammed the blade into the crack between the doorframe and the wall, and thrust the handle sideways. It snapped off and he sent it skittering across the porch and into the bushes. He held up his hands. "I don't want to fight you."

"Then leave." Cyrus thrust his knife upward like he was gutting an animal.

Something caught my eye as Ehtishem shifted to match his enemies' movements. A blue stain bloomed on the left side of his green shirt and spread along his ribcage as blood seeped into the fabric. My grip tightened on the shotgun. "Ehtishem, move. I don't want to shoot you."

The Ohnenran ignored me, but Lot barked a sharp laugh.

Cyrus snorted. "There's nothing frightening about an unloaded gun, woman."

I brought the weapon's barrel up past Ehtishem's right arm and snugged it against my shoulder. "Please move, Stranger." This time he shifted to the left. I stepped past the doorway and sighted Cyrus. "Want to test that, Elder?" I slipped the safety off.

Luis stood, wavered, and gaped at me. Cyrus sneered. "Everyone knows you have no ammunition, Rachel. Stop playing cowgirl."

I lowered the barrel and fired. The porch step exploded into shrapnel and dirt kicked out toward the men as they jumped back. I pumped the gun and noticed even Ehtishem eyed me with arched brows. I brought the muzzle back up to point at Cyrus's chest. "Now. Get out of my yard and out of my life. Pearl and I are leaving with Ehtishem's help. Anyone who follows us will be shot. I welcome hell's warmth."

Cyrus opened his mouth, but I interrupted. "It won't be the first time I've killed a man, Elder. I've tolerated you for far too long, fear monger. Hypocrite." *Rapist. Murderer.*

Jonah stepped forward. "Leave then, Rachel. Throw your lives to the Devil. But don't come home crying when he's had his way and tossed you aside. That child's blood is on your hands, woman, not ours. Go sleep with dogs and devils."

"Rachel, please don't do this." Lot's plea might have swayed me before Ehtishem arrived in my yard, muddy and bloody. But now it was oil on water.

"We're leaving Goat-Goat and the chickens, Lot. Please return for them this afternoon. I want to know they're cared for. Tell Judith I'm sorry." I swallowed but couldn't afford remorse for leaving my best friend. She had a better life than Pearl and I ever would.

"Rachel—"

"My decision's done, Lot Jones."

We remained in the doorway. Ehtishem stood beside me, blood soaking his shirt. Pearl and the dogs were behind me. Her sobs and their gentle whines filled my ears. I kept the gun wedged hard against my bruised shoulder, the safety now on.

Pale blue and pink tinted the sky when our assailants' voices faded and Ehtishem grasped the cooling gun barrel. "Let go, Rachel."

I nodded and did as he said. I sucked in a breath. "Let me see that wound."

Ehtishem shrugged. "It's minor. We haven't time to bother with it."

I blocked him as he turned to the door. "It needs stitches. I can't drag your enormous carcass through the woods if you keel over from blood loss."

A smile twitched his lips. "Sew quickly."

"Pearl." Speaking sharply to cut through her fear, I turned and moved to the kitchen. Ehtishem followed.

"Yes, Momma?" She sniffed and gasped.

"Fetch scissors, thread, needle. Be quick."

She dragged the medical bag to the table. Ehtishem placed the gun on the counter and pulled his bloody shirt over his head. He tossed it on the floor, turned toward the sunlight streaming through the kitchen window, then raised his arm and rested it atop his head.

The wound stretched from stomach to back—beneath his ribs, around and up to his shoulder blade, and in some spots I could see black bone. I poured water from the kettle into a bowl then sponged the blood away and cleaned the gash. "No time for a pretty scar."

Ehtishem grunted, drew a deep breath, and released it. He remained still as I stitched the slice, smeared it with antibiotic ointment, and bandaged him. He lowered his arm and accepted the shirt Pearl offered.

She put extra bandages and ointment in my pack.

Ehtishem shouldered his pack and winced. "Aiya." I fetched a towel from the bedroom and wrapped it around the straps to pad where they hit his wound. "Ferahi-va," he said.

"Don't tear out those stitches."

He nodded as he adjusted the straps on Jack's saddlebag.

I settled a pack on Audie then straightened. The dog's whole body waggled as he watched me with intent brown eyes and pricked ears. I scratched his chin and smiled. Though I couldn't match his excitement, it did keep me from sinking into despair.

The Stranger strode to the door and looked at me. "Ready?"

I nodded. "Pearl?"

She grabbed her doll, took my hand, and we set off.

I paused at the gate, ran my hand over the carved roses, and stared down the length of ragtag fencing. I exhaled and stepped through.

Goat-Goat's bell followed us for a long way until it blended with the whooshing wind, the creaking trees, and the birds singing in the morning.

PART TWO
SPLIT

NINE

PEARL'S HEAD rested against Ehtishem's broad back. "Momma, I'm tired."

I heard the exhaustion behind her words and came abreast of her. Tears welled in her big green eyes and spilled down her cheeks leaving white paths through dirt and dropping dark splotches on his green jacket. "I know, Pearly Girly. We all are."

"We'll stop soon." Even Ehtishem's words came slowly.

I hadn't missed the limp creeping into his pace. "I should look at your ankle. It probably needs to be re-dressed. And I don't want you reopening that wound."

He nodded. "I'm looking for a safe place to stop."

"Okay." I touched Pearl's face. "Soon, baby, we'll stop soon. Then you can sleep."

"I wanna stop now, Momma."

The whine behind her words raked my nerves and it took all my patience not to snap at her. "I know, Pearl. Not long now. You can do this."

We continued up into the trees, moving deeper and deeper into the dark forest. The dense canopy enclosed us and I'd long ago lost my sense of time and place. I saw only gray bark and green leaves, moss hanging down and ferns climbing up. We could so easily hide in the unending forest but so could spying eyes. And each snap of a branch, every creak of a tree made me twitch.

But Ehtishem just kept moving up into the trees, unwavering in his pace and direction as if he knew this land like his own, as if he'd lived his whole life in these mountains.

Now exhaustion filled *my* voice as I said, "Ehtishem—"

"Here." We'd emerged onto a rocky, south-facing slope. He eased Pearl into my arms, dropped his pack off his chest, and looked around. "Stay here."

Pearl curled against me and began to cry. "I'm hungry. Hungry."

"Here." I offered her a piece of dried rabbit and some bread, then opened the water bottle. Our supply had halved during the day, but I knew Ehtishem wasn't drinking enough.

Returning with several large pine boughs, he found a flat area among the boulders and trees and began erecting a shelter. He came and went bringing more branches, then pine needles, until he'd constructed a crude, dense shelter.

I spread a blanket within it and settled Pearl beneath the branches. She whimpered and cried. I stroked her hair. "Hush, Pearl. Remember, you control your emotions, they don't control you." I tucked one of Ehtishem's thermals and another blanket around her and directed Jack to lay against her back, Audie to her front. She sighed and her breathing had slowed and deepened before I straightened from her shelter. I turned.

Ehtishem was watching me. "What does that mean?"

I returned his gaze, surprised by his question. "You know what it means." I stepped away from the shelter and leaned against a rock outcrop. "We've had this conversation before."

"Have you changed your opinion about my emotions?"

I reached back and tugged the tie from my braid. "You're only one man, Ehtishem. That's not enough to undo a lifetime of horror." I untwisted my hair, hissing as my fingers caught knots. I shook my head. "I'm sorry."

He turned away and descended into the forest.

I watched Ehtishem come and go, constructing another shelter opposite Pearl's.

"I'll sleep between the two." The inflection that had begun to color his sentences was gone. He stood as he finished the shelter, stretched, and grimaced. Then he fished two thin plastic bags from his pack. "I'll be back in a while. Don't worry. I'm setting these for water." He disappeared down the mountain as a response died on my lips.

I listened to the creak of the trees and the whoosh of wind through their branches. I slumped, fatigued all the way to my bones, but I wouldn't sleep, not until Ehtishem returned. *When did he become just Ehtishem to me?*

He finally came through the trees and settled beside me between the shelters. "Ten trees straight down; the bags are on a large maple." The monotone I hated robbed all the humanity from his words.

I handed him a piece of meat and the canteen. "You're not drinking enough, and I should look at your stitches and check that ankle." He took a small sip of water, popped the jerky into his mouth, and shrugged out of his jacket. I lifted his shirt and unwound the gauze and bandages. The long knife wound looked better than I'd expected—purplish but not infected. I smeared on more ointment, replaced the bandaging, and then sat back on my heels hoping he hadn't noticed the tremor in my hands when I touched him.

He ate a few dried apple slices and some dried strawberries, and otherwise remained still and silent. I drew spirals in the dirt with a stick. "Why are you supposed to be dead?"

"I stood in the way of a very powerful man."

"Military?" I looked up. He nodded and sipped the water. I chewed on my chapped lower lip and glanced at Pearl and the dogs. "But you said you're not a criminal."

"I guess that depends upon whom you ask. I'm an Ohnenrai soldier, Rachel. Doesn't that make me a criminal to you?"

I exhaled and tilted my head as I gazed at him. "Don't do that to me. Right now you're the lesser of two evils."

Ehtishem looked at me for a long moment. "My people don't think I'm a criminal, but they do think I'm dead." He took another longer drink from the canteen and looked away again.

I stared at my nails and noticed for the first time how calloused my fingers and palms were. "And no one searches for a dead man."

"If you knew more about me, Rachel, you'd want to finish the job."

I lowered my head and pressed my palms to my forehead. "*Goddamn you,* don't make me regret this decision." There was more anger behind my words than I'd expected, but it was the only way to keep fear at bay. If he was misleading me, as Jonah and Cyrus had accused, I would be incapable of stopping him. But I could not, would not, believe I had taken Pearl from Cyrus only to watch her suffer and die at Ehtishem's hands. I needed an ally and, like it or not, he was it.

"All right," he said.

He offered the canteen. I snatched it away. I took a deep drink then capped it and threw it on my bag. It made an unsatisfying slosh, and a scowl pulled my mood down a black hole. I yanked the medical bag toward me as I knelt beside Ehtishem's ankle. "Get your boot off. Please."

He eased it off and rested his heel on my knee. I pulled down his sock and unwound the pressure bandage. His ankle appeared normal. "Look away. Tell me if you feel this." I refused to look at his face. I pulled scissors from the bag and methodically poked and scraped his foot and toes, top and bottom. Each jab or scratch, a bit harder than necessary, elicited a simple "yes" from my patient. His quiet acceptance of my anger only fueled my ire. "It looks fine." I rewrapped the bandage. "Put on your boot."

Ehtishem did so, snapping each row of fasteners, tightening each strap with two strong tugs, and securing the ends into their slots on the side of each boot. He straightened and regarded me. "Rachel, don't deny what I am. Because I don't deny what you are."

I glared at him. "Oh? What am I?"

He paused before answering. "A prisoner. The child of accused terrorists."

I turned away and bit my lip, struggling to contain my emotions as I'd just counseled Pearl, but I lost the battle. "You didn't know my parents, Ohnenran. My mother was a doctor. My father was one of the first interpreters for the Ohnenrai. They were good people." I faced him and leaned forward. "Your soldiers *murdered* them." I shoved my scissors back in their case before I used them unwisely.

Nothing changed on his face. No shift in his posture. Nothing. His calm, his control, his complete acceptance or dismissal of my feelings crystallized my rage. I stared at my fists as they curled around the brown leather strap of my medical bag. My self-control slipped as the memories of my parents' last moments spilled into my brain.

My father striking an Ohnenrai soldier as the man tore me from my mother's arms. The sickening *crunch* as another soldier struck my father's face with his rifle. My father's bright red blood staining my mother's white coat. Her broken shriek as the sound of a weapon cracked the black night. An Ohnenran throwing me into a transport with a pile of terrified children. A whining shockgun pressed to the back of my mother's bowed head as she sobbed. *"I'm sorry, Rachel."*

I looked up at Ehtishem. I wanted to strike him, to beat him into a reaction. I wanted to make him angry, sad, hurt, something. Anything.

"I'm sorry, Rachel."

My mother's words from his mouth. A lump filled my throat, and I couldn't swallow or breathe. I jerked up, away, and stumbled to where Pearl slept. The dogs eyed me. Tears blurred my vision. As much as I wanted to deny his words, I couldn't. I knew they were true, had always known. I remembered hushed conversations when my father and mother and their friends had thought I slept. The diagrams and drills and safe houses. My mother hoarding medical supplies and showing me how to care for burns, broken bones, shrapnel wounds. How to amputate limbs, rudimentary plastic surgery. Fleeing to Fairbanks. Hiding in the woods. Innocent people didn't run and hide.

Ehtishem approached but stopped at arm's length. I looked up, tears making cold, thin tracks down my cheeks. His face wavered beyond my tears. I inhaled, released the breath slowly, and wiped my eyes with my dirty sleeve. Squaring my shoulders, I stepped toward him meaning to move past, but he held his ground. He raised his hand as if to touch my face but arrested the movement, a question behind the gesture and his eyes.

Never had I longed for a man's touch. Never had a man given me the choice. The men of Suffer had only taken. Even good, kind Joshua had claimed me like a piece of property. But not Ehtishem. "What do you want from me?" I whispered.

"Only what you want to give." His long, strong fingers hovered inches from my cheek. He shook his head. "I've never felt this, Rachel."

I looked past his hand to his parted lips then up to his hazel eyes. In those eyes I saw something unexpected—an unblinking intensity that drew me toward him until my tear-stained face rested against his palm. I closed my eyes and sighed.

Ehtishem echoed me and his breath warmed my skin. His lips brushed mine, withdrew, waited.

Which way to tilt? Toward the man or away? Toward the unknown or back to fear? *Maybe.* I tipped forward and pressed my lips to his. Ehtishem's hand slid through my hair to the nape of my neck and he pulled us together. His lips parted, our tongues touched, and we exhaled into each other.

All the fear and effort of the last three days, six weeks, and twelve years coalesced within me and I collapsed against him. Ehtishem's body, damaged by illness and injury, pushed by the need to defend and flee, should have given way to mine. Instead he was like the unbending oak, warm and living, pulling me into his sheltering arms, protecting me from the storms within and without.

His left arm encircled my back and his fingers caressed the curve of my waist just below my breast. My breath caught, then quickened. I wanted him. And that wanting escaped me in a low moan as his lips traveled my jaw to my ear and I tilted my head. Then our mouths met again, and I was lost in the feel of his skin as my hands slid beneath his shirt, up his back, around to his stomach and chest. They skimmed the bandage, a reminder of his efforts to protect me, to protect Pearl.

He pulled back. "Rachel." Longing and emotion deepened his voice, something I wouldn't have thought possible six weeks ago.

"No," I refused to release him. "Don't stop, Ehtishem."

"You're tired."

"I'm certain."

He cradled my face, tilted my head back, and peered down into my eyes. He seemed to be searching my soul. *"Rahzhel."* His voice dropped into the singsong Ohnenrai accent that he'd stifled all this time. He drew me back against him and pressed his lips to mine. His intensity was different, deliberate. He had made a decision and, as I now understood, Ehtishem Zain would follow that decision to the end of its course.

Ehtishem's lips tickled my ear. I turned my face, wanting to capture those lips with mine. "Rahzhel." I was snuggled and warm against his chest and felt his muscles shift as he tightened his arms. One pillowed my head and the other was wrapped around my hips, his hand splayed across my spine. "Don't bewitch me, Pairika."

I smiled at the nickname. It meant sorceress. But the sound of a dog's thumping tail brought me up. I opened my eyes and shifted, searching for Pearl.

"She's fine." Ehtishem kissed my shoulder. I shivered. "Still asleep. The sun is just rising and she's nowhere near waking."

I glanced past the opening of our bower and saw the stars still winking in a blue-black sky. They'd seemed so near last night. *As if I could pluck them from the heavens and string them into a crown for Pearl.* I shivered again as Ehtishem gently drew my hair back and trailed his lips over the soft skin where my neck and shoulder joined. I inhaled and tilted my head as he nuzzled his way toward my ear. But one of the dogs snuffled. "Wait. Please. I should dress."

Ehtishem stopped. "You do not want her to see us?"

I rolled onto my back. "That's not it. I don't know what to tell her. I don't know what this is."

He planted his hands on each side of my body, lifted himself over me, and gazed into my eyes. "This is what you chose last night, Rachel."

Warmth flushed my face and chest then spread through my body. "Ferahi-va."

Ehtishem exhaled and crushed his mouth to mine. He slid one strong arm beneath me and lifted me to him. I felt him between my thighs, against me, within me. I groaned and wrapped my legs around him.

We pushed and pulled, our bodies sliding together and apart, as the world turned around us, the heavens wheeled above us, and unseen forces moved against us.

When he came I lifted my hips, drew him in, and tried to fill myself with his strength. Then the thought of Ehtishem's quiet power pushed me over the edge into unreason and I buried my shuddering cries against his neck as he held me. He rocked me, stroked my damp hair, kissed away my tears. And I sank back into sleep's heavy darkness.

I opened me eyes to movement. Ehtishem was dressed and sat surrounded by our possessions in the space between the two pine shelters. I sat up, shivered in the cold morning air, and dragged my sweater over my head. "Why are you repacking?" I glanced past him at Pearl. She slept, her arm over Jack. And Audie's head, resting atop her hip, gently rose and fell with her deep, even breathing.

Ehtishem stopped and considered the rolled socks in his hand. "I never meant to feel this for you, and now I've endangered you and Pearl." He shook his head. "I only ever wanted to protect you."

"I don't understand."

Ehtishem dropped the socks and grabbed a pair of binoculars from atop his bag. He stood and focused on the sky. I heard a high-pitched whine and wanted to crawl beneath my blanket. The sound of an Ohnenrai spy drone was all too familiar.

"That's the second in as many hours." He turned and I saw regret in his eyes. "I wasn't lying when I said I wouldn't hurt you or Pearl, but it seems Cyrus made good on his threat to contact the Gate Patrol about me." He threw the binoculars onto the blanket.

Cold spread up my spine. "Why would they pay any attention to that lunatic?" I shook my head and dragged my skirt on. "How could he even reach them?"

Ehtishem crouched at the opening of the shelter. "All colonies have access to a comtab for emergencies."

"No one ever mentioned that. *You* never mentioned it."

"It only relays messages to and from your area's Gate Patrol."

I stared at him as my tired brain processed his words. "They've sent someone for you." His lips pressed into a thin line as he nodded. I looked at Pearl. "And Cyrus told them about us." My gaze returned to him. "And they'll follow my tracker." The Ohnenrai implanted location trackers in all their prisoners. I touched the back of my skull, recalling the staples that had closed the incision.

"Yes." Bitterness lowered his tone. He plucked an errant brown pinecone from our bower and crushed it with one hand. The seeds crunched and crackled beneath his anger.

I closed my eyes. "Goddamn him."

"Indeed." He plucked another cone, a closed green one, and pried apart the seeds. "You have a few days, maybe less. When he contacted them a second time to report you missing they became more motivated to push the matter up the chain of command."

I clenched my teeth and my fists as I let out an angry groan. "Why?"

"Why?"

"Why can't he just let us go?" I blinked, swallowed, and looked away. My gaze settled on the medical bag. "Wait. Why can't we remove the tracker?"

"Nava. It's not so simple, Rachel." His words chilled my hope. "Trackers are implanted in the brain and they're designed to destroy if tampered with. I can't deactivate it. I haven't the skills or the tools." His face shimmered and distorted behind my tears. I would die if Ehtishem tried to free us from his own military.

He stroked my damp cheeks. "I knew I was placing you in jeopardy, but I couldn't leave you and Pearl behind."

I shook my head. "It would've happened anyway. I'd planned to follow you when you left."

A smiled tugged up the right side of his mouth. "You're mad and brave, Pairika." He gazed at Pearl for a long moment then returned to sorting and packing. "We cannot linger."

I pulled on my boots and stood. "I'll fetch the water."

Ehtishem also stood. He slid his hand into the hair at the nape of my neck and pulled me to him. His other hand pressed into the curve of my back. "For so long I fought my feelings for you. I knew they were dangerous, and now you understand. I must leave you and Pearl. I'm the greater prize and can draw them away."

"No." I shook my head, but his grip tightened. He endangered us. If we stayed with him, they would find him, and they would find Pearl. I knew he spoke the truth even as I fought it. "We're better off with you. I'm not strong enough."

Ehtishem kissed me and kissed me and kissed me. He buried his face in my hair, and I clung to him. "You are the strongest woman I've ever known, Rachel." His lips brushed my skin as he spoke. "You will do what you must to keep her safe. You always have."

I inhaled. Ehtishem smelled like a warm day when the summer sun scorches the grass brown. I pulled away and nodded. "Pearl comes first." I swallowed my fears. They served no good purpose here. "What now?"

He stepped back, the emotion left his face and body, and he became the aloof Ohnenrai soldier once again. "I'm counting on the patrol to choose me over you. Without a tracker, Pearl won't show on their screen, and you're a low priority." He stripped the needles off a stick and sketched in the dirt a small circle, an X below, and a larger circle beneath that. "We're here." He tapped the X.

Both dogs rolled over and whined. Pearl stretched and yawned, then giggled as Jack and Audie snuffled and snuggled her.

I grabbed the canteen. The icy water made my teeth ache but focused my mind. I got dried fruit, crackers, and cheese for Pearl then returned my attention to Ehtishem's sketch as she ate and watched.

"The North Pacific U.S. Gate runs from the Canadian border to the Oregon/California border." He glanced up. "Do you know that geography?"

I nodded. "Yeah. Basically."

He pointed to the smaller circle. "This is Suffer." Then he dragged the stick to make a line that ran past our X to the larger circle. "This line is a north-south railroad track and the larger circle is the ruins of Seattle. Haven is beneath them."

Pearl leaned forward. "How can a community be beneath a city?" I cocked my head. "And how do you know about it?"

"Seattle was destroyed by a fire over a Terran century ago, Pearl. The street level was raised when it was rebuilt." Ehtishem returned my gaze. "I know about it because I've been there." I opened my mouth, but he interrupted me. "There's a lot you don't know about me, but you're right that I should keep it to myself ... for now." I nodded. He returned to his sketch. "The railroad will lead you right to Seattle. Once there you'll be noticed and taken underground. You can trust those people."

"What's Haven?" Pearl handed Ehtishem his jacket and rolled up her blankets.

"A free colony that only a few Ohnenrai and Terrans know still exists."

I studied him. "A free colony? The Ohnenrai know about it, but it still exists? How is that possible?"

"Because the ones who know about it live there."

Pearl gaped at him. "Really? As friends?"

Ehtishem watched me as he answered. "Yes. Live and work together."

I returned his gaze. "You're not just some soldier." I heard the wind blowing past my ears and whistling between boulders in the silence that followed my question.

"No. I'm not."

I nodded. "Something else you need to keep to yourself?"

"You and Pearl must get as far from me as possible. I'll head north for the U.S./Canada Gate to draw them away. You follow the train tracks south. Avoid contact—Ohnenrai and Terran—until you reach Seattle. If you cannot, remain calm and say as little as possible. Pearl?" He looked at her. "This is very important. Do *not* reveal that you can speak Ohnenrai to *anyone*, Terran or Ohnenrai. Especially Ohnenrai."

"Why not?" Her serious manner and expression mirrored his.

"Because you and your mother won't be safe."

She straightened. "Okay. I won't forget. Momma has to stay safe."

I swallowed a lump as Ehtishem replied, "You both do." He finished repacking Pearl's backpack with light necessities—clothes, bandages, the bread, cheese, dried meat, plastic bags, filament. He stopped to demonstrate his flint, making sure she knew how to use it. The heavy things—water, medical instruments, alcohol, dried fruit and nuts, blankets, spare boots and my clothing, shotgun shells—went into my pack or the dogs' saddlebags.

Pearl dressed while I fed Audie and Jack, and Ehtishem went down the mountain to fetch the water bags. We brushed the dogs and inspected their feet, and I choked down some cheese and fruit.

Ehtishem came through the trees carrying the plastic bags. "Canteen?" He held out his hand. I gave it over and he carefully emptied the bag into it. "Potable water." His gaze still held no emotion. "Reset these each night and you'll have safe water every morning."

We secured the saddlebags across the dogs' backs and I helped Pearl with hers. I slung the shotgun belt across my body like a bandolier. Ehtishem hefted my pack onto my shoulders.

"Is it all right?" He held the weight as I adjusted my jacket.

I tightened the shoulder straps, ran the waist belt beneath the bandolier, and snapped everything in place. "Yes. It's fine, not too heavy."

Ehtishem ran my knife belt around my hips, and I realized he'd exchanged my knife for his. I protested, but he shook his head. "You'll need it more. It's much better than yours. You can strike the flint against it, and you'll need the compass in the handle."

"Ehtishem—"

"Take it." I couldn't argue against the edge in his voice. And I didn't fight him when he clipped his Faraday light to my belt.

He turned to Pearl. "Care for your mother."

"Why can't you come with us?"

"Trust me, you're safer this way. There are people who want to find me much more than they want you and your mother. I need to draw them away from you." He shouldered his own pack.

"They're Ohnenrai? Can't you just order them to leave us alone?"

"No." He knelt before her. "It's not that simple."

Pearl said, "But—" then stopped when Ehtishem raised his finger.

"I have to leave you. Believe me, I don't want to. You must be as brave and smart and strong as I know you are. Help your mother. Follow her lead and her instructions as you always have. Stick close to the dogs. You have a long way to go, but I know you'll be fine. All right, Pearly Girly?"

Pearl nodded then threw her arms around him. His use of her

nickname surprised me but not as much as the affection and pain I saw cross his face as he returned her hug.

As he eased her back reserve returned to his countenance. He stood and stared up the mountain. "Keep heading west until you reach the train tracks. They run along the ocean in this area. Turn south and follow them. It'll be safer than taking the roads. This is a good time to travel. The storms won't be too fierce." He turned to me. "Watch your water supply. Use the purification tablets only if you can't get water from the trees."

I nodded at his monotone instructions, my mind growing numb with each word, as if every syllable carried him further from me. I stared at his chest, at Jack, at nothing. Silence fell between us, its space filled with the whistling wind, the slow creak of the towering pines all around, the whoosh of their branches.

Ehtishem scratched both dogs. "Be good and vigilant," he told them.

I turned to Pearl. "Ready?" She nodded and slapped her thigh. Jack and Audie went to her. "All right," I added as I shifted.

Ehtishem captured my face between his hands and kissed me. I surrendered to him as his lips and tongue caressed mine as we inhaled each other's breath and exhaled into one another. He pulled away, pressed his forehead to mine, and looked into my eyes. "Va thrayoshta."

"We *will* be safe." I stepped back and squared my shoulders. "Join us soon, Ehtishem Zain."

"I will find you."

I took Pearl's hand, turned, and headed up the slope. "Close your mouth, baby girl, or bugs will fly in."

TEN

I DRAGGED Pearl toward the unknown, choosing to believe that it had to be safer than the known dangers we'd left behind. When she stumbled, I hoisted her onto my back, steadied myself with a makeshift walking stick, and continued the trek. We had enough water to last two days, enough food to last five beyond that.

"I'm glad you like Ehtishem now, Momma."

Jack had found a worn tennis ball and he and Audie scrambled after it as Pearl lobbed it up the tracks. The game had entertained all of us for three days, and when Pearl's arm tired, I took a turn. Now our big, black hound loped back, the grayish-yellow ball in his mouth, as Audie ran beside him and tried to steal it.

"You are? Why?"

"Because he's nice and he's nice to you. He makes you happy. And me." She laughed as Audie knocked the ball from Jack. Both dogs scrabbled after it, grumbling and yipping at each other. "Even the dogs like him."

"True." I took a gulp of water and passed her the canteen. I didn't want to discuss the Ohnenran. I had nothing to hide from

Pearl, but I didn't want to think of what I'd so briefly held and so quickly lost.

Jack regained the tennis ball and triumphantly delivered it to Pearl then joined Audie to drink from a deep puddle between rail slats.

"Ew." She wiped her hands on her skirt and rolled the drooly ball in the grass as I laughed. She looked up and grinned. "Don't worry. Ehtishem will ditch the patrol and catch up to us before we get to Haven."

My mouth went dry. "Are you hungry? Let's get off the tracks and have a little snack and rest."

We skirted a salt marsh, the ground squelching beneath our feet, and climbed a gentle rise to settle on a grassy patch within a thick stand of pines. From our vantage we could see the tracks and quickly disappear from sight. Not that we'd seen any signs of humanity since leaving the mountain and Ehtishem. We shared an apple, and I peeled an egg for each of the dogs.

"Pearl?" I looked down and noticed spring shoots emerging from the ground. Crocuses. "You need to realize we're unlikely to see Ehtishem again."

The apple crunched as she took a big bite. "Here." She held it out to me and replied as she chewed, "No I don't, Momma." She wiped her chin with her sleeve.

I shook my head. "You finish it. I'm not hungry."

She studied the apple, turning it this way and that. "He'll find us because he loves you." She punctuated her response with a big bite and watched me as she chewed. I sighed and took another gulp of water. I didn't have the will to deflate her bubble. Time would do it for me.

We watched sparrows and juncos flit and twitch and hop in search of seeds and insect eggs.

"Were my grandparents terrorists?"

"What?"

Pearl scratched Audie's chin and murmured love to him as he waggled. "I heard Ehtishem say you're the child of terrorists. Is it true?"

I didn't know what shocked me more—that she'd heard his accusation or that she'd heard us make love. Jack rolled over at my feet with a yawn and gazed at me, an unspoken request for a belly rub. I obliged, happy to have the soothing distraction. "I'm not sure how to answer that." I looked up. She was watching me. "What do you want to know? *Why* do you want to know?"

She shrugged. "I guess I just want to know if they killed people."

"No, they didn't. But I have. And so has Ehtishem, I'm sure."

"Do you wish you hadn't?" She received a kiss from Audie.

"Yes...and no. The man I killed was trying to hurt your grandparents and me. I was fourteen, but I still regret it." He was my Uncle John, and he was desperate and stupid.

Jack groaned, yawned, and closed his eyes with a sigh.

"Your grandparents felt betrayed when the Ohnenrai seized control. They did what they thought was right to protect me. But I do think they had a lot of regrets, Pearl." I stood and lifted her pack. "We should get going."

Both dogs were on their feet, stretching and wagging, before we had our backpacks settled. Then we returned to the tracks and the ball game commenced again.

"Baby girl?" I took Pearl's hand, and she met my gaze. "Killing someone changes you. It leaves a mark. It's not something you can see, but it's there. Always."

She nodded.

"I pray you never have to wear that mark, Pearly Girly."

To the west, over the ocean, the setting sun broke below the leading edge of a storm to cast golden light below the clouds, lighting their iron undersides.

"Look at that, Momma."

"There's our God, Pearl. He's not in a book or a madman's words. He's in the rain and sun and the air we breathe."

She twined our fingers together. "He's in Judith's baby."

I looked down at her and smiled. "He's in you."

"And you." She looked at the dogs. "He's in Jack and Audie."

"Yes, definitely." I laughed as the dogs snuffled through grass so tall only their tails showed like periscopes. Pearl's fingers tightened, and I looked back at her.

"God's in Ehtishem too, Momma."

I squeezed her hand, swallowed, nodded.

"God will guide him, just as he guides us to Haven," she said. "We'll see him again."

I held her gaze. She had such conviction in her eyes and her words. "I hope you're right." I looked back to the iron and gold sky. *God, make it so.* I inhaled. "I smell rain. Let's find shelter."

We held to the tracks bordered on one side by ocean, the other by forest. We passed abandoned houses, dilapidated houses, burned-out shells of houses. They made me nervous with their staring, empty-window eyes.

Finally, with thunder rumbling, we rounded a curve and Pearl said, "Hey, a tunnel."

We faced a railway tunnel, its concrete arch charred and half-collapsed. Jack and Audie scampered over the debris. We followed. The white glow of Ehtishem's light revealed a collapsed roof not ten feet in from the tunnel mouth. Something reflected the light and I stopped the beam. Distorted, dead headlights of a pancaked train stared at me. The engineer's compartment was lost beneath concrete and rock.

This isn't a tunnel. It's a tomb. Even as I reconsidered our choice, thunder boomed and lightning illuminated the graffitied walls. Pearl and I jumped, the dogs whined. *Okay, tonight it's home.* The unmistakable drum of hail on the roadway confirmed my decision.

We set out plastic bags to collect rainwater then fed the dogs and ourselves. I settled the clothing packs into a bed of sorts beside the wall and dozed as Pearl slept in my arms. She twitched and murmured, cried out once, then settled back into uneasy sleep. The dogs snuggled beside us for warmth and safety. The shotgun rested against my right leg.

I awoke to Audie and Jack growling. Some animal snuffled and shuffled around the tunnel mouth. The dogs' warnings grew louder and the creature scuttled away. I patted our protectors, shushed and praised them until they settled and sighed and closed their eyes. But mine remained open. I peered into the darkness looking for ghosts of long-dead conductors, panicked families, strangers encased in a mountain of charred and broken stone. I wondered who held blame for this death scene. Us? Or them? Then I wondered if it mattered anymore.

Audie and Jack lifted their heads, their ears perked, their eyes intent. Pearl opened her mouth but shut it as I held up my hand.

I hefted the shotgun, checked the safety, then chambered a round. Keeping my eyes on the tunnel entrance, I caught a new round between my pinky and index fingers and slid my hand forward from the trigger guard. I popped another round up into the magazine and pushed it forward with my thumb, and then another and another until the gun held a full load. Aside from nearly killing Cyrus, I hadn't used the gun in years, but I'd kept it clean and had practiced quick loading. Now I lodged it against my shoulder and looked down the short black barrel at the bead, then beyond as Jack and Audie growled and rose.

Voices drifted into the tunnel. Male voices.

"Behind me, Pearl. Now. Stuff your ears. Cover the dogs' ears too."

She scrambled back, grabbed the blanket, and covered herself. Just as we'd practiced so many times at home.

"Quiet, dogs. Go to Pearl."

Both obeyed, slinking back, their teeth bared and their hackles up. A zipper growled and fabric rustled as Pearl opened a pack and fished out cotton. "Come here, dogs," she whispered. I hoped they'd let her protect their ears. If I fired the gun in this concrete tunnel the sound would deafen them and, quite probably, me as well.

Feet scuffed. "Those bags weren't there yesterday."

"Nope. They've been set out for rainwater. See?"

"Yep. Think it's the convicts the Gate techs were talkin' about?"

"Pretty likely. Haven't seen anyone else around since last fall." The feet crunched gravel. "They probably followed the tracks to here."

"That sure-as-shit is a lotta land to search, Fred."

"The Ohnaries have trackers, dipshit."

"Whaddya think, Pops?"

A third man joined the conversation. "I think they couldn't've gone too far. They'd've stayed close to the railroad. Too hard to move through all that wilderness. Why do that when you've got tracks to follow?" Feet crunched gravel and the tunnel darkened as a body blocked it. The man leaned over and squinted at me. "And there they are. Hello, pretty lady."

Audie and Jack snarled.

"Aw, you tell your mutts to shut it or we'll have 'em for dinner," he said.

One of the men cackled. "I haven't had dog in months. That's good eatin', Pops."

"C'mon out, girl. We're not gonna hurt you."

"Much," one of the others added, and all three laughed.

That was enough for me. I thumbed off the safety and snugged the gun butt tighter. "Quiet, dogs."

"That's it. Call off them doggies." The lech squatted less than ten feet from the muzzle of my gun, his arms stretched wide as he gripped the sides of the narrow opening. More light illuminated the tunnel. "Whatcha got?"

"More time than you." I squeezed the trigger.

The concrete tunnel amplified the gun's roar. Explosive pain jolted me as my eardrums burst. The man's chest erupted in a fine spray of red and he tumbled backwards. I heard muffled sounds and both dogs shot past me as I pumped the gun. "Stay put!" I barely heard my own voice as I shouted at Pearl. I crawled forward, trying to ignore nausea and dizziness and blinking back tears. I reached the entrance, knelt, and brought the shotgun to my shoulder. A figure loomed before me. Another man, his face twisted and evil, a large, serrated hunting knife in his hand.

I fired.

His face disappeared and I ducked as blood and tissue sprayed me. I wiped away his gore with my sleeve, pumped the shotgun, and lunged from the tunnel. I pivoted as I shouldered the weapon and saw Audie take a blow from the remaining man. The brindle dropped back and crouched for the next attack.

"Audie! To me!"

The dog whirled and charged across the tracks to my side. Ignoring the two twitching bodies at my feet, I kept the shotgun trained on my final target. The man, bloodied and torn by the dog, clenched his fists and roared at me. I heard nothing. And his contorted, wild expression seemed all the more terrifying in my silence as he ran at me.

I fired.

The shot caught his right shoulder and knocked him back, but he got up, lurched, and kept coming. I pumped and fired again. This time the round hit him in the gut and he went down. I staggered toward him, saw that he still lived, and knew I couldn't leave him to a slow death. I pumped the gun, put the barrel between his eyes, and pulled the trigger. Then I dropped to my knees and retched.

Pearl tugged my arm. Tears streaked her face and she clung to me, shaking. But she wasn't hysterical. Which I knew wasn't normal, but I was thankful anyway. Pearl had never been the fall-to-pieces type.

"Oh, baby, I can't hear you. Nod if you're okay." She did and pointed. I followed her finger and saw Jack. I rose and stumbled after her, my feet unsteady and the world tilting and turning. Our big black dog was dead, stabbed in the skull and the chest. Audie circled us, his tail tucked. He sniffed Jack, backed away, and circled again.

"Audie." I patted my thigh. He came to me. I pressed my hand to his chest and felt him whimpering, shaking. "Stay with Pearl."

She sobbed into Jack's soft fur as I rose and went through the dead men's pockets. I found matches, winter gloves, and a butterfly knife. Then I dragged each corpse to the side of the tracks where a slope dropped off into rocks and weeds and ocean. I shoved them over. More than once, I had to lie down until the spinning and nausea subsided.

Then I returned to Pearl. Her tears spent, she looked up and said something. I knelt. "I can't hear you. I won't be able to for a few days." She nodded and made a digging motion. She wanted to bury Jack. I was terrified that the shotgun blasts would bring more attention, but I couldn't abandon my dog. Pearl helped me carry him into the tunnel and cover him with a cairn of rubble.

Audie paced from the entrance to the burial mound while we redistributed the goods from Jack's saddlebags. I shed my gory clothes and tried to get strangers' blood and tissue off my skin and out of my hair. The vertigo and nausea eased, but a never-ending bell choir now filled my aching head.

Before we left the tunnel I rested my hand on the cairn. "Thank you, Jack, for everything. I...god...I'm sorry." I sobbed and swallowed a lump as Pearl clung to me and cried. I straightened and wiped tears and snot on my sleeve, drew a deep breath, and dragged her out of the tunnel. I looked back once. "Goodbye, Jack." Tears flowing unchecked, I slapped my thigh for Audie. "C'mon, Pearl, we need to find where the tracks pick up." She nodded and wiped her tears with her sleeve.

A steep ravine towered over us. I didn't want to move, but I hadn't forgotten our attackers' conversation. The Ohnenrai were looking for someone, quite likely Pearl and me.

One step at a time.

We clambered over huge, fallen trees, scrambled around enormous swaths of blackberry brambles, and hauled ourselves over boulders. Trees jutted out over the train tracks at impossible angles, clinging to the ravine by bulging roots. The blackberry vines reached for us, wicked and thorny.

Pearl clung to Audie's pack and let him pull her upward. I followed and tried not to think of Jack, tried not to catch my daughter's sorrow. I couldn't afford the luxury of mourning. When I stopped to vomit or lay flat, my face in the dirt, Pearl tugged, Audie nuzzled, and I pushed myself harder than I thought possible.

When we finally reached the top, scratched, bruised, and filthy, a narrow ridge lay before us, covered in crumbling, ruined mansions. What once had been a wealthy neighborhood overlooking the Pacific Ocean now was blackened debris. Here and there, empty windows stared from singed walls and homeless chimneys stood, fragmented and falling. Most of the homes were no more than rubble-strewn foundations and overgrown driveways. Where garages once stood, twisted cars still awaited drivers who would never return to load them for vacation, head for work, take the kids to school or Boy Scouts or ballet.

"C'mon, baby. Let's get to the other side of the ridge. We're too exposed here." I rubbed my forehead, fighting a low, pulsing pressure in my skull. Pearl nodded and kept me steady as we wound through the ruins. Audie stayed close. I wondered how long he would mourn his brother's death. We reached the end of a street, cut through a weedy yard, and climbed a small rise. Ahead of me, Pearl stopped. She pointed and mouthed something. I reached her side and stared.

"Jesus H. Christ. That's not supposed to be there."

ELEVEN

A GATE—A barren, twenty-foot-wide swath—stretched to the horizon from east to west. Regularly placed stanchions followed the center of the scorched path, and pale amber light, beautiful and deadly, flickered between each post. Piles of bones and fur and feathers littered both sides of the glowing barrier. A breeze ruffled my hair, and the acrid stink of burned flesh filled my nose and mouth. Pearl gagged, pulled her sleeve over her palm, and filtered the stench through the fabric. A constant, pulsing hum punctuated the air, almost too low to hear, but vibrating my skull and bones. It was the source of the pressure in my head.

Pearl tugged my hand. I read her lips as she exaggerated her question: "Is that a Gate?"

"Yes. And it's not supposed to be here." I glared at the beautiful monstrosity. "Ehtishem didn't say anything about this. He said we could travel all the way to the Oregon/California border."

My gaze tracked the Gate to where the land dived off a cliff into the ocean. The deadly wall followed the drop stretching vertically between horizontal posts embedded in the cliff face. It marched out to sea on massive stanchions and I wondered how far it went.

The ridge was more gradual on this side and ran into a winding, two-lane road. I took Pearl's hand and we moved downward.

It took much of the morning to reach the eerie wall, and when we finally did I only wanted to run away. The hair on my arms, even on my head, rose as electricity crackled the air. My skin, my eyes, and my mouth all went dry as moisture was sucked from my cells. I studied the menace while Pearl clung to me and Audie whined with his tail tucked between his legs. Most of the carcasses littering the area were still decomposing. The wall robbed moisture from everything, so if they'd been long exposed to the elements they would've been more decayed. "This was recently built."

Pearl tugged my hand and I read her lips again. "After Ehtishem came north?" I repeated her question. She nodded. "Yes, after that. Which means he didn't know." I exhaled relief. The thought of betrayal had gnawed at me since we'd spotted the Gate. "All right." I looked around then pulled Pearl back into the forest. "Let's follow this thing eastward. Maybe we can find a gateway."

I checked and rechecked Ehtishem's compass and watched for threats from all directions. We were on a gradual southeast course and the terrain following the Gate's scorched earth gradually changed from dense, pine forest to grassy knolls to an expansive, lush flood plain.

We walked the rest of the day then found shelter in a collapsing barn and rested for three. The nausea and dizziness subsided. The ringing continued. But I regained some hearing, mostly in my left ear. Pearl set a snare and caught a rabbit on the second day. Audie dined on moles, mice, and countless flies.

When we set out again, I felt stronger and we made better time, dashing across a four-lane roadway littered with burned and obliterated cars and ducking back into overgrown fields. The patchwork terrain had been farmland, and we found peas and lettuce and apple trees near a collapsed barn. By the end of the day, however, our course had begun an upward climb into the mountains.

"Momma?"

We'd found an unlocked car in an abandoned garage—all that remained of a neighborhood—and had settled in for the night.

"Hmm?"

"What if we don't find a gateway? We won't go back to Suffer, will we?" Pearl lay across the backseat with Audie. I was snuggled into the reclined front passenger seat. The car felt surprisingly safe and cozy.

"No. We'll never go back there."

"Will we head north and look for Ehtishem?" Her words were slow and thick with sleep.

"Maybe. I don't know. Go to sleep, Pearl."

I stared at rusty pliers and some empty parts boxes on the floorboard. One had held an overflow hose, another was for a planetary gear—I didn't know what those things did. "Planetary" made me look past the windshield and through a hole in the garage roof. Stars sparkled, planets glowed, and I swallowed a lump and took a few slow breaths. *Shit*. It had been stupid to sleep with him. I wiped my eyes and nose with my sleeve. And it was stupid to miss him.

I glanced in the rearview mirror at Pearl, then closed my eyes and started counting in my head. I fell asleep somewhere in the five hundreds.

The next morning, after eating and changing, I climbed into the car's driver seat and hit the starter button on a whim. I nearly jumped from my skin when the engine buzzed then hummed to life. Audie yelped and ran from one end of the garage to the other while Pearl clapped and squealed. And I laughed madly, all the while silently grateful that my father had taught me to drive the summer before he'd died. Then I wondered where the owner was. Someone had maintained the car and I was sure he or she would be pissed as shit to find us in it. We'd had stupid luck, best not to push it.

"Let's go before someone comes looking for this, Pearl." We loaded the bags and the dog into the car and headed east on a deserted, winding road. "I don't know how far this will get us, but I'll take what I can get."

The car coasted to a stop. I hit the starter. It buzzed, the engine hummed then died. I heard hissing and gurgling. "Uh, that's not good."

Pearl shook her head, her mouth pressed into a grim white line. "Nope."

We'd driven much of the morning, singing and playing I Spy. We'd seen waterfalls and deer, cattle and countless flattened buildings and burned-out cars, but we hadn't spied a gateway interrupting the endless Gate's amber glow.

Towering pines and maples obscured the road as it curved up and around a bend. To our left, gray and white granite loomed over the road. To our right, a break in the trees followed a broken asphalt lane. I peered down the track and saw the straight angles of white stucco buildings jutting through the mounded, thorny tentacles of blackberry bushes.

I rested my forehead on the steering wheel and sighed then reached beneath the dashboard until my fingers found a lever. I pulled it and the hood released with a *clunk*. I looked around, searching for movement, people, threats. There was nothing, so I pushed open the door and listened. "Do you hear anything?"

"A hawk. The wind. And the car is gurgling."

The silence made my shoulders hunch and my skin crawl. "Stay put."

"Okay." Pearl's hand went to Audie's scruff.

I grabbed the shotgun, stepped from the car, and turned back. "Keep Audie in the car." The brindle whined and thumped his tail against Pearl's chest. She captured it. I scratched his ears then closed the door and stood against it, listening and looking. I didn't miss the long rivulet running from beneath the car down the road we'd traveled. "Hell and a half." I shouldered the gun and went to the hood. I fumbled with the catch, lifted it, and stared at the hoses and batteries and machinery, hopeless and helpless. I fixed people, not cars.

A sound reached me—panting, a whine.

I straightened, lowered the hood, and looked at Pearl. Her eyes focused past my shoulder and widened. Audie sat on the seat, his ears back, and his lips curling away from his teeth.

"Mom-ma?"

I knew what stood behind me and I didn't move. "How many? How far?" I kept my tone low and even.

"Four." Pearl held up her fingers and pointed. "At the bend in the road. Now five." Her voice rose and tightened with the last word.

Audie gnashed his teeth. His tongue flicked forth.

Too close. I couldn't get back into the car before they caught me. "Watch out for Audie. He's gonna go nuts. Do not let him out."

"But, Momma." Fat tears spilled down her cheeks.

"Pearl. Do as I say and stay in the car with Audie. No matter what happens."

Audie rocked back and forth on the seat snarling and barking, his fur spiky from nose to tail.

At the first low growl I scrambled up the hood and jumped to the roof, swinging the shotgun off my shoulder. A dog leapt onto the hood, its claws scraping and scrabbling. As I turned, it snapped its slobbering teeth at my ankle, barely missing. I bashed the mongrel aside with the gun. It hit the ground with a yelp as my backswing caught a second bony beast. Somehow, I sighted and fired. I missed, but the sound ricocheted off the rock face and the dogs flinched away, their tails tucked and ears back. The sound stung my ears. If I'd had a tail, it would've been tucked too.

But the diseased curs weren't so easily deterred. They circled the car, snapping, drooling, snarling. The whites of their eyes were yellowed with sickness and their fur was dull, matted, and mangy.

I stood now, the gun pumped and shouldered. My ears ached and rang. The car rocked beneath me as Audie hurled his body at the windows and windshield, desperate to defend against the attackers. A hound lunged at Pearl's window and I blew a hole in the poor mutt's chest. The first dog still staggered around, shaking its bloodied head and whining. I shot it as the other three descended upon their dead companion.

My attention snapped to the road's bend. Four new dogs charged toward the car, howling and yelping. Audie snarled and bellowed. Pearl shrieked. I fired, pumped a round. Fired, pumped a round. Fired, pumped, and nearly tore my fingernails off as the round jammed. "Goddamn it!"

"Momma!"

I grabbed the hot barrel and swung the gun back. Two dogs hit the hood, stopped. They crouched and whined, their ears back and tails tucked. I froze. *What the hell?* All the dogs cowered, then as quickly as they'd attacked, they now retreated up the road.

I slipped to the ground, knelt, and slapped the shotgun barrel, but the pump remained immobile. "Fucking c'mon." I pushed the gun's safety and jiggled the pump without luck. "Shit, shit, shit." Giving up, I pulled open the door as I looked left, right, into the trees, up the cliff. A low vibration traveled through the ground, up my legs, all the way to my teeth.

"What is that?" Pearl clung to Audie and stared out the windows.

Now the low, rhythmic *thum-thum-thum* of massive, other-worldly engines joined the vibration.

"Get out!"

Pearl released Audie to me as a phalanx of Ohnenrai gunships cleared the ridge's toothy crags, their reflective exteriors changing like chameleons to match the earth and sky. The dog whined and barked. As the ships split into two groups and maneuvered to surround us, he jerked away from me and raced down the lane.

"Audie!" Pearl scrambled after him.

And I raced after her. "No, baby! Let him go!"

Trees and bushes slashed wildly, their leaves whirling and swirling around me as the gunships descended. My guts felt jellied— an effect of the ships' anti-grav. I cleared the treed lane and came to a compound of buildings.

Pearl stood staring as a handful of people raced past her and up the stairs into a long, low, whitewashed building. Their mouths opened and closed as they shouted to each other, but their words were lost to the thunderous engines. I grabbed her and charged up the stairs. But she pulled away and lunged off the concrete landing, shouting, "Audie! Here, dog! Audie!" as the brindle charged out of the trees toward us.

I pulled on the door. It was locked. "Let us in!" I shouted and pounded to no avail. Trees cracked and snapped all around the compound as landing ships splintered them.

I jumped off the landing and seized Pearl's hand. I grabbed Audie's ruff and dragged both of them to another building, and another. Debris careened around the courtyard and grit stung my skin. "Damn it!" I raged as I encountered only locked doors.

We lurched into the arched entryway of a small, white building. This time the door yielded. Audie whined and skittered around our legs. "Go." I pushed Pearl through the door and into a two-story rotunda. I tried a door to our left but it was locked. A helix staircase spiraled up to a landing above, and I spied an open doorway. "C'mon."

We scrambled up the rusty, rattling stairs, around the landing, and into a long hallway lined with doors on both sides. Windows clattered. Dust rose and rained all around.

"You try that side. I'll try these," I said. Pearl took the left and I went up the right, each of us encountering more locked doors. Audie ran from me to her, from her to me.

Please, God, please. Just one.

"Here!" A door yielded to her with a high, hollow creak but only far enough for me to squeeze through. Buckled floorboards blocked it. Dim yellow light through a dirty window showed a small room devoid of anything but a legless wooden chair, brown leaves, and bird shit. Dead ivy pushed through two broken windowpanes and trailed down the wall, across the floor, and down through a hole big enough to swallow a twin bed.

The thrumming and vibrations increased then slowed and eased as the gunships landed. "Quiet, Pearl. No matter what." I pulled her to the wall behind the door. Audie barked, and I grabbed his muzzle. "Hush."

Gunfire cracked the air followed by the rising whine and boom of Ohnenrai weapons.

Shouts. Orders and protests. Screams.

Audie yelped and charged out the door.

"Audie!" Pearl lunged after him, but I yanked her back. "Let him go!"

"But he—"

"He can take care of himself." I crouched, pressed her to me, and wiped her tears. "Remember, you don't speak Ohnenrai." She stared at me. I shook her. "Pearl. Don't forget."

She nodded. "I don't speak it. I remember, Momma. I'll keep you safe."

We jumped as the building door banged open, and again as the locked door below us yielded with a *crack*. Heavy boots thudded up the stairs, into the hall, through the room below. The hall doors opened to force.

Bang.

Bang.

Bang.

A radio crackled with Ohnenrai commands: "Remember, hold fire, hold fire. You know why we're here, pa'nerem. Let's get our prize and go home."

"I have two here."

"Match?"

"No. This kid's tracked. I'll bundle and go."

Another set of boots scraped the metal stairs.

"Affirmative."

Hard soles crunched crisp, brown leaves.

Pearl and I jerked as the door to the next room slammed open. There was the scrape of wood on wood.

"The dresser? How small do you think these people are?"

"I don't know. Terran kids are small, right?"

The door beside us creaked. Dust danced in the bright light beam that entered the room.

Pearl pushed against me. A black weapon barrel appeared past the door.

"I have them."

The barrel paused.

"Match?"

Boots scraped.

"Affirma— Wait, no. Not a match. Repeat, no match, fra. Bundle and go?"

I raised my shotgun like a baseball bat.

"Affirmative."

A thud came from the ground floor. Pearl and I jumped as a snarl erupted and a soldier shouted. A weapon boomed. A yelp followed.

Pearl gasped. "Audie." It was barely a whisper.

"What was that?"

"Dog, fra."

The soldier standing in the doorway spoke in monotone English. "I heard you. Come out. Sorry about the dog, but he started it. We're not here to hurt anyone." We didn't move. The soldier tapped his foot once. "Don't make me gas you."

I remembered the gas from my childhood. They'd used it to drive us from the woods. It had burned my eyes, my lungs, my throat. My tongue had swelled and I hadn't been able to eat for days. Now, the soldiers had us and I didn't want Pearl to suffer like that. "Okay. We're coming. Don't gas us."

Pearl grabbed me. "Momma, I'm scared."

I kissed her. "I know. Stay close. Don't speak. Remember Ehtishem's warning." I held her tight. "I love you."

"I love you too."

"I'm pushing a gun to you," I said as I pushed the weapon past the door and helped Pearl negotiate the gaping hole in the floor. She molded herself to me.

The soldier was shorter and smaller than Ehtishem. He raised his face shield and watched us with a bland expression, his gun sighted on us. I knew his helmet had intercepted my tracker signal. He pressed a spot on his gun and spoke in Ohnenrai. "I have them. Negative signal on the girl, affirmative match on the woman."

"Good work. Bundle 'em. We have what we came for. Let's clean and carry, pa'nerem." Our captor motioned with his weapon. "Outside."

We obeyed, but when we reached the front doorway Pearl tried to pull away from me. "Audie." She pointed toward a soldier carrying the limp dog.

Two soldiers approached. One kept his weapon on me. The other yanked Pearl from my arms as our captor caught my wrist.

"Let go of her!"

"Momma!" Pearl turned and pounded on the Ohnenran's chest. "Let me go!" The soldier cuffed her hands and hefted her over his shoulder as she arched and twisted and raged.

"No!" I slugged my captor in the face and blood erupted from his nose. He said nothing as he grabbed the back of my neck, slammed me into the rotting door, and threw me to the ground. As I struggled for breath, he pinned my back with his knee, cuffed my hands, and yanked a dark canvas bag over my head.

Pearl shrieked and I felt a hypomatic's stinging pressure against my neck. Fire shot through my veins, into my brain, my heart, my lungs. Everything slowed and became muted, fluid, dense.

The soldier jerked me to my knees and said in Ohnenrai, "Interesting."

"What?"

"She's not down."

I lost track of who was who as the soldiers' voices blended and warped.

"Ahmm. Should I dose her again?"

"Not unless you want her heart to stop."

"I want visual confirmation."

I jerked at this new voice and turned, searching for Pearl. I couldn't focus my eyes in the dark bag, and my breath dragged in and out.

"Fra? Zant, fra."

Boots boomed in my head, growing louder, the sound now taking on color and speed as the Ohnenrai sedative further bent my brain.

Metal fasteners and weaponry rattled. The sound turned everything yellow. Each boot step flashed orange, then red, then redder until they stopped before me.

"Remove the bag."

My head rocked back as the bag ties loosened. Then white light overwhelmed my eyes and brain. It quickly turned a kaleidoscopic world of swirling colors and patterns. I struggled to focus on anything, finally settling my eyes on shiny, black boots that oozed and undulated but remained black. *That* was something to grasp.

"Show me the tracker reading." There was a pause then this new soldier said, "Zant. That's the one."

Each word splotched purple. The boots disappeared, replaced by gray that streaked to red-green-orange. The world warped as a hand tilted my chin. A mouth, nose, eyes—a face—appeared. I struggled to merge the features.

"Hello, Rachel Pryne."

TWELVE

A SLAP JARRED me back to consciousness where the world still warped and distorted like the Devil's idea of a rainbow.

"Rachel Pryne."

I tried to raise my chin from my chest, but my muscles wouldn't cooperate. My shirt was wet. I latched onto that fact like a drowning woman and forced my brain to connect it to the line of drool hanging from my lower lip.

"What is so interesting about you that Ohnenrai Genetics would send a soldier on a suicide mission to retrieve you?"

Sound sped and slowed the swirling rainbow world. My interrogator was speaking English, but the fast and slow pulse of his words across my eardrums and the undulation of his uniform's gray fabric were distracting me away from his questions.

"Rachel, answer me truthfully, then you and your daughter— Pearl—then you and Pearl can go." Her name triggered a lovely, slow waltz of lavender swirls. "Who is Ehtishem Zain?"

He and another soldier had been asking me questions for hours, or maybe it was days, or maybe they'd just begun. He leaned over me. I blinked-blinked-blinked. My eyeballs felt sandy. "Just a soldier," I said and looked down from his warping features. "Isn't he?" I felt his breath with the next question. Its warmth turned everything yellow.

"Where are you from?"

"Terra. Suffer." Thinking made my head hurt. "There was a brick house in D.C. We lived in Virginia, near a big park. I like parks. The grass feels good between my toes." The thought of grass warmed me and everything melted like green ice cream running down a yellow cone.

He straightened and turned to the soldier. "Mem anagava iristahe."

"Frena manaya-hei framru-hei ahn eresh, Zosh," she answered.

I'd lost my ability to understand Ohnenrai. My doped brain just colored their words ice blue. I shivered.

"Zant." He nodded. "Aiwiyo." He reached out. The woman passed him a container, which he pressed to my lips. "Drink. You must be thirsty."

Water. Aiwiyo is water. I remembered as I drank. The world slowed and sped with each swallow of the cool liquid. My skull throbbed. Then he pulled the container from my lips and splashed the icy water in my face. I shrieked and gagged.

"Who sent that soldier for you? Where is he now? What was your destination? Give me answers if you want Pearl to live past this day."

"Pearl?" I looked around. "I don't know where she is. Please help me find her." My voice cracked with the last sentence and a lump closed my throat.

He threw the metal canister at the wall. I jumped as it banged and ricocheted, the sound flashing white lightning in my brain. The water, the sound, the flashing light all combined to plunge me through a black hole of memory.

I walked through the front room of Joshua's house as someone rapped on the door. I wiped my wet hands on my apron and opened it. Wind whipped rain into the house. I stepped aside to admit Elder Cyrus. "Elder. What brings you here on a blustery morning?"

He doffed his hat and smiled. "I've been remiss in checking on you, Rachel. I promised Joshua I would see to you while he Walks."

The house shuddered under a blast of cold wind as I took his hat and coat. "It's a miserable day for a short walk, let alone a God Walk. I hope the men found shelter."

"I'm certain they're fine. God watches over them."

I returned his smile. "Yes, of course. You're kind to be concerned, but I'm fine." I returned to the tiny blue-and-white kitchen. "Tea, Elder?"

He followed. "Tea sounds nice. Thank you."

I put the kettle on the stove and gestured to the small table occupying the center of the room. "Have a seat. I just began the dishes."

He rolled up his sleeves. "Let me wash."

I laughed. "Did you come here to help with chores?" I took the plate that he handed to me.

"We all have needs, Rachel." It seemed a strange answer, but Elder Cyrus often spoke cryptically.

"I'm not sure I need help with my dishes. But I won't pass up pleasant company."

We washed, dried, and chatted about the storm, the delay the bad weather would cause the men Walking, the previous evening's sermon; the storm had cut it short. Rain slammed against the window as the gray sky darkened.

Elder Cyrus picked up the damp dishtowel and twisted it over the sink.

Shaking my head at the wild weather, I turned to put the last cup away but jumped as a crack of thunder rattled the sky, the windows, and the house. Lightning lit up the room. The lights flickered and *went out. "Oh. That was close." I laughed. "I wonder where Joshua left the Faraday."*

Something damp pressed my throat and tightened. I clawed at it, gasping, desperate for air. He was behind me, his body pressed against mine. He pushed me. My hips hit the table. He doubled me over. My skull cracked against the wood and I saw triple. He twisted the garrote; my vision narrowed, blackened. I tried to jerk around, away, tried to escape. Stop! No! I couldn't scream. No air in. No words out. Fabric tore.

Trapped between then and now, I kicked and punched at an attack that wasn't happening. I drew a ragged breath to scream. But another slap snapped my head to the side. It slammed me into reality and out of my chair. Once again, I watched shiny, black boots ooze and undulate as they approached.

"Someone's too interested in your DNA, Rachel Pryne, so I want you kept away from Genetics." The man bent, grabbed my hair, and turned my face to him. "Something tells me leashing you will be advantageous."

"I once was lost but now am found, but now am found, but now am found." I slurred the lyrics again and again as my head lolled on my shoulders in time with no discernible rhythm. People surrounded me, whispering, crying. I was hollow and cold. I moved where they moved, shuffling my lead feet and squinting beneath the room's bright lights. "Was blind, but now I see."

"Give me answers if you want Pearl to live past this day." The meaning of that threat slowly came into focus with each passing hour. Despair and hatred warred for dominance and I swung between the two like a broken pendulum, cracking my case and losing time. *My baby is gone.* I shook my head. The world spun. I

staggered as the pressure in my aching skull shifted and my vision tunneled. I reached out. Hands steadied me. "Pearl?"

Someone replied, "They put your daughter on a different transport. No one's seen her since. I'm sorry." I squinted at the face, forcing the features into their right places. A Terran woman. I nodded and breathed through my mouth to stop the panic that threatened to escape as a scream.

All around were faces of strangers. Eyes wide, mouths pinched, brows twisted. Fear. I was crowded into a white room with other naked women. "Through many dangers, toils, and snares we have already come." My scalp itched, and reaching up I found only fuzz where long, dark curls had been. Suddenly, cold water rained from the ceiling and walls, accompanied by shrieks and gasps. Water ran down my body and I pressed my face against a slick wall, shaking and crying as I relived Cyrus's attack again. Then someone leaned me in a corner like a broken shelf and I closed my eyes.

"I'm sorry, Rachel." Those were Ehtishem's words spoken on the side of a mountain.

What had he done?

"And grace will lead me home."

"PNA466825. B-Level North. Maintenance."

We stood in a line. I wore loose, light gray pants and a matching shirt. No shoes. I didn't recall dressing. An Ohnenrai woman walked down the line, a thin metal compad in her palm. She paused beside each Terran prisoner, read off a code, and named a division in English. Her voice and movements left streaks in my brain, but the world had finally stopped warping like oil on water.

"PNA572662. Northwest Shuttle Bay. Maintenance."

Another Ohnenrai woman followed her with a hypomatic gun.

She pressed it against each prisoner's neck and administered some form of medication. A set of inoculations, I guessed, as none of the women was incapacitated like I'd been by the sedative.

"PNA874442. Northwest Shuttle Bay. Maintenance."

She reached me. "PNA625969." She paused, tapped her screen, and read something. She made a little grunt, so low it was almost inaudible, then continued. "Genetics." She turned to her companion. "Pass this one." She showed the woman something on the reader.

The other woman shook her head and tapped the screen. "No, there's an Elite override. See? Butcher Bay crew." There was a hiss as she triggered the gun to load a dose.

I glanced down. My hands were free. My feet weren't shackled. *To hell with this.* I looked at the women's expressionless faces, the hypomatic coming at me, and slugged the technician in the face. She made a strange little "oof" as she hit the floor. The hypomatic skittered across the room, and her companion stared at me as I made a mad, wobbling dash through the door.

All the corridors looked the same—dark gray flooring, light gray walls, blinding lights. And none of them remained straight for my drugged brain and tripping feet. I staggered down hallways, crashed around corners, and shouted, "Pearl!" But no one answered. A klaxon sounded, red lights strobed high up on the walls, and double doors thudded shut ahead of me. "Pearl! Where are you?"

I spun at the sound of heavy footfalls and ran into another wall. Two soldiers turned the corner behind me. I dodged down a hallway to my left, careened left again, and knew I was doubling back. "Pearl, answer me!" I glanced back. The soldiers were gaining ground.

More doors ahead. The red strobing lights made the walls shimmer pink and my doped brain made them melty. *Thud.* The doors rumbled shut. Unable to stop my momentum, I slammed into them and staggered back.

"Fun's over," one of the soldiers said. I turned to find them filling my escape route. Their weapons were holstered. Both men easily outweighed me. They were all hard muscle and brute strength. I shook my head, as much to clear my mind as to deny their words. They swarmed me. I hit the ground hard and saw triple as my head cracked against the floor.

"Get off!" I kicked out and caught flesh with my heel. But the man I struck didn't react, didn't even flinch. The soldiers flipped me to my stomach, manacled my wrists and ankles, and shot me up with the same fiery sedative. It flashed through my veins and heart, my lungs and brain. "Let go!"

The world warped then went away.

PART THREE
SYNTHESIS

THIRTEEN

"HELLO, RODENTS."

I lay in a bottom bunk and squinted at the backlit figure in the doorway then peered around the long, skinny room. Row after row of beds, no more than metal shelves, jutted from the walls with thin mattresses and thinner blankets. As the Terran women around me sat up, climbed from their bunks, and crowded the narrow center aisle, two shadows slipped into the room.

The Ohnenran who had spoken was our Driver. Her job was to get us to and from the Stoaca Varefshar—the Butcher Bay—where slaughtered livestock was offloaded from Earth, butchered, and distributed to the ship's many kitchens. "Rotation change. Your turn." She spoke English and tapped her lacquered fingernails on the metal doorframe.

Pearl was gone, likely dead. I groaned, pulled the covers over my pounding head, and hoped they'd forget I existed.

"You too, fresh meat." Hands caught my collar and sleeve and dragged me from the bed.

I landed on my stomach and went fetal as dry heaves shot pain through my gut. "*Je*-sus."

A female assistant towered over me. "You Terrans are pathetic." She jerked me up and pushed, slapped, and kicked me into line.

"Humph." The Driver jabbed my shoulder with a long, hard finger. "I don't see why we're bothering with you. Pale, ugly, bony, and sick. You'll be dead in a day."

Then our group set off. We shuffled through conduit-lined corridors, turned corner after corner, took caged freight elevators, and always moved downward. Finally, we passed through scarred, metal double doors and into the cavernous Northwest Shipping Bay. Our group halted and I gawked. Workers moved, ships maneuvered, lights strobed. A continuous earthquake rumbled the floor. Metal groaned, clanked, squealed. People called out orders. I heard both Ohnenrai and English.

"Welcome to the Butcher Bay," the Driver shouted in my ear. "Learn to love it. This is where you'll die." We stood at its opening, which recessed back from the Northwest Shipping Bay's massive straight canyon. The Butcher Bay stretched on and on, covering a length, breadth, and height far greater than I'd imagined could exist within something manmade. Suffer could've fit several times over within the Butcher Bay, and the Northwest Shipping Bay contained many such areas.

A car-sized ship came to a halt in the central lane. With thrusters hissing bursts of air, it pivoted and maneuvered a boxy transport the size of a two-story house into a small bay. The transport cleared the opening with only enough room for a person to pass on each side. I shuddered as its anti-grav washed over us and made my guts feel like they were disintegrating. I hated being near Ohnenrai ships.

The Driver jabbed me in the arm. "You will speak only when ordered. You will obey all commands. You're less valuable than the meat you're unloading today. Got it?" I stared at the floor and nodded. I couldn't speak around the lump in my throat anyway.

"Good. If you pull any of your combative nonsense with the Lead Butcher he'll gut you, and no one will care."

She pivoted and pushed back through the door. The bay's air tried to follow her and left our group awash in a hot, putrid breeze— a mixture of body odor and animal excrement, hot machinery, oil, and the distinct, metallic tang of raw meat.

We went further into the Butcher Bay where more Terrans worked. Some offloaded whole cattle carcasses, some carried crates of eggs and fish and fowl. Some cleaned empty transports. The boxy, multi-leveled containers were large enough to hold all the Sufferns I knew and still have room to spare. *Did we come up in one of those things?* I shuddered.

A pale Terran man was hosing down the open doors of a livestock container, tromping through a pond of piss, blood, and manure. The gore turned my stomach but not as much as his face did. Shirtless, Cyrus wore a breathing mask and gloves, but his oh-so-familiar movements were unmistakable as he wiped his brow and cranked off the hose. He turned toward me.

I twisted away as cold fear constricted my chest. "Oh, shit." We stood against a wall and there was nowhere to go. "Jesus Fucking Christ."

"Rachel," he snarled. I looked back to meet his glare as he came off the transport ramp and stomped toward me, his hands curling into fists. I searched, frantic for cover, frantic to put something between my nemesis and me, but there was nothing. The other women scrambled to escape Cyrus, perhaps sensing my fear and too full of their own to swallow mine.

"Whore!" His blow caught the side of my head and spun me. I crashed to the floor and lost my breath as he landed on my chest. Cyrus leaned over me, his gloved hand around my throat. I pushed and clawed at him. His breath fogged the mask, but I couldn't miss the hatred twisting his face even as my vision tunneled.

But as quickly as he'd attacked, he was lifted off me. I gasped, massaged my throat, sat up. Then I stared.

Ehtishem?

"I should have killed you when I had the chance, parasite." He had Cyrus pinned to the side of another livestock transport. "Now, you'll wish I had," he said in English, his voice as controlled as ever. With one hand, he held my tormentor by the throat and slid him up until his feet kicked free of the ground. Cyrus pulled and scratched, kicked and twisted—a helpless rat in a trap.

An aproned Ohnenran butcher had emerged from a deep bay at the commotion and stood slack-jawed and staring with a wicked blade dangling in his hand. He looked as surprised to see Ehtishem as I was.

Ehtishem dropped Cyrus and stepped back. "Va'gaoshrutavan," he said to the butcher as he held out his hand, palm up. The man fumbled to produce a compad from a pocket beneath his apron. Ehtishem took the device, tapped through screens, paused. As he waited, he put his foot on Cyrus's chest and leaned forward, ignoring the Elder's struggles.

"Aevadasa Enoth Timsai, here. I— *Thrai?*" The man, who'd answered in Ohnenrai, sounded as surprised as the slack-jawed Lead Butcher still looked.

Speaking Ohnenrai, Ehtishem said, "Timsai, I want you and my personal guard detail in the Butcher Bay. Now." He thumbed off the comtab and returned it to the butcher.

I looked around. Work had come to a halt around us as soldiers, workers, technicians, and pilots gathered, stared, whispered. Like a hushed wave, "Thrai" traveled through the growing crowd. I turned my addled brain to translating the word. It was something simple, something obvious.

Ehtishem ignored his audience as he leaned over Cyrus. "This is for knifing me in the back, coward." He cocked his fist and snapped it into the prone man's fogged mask. The mask cracked, Cyrus shouted, and blood replaced fog. "And this is for torturing Rachel." His kick left Cyrus holding his crotch and howling. Ehtishem turned back to the butcher. "This man is not to be assigned to any other work while aboard this ship. I want him to spend the remainder of his life up to his knees in blood and shit."

"Ah, zant, Thrai."

"Frayan, frayan. Idha." Ordering everyone to move aside, three soldiers pushed through the crowd. They stopped before Ehtishem and saluted. Their salute, like a wave, rippled outward until every Ohnenran stood at attention.

I stared at him, at them, and swallowed. *Thrai* had clicked. It meant he was the third in command...of the entire Ohnenrai military. *Holy shit.* I'd been right when I'd said he wasn't just some soldier.

Ehtishem returned the salute and nodded to the new arrivals. "Timsai," he addressed their leader then the soldiers, "Pa'nerem." *Gentlemen.*

"You are a welcome sight, Thrai. We await your orders," Timsai said.

Ehtishem bent to pick me up, but I shrank away. He was the goddamned thrai, one of the Ohnenrai's highest-ranking officers. And he'd duped me.

"I won't hurt you, Rachel," he said in English.

What was going on? What the hell was he doing here? Finding some steel in my spine, I straightened and said, "Too late. Pearl is dead because of you."

His brow furrowed for a second. "How?"

"I was interrogated. They wanted to know about you. They threatened to kill her."

Ehtishem raised his hand to stop me. "Threats are not acts. And this isn't for public discussion. I won't force you to leave, but consider your options."

Threats are not acts. Those words thundered through me. *Pearl could be alive.* I looked past Ehtishem to where Cyrus still cringed. The elder was staying distant while Ehtishem was here, but when he was gone? That bastard wouldn't stop until he got me. I wasn't safe. And going with Ehtishem put me one step closer to knowing if Pearl had been killed—one large step. I nodded. "Okay, but I can walk, you know."

"Not fast enough." Ehtishem lifted me like I weighed no more than Holly Dolly. He ordered his guards to take us to his quarters by the most public route. The soldiers surrounded us and the growing crowd separated to let us pass.

We rode another caged lift and emerged into a bright hallway. Two soldiers snapped to attention then fell in ahead and behind us. They moved with long, even strides and straight spines, as if they knew they were untouchable. All five wore crisp, dark gray uniforms with a dog-head symbol on the jacket front and lapels. But Ehtishem still wore his ragged, gray-and-green fatigues.

A group of soldiers lining the corridor came to attention, their right hands snapping up to the outside corners of their right eyes. "Fra." *Sir.* Ehtishem nodded at them but continued down the hallway toward a set of metal doors. We passed through, turned left, and marched along a wide conduit-lined corridor. The guards tightened their formation around us as we stopped before more double doors. A recessed tablet to the right of the doorway glowed red.

Ehtishem pressed his lips to my ear. "This is a lot more humanity than you've seen in a long time, Rachel. Remember, they're just people. You're safe with me."

Am I?

He addressed the point man. "Huorem?"

The soldier nodded and pressed his palm to the pad. The glow

turned green and the doors slid into the walls to reveal a wide platform crowded with Ohnenrai. My fingers tightened on Ehtishem. A
sea of beautiful, dark faces turned to us, followed by colliding waves
of comments and questions. "Anghu framarez pantham, vana."
Huorem's voice cut through the cacophony as he ordered them to
clear a path. The scrape of shuffling feet replaced words as the
Ohnenrai sea parted.

I shrank away from all the dark brown, questioning eyes as our
group waded into the crowd. There were so many gray-uniformed
men and women standing among the civilians, their bodies at
attention.

"Marez'aste, pa'ratheshto." Ehtishem's voice rumbled through
me as he told the soldiers among the crowd to be at ease.

"Ushta visdi-va, Thrai." *Good to see you, Thrai.*

"Mem kanikar-va, fra." *Welcome back, sir.*

"Thrai, ka fradat visdi-va." *Thrai, what a relief to see you.*

The civilians' comments carried relief and pleasure, but their
gazes scraped over me and their expressions set like concrete. The
military personnel remained quiet and watchful.

Ehtishem approached a coppery energy wall that reminded me
all too much of the Gate on Earth. Beyond the wall, the platform
dropped off to a series of lanes where sleek, white, bullet-shaped cars
flashed past in a blur or came to a gentle stop to release and accept
passengers.

We halted before the energy divider. Huorem palmed another
panel on a doorway set into the glowing barrier and the copper light
disappeared within the frame. The pressure in my ears expanded
and contracted as a car, suspended from two massive grappling
arms, dropped into place before us while another one thundered
past on a lower track. Our group moved forward. I glanced up as we
stepped into the car. There were rows of hooks and cars over the
platform.

Ehtishem settled me into a seat beside the window, but he remained standing.

I stared at him. "Where are you taking me? And where the hell did you come from?" I asked in English.

"I'm sure you're not the only one asking that right now, Rachel," he answered in my language. "But your questions must wait. You will have to trust me and be patient."

"Why the hell should I trust you?"

He continued to face forward even as he said, "You did a few days ago on the side of a mountain."

Screw you. I crossed my arms and glared out the window. My ears popped. I squeaked as the car dropped and accelerated. It shifted to the right then flashed down the empty central lane, the scenery blurring as it whooshed past numerous platforms without pause. It slowed as we entered a cavernous, round station. Eight tunnels converged and cars shifted from lane to lane, platform to platform, up and down in an automated dance.

Ehtishem leaned forward to gaze out the window. "Ahn Maidhya Tarasca—the Central Cross." Bridges arched between the platforms and the cars passed beneath as they entered and exited the interchange. Those releasing passengers rose out of the lanes as oncoming traffic thundered through the Cross.

A guard stepped to the door pad and tapped in several codes. The crossing lights turned orange then flashed between purple and red. Every car halted as ours moved forward, shifting between lanes to reach a central lane.

The Central Cross was larger than anything I could recall. Its mass of humanity dwarfed that of the platform we'd just left, and countless faces had turned toward our car.

"My people don't think I'm a criminal, but they do think I'm dead." Ehtishem had said that he'd crossed a very powerful military leader. Was that what this was all about? Had I been questioned and

Pearl possibly killed because someone wanted Ehtishem dead and we were in the wrong place at the wrong time? *That son of a bitch, Cyrus, is to blame. He reported Ehtishem. He told them about Pearl and me.*

The Central Cross disappeared in a blink as our car shot into the tunnel. *Pearl.* I stared out the window and inhaled against the pain and panic of losing my daughter.

"Are you all right?" Ehtishem asked. I shook my head but couldn't speak. He touched my arm. "I know you're frightened and confused, Rachel. Soon I'll answer all your questions."

The car slowed, entered a hub the same size as our original, and pulled to a platform as all other cars halted. Activity on this platform was different, methodical, its occupants comprised almost entirely of gray-clad military personnel.

Our escorts came to attention as Ehtishem lifted me from the seat. The car doors opened and two of his guards stepped onto the platform, their weapons ready. Timsai followed and pressed a thin, silver tube to his lips. All movement halted at his shrill whistle. The uniformed mass turned and came to rigid attention. "Anghu framarez pantham, vana." His order brought immediate obedience and a path opened through the shifting crowd.

Ehtishem stepped from the car. A murmur traveled through the ranks, followed by the slap of countless left hands against uniformed thighs as every soldier saluted. He told them to stand down and looked neither right nor left as our group passed through another energy wall. We cut through the crowd and entered an elevator, its doors engraved with the dog-head symbol. Two of our escort remained outside as the doors closed.

Ehtishem keyed a series of codes into the panel beside the doors.

"Framru-va nama, vana." *State your name, please.* I turned at the sound of the security computer's voice, but Ehtishem angled my face away from the panel. "Look away, Rachel."

"Nama nava vaeda. Framru-va nama, vana."

He answered its second request for his name. "Thrai Ehtishem Mahle."

A chill climbed my spine and spread across my scalp. *Thrai Ehtishem Mahle. The son of Zosh Zainabahn Mahle.* I'd heard of this man.

My father had mentioned him more than once with awe and admiration. *"Thrai Mahle is a soldier's soldier, Rachel. If I wanted to conquer a world, he's the man I'd recruit to do it. We're fortunate to have him as an ally, because I sure as hell wouldn't want him as an enemy."*

"Vaxsh huxtavist. Ahngano vayaxanem vist. Zasta, vana." *Voice accepted. Face accepted. Palm, please.*

Ehtishem pressed his palm to the panel.

"Kanikar namana, Thrai Ehtishem Mahle." The security computer welcomed him home as the lift ascended.

FOURTEEN

THE ELEVATOR OPENED to a softly lit lobby and a set of brushed metal doors. Ehtishem went through the same security procedure for these doors, crossed through a passway to frosted glass doors, then entered an elegant, cavernous room and set me on a light gray, tufted sofa. He moved to a table in the middle of the room and touched the top of a narrow, black post the size of a pint glass. A series of yellow lights wound their way from top to bottom and back, then a ring around the base glowed green.

I frowned at a faint, throbbing pressure in my skull and touched the back of my shaved head where the tracker was implanted. Ehtishem glanced at me. "You're feeling the interceptor's pulse. It scrambles tracker signals and the monitoring equipment that's standard in all military quarters. Soon you won't notice it."

He addressed our escort in Ohnenrai. "Gentlemen, I appreciate your prompt and careful attention when I called, but this situation is tenuous at best. I won't bargain with your loyalty, and I don't demand it. If it's offered, I'll gratefully accept but only with your clear understanding that pledging it places a target on your backs. If you choose to walk away, I will neither fault you nor withhold my allegiance infield and shipboard."

Timsai stepped forward. "Fra, I don't need to pledge my loyalty. It never faltered. You are the thrai. I will stand with you until old age or war takes me down." Ehtishem clasped his man's hand and murmured his thanks, even as the other guards followed suit and asserted their loyalty.

As his bodyguards took up positions outside the main doors, he and Timsai discussed the past and immediate future. "We can expect visitors, aevadasa," Ehtishem said to his first lieutenant.

I looked away from the men and around the cavernous room. A darkened window ran the length of it and the ceiling rose three stories to a vast skylight through which the Milky Way sparkled like crushed diamonds. I'd never seen it like that.

"No doubt, fra."

And I'd never seen anything like these quarters. There was a kitchen with wide counters and tall wooden cabinets, and a formal eating area with a polished, dark wood table. Opposite the kitchen entrance was a wood and glass stairwell leading to a second floor. Another stairwell led up to a third level. The rest of the room was filled with low tables, chairs, couches, lamps all arranged into small conversation areas. A blue-green glass sculpture of two dogs—a bitch and a pup tugging her ear—sat on the table beside the device Ehtishem had activated. A polished wood grandfather clock tick-tick-ticked against one wall. There was artwork and more sculptures. A reader, transparent and thin as a playing card, sat on a table beside the couch. It all felt elegant and sophisticated. And so much of it had been stolen from Earth.

I folded my arms, tucked my filthy hands beneath my armpits, and glared at Ehtishem and his aevadasa. Without Pearl's presence to temper me, the sharp edge of anger was carving away my self-control.

"Was it an assassination, Thrai?" Timsai squared his shoulders as he asked the question.

"Zant. And I know the organizer's identity but have no living proof to assert my case before the Council." Ehtishem crossed the room to the clock, Timsai on his heels. "The two soldiers assigned to kill me disobeyed the order. They knew it was a suicide mission; they'd die at my hands or Isphahan's. I'm certain his guard was waiting when they returned."

"The zosh? You're certain he ordered it?"

The zosh was the Supreme Command General of the Ohnenrai Military and Civilian Defensive Forces. A council of leaders governed the Ohnenrai, and among them was the zosh. But he or she had the ultimate say in all decisions because the Ohnenrai were driven by military might.

Ehtishem nodded. "Zant, aevadasa." He swiped his fingers across the top of the grandfather clock then scrutinized them.

"That explains a lot," Timsai said. "Isphahan wouldn't leave evidence." The aevadasa mirrored his thrai's stony expression. "The soldiers' names, fra?"

"Dasa Borv and Dasa Nahnesh. When I left them, they were submitting a sealed Refusal of Orders. If the R.O.O. was received, it'll be among their personal files." Ehtishem folded his arms. "I'll get you access to those records. But I expect the search will be difficult, part of an uncategorized data dump."

Timsai glanced at me as he nodded. "Difficult, fra, but not impossible. I'll begin immediately."

"You'll be watched."

"No doubt. I'm certain your resurrection has rattled the zosh."

Ehtishem nodded. "Who's taken my duties?"

"No one, fra. He's undermined all Council attempts to call a Vote of Authority."

"No one." Ehtishem clasped his hands behind his back. "He hasn't named a new dvai?"

Timsai shook his head. "The zosh has retained emergency powers, fra. There's growing discomfort in the ranks, but no one wants a civil war. The Council has been *conservative* in their approach."

"Doubtless. No dvai and no thrai means no one to check the zosh's power. That's an open airlock waiting to suck out any councilor who strays too close." The thrai turned and grasped his man's shoulder. "Discretion, please. And be aware of the danger."

"Zant, Thrai." The assistant then looked at me and asked in English, "And the Terran woman?"

"Her name is Rachel Pryne and she isn't a prisoner. What happens next is her decision. I'll keep you informed."

I straightened. If I wasn't his prisoner, what was I?

"Pryne?" The aevadasa's gaze didn't waver from me. "She holds the complete Code?"

"Zant."

Code? I don't have any code.

He looked at Ehtishem. "That's a weapon worth dying for."

"Good men and women already have, Timsai."

"Then I have work to do, fra."

"Zant. And I want you to inquire about Rachel's daughter, Pearl Pryne. A seven-year-old girl without a tracker who was picked up in the same raid as Rachel."

Timsai tapped a quick note into his compad, saluted, and left. Ehtishem remained stone still in front of the clock.

A weapon worth dying for. A double-edged sword. "Are you my enemy or my friend?" *Strike when you need to.*

He faced me. "I have only ever been your friend, Rachel. And I want your trust and your help."

"Are you fucking kidding? You've been playing me since the

night you showed up in my yard." I crossed my arms. "What's this code your lieutenant talked about? I don't have anything."

"Rachel—"

The security computer announced a visitor: "Sarem Ahremena Uahdimei Mahlei hei jaidhyantai vis."

Ehtishem frowned for a second and strode toward me. But he paused as a compad on the kitchen counter began blinking and emitting a steady, shrill tone. He went to it, said in Ohnenrai, "He can wait," and silenced the tone with a tap on the screen. Then he moved between the entryway and me, and granted entry: "Mem erenavi vis."

I peered around him to see Sarem—Councilor—Ahremena Uahdimei Mahlei.

A tall, hard woman strode through the entryway, her beautiful, mahogany face smooth and expressionless. She held her chin up as she stopped just within the room and scrutinized us. With hawk-like precision she assessed, her gaze lingering on me, then coming to rest upon Ehtishem. "So, you're back from the dead, Ehtishem. That is something to add to your profile," she said in Ohnenrai.

He watched her.

The woman's gaze came back to pin me. "Is this her?"

He answered in English. "You're uncertain? The zosh wasn't. He pulled her from the Genetics roster and redirected her to the Bay."

"Oh? Give me her tracking code." She pulled a small, rectangular scanner from her pocket and tapped the screen, then looked up and around. She waved her hand at the lit interceptor on the table. "Turn that off. I can't take readings with its interference."

"She has a name, Mother." Ehtishem crossed his arms. "Remember?"

I blinked. *This is his* mother? Of course. Mahlei was the feminine form of Mahle.

Ahremena looked back at her device. "I don't deal in names. You know that. I need the woman's code."

"She's Rachel Ellenore Pryne, not a number."

This time the councilor's look not only pinned me, it dissected me too. Then she turned that scalpel gaze upon the thrai and said, "It's interesting that you care." She put the scanner away and added, "I'll send a med tech to examine her."

I stood. "Like hell you will."

A smile flitted across Ehtishem's features. "That's the Rachel I remember."

I turned on him. "I don't need platitudes. I need to know what's so friggin' interesting about me. I need to know what's happened to Pearl. And I don't need anymore goddamned Ohnenrai hands on me."

He came to me and touched my elbow. "Sit, Pairika, before you fall down." I slapped him. "You bastard!"

He didn't release my arm but eyed me, his brow furrowed. "Why did you do that?"

As always, I marveled at Ehtishem's control and, now, his audacity. Yet, for all my anger I still fought the warmth his nearness triggered. "Excuse me for being a little pissed off, but finding out you're one of the bastards in charge of the military that destroyed my planet and murdered my parents has been kinduva a shock."

"Her lack of control is less than charming," Ahremena said, "though I see the attraction she holds for you. She certainly demonstrates a will as powerful as yours. What a pleasant surprise."

Ehtishem released me and turned toward her. "I'll see to her well-being, *Councilor*. And she will remain under my protection."

Ahremena's eyes narrowed and her lips lifted—for a mere second. Was that a hint of satisfaction?

Ehtishem pulled up a chair and sat facing me. "Will you sit,

Rachel? Please." I glared down at him then dropped onto the couch. "I see two hypo marks on your neck. Let me see your arms."

I crossed them. "I don't have to show you shit."

"All right, then I'll assume one was a sedative and the other was a vaccination."

"You'll assume wrong."

"*Two* sedatives?"

"You got it. And I *still* can't think straight."

He frowned, the expression remaining through his next request. "Tell me what happened after I left you."

"I don't have to *tell* you shit, either."

His face relaxed. "True." He stood, went to the kitchen, and returned with two glasses of water.

Anger burned up from the pit of my stomach. "You left us, and now Pearl is dead!"

"You don't know that," he said evenly.

"What? I—no, but the interrogator threatened her. He said she'd be dead if I didn't answer his questions, but I didn't *have* any answers."

"Let's assume she is alive until proven otherwise." Ehtishem handed me a glass and gave the other to Ahremena. "We are fortunate that you didn't have any answers or you, Pearl, and I *would* be dead by now." He appraised the councilor then turned back to me. "It's good that we chose to keep you ignorant."

"*We?*" I looked from mother to son.

She answered in English. "The former zosh, myself, Ehtishem, and Joe and Ellie—your parents."

"My *parents?*" My world was turning upside down and inside out, and it made me dizzy.

Ehtishem touched my arm. I stared at his hand as he said, "This isn't how I wanted you to learn this, Pairika, but I'm certain that Isphahan has figured you out. We have little time and even less room to maneuver. So we're going to drop a lot of information on you now. I need your trust."

I batted his hand away. "You lied about who and what you are."

"No. I am Ehtishem Zain to you, if to no one else."

"You are Thrai Ehtishem Mahle to millions of Ohnenrai!"

"Not one of whom matters to me as much as you do."

"Bullshit. I'm not stupid. That was a very public show you put on today. Obviously, I'm a prop. And you've dragged me—us—*my whole family*—into some horrible mess for reasons I can't even imagine." Water sloshed out of the glass and onto my pants. "You were sent for me, weren't you? You were sent, and you never said a goddamned thing. It was all a charade."

"Nava. I meant everything I said on that mountainside, Rachel." Ehtishem returned to the kitchen for another glass of water. He paused with his back to me then turned. "I told you the truth but not all of it. You are genetically significant to the Ohnenrai. Your parents knew this. They died because of it. And it's why I will always protect you."

Oh, hell. Oh, hell! I'd worked so hard to convince myself my parents' last words were delusions, that learning they weren't hit me in the gut. I looked down at my glass and blinked back tears.

Ahremena said, "Tell her everything, Thrai."

I looked up. "Yes, tell me why I had to watch as my parents were murdered. Tell me why my daughter is probably dead. Tell me why you showed up on my doorstep and screwed with my miserable fucking life!"

Ahremena answered. "Because Ehtishem is a man of honor and duty. He will see an assignment through to the end. Or die trying."

"An assignment? I'm an *assignment*?" Could this get any worse?

Ehtishem's expression remained unchanged, but his gaze never left my face as Ahremena continued. "Zant. As the Hundred Days spread instability, Zosh Mahle, at the request of Ohnenrai Genetics, sent the thrai to extract you and your family from Terra. Someone had placed your parents on a list of wanted terrorists. I finally found you on a detainee report and paid a substantial bribe to get you transferred to Suffer, off the record. But the assassination happened and Isphahan pulled the ships from orbit before I could give Ehtishem your location."

"That terrorist thing is bullshit. And my parents had nothing to do with an assassination." I jabbed my finger at Ehtishem. "They weren't terrorists. They were terrorized."

"I know that, Rachel." Ehtishem came back to sit before me. "I promised Joe and Ellie that their decisions and sacrifices would not be wasted. And I promised them that I would keep you safe."

"You're talking like they were your friends."

"They were. Wormhole travel dissociates time between destinations. I met them when they were young. You know we'd come and gone from orbit over many Terran decades." I did, and I knew that my parents had been abductees.

Ahremena added, "Joe and Ellie were a part of our program long before we revealed our presence to your governments. They were identified as potential genetic donors when they were children."

I closed my eyes, feeling even dizzier. I recalled my mother talking about the abductions, her smile and their excitement as she and my father helped with the first public contact.

"You don't know your significance, Rachel." Ahremena lifted her chin and gazed at me with bright eyes, like I was a prize.

"I will explain this, Sarem." The drop in Ehtishem's tone sounded like a warning. I saw his jaw tense and shift then heard it pop. He glared at her as he took the reader from the side table. Its face darkened as he ran his hand over it. He tapped a few times, swiped the screen a few times, and handed me the device.

He'd pulled up a report read by a female Ohnenran under a visual record of him in uniform with another older commander as they strode through a smoldering battlefield. Behind them the White House burned, black smoke billowing from its innards. A massive Ohnenrai gunship occupied the scorched lawn, and as the camera angle changed the Washington Monument came into view, broken and blackened. It was video from the Hundred Days.

"Offices of the Supreme Command General confirmed reports today that Zosh Zainabahn Mahle and Thrai Ehtishem Mahle were killed when their gunship came under heavy fire."

Eight soldiers, their guns at ready, strode ahead and behind the officers, their eyes scanning and bodies tense. Assistants frantically tapped notes as Ehtishem and his companion dictated orders. Ships rumbled overhead, barely clearing the men and women as they dropped mech-suited soldiers then circled outward, weapons thundering as they blazed a perimeter around the Ohnenrai troops.

I shivered at the sound, at the power, at the memories.

"Zosh Mahle and Thrai Mahle, seen here in archival records from the Battle of D.C., were arriving in New York City for strategic talks with the Terran United Nations when their ship was shot down."

An explosion rocked the camera and all the soldiers ducked as debris showered them—all but Ehtishem and the zosh who looked toward the explosion and brushed dirt from their uniforms.

"The talks—"

Ehtishem reached across me to swipe his hand over the screen. "Druj—lies—to support a coup." He stood and returned the reader to the table. "The soldiers recruited to assassinate me double-crossed Isphahan—my uncle, the current zosh—when they left me in Alaska instead of a grave. Isphahan *did* succeed in assassinating my father, and he believed that he'd done the same to me. Until now." His eyes were intense and he swallowed. "Nineteen months away from Terra for the shipboard Ohnenrai were twelve years earthbound for me, Rachel. You were fourteen years old when these things happened."

He stared at the grandfather clock. My jaw tightened as tension wound around me like a band nearing its breaking point. Finally, he looked back at me. "We knew your parents had family on the Pacific North American coast. I combed every Terran encampment and colony from Alaska and the Northwest Territories to Northern California. My mission was covert because we couldn't reveal your existence to Isphahan's Purists."

"Purists." I exhaled a long breath. "I'm sorry your uncle is a xenophobic son of a bitch, but what does any of this have to do with my family?"

"Our genome is failing," Ahremena answered. "Your parents, like many other Terrans, were helping us create a solution. The Ohnenrai will not survive as a pure species. We need your genes, but Isphahan refuses to accept that. He will annihilate your people to prevent the dilution of ours."

Ehtishem added, "Your parents donated their DNA to our geneticists. And your mother volunteered to carry a fetus. She lost that one and the next and the next. After every miscarriage she came back and demanded we try again. And your father was beside her every time. On the eighth try the pregnancy took. You're as stubborn as your mother, Rachel."

Holy shit. The glass shook in my hands. More water spilled on my lap and I stared at the dark stain. My parents had died for me. I looked back at Ehtishem. They'd died for him too. But had they died in vain?

"I don't make promises in wartime, but I couldn't refuse your father when he asked me to protect you. We all agreed it was best that you not know of your unique genetics." He turned away and stopped beside the dining table, then leaned back, chin-to-chest, and watched me from beneath his brow. "There were too many Purist rumblings among the Ohnenrai *and* the Terrans."

"Your parents planned to tell you once you were shipboard,"

Ahremena added. I glared at her. "But they were killed, and you stuck me in Suffer."

Ehtishem said, "That colony became a place to hide the viable offspring of the Terran volunteers. No one was meant to remain there for more than a few weeks." I looked from mother to son. "All you've ever done was used us."

"We only did what your parents agreed to, Rachel." Ahremena seemed as emotionless as a paperclip.

"I'm pretty damn sure they didn't agree to being shot and having their only child raped and starved for twelve years!"

Her cool expression remained unchanged despite my outburst. "There's no need for hysteria."

Ehtishem pushed away from the table. "You are a decidedly unhelpful woman, Ahremena."

I stood and paced a circle, stopping beside the table. It was set for a meal. "No. No way I'm going to believe my parents gave their DNA freely. That's bullshit. They were abductees. They were *murdered*. And now Pearl's gone, too." My brain was buzzing, maybe from fatigue or a flashback, or maybe I was on the verge of a psychotic break.

You can wound them. Light winked off the polished white china and silverware. *Strike when you need to.* My parents' strange whispered secrets as we hid and ran in the woods while Ohnenrai soldiers hunted us.

I snatched a steak knife from the table and brandished it like a scalpel at Ehtishem. "You tell me what's happened to my daughter or I'll castrate you."

Ahremena crossed her arms. "I prefer she not succeed, Thrai."

In a blink, Ehtishem had seized my wrist. My hand went weak and the knife hit the floor. Catching my other forearm, he jerked me forward until only inches separated us. "Don't make threats you can't fulfill, Pairika." He kicked the knife across the floor and stepped away from me. "I don't have an answer for you."

I swallowed and trembled; my arms ached and my hand tingled. *Jesus Christ, that was stupid, Rachel.*

"Hmm. A surprising level of volatility." Ahremena pulled the scanner from her pocket and began tapping notes into it. "I must review her full genome."

Ehtishem turned on her and said in Ohnenrai, "Councilor, you may leave. Now."

She met his steady gaze, then shrugged. "Ash-ush."

Once she'd departed, Ehtishem held out my water. I accepted it but just stared at the glass as it wept condensation. "You should not have suffered. And your world should not have been destroyed because your people helped us," he said as he picked up his own drink. "Your parents *were* my friends, Rachel. They should not have died." He gently steered me back to the couch and sat opposite me again. "Let's consider Pearl. Tell me everything you remember from the time we parted. I may find some clue to lead me to her."

I peered up at him wanting to massage my anger back into a good, hot rage, but there was no more fight in me. "Pearl. Yeah." I swallowed and told him about the unexpected Gate, the raid, and being picked up. "That's when they took her. They shot Audie and took Pearl." He handed me his water, and I was grateful as the cold liquid washed a lump down my throat. I told of the interrogation, the holding room with the other Terran women, fighting and escaping the techs, and the Driver's brutality.

When I'd finished, he retrieved the reader and pulled up a picture. It showed two older officers listening to a uniformed Ehtishem as they strode past squadrons of Ohnenrai warships. I recognized his father, Zosh Mahle, from the visual record. The other soldier walked a step behind. His arms were crossed and his sullen expression surprised me, accustomed as I was to thinking of all Ohnenrai soldiers as unemotional. Then again, I'd been so very wrong about Ehtishem. "Is this the man who questioned you?" He pointed at the dour officer.

I closed my eyes and tried to assemble the man's features properly. "I'm not sure. Maybe?"

"Did he have a female aevadasa?"

"There was a woman. Yes. An officer." I straightened, remembering. "She called him zosh."

"Aevadasa Vindira." Ehtishem nodded. "As I said, we are fortunate that you knew nothing of your genetics."

"That man is your uncle? He controls everything?"

"Correct."

I stared at the picture. "You think he has Pearl?"

"Assuming she is alive, he knows where she is."

I slouched back against the couch. "And I'm helpless to reach her." Pearl and I were right back where we'd started but even worse off.

"You are not helpless." A woman spoke behind me in Ohnenrai. I jerked around, then clutched my aching skull and groaned as stabbing pain reminded me of the past few days. She continued, "You are tired, overwhelmed, and still suffering the effects of a sedative overdose."

"Good evening, Sree." There was warmth in Ehtishem's voice. "Rachel, Sree is my trainer and one of my most valued advisors."

The silver-haired woman came around the couch and looked me up and down, her lips pursed. By the time she blinked again, I felt autopsied. Finally, she turned to Ehtishem. "Ratheshtolo, you should not have revealed yourself."

"Speak English, Sree."

She batted his words away with a wave of her hand. "Ridiculous. Yesterday you told me the woman speaks perfect Ohnenrai. Don't treat her like an imbecile."

He nodded and said in Ohnenrai, "I agree that the timing was unfortunate, but I had no choice. Rachel was threatened. I couldn't stand by and watch."

"Hmm." She twisted back to face me. "Get rest. And stop doubting yourself. You are a mother, are you not? You have far more power than you know." She contemplated the steak knife. Ehtishem had kicked it so hard it was lodged in a chair leg. Sree glided across the room like a whisper, bent, and worked it free. She deposited it in the kitchen sink then vanished down a dark hallway. I stared after her, my mouth agape.

Ehtishem stood. "Sree keeps my quarters. She is blunt, a quality I admire. And I suspect you will like her."

I let my hands fall to my lap. "I thought you said she's your trainer."

He nodded. "Zant, my most valued teacher. She fulfills many roles. She's been aiding me covertly since I returned to Dathusha."

I stared at my limp fingers, too tired to blink. Ehtishem had known my parents. He'd come to Suffer to get me. Apparently, I was made to fix the Ohnenrai, but instead I'd caused the destruction of everyone I loved. And, to worsen things, he was powerful but maybe not powerful enough to stop an enemy who wanted me, Pearl, and every other Terran dead. I met his gaze. He shimmered behind my tears. "I want my baby."

Ehtishem touched my cheek. "I know. Tomorrow, Rachel. We'll talk more tomorrow. And I'll have better answers. But you need rest tonight." He bent and lifted me again. My head rested against his shoulder as he carried me up the stairs.

"Ka kar Ratheshtolo astu?" Sleep slurred my words as I asked the meaning of his nickname.

"Little warrior."

FIFTEEN

I AWOKE IN A HUGE, soft bed in a room that was larger than my house. Everything was gray and cream except the bright orange flowers on the bedside table. A chaise sat in front of a wall-sized window. Beyond the glass, Earth rotated against star-speckled space. I'd known I wasn't on Terra, but I'd been too doped up and distracted to think about it. Seeing the planet was a kick in the gut. I cried and watched India, Asia, Australia—my home's changing face as the ship orbited. I'd slipped into Ohnenrai with Ehtishem and now I doubted I'd hear my own language for as long as I remained aboard Dathusha.

Finally, I sighed and wiped tears and snot on the sheets. "No more self-pity, Rachel Pryne. You don't have time for that shit." I swung my feet to the floor and realized I was wearing a dark purple gown that I didn't recall putting on. The too-long hem and sleeves were annoying until I found a sash on the bed and cinched the dress. But I gave up on rolling the stupid, flowing sleeves.

I hadn't asked to be part of this experiment, but it had given me power. The Ohnenrai needed me. I was going to use that to my advantage even if it meant destroying myself to destroy all of them, a decision that hinged on Pearl's well-being and whether or not I could trust Ehtishem.

I crossed the room and touched the wall panel beside a set of frosted glass entry doors. They retracted to reveal a long landing that overlooked the cavernous first floor. More closed doors lined the walkway, and stairs bisected the midpoint. The ceiling soared beyond the second and third floors to the vast skylight. The Milky Way still twinkled beyond the glass.

I clung to the polished wood stair rail, my stomach rumbling at the scents of steak and fresh bread as I descended. When I reached the table, I stopped and stared at more food than Pearl and I ate in two weeks. There were peas, potatoes, rolls, steak, chicken, fish, tomatoes, carrots, salad, berries, oranges, almonds, honey, jam, butter, wine, milk, juice, coffee—I hadn't smelled coffee since I was a young girl.

"Sit and eat. Your clothes are falling off you."

I turned and looked up to see Ehtishem and Sree descending from the third floor. "Stop fussing," he responded to her. "You're like an old hen."

"I don't know what that is, but I'm sure it's no good. You'll see I'm right when you run combat drills. That is *if* the med techs certify you."

Their banter might have amused me if his appearance hadn't started nausea twisting in my gut. He'd shaved his head and wore the dark uniform of an Ohnenrai military officer. Charcoal gray with seams pressed straight as razor blades, the clothes made him a loathsome icon of my world's conquerors. Four green and gold bars marked both sleeves over his biceps and were echoed on his left collar and around his cuffs. One side of his chest bore row upon row of colorful insignias. The other held a circle of six blue and six gold stars surrounding a white dog—Draxtu Mainyu. The same symbol decorated his guards' uniforms and the elevator doors. It meant determination under any circumstances.

Thrai Ehtishem Mahle.

The thrai looked up from working his metal jacket fasteners and said in Ohnenrai, "I'm glad you're finally awake, Rachel. Will you join me for evening meal?"

"No. I'm not hungry." I stepped behind a chair as he approached. I didn't care if he said he would always protect me. He'd done a crappy job so far. And when I saw him dressed like that I didn't trust him. Maybe all the things he and his mother had said were lies.

He surveyed the table. His brow furrowed then smoothed out just as quickly. "Sree, I already asked you not to make so much. Do you think I've been without food for twelve years?"

"Nava, but that woman has, Ehtishem."

"Show Rachel the kitchen. She can feed herself. And prepare small meals for me. I will eat aboard Pohru-Mahrko if I'm still hungry."

One of the frayed strands checking my sanity snapped. "We've been starving—hunting and scrounging—while you and your people ate like *this*? While you ate *our food*?" I grabbed a peeled orange and threw it at him. He and Sree ducked. The fruit exploded against the wall behind them. "You son of a bitch!"

I reached for the coffee carafe meaning to do some serious damage, but the security computer announced, "Zosh Isphahan Uahdim requests entry." I stopped.

Ehtishem picked up a cloth napkin and wiped juice and pulp from the back of his neck. "Entry granted." He put his hand on the carafe, leaned over the table and me, and said, "Can you control your temper, Rachel, or do I need to remove you to another room?"

Insulted, I opened my mouth to answer, but the inner door

opened and the zosh entered the room. He was accompanied by a group of soldiers. And Pearl.

"Pearl!" I lurched toward them, but Ehtishem caught my wrist.

"Can you stay silent?" His expression, his voice, his manner were so damned controlled.

I craned to see around him then, failing, met his cool gaze. "Fine. Yes. Just let me see her. *Please.*"

He considered me for a long moment, then nodded and pointed at the couch. I sat as Sree took the coffee. Ehtishem turned to regard his uncle. But for the dog symbol, Ehtishem's uniform matched the zosh's.

"Welcome back from the dead, Thrai." The man looked and sounded as welcoming as an iceberg. Pearl stood several feet back and behind him, and I couldn't see her past his imposing figure. As the two leaders faced each other, I seethed at the hazy memories of the zosh beside a dilapidated building and, later, interrogating me. This man had destroyed my world.

"Thank you, Dvai."

The title meant Second. Isphahan's eyes narrowed.

Ehtishem stepped forward and the zosh's guards shifted like a herd of nervous horses. "Rachel, I regret you and Pearl ever met acting-Zosh Isphahan Uahdim."

Isphahan studied me as he moved into the room. Our eyes met. "Hello, again, Rachel. Thank you for luring my nephew out of hiding." His gaze returned to Ehtishem and something tightened the corners of his eyes and tugged at his lips. "I should have known removing you couldn't be that easy, nephew."

I looked from him to Ehtishem then strained to see Pearl's brunette curls.

Ehtishem drew up straight and tall, folded his arms, and returned his uncle's gaze. "Bold words. Fra."

Pearl shifted. I saw her face and gasped. An elaborate, white serpent mark—more a brand than a tattoo—wound from the middle of her forehead, down her left cheek, to her jaw. Her skin was pink and bruised. The snake glared at me with baleful, yellow eyes and poison glinted on its curved fangs. Ehtishem must have seen Pearl too because he'd stepped back to block me.

"I'll give you credit, Thrai," Isphahan said. "Yesterday's public display shackled my hands. For now."

Heat flushed my chest, neck, and face. I shook as my hands curled into fists. I didn't think anyone could be worse than Cyrus, but Isphahan had not only threatened Pearl's life, he'd dehumanized her by marking her as his own. The serpent on her face matched the one emblazoning his uniform.

"Let them go, Isphahan. Rachel and Pearl have suffered enough. They needn't be pawns in our game."

"I'm not the one who brought them into this. That guilt lies squarely with you and Ahremena. And you know I'll never relinquish a tactical advantage." He pivoted and caught Pearl's braid.

She squeaked.

I lunged off the couch.

But my murderous trajectory was cut short by Ehtishem's hand around my upper arm. My head snapped back as he jerked me against him. "Control yourself or Pearl will pay for your behavior." His low words cooled my anger like ice water and I sat as abruptly as I'd stood. But his gaze hadn't left Isphahan. "You murdered Rachel's parents, destroyed her world, and stole her freedom." While I shook and ground my teeth, Ehtishem's voice and demeanor revealed no emotion as he added, "What more do you want?"

"That's an idiotic question. To end the degradation that began with the Mahles, of course. Your kind doesn't belong on the Elite Level. And *she* has no place aboard this ship." Isphahan jabbed his finger at me. Then he smirked. "Still, you're really quite remarkable,

Ehtishem. You revealed your mother's subterfuge and destroyed a great deal of her work in one simple step. And you brought me your own nice, short leash. Thank you." He twisted his hand in Pearl's braid and added, "Best of all, the girl's a choke collar. She is my property and will remain aboard Dathusha in my messenger corp. For now."

Pearl is no one's property. It was Cyrus all over again. My fingernails bit into my palms as my fists tightened.

Ehtishem nodded. "Well, if she doesn't work out, I'll take her off your hands."

"If she doesn't work out, I'll blow her out the airlock."

I was off the couch before my brain could stop me, but Ehtishem was ready. He caught my waist and spun me into Sree's grasp. "Let me go, damn it!"

"Momma!"

Sree was old and topped me by only a few inches, but she was by no means weak. She pulled me close. "Calm yourself, Mother Rachel, before you get your child killed."

My vision tunneled, my body chilled. I craned to see Pearl. Isphahan had clamped his hand around her upper arm and her face twisted as he pinched flesh to bone. I inhaled and squared my shoulders. My voice wavered only a little as I met the zosh's narrow gaze and said in English, "I'm sorry. I'm tired and upset. Pearl, please remember to control your emotions better than I have." She nodded, and it was all I could do to not go ballistic at the sight of tears streaking her cheeks.

Isphahan grunted. "Remember your place." He shoved Pearl behind him.

Ehtishem stepped forward. "I don't want to hear of harm coming to that child, Isphahan. I would not take that well."

A sneer briefly lifted the corner of the zosh's lip and narrowed his eyes. "I think I've seen enough. *Thrai.* You have two choices:

pledge your loyalty or be charged with treason." With that he left the quarters, Pearl in tow and his guards in lockstep around him.

"How could you provoke him like that?" I yanked my arm from Sree's loosening grip. "He's going to kill her!"

"Avoiding her death is exactly why I said that, Rachel. If Isphahan views Pearl as a means of controlling me, I believe he'll keep her close."

"You *believe*? That's your plan? Leave her in the Devil's den and hope for the best?"

"Zant."

"Why?"

"My uncle is a Purist and an Elitist. He doesn't believe a Terran child is capable of understanding our language. Pearl has hidden her abilities and intellect well. I can use her and the other Terran children in the messenger corp. They can gather information, contact my allies, and identify my enemies, right under the zosh's nose."

"A spy ring? You're endangering her—*them*—for your own gains."

"They're already endangered. But with their help I'll wrest control from Isphahan. He'll do something to expose his throat. I need to be there to tear it open."

"Pearl is all I've got, Thrai. Every minute she's with him, is a minute she could die." I reached up to run my hands through my hair and encountered stubble. I pulled them away, glared at them, and turned that glare on Ehtishem. "The zosh better not take too long to screw up."

"Pearl's not the only one with a gun to her head, Rachel. I've already attended three debriefings today and have an emergency Council hearing this evening." Ehtishem's expression wavered for a blink. "If they find me treasonous, we'll all pay the price."

"Why would they find you treasonous?"

He shrugged. "I was absent from duty and failed to contact our ground forces for twelve Terran years. I've admitted to being with Terrans much of that time. I've returned with a detainee from an unofficially established colony—the existence of which I failed to report. I've refused to acknowledge the zosh's rank. It's not difficult to add that up to treason."

I paced away. He didn't have to define the penalty for treason. No military would permit a traitor to live during wartime. And if they punished him, I'd have no protection and no means of saving Pearl. I faced him. "Since I'm not your prisoner, I'm leaving. My daughter is alive. I'm going to get her."

"You cannot succeed, Rachel."

I waved my middle finger at him as I stomped through the passway and slapped the door pad. The door opened and the guards came to attention. I was being a damned child, but my pride and a new, quite-possibly-stupid level of determination had rushed in to fill the void left by Pearl's absence. Ignoring the men, I lifted my chin, strode to the elevator, and hit the call pad.

Behind me Ehtishem said, low and steady, "Mahzel, Huorem, keep her safe—from herself and anyone foolish enough to get in her way. And, beware, she bites."

The elevator arrived. I stepped inside. So did the two soldiers as the doors whispered shut. "Gatu, vana." The computer, polite as always, requested a destination.

I had no answer, so I crossed my arms and shot daggers at the soldiers. "Here we go again, the Ohnenrai are here to protect the poor little Terran from herself. How noble. Only problem is I've seen how you guys protect and it doesn't work out so well for my people. So you can piss off. I don't need your kind of help."

"Gatu, vana."

Shut up.

"Nava, frei, we have our orders," one of them replied in

Ohnenrai as he reached past my shoulder and tapped a glowing orange bar on the panel.

The elevator thanked him, "Ferahi-va," and descended.

"Oh, I see. I wouldn't want you to disobey orders. Best to blindly follow your leader like a good pair of Nazis."

He asked, "Nazis, frei?"

"Oh, for Christ's sake, look it up, jackass." The elevator panel glowed green. The doors opened to dusky light and a sea of Ohnenrai men and women—soldiers and civilians—hustling to catch cars and lifts. It was evening. The massive ship's lights had changed to reflect the sun's rotation—theirs or mine I didn't know. Street level lights glowed amber as they came on and the overhead lighting —so many hundreds of stories above me in this part of the ship—softened, casting my strange, new world in a rosy glow. "They're going home."

"Most, Barethri Rachel. We follow the Terran twenty-four-hour cycle, and the night shift is in place," the same soldier replied.

Some of my fury evaporated with the ending day and his use of the honorific Barethri— Mother—but I wasn't about to turn around. I struck off along a broad boulevard doing my best to ignore stares. "You're Huorem, right?"

"Zant, frei."

I glanced at his companion, Mahzel, but the man's attention was on the crowd. Apparently, he was the silent one of the pair. "How many Ohnenrai live on this ship, Huorem?"

"Eight million on Dathusha."

Eight million. And they all stop for Ehtishem. "Dathusha is the ship we saw from Earth?"

"Nava. Most likely you saw Pohru-Mahrko in low-Earth orbit or warships on atmospheric patrols. Dathusha generally orbits behind Terra's moon."

"She hides?"

He nodded. "Usually. She's the only home we have. Pohru-Mahrko protects her."

Long, bullet-shaped vehicles passed going both ways, crowded with people. Shops were closing, cafes were filling, and all around I saw the Ohnenrai leading normal lives. I wandered into a large store and found shelves lined with cans and boxes and bags of Terran food and goods. "The Ohnenrai shop?"

Huorem answered, "Citizens receive the BLA—Basic Living Allotment. They come here to buy and barter for what trickles down from the Elite."

There were sneakers, ice cream, makeup. I fled the store after standing before a selection of cereals, staring at the boxes of Cinnamon Life and wiping tears from my eyes and cheeks. My father and I had spent many Saturday mornings having "special picnics" on a blanket in front of the family room TV, watching cartoons and eating Life.

A woman followed me from the store. She approached but was blocked by Mahzel. I turned away from her blank face to wander and stare, to wonder and lick my wounds raw. She trailed me along the street, remaining outside the shops as I came and went but always there. Finally, as I exited the third dress shop, gawked at by both patrons and shopkeeper, I confronted my shadow. "What do you want?" I asked in Ohnenrai.

"I'm wondering what kind of woman helps the enemy of her people."

"Well, have you figured out the answer?"

She shook her head. "You are not what I expected." She glanced at my guards and meandered along with me.

"Which was what?"

"An arrogant woman. A woman much like those of the Ohnenrai Elite. Instead, I see a woman who seems lost."

I considered her comments. "I aided the thrai because I'm a

medic and he was injured. I didn't know his name or rank until I came aboard."

"And had you known his identity?"

"I'd have shot him."

She studied me, a wisp of a smile tugging up her lips. "I think I now understand why he cares about you, Terran."

"Well, maybe you should enlighten me, Stranger."

Her smile morphed into a blank slate. "Maybe you should ask him." She crossed the boulevard and disappeared into a crowd. I turned and continued along, now walking between the two soldiers, my head level with their chests. I paused and glanced back. *How did she know I helped him?*

"Barethri?" Huorem looked down at me.

I moved on. "Who was that woman?"

He shrugged. "Just a citizen."

A kind of marketplace and entertainment district, the area was teeming with people walking, talking, eating. It was strange to see them move out of our little group's path. I'd never imagined the day when an Ohnenran would step aside for *me*.

"How big is Dathusha?"

Huorem answered, "Hmm, about the size of your New York City."

I shook my head. "I've never been there." New York meant nothing to me.

"Ahm. About three hundred square miles." His bushy eyebrows furrowed as he looked around, then he shrugged again. "I cannot think of another equivalent you would know."

I nodded. We rounded another corner and I stopped. The boulevard widened, the structures gained height, and bright, jewel-toned lights lit the night. I'd been so preoccupied with our conversation and, before that, the woman's comments that I hadn't noticed the sounds and lights, but now they rushed in to fill my head.

Signs flashed neon advertisements, some rising six, seven, eight stories. The ceiling had darkened to become a twinkling starry sky. Music blared from restaurant patios, and the lyrical sound of Ohnenrai filled the air. The boulevard split to circumvent a massive building, the face of which was a screen that dominated the glowing, bustling streets. Ohnenrai groups and individuals stood in lines, strolled and admired the lights, and came and went from the buildings.

The massive screen changed to a visual record of a uniformed Ehtishem striding past ranks of soldiers. Words appeared—a list of some kind—as the image zoomed in, froze on his handsome profile, and a man's voice announced: "Power. Intellect. Achievement. Mahle for Proven Superiority. Because You Deserve the Best."

Huorem jerked his chin at the screen. "Look, Mahz, Sarem Mahlei's not wasting any time." Mahzel grunted agreement and continued scanning the street as Huorem added, "You can bet there'll be more takers than ever this time around."

I glanced from one soldier to the other. "What is that?"

Huorem looked away from the screen and began surveying the crowd too. "The viewer or the offering?"

"The offering, I guess. What is it?"

"The Mahle family is opening a new offering for the thrai's genes."

I stopped. "For his *what*?"

"His DNA. It's available like everyone else's."

"Zant," Mahzel interrupted, his voice a solemn bass. "But not everyone's is as desirable as the thrai's."

I jumped as they bellowed, "Drax-*tu*," and reached over me to thump each other in the chest, blows that would've cracked my ribs and deflated my lungs.

"What the hell was *that*?"

Mahzel returned to scanning. Huorem rested his gun across his arms and nodded at the screen. "Look." I did as he continued to speak. "All the thrai's guards have his genes. We're like family. *We* choose who protects him. *We* choose who's around him."

"And we're not easily impressed," Mahzel added as he met my gaze. It was weird; he had Ehtishem's hazel eyes. I hadn't noticed before.

On the screen, a new list appeared, and the announcer was naming locations. Huorem said, "Right. So here's how the offering works. Most Elite sell their DNA. Most Ohnenrai do, for that matter, or barter it, but not the thrai. His offering happens every three cycles—I guess that's like a Terran season, zant, Mahzel?"

The other soldier nodded.

"If you want to try for a child and want the thrai's genes in the mix, you put your name in the draw. The Mahles randomly pull the recipients. Military personnel get an extra draw, but otherwise there's an equal chance of getting some Elite DNA. *The* Elite DNA. Free."

I looked around, beginning to see these people with new eyes. "The thrai must have thousands of children roaming this ship."

The announcer had finished and Ehtishem's picture had been replaced with Draxtu Mainyu. Now Mahzel looked down at me. "Barethri Rachel, have you seen any children since you've been aboard Dathusha?"

"No." Only Pearl.

Huorem shook his head. "Few women conceive. Fewer deliver live children. The babies who survive rarely last a few days. Of the handful that makes it out of the Nest, most go mad. Maybe one or two of them are normal in the head," he tapped his skull, "but the chances that they'll produce offspring is piss-poor, if you'll forgive the Terran phrase, frei."

I swallowed and nodded. *It's like Suffer. How can it be the same?* They were confirming what Ahremena had said—the Ohnenrai genome was failing and the Sufferns were part of a genetic experiment.

"Thrai Mahle, seen here carrying Terran, Rachel Pryne, was presumed dead until his sudden appearance in the Stoaca Varefshar twenty-five hours ago."

I looked up when I heard my name. The image on the screen had changed and a chill crawled into my skull and around my chest. I was seeing myself—dirty, bruised, and nearly bald—in Ehtishem's arms as he strode past saluting crowds and into the marked elevator.

"You are genetically significant to the Ohnenrai."

The announcer continued. "Ohnenrai Genetics confirmed shortly after the thrai's return that the Terran woman's genome holds the complete and active Azatem Code. And Thrai Mahle's disappearance coincided with a covert operation to retrieve her and her female child when Ohnenrai/Terran joint operations failed."

Around me there was clapping, hooting, whistling from the Ohnenrai, loud enough to drown out the announcer. I shrank back until I felt the cold glass of a window. I turned and found the startled gazes of three diners. They said something, pointed at me, and other Ohnenrai faces turned my way. People rose. People pointed.

Everyone on this ship knows my face. "Get me out of here." I wasn't afraid; I was lost and confused. The Ohnenrai woman had been correct.

Huorem caught my elbow. Mahzel led us with his gun at ready-rest and his stride long and sure. Their commands were loud and firm when we encountered crowds: "Anghu framarez pantham. Idha." *Clear a path. Now.*

People moved toward me; hands reached for me. They were blocked by the muzzle of a gun and an order: "Ma'zaste." *Don't touch.*

But as our group moved forward, the excitement of the crowd dimmed and grew discordant. They looked away from me, toward an approaching vehicle, and they seemed at once both attracted and repelled by it as they pushed, fled, jostled, advanced.

Mahzel suddenly seized my arm and thrust me behind him and Huorem. He pivoted, came to attention, and saluted as a high-pitched whistle broke through the crowd's dissonance. I peered between the soldiers and saw that the vehicle had stopped not ten feet from us to release a group of soldiers and the zosh.

Where's Pearl? I shifted to get a better look, searching for her, but Huorem caught my upper arm and held me in place. "Don't move," he murmured. His intensity made me obedient.

The citizens scattered for Isphahan. I held my breath as he passed us. He didn't acknowledge Huorem or Mahzel, nor was my daughter with him. Once he'd entered a building, I leaned against a light post, my head hanging low. *There's no way I can save her without help.*

"Come, Barethri. We will escort you to the thrai's quarters."

I nodded and followed, taking shelter in the shadows of my guards. I'd been a fool in so many ways. Finally, back in the elevator —the Master Lift—and rising toward my non-prison, I sagged against the polished wall. "Ferahi-va, gentlemen. I'm sorry for what I said earlier. I was wrong and rude."

They exchanged glances. Then Mahzel replied in English: "We're just following orders, Mother Rachel."

Ehtishem wasn't waiting when I crept through the passway with my tail tucked. I wandered around the great room, looking at everything and seeing none of it. My mind kept returning to Pearl's marked face, her tears, and Isphahan's callous words. I'd gotten nowhere near her and it had been suicidal to try; Ehtishem was right.

I stopped before the grandfather clock. It was both absurd and appropriate in his quarters and reflected the pendulum swing of my feelings toward him. I hated him for lying. I hated who and what he was. Yet I'd never imagined the genetic enslavement and murderous betrayal he'd faced, even as a leader. Perhaps, *because* he was a leader. I hated that I needed him in order to free Pearl, and I hated that I empathized with him.

Isphahan had all of us under his thumb. Even if I took myself out of their experiment, the zosh would still have Pearl to use against Ehtishem. All the power I'd imagined on my side was useless until she was safe. My surroundings had changed dramatically in the last week, but my circumstances hadn't. And neither had my goal. Pearl and I still weren't free. And working with Ehtishem was my only chance at success, whether I liked it or not.

I watched the pendulum swing to and fro, light glinting from its polished brass surface. For years I'd wondered who would come for me and why, but I'd never expected him to know my parents and count them among his friends. And I certainly hadn't expected to like him. "Damn it." What good was a double-edged sword when you'd wound yourself wielding it? "Double-edged bullshit." I straightened, turned, and trudged up the stairs.

As I reached the second level, a light at the end of the hall drew me away from my door. I found Ehtishem in a small room, sitting at a desk before a vast window. He looked up from carving a wooden block the size of Pearl's palm. Shavings littered the desk and the pungent scent of pine stung my nose. I remembered my daughter's delight as he spun the little wooden top across the porch rail, and I recalled my harsh words to her that day. I looked around, avoiding his gaze.

The room held shelves of books, a side table with a lamp, and the writing desk. A long, squishy sofa occupied one wall, its cushions fraying and lumpy as if Ehtishem had spent many hours upon them.

He paused in his task, the knife hovering over the wood. "Have you returned to begin the next round of abuse?"

I scratched the back of my head then shivered and rubbed goose bumps from my arms. I couldn't wait for my hair to grow back. "I'm too tired to hate you right now. I'll get back to that tomorrow. Tonight I need answers, Thrai."

He lowered the knife and block and said in English: "Please, Rachel. Never call me that. Not you."

I tilted my head and considered him then replied in Ohnenrai. "Why did my parents do this? Why does your mother offer up your genes like you're some prized bull? And what is the Azatem Code?"

Ehtishem frowned and set his project aside. He brushed wood shavings into a small pile then stood and came to perch upon the front of the desk. His loose pajama pants and short-sleeved shirt were the same charcoal gray as his shipboard uniform. "You saw the offering."

I nodded.

"The Ohnenrai creation legend says we were designed to be gods of war. Some of our people embrace that story as the truth and demand the purity of our genome be maintained. But we're not gods, Rachel. We're monsters. And we're not the worst ones out there." He jerked his head toward the window. "That title belongs to the Azatem."

I recalled our hushed conversation from so many weeks ago when he'd told me his people had made a ruthless enemy. He'd called them vengeful. "Are they the ones who destroyed Ohnenrah?"

He nodded. "I'm sure my people seem powerful to you. But all our knowledge is stolen. We're so alike—Terrans and Ohnenrai. It would be comical if it wasn't pathetic. Like you, we were visited by an advanced society. The Azatem sent a ship with a simple message: 'Submit or die.'" He gripped the edge of the desk. "Countless Ohnenrai fought and lost, again and again. Until my father's great-grandfather led a suicide mission to sabotage their ship."

I could only stare and listen.

"We thought we were smart. The Mahle family earned their Elite status and control of the military that day." He was gazing at the floor. "But we'd made a critical mistake."

"What?"

Ehtishem looked up from beneath his brows. "Underestimating the enemy. We soon discovered that we'd merely taken out a small harvester. And our crime wasn't unnoticed. The next visitor was a warship. There was only enough time to evacuate Dathusha and a few other ships before our enemy obliterated Ohnenrah. It's now as inhospitable as your moon."

"Harvester?" I knew I wouldn't like the answer, but I had to ask.

His mouth tightened. "The Azatem—the Unborn—use host bodies to reproduce. Like a virus, their DNA cripples the host's defenses and destroys unwanted chromosomes. Then it combines with the remainder to rebuild the organism as a new hybrid. One Azatem generation can be nearly unrecognizable from its predecessor. Our geneticists had never seen such an aggressively evolving species."

"Oh."

"The Ohnenrai have become a band of thieves running from punishment, Rachel, but they will catch us. The Azatem are heading this way. 'Evolve or die' is their mantra."

He studied me for a moment then continued. "What Ohnenrai Genetics calls the Azatem Code is a complete human genome with one additional rare chromosome. In the few individuals who carry it, that small sequence is fragmented and useless. But in your genome, the code is intact."

I crossed my arms, hunched my shoulders, and tucked my hands into my armpits. "And that means what?"

"Our geneticists inbred and engineered generation after generation of Terrans to produce *you*—a woman with a dominant, functional Azatem Code that she can successfully pass to her offspring."

"You emphasized the Code. You bred for it?" He nodded. "What's so special about it?" Another question I wasn't sure I wanted answered.

"It causes your immune system to aggressively counterattack when Azatem DNA invades your body."

I stared at him, digesting that information. "My genes destroy their DNA?"

"Zant."

I swallowed. "*Je*-sus. I really am a weapon." I straightened and lowered my arms. "And so is Pearl?"

"We hope so."

I cocked my head and studied him. "What about you? You still haven't told me why your mother's spreading your DNA far and wide among the Ohnenrai."

"You have the clarity of an outsider's perspective." He nodded. "I hold the Azatem Code too. It's functional in me but not in the people who have inherited it from me. It appears that functionality is passed through the maternal epigenome. Testing Pearl's immune response will confirm that, if we can get to her. But once we know, Ahremena hopes some simple gene splicing will activate the code in everyone who inherited it from me."

"But if I'm key to stopping the Azatem, why do the Purists hate me? That doesn't make sense."

"My people's DNA was mutilated by the Azatem, Rachel. Isphahan and his followers don't want *any* non-Ohnenrai genes introduced into our genome. They hold a misguided view that genetic engineering is the tool of the enemy." He pushed away from the table and gazed at me for a long moment. "You and I are products of the same engineering process, Pairika. We are weapons designed to destroy the Azatem."

SIXTEEN

I WAS SITTING on the couch in Ehtishem's office, wrapped in a soft orange blanket. The only light came from the rectangular lamp on the side table. The room still smelled faintly of pine, but all signs of his whittling were gone. I'd remained even after he'd finished his project and pressed it into my palm—a delicate carved leaf. I'd spent the good part of the night telling myself that I didn't give a shit about the failing Ohnenrai genome or their big, nasty enemy. Telling myself that they could all die a horrible death as far as I was concerned. Especially Isphahan.

In other words, lying to myself. Because Ehtishem had planted a new litany in my mind and I couldn't shut it out: *We are weapons designed to destroy the Azatem.* It meant I didn't have to be alone, even if I still hadn't decided whether or not to trust him again. But it also tied Pearl and me to these people. And it knocked down the walls of my world to reveal a universe that was so much larger and scarier than I'd ever imagined.

I turned the wooden leaf over and over, studying the strange grooves on its back and marveling at the curling edges and the delicacy of each scored vein. *Why did he give me this?* I shoved it into my pocket, stood, and left the room. I needed to talk to him. I needed to know if he really, honestly cared about *me*. I needed to do, go, save Pearl and, maybe, everyone else too.

As I reached the first floor, Sree emerged from her quarters speaking to someone in English. "Bedding and towels are in that cupboard. Keep your quarters neat and your clothing clean. Here's the laundry drop. If you require additional uniforms, don't wait until you've run out of decent ones. It takes several days to get the orders filled. As the thrai's messenger you represent him. You will be neat and clean and polite at all times."

"Zant, frei."

"No. Do not speak our tongue. You will use your Terran language only, unless you are delivering the Ohnenrai messages you are given by your thrai or another messenger. Do you understand?"

"Uh, yes, ma'am."

The crack in his voice told me she was speaking to a boy, and I turned away from the kitchen to see him. Sree came into the main room, the messenger behind her. "Adam? Oh, my god, Adam!" I almost fell over a chair getting to him.

He glanced at Sree then stepped back as I reached him. "I, uh—" He blinked then gawked. "Rachel? What are *you* doing here?"

Adam's face was marked with Draxtu Mainyu in profile. The dog's ears flattened on the boy's forehead, its snarl ended beside his nose, and his eye was the animal's eye. It was an eerie sight as he and the dog stared at me.

"What happened to your hair?" he asked.

I touched my scalp. "I was picked up, too, and ended up in the Butcher Bay before the thrai found me." I pulled him into a hug but let go immediately as he flinched. "Your back. Turn around. Let me see."

He looked away. "I'm fine."

"Obey your medic." Ehtishem spoke English as he descended

from the third floor. "I don't want you in pain." Adam swallowed then pulled his shirt from his waistband as he turned. The welts were red, swollen, and weeping.

"Damn it, Thrai, why hasn't he had treatment?" I glared at Ehtishem as I caught the boy's arm and pulled him to the couch. "Sit and take your shirt off."

"Excellent question, Rachel. I have no answer."

"I'll get some towels and warm water," Sree said as she headed into the kitchen. "What else do you need, Mother Rachel?"

"Antiseptic, antibiotic, bandages, and something for his pain."

"I'll get the medicine and the bandages," Ehtishem said and turned down the hall toward Sree's quarters.

I straightened and stared at his retreating figure. I hadn't expected the note of concern and contrition that colored his voice. I turned back. "Have you seen any other Sufferns?"

"You don't know?" Adam asked.

His question and the way his voice squeaked up an octave scared me. "No. I saw Cyrus but no one else."

"That—that *bastard*!" Adam said.

I stared at him. I'd never heard him curse.

"Enough." Ehtishem had returned with a medical kit. "I'm expected aboard Pohru-Mahrko, Rachel, and I need Adam with me. Treat his wounds quickly. Your questions must await our return."

I glared at him even as I set to ministering welts that should've been well on their way to healing. "What are you hiding?"

"Nothing." He met my gaze without emotion. "We don't have time for this discussion. It's not something I want to start and leave unfinished. We'll address it later."

I ground my teeth at his stonewalling, but the emotionless expression on Ehtishem's face told me not to waste my breath arguing.

Once I was done, and Adam's pain had eased, Ehtishem

gestured to the boy. "Come." He turned to me as Adam dressed. "You'll be alone for the remainder of the day. I anticipate another long debriefing and have several meetings scheduled." He'd returned to Ohnenrai; it seemed only Adam would hear English from the thrai's lips.

I crossed my arms and watched them leave.

Sree excused herself too. She needed to organize supplies for Adam. The boy would be staying in the rooms beside hers. They were attached to Ehtishem's quarters by the long hallway.

Like a mouse in a maze I circled the main room. But there didn't appear to be an end to my conundrum, or any cheese. The Ohnenrai had raided Suffer, that much I could guess. But what had they done with everyone? Were they sent to other camps? Had they been brought aboard? I tried to remember familiar faces from the shipboard quarantine, but I had only hazy memories of frightened strangers. There was an obvious answer, but I didn't want to consider that. It was impossible to imagine all of them gone.

I stopped before the wall window and stared. Undulating across Earth's night sky, the aurora borealis glowed green and purple and ghostly, as surreal from above as it was from below. The last time I'd seen it was the night my parents had died. My world felt no less eerie and upside down now.

Outside the passway, a baritone voice asked, "Is she here?" *Ehtishem?* My traitorous heart thumped against my ribs.

One of Ehtihhem's guards replied, "Zant, Zosh."

The door opened and I turned as Isphahan strode into the main room. Once again, Pearl wasn't with him. He had the same maddening control as his nephew, but the way he studied me through half-lidded eyes made me think of Cyrus.

I inhaled against the chill that gripped me and said in English: "Zosh, welcome. I'm surprised to see you. I'm sorry, but the thrai has gone to Pohru-Mahrko for a meeting."

"I know that, woman. I just left him," he replied in my language. "I came to see you."

"What a privilege."

Sree emerged from her wing, bowed to the zosh, then me. "May I bring you a refreshment, Zosh?"

I was never so happy to see Ehtishem's trainer.

Isphahan eyed her. "No, thank you. I won't stay long."

Sree bowed again and looked at me. I shook my head then wondered if my expression had held a plea as she stepped back to the kitchen entry and remained, ostensibly, at my service. I hadn't expected her to stay, but I was glad for her presence. "Will you sit, fra?" I asked.

Isphahan remained ramrod straight in the middle of the vast room. "I prefer to stand."

I turned for the couch. "I'm sure you won't mind if I sit. That is *my* preference." I sat without awaiting his reply. None came. He studied me, his hands clasped behind his back. I returned his gaze and thought of ice, concrete, marble. I wanted to match his demeanor, afraid that if I didn't I'd crumble. This man wanted my child and me dead, and I knew he was just biding his time.

"I understand you are a religious woman."

I blinked, surprised by his choice of topic. "I believe in God, I pray, and I doubt."

"Prayer. That doesn't do much good. Religion is a method of control, quite effective if done correctly. Wouldn't you agree?"

"Yes. I've seen it used that way."

His gaze never left me. "And destructive, when done incorrectly, as you know. Shame, that mess in Suffer. That's why I'm here to offer my condolences. I understand you lost many friends."

Oh, God. "I left some good people behind. Yes, Zosh. Thank you." I swallowed as that old, familiar chill crept up my spine.

"A complete investigation was carried out. I just reviewed it with the thrai. My troops were unprepared for such an intense level of fanaticism." He shook his head. "I didn't want it to end that way, especially for the children. But I don't think anyone can be blamed, except the Suffern leadership, of course."

The cold spread over my scalp, down my arms, and into my chest to seize my heart.

"Weakness. That is the problem with your genome, Terran. But some people refuse to recognize that." He returned to the passway but paused before leaving. "My people have been weakened enough." I jerked at the slap of the soldiers' salute as he disappeared through the passway, an indistinct figure beyond the doors' frosted glass.

He'd left me with cold silence and abject terror. Only the ever-present thrum of the ship carried to me, and it grew louder in my ears. Sree cleared her throat. I glanced at her. "I want to know exactly what happened in Suffer after we left." The calm in my voice surprised me.

She shook her head. "I'm sorry, Mother Rachel, I don't know. That's controlled information. You will have to ask the thrai."

I fled to my room where I paced and dissected Isphahan's one-sided conversation. I kept getting stuck on *"I didn't want it to end that way, especially for the children."*

Finally, I seized the comtab from the dressing table and stared at the black screen. *How the hell do I reach him?* Until this moment, it hadn't occurred to me that I might want to contact Ehtishem. Recalling how he used the device, I ran my fingers down the sides of the tablet. It darkened and a flashing bar appeared at the bottom. I tapped it. A computer voice asked me to input the receiver: "Vana framru va hantaoj."

"How?" No keys appeared on the screen.

"Mem ashaishtem, nama nava vaeda." The compad directory

apologized for not know what the hell I was talking about. "Vana framru va hantaoj."

Oh. "Ehtishem."

But the directory still refused my request.

I stared at the screen. *For Christ's sake, Rachel.* "Thrai Ehtishem Mahle."

"Va upaman, vana." The device asked me to wait and the screen turned amber.

A woman appeared, her symmetrical features composed and neutral as she greeted me in Ohnenrai. "This is Thrai Ehtishem Mahle's office in the Offices of the Supreme Command General. I am Devhi Omrai, assistant to the thrai. How may I help you?"

"Is the thrai available? I need to speak with him. Please."

The woman blinked and switched to English: "On whose behalf are you calling?"

"I'm trying to reach Ehtishem."

Her expression darkened, a ripple of irritation that pulled down the corners of her mouth and narrowed her eyes. "You do not belong on this line. I'm reporting that com as stolen."

"What? I haven't stolen anything. This is the thrai's home comtab. I want to talk to him." Was she the only Ohnenran who hadn't seen my rescue? Or was she just a bitch?

"Thrai Mahle does not speak with your kind. And I'm quite sure he won't appreciate your theft of his personal property." Her gaze traveled to the bottom of the screen and her brows pulled together. Then she turned away. "Fra?" Something passed before the screen and it changed to slow flashing amber.

Did she disconnect me? I stared at the device. The bar still showed the office ID. As I reached forward to tap it, the woman reappeared. Her words sounded constricted and her face was flushed. "Transferring you now."

The screen flashed amber then Ehtishem appeared. "Zant?" The stony neutrality in his voice slapped me.

"Thrai Mahle does not speak with your kind." The sting of those words flared and I bit my lip to keep from crying. *No. More. Crying.*

"Rachel, what's wrong?" Emotion returned to his tone as he spoke in English.

I sucked a breath and swallowed the lump blocking my response. "I shouldn't've bothered you. Never mind." I reached toward the screen.

"Don't end the connection." His low order arrested my hand. "You're not a bother. Tell me why you called."

His softer tone did little to ease my distress. I pressed my lips together then answered, "Um, the zosh was here."

Ehtishem's head tilted. "What did he want?"

"He apologized for what happened in Suffer."

"I see. What did he tell you?"

I rubbed my eyes with my sleeve. "Something happened after we left. Something about soldiers and the leaders. Something happened to the children." Hysteria tightened my throat.

"I wish he hadn't spoken of that. But what I said before stands and I want to have this conversation in person. Can you remain calm until I return?"

I nodded, though I had my doubts.

"Good." He looked away from the screen to address someone. "I'll be right there," he said in Ohnenrai, then he returned to English and me. "I have to go."

I blinked as Ehtishem disappeared from the screen. *He hung up? Yes.* I tapped the bar to disconnect and began pacing. "No more crying, Rachel. I mean it." If I didn't find something to occupy my mind I'd go stir-crazy. I was probably halfway there already.

I exchanged the compad for a reader and dropped onto the chaise. I swiped the screen and began tapping icons. "If I could read the damned language this would be a lot easier." Finding a viewer, I began randomly selecting icons. They all seemed to be visual records of the military or meetings—soldiers working or civilians blathering. "No wonder he likes reading my books. This shit's boring."

A picture of a brown planet caught my attention and I selected it. This footage was different. It was outside looking down on a park-like area and slowly surveying the scene. There was a horrible droning noise. And there was a group of Ohnenrai soldiers doing something I'd never imagined I'd see. They were retreating. Then they were stumbling, scrambling over each other, shouting. The droning gained pitch until my own eardrums vibrated with it. But I didn't know how to mute the reader, and I was too horrified to look away as the soldiers, one-by-one, dropped their weapons, covered their ears, and went to their knees.

"Jesus Fucking Christ."

A strange monstrosity appeared. It was a machine, a creature, or some freakish combination of both. The size of a house, its oval body looked ribbed and rigid, like leathery skin plates had been stretched between its metal bones. But its fleshy gray underside warped and oozed. The horrible noise was coming from it and now was joined by screams from the soldiers as the machine landed on them. But instead of crushing them, its belly bulged, spread, and swallowed the men. Death wasn't taking the soldiers fast enough. The thing was digesting them. *Alive.*

I hit the screen, then again and again, frantic to cut off my view, frantic to stop the screams, then even more frantic when the screams stopped but the humming continued. I threw the reader on the bed and covered my own ears. The record ended. I lurched to the bathroom and threw up on the floor.

I went to my knees then curled up fetal, unable to stop a flashback as I was pulled into grief and loss. But it wasn't Cyrus this time. I was fourteen, again, surrounded by other sobbing children. And all

I heard was my mother screaming as my father was killed, then the sudden silence that followed as her screams were cut off by death.

Ehtishem's weight against my hip awakened me from a dreamless sleep. I was back on the chaise. I'd passed out, but I still felt separated from my body as I stared up at him.

"Are you all right?" he asked. I covered my face with my hands and dragged in a deep breath. "Rachel, look at me. Are you all right?"

"I—uh." I was struggling to remember what I needed to do to get back to here and now. "You are Ehtishem." I touched his hand. "You are sitting beside me. I'm in a bedroom. I'm on a ship."

"You're safe, Rachel."

"I'm safe." My gaze strayed to the reader. "Oh, *shit*. I'm safe. I'm aboard a ship. That ship is called Dathusha. And you are the thrai."

He caught my hand. "You had a flashback."

I nodded and clutched his fingers. He felt so solid, so warm. He felt like safety. Then I remembered that I was pissed off and unsure about him, and I pulled my hand away and crossed my arms. "What time is it?"

"Late."

I rolled away as I remembered my hysteria. "I didn't mean to cause trouble. It's my problem. I'll deal with it."

"Rachel." He put his hand on my shoulder. "You're *not* trouble. And you don't even know what you're dealing with." He stood, grabbed a chair, and once again sat opposite me. He leaned forward, his forearms across his knees, as he studied me. "Should we have this conversation later?"

This conversation. Remembering the zosh's visit, I returned

Ehtishem's gaze and swallowed the fear clawing up my throat. "I need to know what happened. Now or later, it won't change things."

He gazed past my shoulder at Earth. "I wanted to be the one to tell you this, but Isphahan has knifed me in the back with it." He ran his hands over his head. "I don't know how to do this, what to say to mitigate your emotions."

"I already know what's coming, so just say it."

He nodded. "As I left Terra, I passed a patrol on its way to Suffer. Their arrival brought an attack from the men of your community. The patrol called for reinforcements. By the time the troops arrived, Cyrus had gathered all the members into God's House. He was shouting that the soldiers would send their souls to hell. He told the Sufferns they could escape Satan if they sent themselves to heaven. He poisoned them, said with God in their hearts they would overcome the Devil. He drank it too, then set the building on fire."

I stared at him. "This came from a report?"

Ehtishem shook his head. "Adam pretended to drink the poison then unlocked the hall doors. The soldiers pulled Cyrus off him. He doesn't think any other Sufferns survived. Except Lot Jones, who was away from the compound when the soldiers arrived."

"They're all dead."

"Zant."

"Because of me."

Ehtishem clenched his fist. "Nava, Rachel. Because of Cyrus." I couldn't wrap my mind around his words. He leaned forward again. "You had to leave, Rachel; you know that. You had a responsibility. If you'd stayed, where would Pearl be?"

"Look where she is now." I raised my hands and let them fall with a slap to my knees. "I should've left sooner. I shouldn't have left with you. Cyrus poisoned them, but I *condemned* them."

He stood. "I don't understand why you mourn the people who

shunned you and your child. They starved you both and ignored years of Cyrus's predation, yet you shed tears for them."

I stood too. "Of course you don't understand. You've always been the conqueror. Your people killed billions from the comfort of orbit. Life is worthless until you touch it, and I touched *all* of those people, Thrai. I helped birth every child, set every broken bone, treated every fever. I'll never forgive them for what they allowed to happen, but that doesn't mean I wanted them to die." I was in a position I didn't want and had never asked for. And the list of people I needed to avenge kept growing, but most of them had been knifed by me.

Ehtishem rubbed his forehead. He turned toward the door.

"Where are you going?"

"To bed, Rachel. It's late and I'm tired. Perhaps with some sleep I will know better how to help you."

I stumbled into the bathroom. The only remaining trace of my personal hell was the taste of puke in my mouth and I rinsed and swallowed that a few times. I splashed my face and stared at my distorted reflection in the metal basin as water droplets escaped down the drain. I straightened and took in the gray walls. I was a caged rat. "Christ, I've gotta get outta here." I couldn't stand being cooped up in the thrai's quarters for one more minute. Though they were enormous compared to my rotting little cabin, I suddenly missed the open space and fresh air of the woods. I missed grass and trees and dirt. I knew I couldn't really escape, but maybe I could find someplace to hide for a little while.

Out in the hall I ascended to the third level. Once atop the landing, I noted the glow behind the frosted glass double doors to my left —Ehtishem's room. I went right. The first room was a tiled bathing room with a padded massage table and a pool of swirling water. The next held a large table surrounded by chairs—some kind of meeting room or office. The last room was enormous and housed fitness equipment—weights, mats, and a mirrored wall that scared the piss outta me when I unexpectedly encountered my reflection.

I backed out of that room and followed a narrow hall to another door. This one was heavy, like the doors I'd seen as we left the shipping bay, and the floor leading up to it was metal, rather than the wood in the rest of the quarters. Its wall panel glowed green. I palmed it, the door opened, and I gaped.

A huge, three-tiered garden spread out before me, equal in size to Ehtishem's quarters. Lush and beautiful, it was a piece of heaven. Not ten feet from me a stream emerged from a vine-covered wall sluice, meandered past, and ended in a waterfall. A slate path paralleled the stream. I followed it to where the water plunged off the edge to fill a boulder-strewn pond three stories below. Stairs had been cut into the stacked stone cliff. Flowering vines climbed the walls and spilled over the edge. Everywhere bushes, trees, flowers, and grass grew pell-mell to create the feel of a natural wilderness, not a man-made habitat. The creek burbled over rocks and eddied among the cattails lining its edges.

Following the path, I negotiated the stairs, peered into the cave that recessed into the rock face behind the falls, and inhaled the mist rising from the shimmering, turquoise pool as the water crashed into its rocky surface. Reaching the garden floor, I hiked up my dress hem and waded in up to my knees. I laughed as my toes sank into mud. "Jesus. Real, squishy mud."

Leaving the pool behind, I forged into the garden, marveling at the blooms. Some were familiar—purple-and-gold Johnny jump ups, red salvia, mounding pink butterfly bushes, the distinctive cross of creamy dogwood blossoms. Others I had no names for, but every hue and shape vied for my attention.

The air was fresh and sweet, and as I moved away from the noise of the waterfall I heard the hum of insects. One landed on a mound of blanket flowers. I leaned close and stared as it clambered around the red and yellow blooms collecting pollen on its legs. The bug looked like a cross between a dragonfly and a bumblebee. But it wasn't an insect. It was a machine. A tiny robot created to pollinate, and it used a retractable straw to collect nectar, too. "Is that your fuel? Or is someone making honey?"

I dropped into the tall grass, feeling disoriented and chagrined that I'd forgotten I was shipboard for a few minutes. Then the thought of the Sufferns' horrible deaths and even the Ohnenrai soldiers' terrifying end obliterated my self-imposed ban on crying. I curled into a ball and sobbed. I had no control over my fate or Pearl's, I didn't know whom to trust, and I was scared shitless. If I'd stayed in Suffer none of this would have happened. But Ehtishem was right. That hadn't ever been an option.

I finally stopped crying, but I didn't move. I didn't want to. I watched the bugbot mindlessly drone among the flowers. *If I crushed you, would you care?* I sat up and plucked it from an iris. *No. But I would.* It scrambled across my palm, its feet tickling me and leaving a bright yellow pollen path. "You're just screws, processors, little bits of metal. But you're creating life, not taking it. In some way, you're alive too and more humane than the rest of us." I glanced around the garden. "Cyrus. Isphahan. Terran, Ohnenrai, Azatem. What's the difference?" The bugbot lifted off and headed for a mound of white lilacs. "I don't get it." I followed the robot with my eyes and my gaze settled upon another something unexpected—an open door.

I stood and crept toward the dark opening. It resembled the lock through which I'd entered the garden. I halted at the threshold and peered in. Like the one on the third level, metal flooring gave way to wood. But these walls were painted soft green and held vibrant abstract art that brought the garden inside. Who lived here? Were these part of Ehtishem's quarters, too?

"Are you in the habit of entering homes uninvited, Ms. Pryne?"

I froze. The man stood behind me, and he wasn't Ehtishem. I sucked a sharp breath and exhaled slowly to gain some calm. "No. I was just looking. I didn't intend to enter." I turned to face him. He wore a black uniform, but he didn't have the ramrod intensity of an Ohnenrai soldier. "I'm sorry. I would never invade your privacy." It was a lie, of course. Maybe he knew that, maybe not.

"I am Fravaz Ahnoru. I'm sorry we haven't been introduced, but the thrai has a great many demands upon him. Being neighborly isn't among them." Fravaz was equivalent to Captain and meant that this man controlled Dathusha.

"I'm Rachel Pryne. But you already know that."

"Zant." He gestured toward the falls but didn't look away from me as he asked, "Do you like the garden?"

"Very much. Where I lived we were surrounded by nature." I looked into the trees. "I needed this."

"There's much pressure upon you, as well. You are in an unusual position, Ms. Pryne."

"Rachel, please. And unusual, Fravaz?"

He inclined his head. "Rachel. We need you as much as we need the thrai. Do you know how difficult that is for the Ohnenrai? We are a powerful, proud, independent people, yet we desperately need a little wisp of a woman, an alien, to save us. Ironic, considering it was aliens that have destroyed us."

"Not everyone agrees I'm needed, fra."

His eyes narrowed as he studied me. "As I said, pressure." He pivoted and sidestepped as he asked, "Since you are keeping late hours, will you join me for tea?" Beyond him and behind a screen of lavender bushes was a stone patio with an iron café table and chairs. A china teapot sat upon the table, steam curling from its spout.

"Ahnoru. Are you a thief or a finder?" I jerked around at Ehtishem's voice. He was striding through the tall grass toward us.

"Neither, Thrai. Your little lost one wandered into my clutches."

There was a smile behind his voice, and Ehtishem laughed as he approached. "Will you stay?" the captain added, "I've just brewed suxra."

Ehtishem stopped beside me. "Suxra? That'll strip Rachel's stomach."

"I'll dilute it. I'm not a monster."

Ehtishem shook his head. "Ferahi-va, but it is late, Fravaz." He touched my arm. "Come back to my quarters, Rachel."

Part of me wanted to stay and pepper the captain with questions, but caution won me over. I didn't know this man, his intentions, or his stand on my presence aboard the ship. "Thank you for your offered hospitality, Fravaz Ahnoru," I said.

He inclined his head. "Va kanikar—you're welcome. We'll talk another time."

Ehtishem gestured for me to go ahead of him then he turned to the captain and spoke in Ohnenrai. "Please lock your door, Ahnoru."

"Zant, fra."

As we made our way back into his quarters, Ehtishem explained that many Elite Level homes shared gardens. "Some Elite Ohnenrai never leave this level of the ship."

"Why?"

"Ignorance." We'd reached my room. "Rachel, the tensions between the castes are held in check only by tight quarters and fear of the Azatem. Before that harvester arrived, Ohnenrah hovered on the brink of civil war. My family's ascent from the lower level to here has been singular and not welcomed by all. As you've witnessed with my uncle."

I stopped before the closed door and faced him. "Then why did your mother marry down?"

"Genetics." Ehtishem placed his palm over the call pad but didn't open the door, and I looked at the floor, aware of our closeness and his gaze. His voiced softened, deepened as he added, "The

Uahdim family is the longest unbroken bloodline. Their genes are old and exhibit abnormalities born from inbreeding." He inclined over me. "Traditionally, the lower castes have been more *liberal* with their DNA."

I'd been holding my breath and now inhaled. "I see."

He lowered his head until his lips were so close his breath caressed my ear. "Get some sleep, Pairika." The door slid open, brushing my skin, and he stepped away. I backed into the room as Ehtishem disappeared up the stairs.

SEVENTEEN

A GLOWING blue clock on the bedside table said it was 5:01 a.m. somewhere on Earth. I stared at the readout. *The Ohnenrai didn't build that. Stolen clock. Stolen time.* I hadn't slept, too scared of the nightmares lurking behind my eyeballs and too full of confusion. I needed to ask Ehtishem about the things I'd seen on the reader. I needed to figure out if he was screwing with me or being honest. I needed to decide whether or not to trust him. I needed to decide how I felt about him, once and for all.

"Window. Half-light." Swinging my feet to the floor, I braced my hand on the bedside table and rose, groaning as the stiffness of my muscles joined a headache to create a chorus of discomfort.

In the hall, the sharp slap of hands striking flesh, the harsh exhalation of a curse, and the thud of a body hitting the wood floor carried down from Ehtishem's level. My chest tightened. The last time I'd seen him fight, he'd faced four armed Suffern men in our defense. I stopped, held my breath, and listened, my aches and pains forgotten.

Then there was conversation in Ohnenrai and low laughter—Ehtishem's voice and others. "What do you call that?"

I ascended the stairs and saw that the fitness room door was open.

"Tripping."

"Ha! More like dying."

I stopped at the door and peered around the corner.

Ehtishem saw me and said, "Varet."

Three soldiers surrounded him—two men and a woman. Sree stood a few steps apart, and two med techs sat on a bench against a mirrored wall. The weights, benches, mats, and training equipment were cleared to the room's perimeter and an open space dominated the area.

"Rest break." Ehtishem spoke to his soldiers in Ohnenrai as he relaxed his arms to his sides, straightened, and left the circle. He popped a clear guard from his mouth.

They stretched, drank from canteens, checked the white bandages around their knuckles. The woman wiped bright blue blood from her lower lip. Their glances slid my way, assessing, even as their expressions remained neutral. And Sree watched Ehtishem, her eyes narrow and unblinking.

"Do you need something?" He towered over me. Somehow I'd forgotten how intimidating he was, but his bloody, taped knuckles now reminded me.

I looked down at my bare feet. "No, I was just curious."

"We're warming up."

I glanced back at the bloodied soldier. "This is the *warm-up*?"

Ehtishem nodded. "You may observe if you wish, but you must stay on the bench and remain quiet. This isn't a game, but no one will be seriously injured."

I jerked my chin toward the med techs. "Then why are they here?"

"A precaution." A small smirk lifted his lip then disappeared. "Do you want to observe?"

I nodded. "I'll be quiet and stay put."

"Fine." He touched my elbow and pointed at a bench to the left of the doorway. I sat as he returned to the circle. "Pa'nerem, this is Rachel Pryne. She'll observe our practice." He introduced his sparring partners—Timsai, whom I already knew, Mirwai, and Gohra. Ehtishem slipped the guard between his teeth and settled into a relaxed stance. He rolled his shoulders and flexed his fingers. "Adhem."

Gohra and Mirwai turned toward him, smoothing the bandages across their knuckles and chatting. Then Timsai attacked and was dropped by a kick to the groin as the other soldiers set upon Ehtishem.

Gohra lunged forward, a knife in her hand, produced from nowhere that I'd seen. Ehtishem leaned away from the blade even as he kicked the woman in the stomach, pivoted, and kicked again into the back of her knee. As the soldier went down, he slammed his foot into her shoulder then turned.

Mirwai hammered a club down toward Ehtishem's head. The thrai moved into the attack, dropping his chin to his chest and blocking the blow with his upraised hands. As the soldier collided with him, Ehtishem grabbed Mirwai's right shoulder and neck and yanked the man's torso forward and down as he thrust his knee upward again and again into the soldier's chest. Mirwai collapsed to the floor under a barrage of elbow strikes to the back of his neck.

Then Timsai caught the thrai from behind, an arm around his neck and a shockgun to his head. Ehtishem tapped his captor's hand to distract him, then grabbed and redirected the gun barrel. He seized the back of the gun with his left hand, bent at the waist, and extended the weapon forward and away from Timsai. Ehtishem then slammed his right elbow back into his aevadasa's ribs and face. As the man staggered, the thrai stepped forward and back-kicked into Timsai's chest, then turned and pointed the gun at him.

Each movement was short and sharp, natural and vicious. There was nothing graceful or flowing about the fight. Ehtishem devastated his attackers with relentless efficiency.

"Varet." Sree stepped into the group to hand Timsai a towel. The soldier's nose bled steadily from both nostrils. Ehtishem took another towel and wiped the floor as one of the med techs squirted a fine powder into Timsai's nose. The first lieutenant shook his head, squinted, and muttered, "Aiya." But the bleeding stopped.

"Mem visdi-va." Ehtishem faced him. Timsai returned his thrai's critical gaze. Ehtishem shook his head, tapped his wounded aevadasa's chest, and pointed to another bench. "Va nishidet." Timsai nodded and obeyed the order to sit out the next round. As he sat, voices carried into the room. Half a dozen dressed-down soldiers entered. I recognized Tinish, Gahlen, Huorem, and Mahzel; the others were new faces. Four more followed the first group. Ehtishem's warm-up had ended.

The next four hours were filled with kicks, jabs, and blows. More blood spilled, some of it Ehtishem's, most of it belonging to his attackers. Whenever an opponent landed a strike, Sree called, "Varet," and Ehtishem ran and reran the action and a correction. The fighting remained close and aggressive, with the thrai pushing into every situation, never away, using every opening to attack, wound, learn, perfect.

Then I knew how much he'd held back the night he'd defended us. He'd pulled every blow and taken the knife with his flesh rather than taken Terran lives.

I watched Sree, too. She studied every move, corrected and directed Ehtishem. Her body shifted with the rhythm of the attacks and counterattacks. Her words were sharp and critical, and the thrai gave her his complete attention, nodding and thanking her for the instructions. Finally, she called, "Karana," and all the combatants relaxed.

Sweat had turned their gray shirts black. The tape around Ehtishem's knuckles was bluish-gray—stained with blood, sweat, and dirt. The men and women stretched, talked, picked up bloody, sweaty towels, cleaned the floor, and returned the equipment and mats to their orderly places. The thrai worked side-by-side with his officers. I saw relaxed expressions, heard light laughter, saw an easy camaraderie among the Ohnenrai that I hadn't known existed. They weren't just soldiers, they were people.

When they'd left, with nods to me as they passed, Ehtishem dropped to a mat at my feet and lay back with a groan. "I'm rustier than I thought."

"That was rusty?" I stretched my legs and arched my back.

A brief smile lifted his face. "There was a time when no opponent could land a blow."

"I'm surprised you trust them after what happened to your father."

He cocked his head and studied me. "Loyalty means a lot to the Ohnenrai military, Rachel. I trust them. I have to. Or they won't trust me."

Sree sat beside Ehtishem. "Slow and scrawny." She lifted his left hand and tugged at the worn tape. "I don't know how you survived down there."

He closed his eyes. "I had help."

"Humph." She yanked off the tape and turned to do the same with his right hand. "Time to put you on a training regimen and address your diet. You need muscle." She wadded up the tape as she stood. "Up." She toed his left thigh. "Before you tighten, Ratheshtolo."

Ehtishem grunted, rose, and followed his trainer.

"Why are there only two place settings?" The smell of roasting meat had made my mouth water for the past two hours, and I'd paced my room like a starving dog until Sree rang the meal chime. Now, however, I stood beside the table as Ehtishem dried his hands on a kitchen towel. I was surprised that he'd cooked the meal and shocked to see no settings for Sree and Adam.

The trainer shook her head and put down the water pitcher. "Only the thrai and his guests dine together."

Ehtishem pulled out my chair and picked up a napkin.

I glared at him. "That's a load of crap. I'm no better than Adam or Sree. And neither are *you*."

"Proprieties must be maintained." Sree lifted the lid from three dishes to reveal roasted duck, julienned carrots, and rolls so beautifully browned my stomach gurgled at the sight.

"Why? That's idiotic."

"No." Ehtishem still held the chair and the napkin. "Maintaining standards creates the perception of stability, and that gives people security. Whether it's true security matters far less than their willingness to accept it. Take that away and anarchy follows. You cannot deny that, Rachel."

"But who's going to know?" I dropped into the chair and snatched the napkin from his hand. "I don't see why they can't share our meal."

"They do, just not our table."

Sree added, "We dine after the thrai is finished."

"That's unfair."

"Life is unfair." Ehtishem sat as Sree cut and served and left. He returned my gaze, but I didn't find the hardness in his expression that his words had implied.

I picked at the roll, pushed around the vegetables, and ignored the duck. Ehtishem ate and watched me, his expression calm.

Finally, his silverware clinked as he put it down. "Sree has refused my invitations, Rachel."

I looked up from turning my roll into a mountain of crumbs.

"Yes, I've asked her many times to join me at this table. It is not conventional behavior, and she will never place her comfort over the well-being of the Ohnenrai." He drained his water glass. "Believe me, that familiar argument would be preferable to the silence I'm receiving from my current guest. That is *when* she bothers coming to my table." I folded my arms and looked away, refusing to care if I'd insulted him.

His chair scraped the floor. He came to stand behind me, his hands on the back of my chair. Then I squeaked as he yanked the chair away from the table and turned it so that we were face-to-face. "You're not eating, Pairika. You cannot afford to skip meals."

"What does that mean?"

"It means you look like a walking corpse. It means even Pearl noticed and asked Adam if you're sick."

"Pearl?"

He squatted, his hands resting upon the chair on either side of my knees. "Yes. Rachel, you can loathe me until the day I die, but stop punishing yourself."

I looked down at the roll in my hand. I wanted to hold onto my resentment, but once again Ehtishem had found my soft spot and pressed it until I folded. Still, there was a shard of anger left, and I clutched it like a weapon and lifted my chin. "I will eat when I damn well feel like it, Thrai." He straightened as I rose. "And don't you *ever* try to use my child to manipulate me again." I pulled his coat pocket open, shoved the roll into it, and headed for the second floor. But even as I reached my bedroom door, I wanted to go back down and beg to see Pearl. I wanted to promise to eat everything he served me at every meal if I could only have her share our table. I turned, took two steps, and stopped.

Sree's scratchy voice joined the clink of dishes. "Is Mother Rachel your prisoner or not?"

"She's not imprisoned here. She knows that." Ehtishem's emotionless baritone filled the room even when he spoke quietly.

"Oh? Perhaps you should stop treating her like one."

"Meaning?"

"Show her the ship. She's seen these quarters and the workers' barracks, the Butcher Bay and the quarantine rooms. You've been unforgivably lax as her host. And stop bullying her. She is mourning the loss of her people, Ehtishem, even if *she* doesn't realize it. The woman has a child to live for. You've told me how powerful that bond is. She will regain her appetite."

He talked about me? I hadn't expected that. Sure he'd said he cared about me, that my parents were his friends, but those were just words. And I didn't put a lot of faith in men's words. After all, I was an assignment.

Silence greeted Sree's criticism, broken finally by a grunt. Ehtishem replied, "True and fair. I'm out of my element here."

"That's obvious."

"Now you're being *un*fair."

Cabinet doors thudded and Sree's voice grew louder as she joined Ehtishem in the eating area. "Why do you feel uncertain? Are circumstances so different shipboard?"

"Zant."

"How?"

A chair creaked. I slipped into a shadow as Ehtishem crossed the sitting area to the grandfather clock. He took a small crank from its lower cabinet, opened the case, and wound the clock at three points. Then he returned the crank and stood straight and tall, his hands clasped behind his back as the clock chimed twelve times. When the gong faded, he answered, "Dirtside, there was nothing to lose—for either of us. Here, everything is at stake."

Sree stopped beside him. "You value your life so little?" Her tone was quiet and low, filled with the emotion that I'd always thought so rare among their people.

Ehtishem glanced at her. "You misunderstand. On Terra I knew what I needed to do and why. Here, everything is muddied and snakes slither through the thick of it. Rachel blames me for her captivity, her separation from Pearl. They're in greater danger than ever, and I can't deny my culpability. My weakness may have doomed us all. As you said, I should have left her in the Butcher Bay. I should not have revealed myself so soon."

He sounded *vulnerable.*

She touched his arm. "An open wound doesn't heal with stabbing, Ratheshtolo. Snakes or not, you cannot keep her locked away. Perhaps showing her there's more to the Ohnenrai than soldiers and destruction will benefit both of you."

He covered her hand with his. "You always have something to teach me."

"Frena va'ngho dam asmanaca."

I slipped back to my room as I swallowed a laugh at Sree's answer: *"Because you're stupid as stone."*

"I haven't treated you as anything other than a prisoner in my own home, Rachel. I should have seen that. I regret that I've been preoccupied."

Ehtishem had brought me to a rolling, treed park in the center of Dathusha. Men and women—alone, paired, and in groups—strolled, lounged, and enjoyed the setting. He'd called the place Barathrishma—The Womb—and said it rested between the ship's heart and her brain—the command deck and the generator level. Beside trees and grass and paths, there were elaborate flower gardens, game areas, and a wide blue lake. But for the lighted ceiling many stories overhead, I could almost forget I wasn't outside.

The low hum of the ship's generators mingled with the rise and fall of voices and was punctuated by laughter, sometimes shouts, and the occasional dog bark. But I missed the high-pitched enthusiasm of children.

I peered up at him. Despite the apology, his voice kept its standard monotone and his face revealed even less. I wanted to ask about the freakish machine I'd seen on the reader. Being in the park had brought the horrifying thing to mind, but he was so aloof and I didn't want to fall apart in public. I sighed as my gaze drifted to where my hand hooked around his elbow. He'd placed it there as we'd entered the park—pretend affection for prying eyes or real? "I want to believe you but, once again, you're a stranger to me and I can't read you. I can't tell truth from lie. So maybe it's best if we return to saying little or nothing at all, Thrai."

"Utha." The word came out beneath his breath. I looked away; I'd never heard him curse. Utha was the shit that leaks from rotting corpses. Ehtishem stopped. "Forgive me. I shouldn't speak that way. It's beneath me and an affront to you. But—" His pause pulled my gaze back to meet his. "Hearing my title from your lips turns my stomach. That can't be all you see in me now."

My reply was stopped by Adam's sudden appearance on our path. "You should take his message," I said and stepped back. I turned and walked toward Sree.

She stood beside a stone arbor. Snow-white flowers twined up, around, and over the arch. As I halted beside her she brushed her fingers over a cluster and the sweetest scent filled the air. I thought of honeysuckle and peaches and the white jasmine my mother had grown in a terracotta pot on the back patio the year we lived in San Diego.

"What kind of flower is this?" I touched its blue-green leaves and trailed my finger along one of its twisting tendrils.

"A mahle."

"Like the thrai's name?"

A smile created crow's feet at the corners of her eyes. "Yes, like his name. The mahle flower lulls you with its sweetness and beauty, but once it takes hold it's impossible to eradicate. Its vines will pull down a tree and the roots yield a deadly toxin when burned or boiled." She turned to me. "And there's no environment where it does not thrive." Her gaze traveled past me. I followed it to where Ehtishem conferred with Mahzel and Huorem while Adam waited at his heels. "Suitable to the man, don't you agree, Mother Rachel?"

"Very." The flowers looked like small magnolias with elegant, arched pistils. I looked back at the soldiers. Ehtishem crouched, his hand on Adam's shoulder as he gave the boy a message.

"Mom."

I looked away, around, and spied Pearl tucked between two flowering bushes. I glanced at Sree. She was watching me. "Go, but be casual," she murmured.

I strolled to the bushes and angled my body to block my daughter from prying eyes. Faking interest in the leaves and blossoms, I stroked Pearl's cheek and swallowed a lump as she caught my hand and kissed it. Her left eye was blackened with a new bruise and the damned serpent glared at me from her face. I wanted so much to erase it from her skin. "Oh, baby. Are you all right?"

"Yeah. The zosh isn't so bad when he's not around Ehtishem." She averted her gaze. "Mostly he ignores me." We both knew it was a lie. I swallowed another lump, this one made of regret. Pearl was enduring; something she'd watched me do for almost eight years.

Sree stopped beside me. "You needn't worry about me, Mother Rachel. I'm here to disguise your conversation." I nodded, not caring if she relayed every word back to Ehtishem; I had nothing to hide.

I cleared my throat. "Do you know about the thrai's plan to use you and the other messengers, baby girl?" I sniffed the flowers and managed a quick kiss atop her head.

"Uh-huh. We're checking messages for him."

"I don't like it. He's endangering all of you."

"Hold on—" She turned to scan the park past the bushes behind her then pivoted back. "Mom, Ehtishem is my friend. He'd never hurt you or me."

Sree pointed to a cluster of flowers. I nodded as I answered Pearl. "Yes, he has. You don't know."

"I do too. Just 'cause I'm a kid doesn't mean I don't know things. You need to listen to me, Mom." Anger darkened her expression and I caught a glimpse of how she would look when she was an adult— beautiful and intense. "He's helping us and you need to help too."

I straightened. "Enough, Pearl."

"No. You can't say that to me. I love Ehtishem and so do you. You're just mad. You don't know things, like when you're having a flashback. You don't know what's real."

I gasped and stared at her. Pearl's wisdom was too adult and had hit me in the gut.

She looked around. "I have to go. I don't wanna get in trouble." She grabbed my hand and pressed it to her cheek again. "I love you, Mom. Please don't be mad at Ehtishem. Okay?"

I nodded. "I'll try." As she pulled away I said, "I love you too, Pearly Girly." She gave me the bright smile I missed so much then disappeared into the bushes.

I followed Sree as she pointed out an unusual spindly tree, and I spied Pearl scampering through the lakeside crowds. The lump was back in my throat. I swallowed and moved away from Ehtishem's trainer, wanting to be alone. "Why don't you call me 'Momma' anymore?" I whispered. My baby was growing up so much faster than was right or fair. *I'm failing her. Oh, god, I'm failing her.*

Ehtishem spoke behind me and I jumped. "I'm needed aboard

Pohru-Mahrko, Rachel. Huorem and Mahzel will return you to my quarters. I apologize for ending our conversation this way." Adam had departed. Huorem and Mahzel accompanied the thrai, but they'd paused at a respectful distance to speak with Tinish and Gahlen. I nodded and turned away, but Ehtishem's hand on my wrist stopped me. "We can continue our discussion when I return." It was as much a question as a statement.

"All right." The words stuck in my throat. Ehtishem's hand and gaze lingered, and I twitched like a butterfly pinned to a board. Finally, he nodded, pivoted, and pulled his compad from his pocket. He paced through the crowd, his stride sure as civilians and soldiers moved aside. Tinish and Gahlen marched fore and aft of their thrai, eyes roaming and guns at ready-rest.

Our group was quiet as we journeyed across and up the ship to the Elite Level. At Ehtishem's quarters, Huorem and Mahzel took their post outside the entrance and Sree headed for the kitchen, saying, "I'll fix your evening meal."

"Don't bother." I dropped to the couch. "I'm not hungry." I stared at the floor, immersed in thoughts of Pearl, wondering how I'd gotten her into this mess, and how the hell I'd get her out.

Ice clinked into glasses, water ran. Sree exited the kitchen, handed me a drink, and settled beside me. "Do you know much about Ohnenrai children, Mother Rachel?"

I looked up from the drink. She was gazing over her glass at me. The ice settled and popped in my glass. "I—ah. No. Not really. Just that they're raised in groups instead of with their families."

"Ehtishem lived with peers and several trainers until he turned eight. Then he was moved to these quarters."

"Here?" I glanced around. "These were his family's quarters?"

She sipped the water. "No, they've always been his. I lived here with him until he learned vairim. Then I left and he began Service."

I rested the glass on my leg and a cold ring dampened my dress.

"What's vairim?"

"Self-discipline, emotional control. Ehtishem struggled more than most and was more...unpredictable, more dangerous." Her attention didn't leave me.

"More dangerous how?"

"Ohnenrai children are raised in groups, trained from the outset for service in specific sectors. The Mahle family's military control spans five generations. Ehtishem was designed and raised with military rule in mind. His group trainers encouraged his domination. He climbed over the other children, beat them down, and used whatever means necessary to accomplish his goals." She took another sip. "He was nyancyo, a destroyer."

I shook my head. "I don't understand."

Sree put her glass on the table. "I cannot recall the Terran word that means you do not care about anyone when you want something. How do you say that?"

I shrugged. "Ruthless? Remorseless? Merciless. We have so many."

She nodded. "That was Ratheshtolo and why he was separated from his group. He'd already killed when I became his trainer."

"What?" Water sloshed onto my sleeve and hand. I put my glass beside Sree's and wiped my hand across my skirt. "But he was a *boy*."

"Ehtishem was bred for brutality." A smile twitched her lips. "He calls me vanvuisha."

"Conqueror?"

She laughed. "I prefer tahkaesha—trainer. But that negates the danger he posed to me and everyone else when he walked through those doors as a boy." She waved her hand toward the entry.

"How did you stop him?"

"Patience, will, consistency, and a nerve seizer."

"What's that?"

"It triggers seizures. They're illegal."

"How awful. And you used it on a child?" I leaned away from her.

"His mother gave it to me. If she had not, I would be dead."

"You talk about him like he was an animal."

"He had killed two boys with his bare fists, Mother Rachel." Sree regarded me with a frightening calm. "When Ehtishem wanted something, anyone or anything that stood in his way was decimated. The seizer was cruel, but it got his respect. I used it for self-defense."

She was confirming what Ehtishem had told me, that he was designed to destroy. But I'd never dreamed he'd been born a monster. "Why are you telling me this?"

She lifted her glass and studied me over its rim as she drank. Then she said, "Because I taught Ratheshtolo vairim, but he learned spenta-vohyatem—compassion—from you."

I shook my head and stood, "No." I stood and went to the stairs. "I disagree." I didn't want to think of Ehtishem as compassionate, because I had to be able to turn my back on him and his people if that's what it took to save Pearl. Seeing him as human made it too hard to wound him. I was already struggling to carve away the grip he had upon me, and now my daughter.

Sree followed me as I trotted to the second level. "You were the first person to trust the *man*, Mother Rachel, not the soldier. Don't take that away from him."

I moved down the hall but paused before my door and turned to her. "Why does it matter?"

Sree gripped the wood wall cap, her black knuckles pressing up against her dark skin. "The geneticists and his teachers made him a good leader. You can make him *great*."

"Don't do that to her, Sree." We both jumped at Ehtishem's baritone. He took the stairs three at a time and stopped before his teacher. I wondered how much he'd heard.

She stared up at him. "She has the right to know her importance,

Ratheshtolo."

His brow furrowed for a moment. "Agreed. And Rachel already knows a great deal, but it is not your place to speak of these matters."

Sree's mouth tightened and I thought she would argue, but she proved me wrong with a nod. "Very well." She slipped around him and down the stairs.

I turned back and entered my room, closing the door behind me. Not a moment later, Ehtishem tapped on it. "Rachel, may I speak with you?"

"Window. Full dark." The universe disappeared and I was left staring at myself in the blackened glass. "What do you want?" I didn't know if I was asking Ehtishem or myself.

"To finish our conversation. In the same room."

I turned away from myself. "Come in."

He entered. He'd shed his coat, shirt, and shoes, and had pulled his gray undershirt out from his waistband. He looked less the military man and more...Ehtishem.

I crossed my arms. "What happened to your urgent meeting?"

"They can wait. I have business here."

I shook my head. "More bullshit."

"Rachel, I don't want you and Pearl on this ship. I want you on Terra, free and happy."

"What did you stop Sree from telling me?"

He didn't answer and, once again, I felt the weight of his scrutiny. Finally, he said, "I *need* your trust. Sree's right, but it's not—" He folded his arms and looked away.

"It's not *what*?"

"It's not familiar territory—caring about people for any reason other than what they can do for or against me. Needing someone to trust me. *Me*, not Thrai Ehtishem Mahle." He crossed the room in three strides. I stepped back, caught the chaise with my calves, and sat abruptly. He knelt before me and took my hands. "None of this ever should have happened. But it did. Isphahan tried to assassinate me, and good people died to hide my survival. I shouldn't have been the one sent to look for your family, but I was and I saw you. I wasn't designed to feel this, but I do. And that's changed me. Where my uncle failed, you succeeded."

I pulled back. "What?"

He tightened his grip. "You destroyed Thrai Ehtishem Mahle, and I am grateful. He was a monster."

I stared at him, aware of a tingling in my hands that wasn't entirely caused by his fingers fettering my wrists. Once again, I teetered on the brink of decision, but this time I rejected the truth in his eyes and yanked my hands from his grasp. "Get out." I sat on my hands. "Take your lies and get out. *Thrai*."

His mouth tightened as his brow furrowed and he looked genuinely hurt as his chin sank to his chest. After a heavy moment, he stood and stepped toward the door. But he paused and asked, "What will it take to make you trust me again, Rachel?"

"Do you really believe that's possible? You took my world, my parents, my freedom, my daughter, even my dogs, and you want my faith *too*?" I stood, stepped toward him, and jabbed my finger into his chest. "All right. When Pearl stands beside me free from servitude and these two shit buckets you call ships—along with every goddamned Ohnenrai man, woman, and child—have left Terran orbit, *then* you'll have earned my trust. Until then, go the fuck to hell." I stomped into the bathroom and smacked the door panel. Then I leaned back against the cold, white door and gripped my finger. Ehtishem's chest was rock hard.

I heard the bedroom door whoosh open and shut.

"Bastard." But alienating Ehtishem was a mistake and I knew it. Allying myself with him was my only hope for saving my daughter.

"You only have to ask. You only have to trust."

I closed my eyes, shook my head. "I don't know how."

EIGHTEEN

I'D SPENT the morning lying in the garden, staring at infinity through the glass roof and feeling pressed flat, like a lab specimen sandwiched between slides. I was looking for God's eye, awaiting dissection, and trying not to think.

For hours there'd been nothing but the ever-present thrum of the massive ship's generators and the burble of water over rocks from the stream and falls. Now a strange noise caught my attention. I closed my eyes and listened. It sounded like a dog whining and Ohnenrai commands. The sounds emanated from the third level hall. I sat up as the lock opened to the thrai with a dog at his side.

"Audie?" The brindle bolted into the garden and knocked me over. I wrapped my arms around his wriggling body and buried my face in his warm fur, laughing and crying as he snuffled and whined and licked my face and hands. "Oh, my god, I can't believe it." I looked up to ask Ehtishem how he'd found my dog but he was gone.

Audie's coat was shiny and his body was lean and strong. His dark gray harness bore a charging bull-like animal symbol and the name Namanyu, which meant Guardian. Someone had cared for him and renamed him. I slouched in the grass and scratched his ears.

He curled up at my side, his head in my lap. But things would never be the same. Audie and I had lost too much.

Tree shadows were wrapping around us under Dathusha's setting artificial sun when Ehtishem returned with a long, canvas tether looped in his hand. Audie sat up, his ears pricked and his gaze intent. "Audie. Va'jam." My dog charged across the small field, leapt the creek, and skidded to a stop before the thrai.

I stood as Ehtishem attached the tether to the dog's harness, straightened, and asked, "Would you like to see his kennel?"

"He'll stay with us?"

"He'll remain to guard my quarters."

We went into the living area and down to a small, second-floor room by the stairs. A kennel had been constructed complete with a bed, a large litter area, an automatic waterer, and a food bowl.

A refrigerator and cabinet occupied the wall to the left of the door. Ehtishem hung Audie's harness and tether on a hook jutting from the cabinet. He retrieved the dog's bowl and took something wrapped in butcher paper from the fridge as Audie nosed around his new home.

"I can feed him." I reached for the package, but Ehtishem held it away.

"No, Rachel, you cannot." He met my gaze. "Audie will be fed by his master," he touched his chest with his thumb, "or his trainer, Mahzel." He unwrapped raw, deboned chicken and gave it to Audie. He put the paper in the recycler and added, as he washed his hands, "I don't want him confused in battle. His chain of command must be clear."

My dog's days of lounging in the sun and chasing squirrels were over. Fine, but he was still *my* dog. "That's a load of crap and you know it. It's not like I'll be going into battle with you."

"I am his master. Mahzel is his trainer. We will feed him."

That got my hackles up and I crossed my arms. But I didn't want to be ungrateful, so I swallowed more spiteful words. "How did you find him?"

Ehtishem closed the kennel and returned to my side. Hands behind his back, he watched the dog. "When you said I'd taken your dogs, I wondered what had happened to them. Adam spoke with Pearl and told me Audie had been taken in the Cascade assault. Timsai made some inquiries and found the dog was alive and undergoing patrol training."

"But I heard the shot."

"You heard a shockround. The troops had strict orders to employ non-lethal force in that raid, as well as in Suffer."

Audie slurped some water, sat back, and licked his chops.

"Rachel." Ehtishem didn't continue until I glanced up. "I'm sorry about Jack."

I nodded and looked down at my hands. "Me too." I was picking my nails. "Thank you. For finding Audie."

He turned. "He needs to grow accustomed to his kennel. Mahzel will take him out daily for training. Leave him alone now. Please."

I glanced back as I followed him from the room. Audie yawned, circled, and flopped down for a nap. It seemed he'd adjusted to his new role already.

I sighed as we descended the stairs. Ehtishem stopped at the first floor and faced me. "This isn't your preferred arrangement, I know, but I have to justify taking a working dog from a battalion." Even standing one step above him, I had to look up to meet his hard gaze as he added, "Under any other circumstances I would not have asserted my rank this way."

My hackles rose again. "So you're uncomfortable throwing around your weight and you want to blame me? Well, too bad. He was my dog first. Remember? I raised him from a starving, flea-bitten pup. I gave up food to keep him and Jack alive. I'm not interested in your regrets, Thrai."

The security computer announced Ahremena.

Ehtishem folded his arms. "Step outside of yourself, Rachel. I know you can. I have concerned myself with you when I should've been fulfilling responsibilities." He leaned over me. "You're a distraction I cannot afford, but one I cannot ignore." Then his maddening reserve automatically cooled his demeanor, like the ship's windows dimmed to shut out the universe. He straightened, smoothed his uniform, and turned to the door. "Entry granted."

Sree appeared from nowhere to greet the geneticist.

I knew it was impolite to keep up the fight, but I was too damn mad to give a shit. "Well, I never asked to be here. Why didn't you leave me in the Butcher Bay if I'd become such an inconvenience?"

He took a step toward the door, but I blocked him, and he asked, "Rachel, why are you fighting me?"

"Thrai?" Adam had appeared in the hall that led to his quarters.

"What else am I supposed to do? I hate being helpless, and I'm not gonna just lay down and die."

Ahremena cleared the passway but stopped just inside the room.

Ehtishem looked at his messenger. "Do you have it?" The boy nodded and held up a standard white envelope. "Wait in your quarters. I'll get it in a few moments." Adam disappeared down the hall as the thrai turned toward Ahremena. "Why are you here?"

She raised her chin and met his glare. "To tell you that I cannot stall the Council's treason vote much longer. But you have allies."

"Who?"

"Everything is tenuous." She shook her head. "There are two unregistered votes upon which your fate teeters, Ehtishem. Councilor Athusha is one, and I've asked her to speak with you. She has questions. And I believe Fravaz Ahnoru wishes to ask her some questions," she nodded at me, "before he casts his vote. I am organizing a meeting with them, your Council supporters, and several ranking soldiers."

"Anything else?"

"Nava."

"Ferahi-va. Now, get out."

His mother's brow rose and her mouth tightened—the first crack I'd seen in her diamond shell. But she obeyed.

Ehtishem pivoted back to me. "Wait here. I have something for you." He strode down the hall to Adam's room and disappeared through the door. After a moment, he returned, but I didn't look at him. "Your parents gave me this." He held out the envelope that Adam had proffered. *For Rachel* was written diagonally across the sealed flap.

I took it and turned it over. Something round shifted beneath my fingers. "What is it?"

Ehtishem shook his head. "Not my business. I was charged with keeping it safe and delivering it to you should your mother and father not make it aboard Dathusha." He raised his hand as if to touch my face.

"Leave me alone." I sounded emotionless, like him.

Ehtishem's hand stopped. "All right." He stepped around the couch. "Sree, you are dismissed. Please inform Adam of the same."

She stood for a long moment before saying, "Good night, Mother Rachel," and heading down the corridor to her rooms.

Ehtishem went to the stairs but paused before ascending. "I will be in the fitness room."

Silence filled the living area broken only by the low thrum of the ship's generators and the steady ticking of the grandfather clock. I wandered the room, the unopened envelope in my hand, taking in the elegant leather and wood furniture, the undulating blue-green sea glass sculptures, the glowing green signal from the interceptor. I saw my reflection in the darkened room-length window that hid Earth from view. I felt the dark, smooth wood beneath my bare feet, touched the etched glass table, saw the fine bone china, the sculpted silverware. All were stolen from my planet—the riches of a world plundered. Everything of value, even the very foundation of life, had been taken to serve the Ohnenrai.

My dog. My parents. My daughter. Even me.

That thought mixed with the mad brew boiling in my brain, and the whole mess bubbled over. I wanted to vent all the pain, horror, fear, loneliness, loss, insanity I'd witnessed, felt, swallowed for so damn long.

The envelope slipped from my fingers.

I scrambled up the stairs past Audie's kennel to the third level. My bare feet slapped an angry rhythm on the cold, wood floor as I stomped past Ehtishem's sleeping room, the luxurious bathing room, and the darkened study. I stopped at the open door to the fitness room, shaking, my heart thudding.

His back to me, Ehtishem grasped an overhead bar with a wide grip and, chin to chest, he pulled his body up until the back of his neck touched the bar. He held the position, counting beneath his breath, "Aeva, aev'avare. Dva, aev'avare. Thrish, aev'avare." He lowered his body, rested for a few more counts, and began again.

He wore no shirt and I stared as his muscles rippled beneath the long, raised scar that wrapped from stomach to spine. I closed my eyes and saw him blocking the four Suffern men from taking Pearl. I saw him, crippled and feverish, ready to protect me from Cyrus, not making me feel ashamed that the Elder's very presence had made me puke. I felt Ehtishem's gentle touch, his soft lips, his strong, sure body as we made love on the side of a mountain.

He's always protected me.

"Rachel?"

I jumped.

He stood an arm's length from me, his brow pulled down. "Are you ill?"

I shook my head. My tongue felt fat and my heart slammed

inside my chest. "I—I was so pissed off at you. I was downstairs feeling robbed and alone and mad and-and *confused*. And I stomped up here wanting to... I don't know... Wanting to *hurt* you. But—"

Ehtishem waited.

I drew a shaky breath and placed my finger on the leading edge of his scar. "But I saw this." As if my body had a mind of its own, I stepped toward him and slowly ran my hand along the scar and up his back. When my fingers stopped, I was pressed against him.

He held his arms away from his sides, his palms facing me as if to show he meant no harm.

"And I remembered everything you've done for us, for me." My words dropped to a whisper. "I don't know if you're my friend or my enemy, but I know I can't hurt you."

He didn't reach for me, didn't speak or blink or breathe. I feathered my fingers from his temple to his jaw and brought my hand to rest upon his smooth chest. "And, no matter how hard I try, I can't deny you. Ehtishem."

He exhaled, cradled my face in his hands, brought his lips to mine, and pressed me against the wall. I moaned and pushed against him, drew my arms up around his neck, and felt him lift me off the ground. I wrapped my legs around him as he pushed my gown up. Then he was hard against me, inside me, pushing. I cried out. Ehtishem stopped.

"I'm sorry," he panted, "I don't want to frighten you. I—" My tongue stopped his words. My hips gave him all the encouragement he needed. I clung to him as he drove into me, pinned me against the wall, made me moan and pant and scream and shake.

We came together, twined and intertwined; our lives, our bodies, our love inextricably connected. Then Ehtishem carried me to my bathing room, washed me, kissed me, and made love to me again and again and again.

Ehtishem had left the unopened envelope on my bedside table. I lay in bed staring at it and listening to his deep, even breathing. Finally, I sat up, retrieved it, and tore open the flap. Inside was a title page ripped from *Jane Eyre* and folded around two wedding bands. I swallowed a lump. I knew the rings immediately. My parents' wedding bands were unique—plain platinum on the face with elaborately carved flowers adorning the inner surfaces. My father had commissioned them from a local artist when he was stationed at Ramstein. I'd always wondered about the flowers. My mother had said they were like magnolias, but now I recognized the mahle's distinctive arched pistil.

I saw my father's upright printing as I unfolded the page.

Dear Rachel,

We love you more than anything in the world. If you are reading this, you are safe, though your mother and I are likely dead. I'm sorry things went wrong so quickly but know that you are safe with Thrai Ehtishem Mahle. He and his people have trusted us with their future, and we have trusted him with yours—they are one and the same. You hold the key to everyone's survival, my precious daughter. We regret only that we cannot be with you to see this journey to its end. We will always love you and take comfort in knowing that you will be protected and that we will live on within you, within your children, and within your children's children.

All our love,

Daddy and Momma

I stared at the page, waiting to feel sad, waiting to feel angry, waiting for something, anything. But I'd already mourned my parents; I had nothing left to give them. Even if I did, I didn't think they'd want it. Self-pity had never been their thing.

My father had written this note *before* they'd returned to Fairbanks. *Strike when you need to.* Something had changed his mind about trusting the Ohnenrai, but had he lost faith in Ehtishem, too? The last thing he'd told me was to cut them down when I had the chance. Or had he? I'd learned so much since that horrific night that I didn't trust my memories anymore; they may not have been delusions, but I doubted they were accurate. I couldn't rely on the ghosts of my childhood for guidance. They'd been useless in Suffer. They were useless here. *I'm on my own.* I looked at Ehtishem. He was awake and watching me. *But I'm not alone.*

As far as I could tell, Ehtishem had been nothing but honest with me. My parents had made him part of my life, then they'd died. But *I* was still alive. And so was Pearl. I was a double-edged sword, but I didn't want to wound my daughter or myself. We'd suffered enough. I had to strike the real targets.

I refolded the letter. "Why didn't you tell me you knew my parents when we met?"

Ehtishem sat up. "Would you have been more or less likely to leave Suffer with me?" We both knew the answer. He swung his legs off the bed to sit with his back to me. "The afternoon I finally found your colony I heard voices and followed the path toward your house. I saw Cyrus leaving and I trailed you to the river. Snow dusted the ground, yet you plunged into that icy water and stayed under so long I thought I'd have to rescue you. Then Pearl called and you went to her as if nothing had happened."

I gripped the sheets and stared at my trembling hands. He'd known about the rapes all along.

"When I realized you were Joe and Ellie's daughter, I wasn't sure what to do. Your parents' faith set me on the path that carried me away from myself, Rachel. But knowing you were their daughter made me loathe you."

"Loathe?" I stared at the hills and valleys of his wide back.

"You were a reminder of my failure, a reminder of the monstrous things I'd done on other planets. I'd believed I was a god; you were proof that I was only mortal and very flawed." Ehtishem dragged his trousers across the bed and slipped them on. He stood and faced me. "You're still proving that." He garroted his left hand with his belt, the leather creaking with each twist. "My feelings changed when I saw you withstand the hatred and pressure of your own community. I understood betrayal, and I saw how much worse it was for you because you couldn't escape Cyrus." He looked down at his twisting hands, the bones pressed so hard against the skin that every ridge was visible. "And you showed greater self-control for the sake of your child than any Ohnenran ever could."

He relaxed the belt and looked up. I saw grief in his tight jaw, his downturned mouth, his guarded eyes. "And I hated myself even more. Every indignity placed upon your shoulders weighed me down even as you stood straighter and grew stronger because you had to protect Pearl. Even as you did what I could not."

"Stop, Ehtishem." I slid my legs over the side of the bed and turned my back to him. "I don't want to hear this." I closed my eyes. I didn't want a confession that might loosen our renewed bond.

He came around the bed and knelt. "You have to hear this, Rachel. We cannot keep secrets. Isphahan will use them against us."

I slipped my mother's ring on my right hand and twisted my father's around on my thumb. "What do you mean?"

"It's his favorite tactic. Spread conflict among your enemies to create distrust and disorder. Then crush them. You've seen it in action already."

"I have?" I looked up at him. "When?"

"The evening before my father was assassinated, I gave him evidence that Isphahan had orchestrated the Hundred Days."

I gaped at him. "Why would your uncle do that?"

He rested his hands beside my hips and leaned forward. "To justify everything that has followed on Terra."

"To save us from ourselves," I whispered.

"Isphahan knew his window of opportunity was narrow. It's obvious that the assassinations were planned in haste. Which is how I survived. And he's employing conflict with you. That's why I'm telling you all of this. I have to take this weapon from his armory, Rachel. I will not allow him to create a war between us."

He pulled back and lifted his chin. "The night I came to your home, I'd intended to abandon the Ohnenrai to extinction. I couldn't watch you and your world be destroyed anymore." He shook his head. "It was idiocy that sent me into the mountains in that storm and luck that placed my foot on that weakened log." His expression softened. "Had I not broken my ankle, I would not have needed you, Pairika. I would not have felt your hands, smelled your skin, known your kindness."

He reached for me. I slipped off the bed and into his arms.

NINETEEN

ADAM KNELT IN THE KENNEL, brushing Audie's coat. His every stroke brought me a wave of longing for Pearl. She'd always taken her time when brushing the dogs, checking their coats for ticks and fleas and their feet for thorns.

Ehtishem was meeting with his security team and advisors on the first floor. The debriefings and Council inquiries had ended two days ago and the thrai had been sent home to await judgment. But he hadn't sat idle. He'd met with Elite and military supporters, gathered information from his soldiers, and received messages from the boy before me.

"Adam?" He looked up. "What's the thrai having you do to sniff out the zosh?"

He sat back on his heels. "All the kids are relaying their messages to Pearl. If they have anything to do with the thrai, you or her, or genetics, she gives them to me and I repeat them to him." He stood, scratched Audie's ears, and left the kennel. He returned the brush to its cupboard and wiped down the bowl for the auto-waterer.

"What's he looking for?"

Adam's back was healing and he seemed to be coping well with

his circumstances. Better than I was, anyway. "A mistake, he said."
He returned to the kennel and began cleaning the litter area. "The
thrai said that he makes the zosh nervous, and that would make him
slip up."

"Any luck?"

He paused and his eyes narrowed, then he shrugged. "Dunno.
The thrai's hard to read." I nodded and looked up as Ehtishem
topped the second floor landing.

"Will you join me downstairs, Rachel?"

I pushed away from the doorframe. "Sure."

Ehtishem turned to his messenger. "When you're finished with
Audie get some sleep, Adam. I need you rested and alert."

"Yes, sir. Thank you."

I glanced back at the boy as Ehtishem led me to the stairs. Like
Audie and Pearl, Adam was adapting to this life. I fingered the
carved wooden leaf in my pocket. While Ehtishem and I had spent
no more time together since making love, I'd begun carrying this
piece and wearing my parents' rings. When I asked him about the
leaf, he'd smiled and said, "It's a piece of the puzzle," but would say
no more. Somehow, this life didn't feel so much like a mistake when
I felt the polished wood.

We reached the first floor and Timsai stood. He was alone.
Ehtishem settled me on the couch, sat beside me, and said in Ohnenrai, "All right, let's discuss the facts. What's the public opinion of my
return and Rachel's presence here?"

His aevadasa nodded. "They speak of the thrai who rose from
the dead. Many Elites fear you more than ever. Your acceptance of
your father's unorthodox methods with Terra has been warped into a
dangerous and, in some people's minds, anti-Ohnenrai approach.
Publicly displaying your bond with this woman only furthered their
disaffection, fra."

"What is the mood among the troops?"

"You're their thrai. The men will follow you. But there are some dasas who've been bought. Their words and deeds are unlikely to match." He glanced at me and cleared his throat.

Ehtishem leaned forward. "Speak freely, Timsai. I value your judgment."

"It would have been better had you left her in the Butcher Bay. Her presence complicates matters."

"Because of the Purists. I agree. But it was not an option."

Timsai nodded and studied me. When I lifted my chin and returned his gaze, he tilted his head fractionally. "Protect her as quickly as possible, fra." I straightened and glanced at Ehtishem, who nodded and rested his hand atop mine. I didn't miss the aevadasa's gaze follow the move then dart away. Ehtishem's first lieutenant shifted. "Yes, well, it's a simple matter of submitting the claim. And making a mark, of course."

"Zant. A simple matter." Ehtishem rose and went to the passway door, Timsai at his side. Their voices dropped and the room swallowed their words. When he returned, Ehtishem strode to the kitchen for a glass of water. He stared out the window as he drank.

"What's wrong?"

He didn't answer for a long time. I was about to rise when he finally faced me. "I dislike being cornered, having limited options." He drained the glass, set it in the sink, but remained leaning against the counter. "I'm looking for reasons to continue this fight, Rachel."

"What? Why?" I stood.

"It's hopeless. Even if I give you what you want—your freedom, Pearl's, Terra's—there's no future."

"What does *that* mean?"

"The Azatem don't care about our brewing little civil war. And my uncle's lunacy has delayed any progress we've made toward stopping them. But you can be sure they haven't paused in their search for us. All they want is to suck the life out of every creature in this galaxy and beyond. They are relentless." He fell silent, looking into the room at nothing, seemingly lost in thought.

My chest had constricted. I swallowed a lump. His description of the Azatem's goals had struck a chord. "Ehtishem?" He met my gaze. "That flashback I had in my quarters, it wasn't triggered by what happened in Suffer." His mouth tightened, but he waited.

"I saw something on the reader. A machine, a—a *thing* was killing Ohnenrai soldiers. They were panicking and screaming." I twisted my fingers together until the joints hurt. "Jesus Christ, Ehtishem, their screams. That's what did it. That's what set me off." I inhaled, held my breath, exhaled. And again as he crossed the room and took my hands.

"I don't know how you found that visual record, Rachel. I wish you hadn't. It's part of the material Ahremena used to persuade donors, like your parents."

"Those things belong to the Azatem?"

"Pa'vikeret—reapers. The harvester sent them to gather my people's DNA. They're as much creature as machine. But they're amoral, like the Azatem."

I swallowed. Now I truly understood my parents' actions. The Azatem could send reapers for Pearl, for everyone on Terra, for Ehtishem.

I pulled my hands from his, took several steps away, and turned to look at him. Even on the edge of disaster, he stood tall and strong, and I had the impression of a granite mountain as I took in his pressed uniform, his broad shoulders, his handsome face. He was created to stop the Azatem. And so was I. If I could prevent that kind of horror from spreading to Earth and beyond, I would. I had to. "Okay." I nodded. I would help Ehtishem and protect Pearl, or die trying. Just like my mother and father had.

"Okay what?"

I met his gaze. "Your family and people beat them once. You'll do it again, this time with better weapons. I won't let you give up, you big, old son of a bitch, because I've been through too goddamned much to just quit. I'm not gonna let Cyrus, Isphahan, or those Azatem bastards finish Pearl and me off. And neither are you."

He didn't react, and I wondered if my little rah-rah speech had penetrated his thick skull. Then he strode to me, caught my shoulders, and bent to gaze into my eyes. He searched as if some answer lay within me. "Are you willing to surrender *all* your freedom before I can return it to you and your people?"

I sucked a breath between my teeth. "This is about your conversation with Timsai."

"Zant."

"All right. Let me have it."

Ehtishem paced away from me, his hands clasped behind his back. "Ohnenrai property laws are clear and strictly enforced. Claiming you as my vira—my property," he faced me again, "as distasteful as it is, keeps you safer than any other option."

"It's a simple matter of submitting the claim, and making a mark, of course." The full meaning of Timsai's words hit me. "You need to mark me. Like Pearl has Isphahan's mark. Like Adam."

"But not Draxtu Mainyu; that's a military mark. This will be the mahle flower."

"Where?" He looked away and I had my answer. "On my face."

Ehtishem met my gaze. "The law is very clear."

"And so is the mark. You can't hide it if it covers half your face." I touched my cheek.

"It won't be so large."

"But it won't be missed, either. And it's permanent."

Ehtishem returned to me and touched my cheek. "It will be white but not like a Terran tattoo. So, zant, it'll be impossible to remove."

"It's dehumanizing."

"I know."

I held his gaze and my breath then exhaled. "Do it, before I change my mind."

He nodded and called Adam as I returned to the couch. When the boy arrived Ehtishem said, "Take this message to Timsai: 'Mareza daitim vaedhem. Vayem nisirinu hayem at fratem daxshtem adha.' Repeat it." Adam did, several times, until Ehtishem was satisfied, then he left.

The message had been simple: "Prepare the property records. We'll submit them and make the mark today." I rose but had no place to go and nothing to do, so I stood beside the couch and said, "Today."

"We cannot wait. I'll meet Timsai in the Records Office for the filing." Ehtishem pulled on his boots—snapping and tightening and tucking—then returned to me. "*Rahzhel.*" I was staring at those boots, remembering Pearl clomping around in them but looked up at his quiet inflection. Ehtishem cradled my face between his palms. "I hate what they've done to you, what I'm about to do to you." He pulled me against him, tilted my face, searched my eyes. He pressed his forehead to mine and said, "Don't break."

I shook my head. "'He will my shield and portion be as long as life endures.'"

"I never understood that part of the song."

I smiled. "I used to think it meant God would protect and provide for me, but I've changed my mind."

He kissed me and stepped back. "*Mem gered.*" He disappeared through the passway, snapping the closures on his jacket.

"I know you're trying," I said to the closing door. "So am I." I wandered upstairs and into the kennel and jumped at Sree's unexpected presence there.

She smiled as she straightened from petting Audie. "I surprised you."

Hand to my chest, I nodded. "Yes. I was thinking." The dog was chewing and, again, I was surprised. "You fed him?"

She gave me a sly smile and offered a piece of jerky to Audie. "A small treat. I like dogs and Audie should be rewarded for his loyalty." She scratched his head and left the kennel, pausing beside me. "Our secret?"

I nodded and met her gaze. "He is a good dog."

"Zant." Her smiled broadened. "I am off to get Ehtishem's altered uniforms and visit a friend. Unless you require my service?"

"No. Thank you."

She left, I heard her feet on the stairs, then the front door opened and closed. Audie dropped a slobbery ball at the gate. I laughed. "Some things never change, right, dog?" I reached through the links to scratch his ears. "Your affection always comes without a price." It wasn't really a fair thing to say; Ehtishem had never asked for more than I was willing to give.

Adam's and Pearl's marks were large and fierce, meant to intimidate and show who was in control. I trailed my fingers from my cheek to my forehead. How large would the mark be? "Will you recognize me, Audie? Will I?" I sighed. "Does it even matter?" I scratched his chin. "Maybe not." I'd changed so much in such a short time. What was one more alteration other than the opportunity to remake myself?

I remained in the kennel for a while, giving and getting love. Finally, I sighed and straightened. "I should go. I'm not supposed to spoil you."

He sat, tilted his head, and pricked his ears as if asking, "Why not?"

I smiled. "Why not, indeed? I've already been dissected, what's left to do? They can hook up the electrodes and see if I jump for all I care." I opened the gate and slapped my thigh. "Heel, Audie." We headed for the third level lock and the peaceful garden beyond.

Fresh, cool air and moisture filled my sinuses as we crossed from metal flooring to lush green grass. "Go on, dog." His nose and tail wiggling, Audie raced down the terraced steps and disappeared among the bushes and flowers while I negotiated the rocks to cross the stream.

The opposite bank offered a view of the lush mahle vine that dominated the third floor entrance we'd just used. These flowers were crimson with white splattered like paint in their centers, and their heady scent permeated the upper terrace.

I sat on the stream bank with my knees tucked beneath me and closed my eyes. The sound of the water tumbling, splashing, and bubbling around and over the rocks made me think of my bathing hole. The only thing missing was the tick-tick-tick of blackbirds among the cattails.

By tomorrow I'll be property. My throat tightened and I sucked a deep breath as I touched my face. *Ehtishem.* I'd been delivered to the heart of the beast but had found it to be a warm, caring heart, not the cold, dead one I'd expected. And I was relieved and strengthened for finally recognizing that. I'd wasted too many days on anger and confusion, days that should've been spent figuring out how to help Pearl and, now, how to stop the greater enemy.

But when I thought about the Azatem reaper, panic shimmered at the edge of my mind and I had to pull away. *How the hell am I gonna be any use to Ehtishem if I'm freaked out just thinking about them?* It was impossible to comprehend their existence. Especially surrounded by tranquility, artificial or not.

Movement in the bushes behind me drew me from my ping-pong thoughts. "There are no squirrels or rabbits here, Audie," I said as I glanced behind me.

It wasn't my brindle hound.

I gasped and jerked away from the marked, familiar face, but he tackled me and we tumbled into the water. Cyrus locked his arm around my neck and pulled me to my knees, my back arching against his body. His breath warmed my ear. "I don't want to kill you, but he insisted, Rachel. Shame, really. Fucking you took me closer to God than prayer ever could. But the zosh agreed to a trade—your life for Pearl's."

I clawed at his flesh, kicked and twisted and fought, but his grip only tightened. I couldn't scream; no air went in, no sound came out. My pulse pounded in my ears, my vision tunneled.

Something damp pressed my throat and tightened. I clawed at it, gasping for air. He was behind me, his body pressed against mine. He pushed me. There was barking, a shout, and I was falling, falling, falling, and drowning. I sank beneath the surface of the swimming hole and looked up into Ehtishem's emotionless face.

I jerked awake. A man was leaning over me. I slapped at him. "Bastard! Get away!" Strong hands caught me.

"Calm down, Mother Rachel. I'm not attacking you."

At Huorem's words I blinked the nightmare from my eyes, though it held on and I trembled. "I was dreaming."

"Nava."

"What?" I was on my back in the grass, soaked and disoriented. "How did I get wet? Why are you here?"

"Huorem, is she hurt?" Mahzel's voice came from beyond the waterfall.

"She's conscious." He leaned over me. "Do you see more than one of me?"

I shook my head. "Just one."

"Do you have any pain?"

"I'm confused."

"Do you know who attacked you?"

"Attacked? I was dreaming of Cyrus. He *attacked* me?" I shook my head and pressed my hands to my face. "But how could he get here? He's a worker in the Butcher Bay."

Mahzel appeared above the falls with Audie tethered. "Are you all right?" he called as Huorem helped me sit up.

I nodded though I was still shaking. I knotted my fingers together and stared at the dog. "I'm sorry I took Audie out. I know I'm not supposed to."

Mahzel's com buzzed. He pulled it from his pocket. "Fra. Zant, Thrai, I did. Barethri Rachel was attacked in the garden. Zant, zant, she's disoriented but unharmed." He listened and shook his head. "She's uncertain, Thrai, but the assailant came through Fravaz Ahnoru's quarters." He listened again. "She had the dog with her. He chased the man off." He paused. "Zant, zant, I agree, Thrai." He listened then said, "Zant, fra. I'll do it now." He made another call as he descended to the first level.

Huorem disappeared through the third floor lock then returned a few moments later with a blanket and a towel. He wrapped me up while I dried my face. I focused on him and Mahzel and Audie, trying to stave off the weird, outside-of-myself feeling that came with a flashback. *Oh, shit, no. Not another.*

Ehtishem arrived, accompanied by Fravaz Ahnoru. Someone had let Cyrus into the garden through the captain's quarters. It was the only other entrance to the shared sanctuary.

Stillness radiated from Ehtishem, like the dead, weighty silence that preceded an Ohnenrai orbital bomb as it struck the ground. Hell followed that bomb, but a split-second of utter silence and abject terror preceded it. Ehtishem was that moment suspended and his security team circled him but never got close, as if touching him might set off an unstoppable chain reaction.

"Thrai," the fravaz turned to Ehtishem, "I have no explanation."

Ehtishem nodded. "I don't expect one from you, Ahnoru. You are not responsible for this. I'm familiar with these tactics, and I'm not foolish enough to step into the trap."

"I don't understand, fra."

241

Ehtishem looked at the man. "No, but the zosh does."

Med techs checked me as I watched Ehtishem order a search of the captain's quarters and his own "from crack to crevice." He wanted Cyrus's head, but Timsai told him it was impossible. The Uahdim family had invoked the Right to Property—their serpent was the mark I'd seen on Cyrus's face. He was untouchable property now.

When Ehtishem's quarters were cleared, Huorem and Mahzel accompanied me to my room and took posts at the top and bottom of the stairwell. As we'd entered the third-floor airlock, I'd heard Ehtishem tell Sree, "There is a time for vairim, and there is a time for violence."

In my bathing room, I cranked on the cold water, grabbed the soap, and scrubbed my hands, but I couldn't wash away Cyrus. And I couldn't stop shaking. The emotional storm that was a flashback was pushing me outside of myself. I'd known I couldn't avoid it for long. I gripped the cold sink basin and squeezed my eyes shut. "Fuck."

"Rachel."

I jerked around with a little cry.

"You're safe now." Ehtishem reached for me.

I stiffened and stared at his outstretched fingers. I couldn't stop fear. And I couldn't block the nauseating memory of Cyrus's arm tightening around my throat, constricting my skin, his will violating and dominating. I turned away from the question behind Ehtishem's eyes and slipped past him into my bedroom. Logic said he was here to protect me, but I was fighting my own illogical mind. "I...ah... Am I?" I struggled to swallow the dry lump in my throat.

"Zant. Yes." He approached. I shifted to put the bed between us. Ehtishem moved toward me and, again, I skittered away.

"Stop." His word contained enough power to hold me to my spot, will controlling instinct if only for a heartbeat. But Ehtishem's next act released that hold and an explosion of terror. He stepped forward and placed his hands on my shoulders.

"Don't!" I jerked around so suddenly that he moved into an attack that wasn't coming. He straightened and caught my wrists as I lunged backward, my hands raised against assault. I yanked them free, stumbled back, and hit the wall hard enough to bite my tongue. Watching his every move, I scuttled into the corner.

Ehtishem remained still. "Pairika, I didn't mean to scare you. Shh, don't cry."

But I couldn't stop. I'd been sticking my fingers and toes into so many cracks in that dam for so many years, the day was bound to come when I ran out of digits and the cracks overwhelmed me. I sobbed and sank into a crouch, my hands over my head and my face hidden.

"Rachel, I'm coming to you now. I won't hurt you. I won't touch you."

But that wasn't what I wanted. As Ehtishem knelt before me I whispered, "Hold me, please."

"Are you certain?"

I nodded. I needed to let this all go.

We sat at the dressing table in my bedroom and Huorem showed me his design. "If you don't like it, I'll do another."

I looked at him then past his shoulder to Ehtishem, who stood, arms folded, face blank. "Is that normal?" I asked in Ohnenrai.

Huorem shook his head. "The thrai and, well, all of us thought you would like having some input."

Concessions. I bit my upper lip, ducked my head, and nodded. "Okay. Show me how it'll be placed." I glanced at Ehtishem, but his expression remained unchanged, even as I added, "Then we can decide."

Huorem shifted the mirror between us. "I'll sketch it on so you can see the size and placement." I composed my expression and he quickly drew on my face. His large hand was gentle. The brush tickled. "You can look, Barethri."

When I opened my eyes, I wasn't prepared for my reaction. I had expected to be horrified. But I wasn't.

A white flower bud unfurled on my forehead. Leaves, vines, and tendrils trailed and curled over my temple, around my left eye, and along my jaw. And a mahle bloomed across my cheek. The design was elegant, delicate, beautiful, and the right side of my face now looked plain.

The chair creaked as I pushed back from the table. "Give me a minute." I went to the window to look at the stars but stared at my reflection instead.

"Dasa, sadayeiti amat." Ehtishem told Huorem to leave us.

"Fra." Huorem stepped away from the table.

I watched the soldier go and met Ehtishem's gaze in the glass.

"Do you want privacy?" he asked in English.

"Nava."

He clasped his hands behind his back, dropped his chin, and waited.

"In the barracks, the Driver said I was pale, ugly, bony, and sick. Honestly? I've always felt like a giraffe among gazelles."

"Hmm." He circled me. "Well, you are pale, but you're not sick." He stopped and assessed me from head to toe and back again. "And you're bony, but better nutrition will soften your angles and pad your curves."

"Ehtishem, I—"

He slid his hand along my jaw, over my ear, to cup the nape of my neck. He leaned so close his breath brushed my lips. "But,

Pairika, you *are* a gazelle, and I'll only ever think you are beautiful."
He kissed me.

I pulled back. "You don't hate this?" I touched my left cheek.

"No."

I bit my lip. "Neither do I. And that's messing with my head. I'm becoming a possession. A *thing*. And this mark announces that to everyone. I should hate it and you."

Ehtishem covered my hand with his. "You will never be my possession. I don't care what the law says. If there was another way I would take it, but I have to protect you."

I nodded.

"I regret that this—all of this—happened, Rachel."

"I know. But if it hadn't, I wouldn't exist."

"And I wouldn't have found you."

"And we need to be here. We have things to do. I'm glad you came to Earth and found me." I shut my eyes. "But I also feel guilty, and that has me spinning, too."

"I understand."

I looked at him again. "Let's finish this."

Huorem returned. He cleaned my skin and transferred the final design onto my face. With long, sure strokes, he painted a white liquid along the lines. "Last chance to block the pain, Mother Rachel."

I met his gaze. "Sometimes you need pain to remind you of your strength, dasa."

He nodded and cleaned my skin again. The lines felt stiff and my face tingled. Huorem opened a jar of green gel and picked up a wide brush. "Keep your eyes closed until the burning fades." I closed them. He painted my face with broad strokes.

Pads were pressed over my eyes. Ehtishem said, "Eyes closed, Rachel." He sat beside me, his hands holding mine.

The burning began, like Huorem had dragged a lit match over

my skin and followed it with an acid bath. "Jesus-Christ-oh-my-fucking-god." I gasped and dug my fingers into Ehtishem's flesh. As always, he was unyielding. I thought of Pearl enduring this. I thought of laboring to deliver her. And I remembered to breathe—one deep inhalation, four short and one long exhalations—and I focused on that. After several long minutes, the burning eased, faded. The pads were lifted from my eyes, I blinked, and my hand shook as I wiped tears with a cloth Ehtishem held out.

Huorem was watching me, his brow pulled into a straight, bushy line. "Barethri Rachel, you may be small and you may be Terran, but you're as tough as any Ohnenrai soldier I've known."

I cleared my dry throat and swallowed. "Dasa, I doubt you know any Ohnenrai soldiers who've given birth."

Ehtishem gave his little laugh and Huorem grinned. The dasa uncapped a tube and squeezed out some blue gel. "This will soothe the burn." Once again, I closed my eyes as he painted it on my skin. "Better?"

I nodded. "Yeah, already."

As Huorem shifted the mirror, the sound of raised voices and stomping boots carried up the stairs. Ehtishem stood. He moved between the doorway and me as the door opened. The zosh entered. Behind him strode Tinish and Gahlen. Mahzel stopped in the doorway to block Isphahan's guards.

I wished to God I could slap the crap out of the man. "I believe it's customary and polite among the Ohnenrai to ask permission before entering a woman's room."

"You're no woman. You're property," Isphahan replied.

"She is correct, nonetheless." Ehtishem emanated the same still fury that had rattled everyone in the garden. But his tone betrayed none of it as he asked, "Do you require assistance, Dvai?"

His uncle closed the gap between them. "I sent a vira this way on an errand. He answers to 'Cyrus' and expressed interest in your Terran. Have you seen him?"

Ehtishem said, "I have not."

Isphahan crossed his arms and watched me as he said, "That's surprising. I promised him a little reward when he returned."

"You bastard!"

Huorem caught my shoulders and pinned me to my chair. "Don't," he said beneath his breath.

The zosh laughed. "Your jahika certainly has a temper, Thrai."

He'd called me a slut. Ehtishem's chin lifted. "I would appreciate you controlling your language, Dvai. There is a lady present."

"Where? All I see is a canker."

Ehtishem gestured to his soldiers. "Tinish, Gahlen, escort the dvai from my quarters. His lack of self-control is alarming."

Isphahan drew up tall and his smirk turned to stone. "Once the debriefing is released and the judgment is finalized, Ehtishem, you have one hour to present your oath. After that you, and anyone associating with you, will be arrested and charged with treason. Then I can finally flush the rest of the Terran utha your mother's been mixing into our blood." He crossed the room but paused in the doorway. "And don't think your mark will protect *her*," he stabbed a finger at me, "when your property is confiscated. Thrai."

The door closed. And Ehtishem smiled. I gaped at him as he looked at where his uncle had stood and said, "I've got you, ahzish." His gaze met mine. "I know what we're looking for." He raised his hand to Mahzel and Huorem. "Find Adam."

The soldiers saluted and left.

He brought a cool damp towel from my bathing room. "This will help with the redness."

I took the towel. "What's going on?"

He leaned against my bed, his long legs stretched out and his ankles crossed. "Isphahan plans to execute anyone aboard Dathusha who has Terran DNA. And I plan to stop him."

My mouth had gone dry. "You have to get them off this ship."

He nodded. "And leave Terran orbit." He frowned and gestured toward the towel. "Come. Let me help."

I stood before him and closed my eyes as he gently wiped the gel from my face. My mind went to the zosh's words about Cyrus. I looked at Ehtishem. "What about Pearl?"

He tossed the towel onto my dressing table and captured my hands. "She's safe, Rachel. She's too useful a tool for Isphahan to toss aside so easily. Not yet." I bit my lip and nodded. "I'm far more concerned about getting everyone off Dathusha. I can't use ships, but I need something large."

"What about the livestock transports?"

He gazed at me, his lips lifting into a gentle, brief smile. "*That* is a smart idea."

TWENTY

THE DRONE of voices filled the main room of Ehtishem's quarters and overcame the ceaseless hum of the ship's generators. The first to arrive had been ten military commanders, all stone-faced and ramrod straight. Each of their pressed, gray uniforms bore a different creature emblem. Ehtishem had introduced me. They represented factions of the Ohnenrai military.

A woman with hair as short-shorn as her male colleagues spoke for the group. Her uniform bore the same bull-like animal that had appeared on Audie's harness when Ehtishem had found him. "The military, with the exception of a few weak-willed dasas, supports you, Thrai. We don't want an escalation of this situation, but we won't stand idle as the zosh tramples process. The people need order or they'll lose confidence."

Ahremena had arrived with a towering, long-limbed woman whose cool expression rivaled the geneticist's. Councilor Athusha oversaw the Ohnenrai Office of Military and Civil Records. Much like Ehtishem's mother, the councilor assessed me with an eagle eye and I felt weighed, measured, and judged when she'd finally finished and turned her attention to the thrai. Her gaze stopped at his hand upon mine. "Is she your lover or your property?"

Ehtishem replied, "My lover by choice, my property by necessity, Sarem."

Behind the two women, Fravaz Ahnoru paced, his hands clasped behind his back as he took in the room's occupants. He stopped beside the interceptor and touched its green light. "Well, no one on the Council appears willing to address recent matters, so I will. I was relieved to see the thrai's return." He straightened. "Emergency measures are understandable in the moment of immediacy, but it's been nineteen months and no Vote of Authority has occurred. Zosh Uahdim has overstepped his entitlement."

He crossed his arms. "The thrai's return was treated not as a cause for celebration but one for suspicion. And now this." The captain gestured toward me then looked at Ehtishem. "There's not enough space aboard this ship to accommodate a dictator, fra. Violating the privacy of a citizen is bad enough, but to blatantly attack a man of your stature throws doubt on the zosh's willingness to respect citizens' rights." His gaze swung to the gathering. "What's next on the Purist agenda? My maternal line were laborers from the middle caste. Will I be subject to scrutiny because I don't carry one hundred percent Elite blood?"

"Surely you don't feel it's heading to such an extreme, Fravaz?" The speaker, Councilor Athusha, was looking at Ehtishem.

But it was Ahremena who answered. "The Purists' actions are explained by my department's recent successes. Working with the Terrans conflicted with their goals. We have within our grasp the mechanism of survival, but it means a compromise the Purists reject."

A female officer asked, "So the report about the Terran woman's Azatem Code was correct?"

"Zant. Rachel Pryne has a complete and functional Azatem Code. Once we've confirmed that it is functional in her female child, we'll know we have an inheritable solution and can begin introducing it into the Ohnenrai genome. We also hope to use it to activate nonfunctioning genes."

"Do we know it's safe and not just another false lead or ticking bomb?" The question came from a soldier.

"We're proceeding cautiously, aevadasa. We now know the gene's functionality is controlled by the maternal epigenome."

The captain asked, "What's preventing you from confirming inheritance, Councilor?"

Ahremena shook her head. "We haven't been able to access Rachel Pryne's child to sequence her genome and test her immunity. The zosh continues to block us at every turn."

"This is ridiculous. He'll have us go extinct, rather than dilute our blood," someone said.

"Zant, and for no good reason. Our genome is already impure. The Azatem saw to that," an officer remarked.

"If the zosh would only listen to reason. There is unquestionable proof sitting in this room that demonstrates the strength of hybridization," Ahremena said.

All eyes turned to me. Councilor Athusha leaned forward. "The Terran shares our genes?"

"Nava." Ehtishem released my hand and stood. "I am the hybrid."

Then the room was filled with questions that careened out of control and into each other. My brain buzzed. What would happen when this information got out? How would the military react? And the civilians?

"Varet!" Ehtishem's order flattened all the confusion and made me jump.

Ahremena continued. "Ohnenrai Genetics saw the need to take many approaches to combating the Azatem. When we found its fragments in the Terrans, we began inbreeding and engineering to create a complete and active Azatem Code. At the same time, we began engineering Azatem DNA in hopes of understanding how it attacks so efficiently, how it selects chromosomes, and the mechanism of mutation. The vast majority of our results were failures, but we found that combining Azatem, Terran, and Ohnenrai DNA garnered some powerful results. And, in one case, a tremendous success."

I gazed up at my lover. He was a hybrid. And I was probably the only genetically pure humanoid aboard Dathusha. *Goddamn.*

"Did you hear my question, Ms. Pryne?"

I looked around. All eyes were on me. "No. I'm sorry."

Fravaz Ahnoru nodded. "I asked if you knew that your DNA makes you dangerous to the Azatem *and* to us."

I met his gaze. "Well, yeah, though I'm not feeling very dangerous right now."

Several officers laughed. One of them said, "It also makes your child significant."

I straightened. "My child has always been significant, if only to me, fra."

Ehtishem sat and took my hand again as murmurs traveled the room. Councilor Athusha spoke. "Ms. Pryne, returning to the fravaz's point, if you will?"

"Yes?"

"Do you comprehend the solution as well as the threat you pose to our people?"

I looked around. *All these leaders waiting, hanging on my words.* The weight of their hopes and fears settled upon me. "The Azatem and their code may be pretty new to me, but I've known I was a double-edged sword since the day your soldiers executed my parents." My gaze dropped to my fingers entwined with Ehtishem's. "I knew someone would come for me." I met his gaze. "I knew you needed me." Then I looked at the councilor once more. "And I'd planned to stab all of you in the heart at the first opportunity, Councilor."

Ehtishem didn't react, and only the ship's generators and the ticking clock broke the room's heavy silence.

The captain finally spoke. "Why haven't you?"

"Because it would be pointless." Ehtishem's fingers tightened on mine as I added, "The dead don't care about revenge and the Azatem have already punished you far more than I ever could." I looked up and found him gazing at me. "And I have a child to protect. I need to do what's best for her, just like my parents did for me."

After all the people had left, Ehtishem held me. "You weren't surprised by my confession," I said as I studied Draxtu Mainyu's visage on his uniform.

"No. I knew you were waiting for me the night I appeared in your yard."

I leaned back to look at him. "How?"

Ehtishem traced one of the vines marking my face. "You didn't shoot me."

I smiled. "True."

He cradled my face between his palms and kissed the mahle bud on my forehead. "Were you surprised by *my* confession?"

"Yeah, I didn't expect that."

A smile tugged up his lips and narrowed his eyes. "I know. Does it change anything?"

"Well, since you're not a reaper and you *do* seem to have some moral fiber, no, I think we're good." He laughed. I asked, "Once we get Pearl what will Ahremena do?"

"Confirm that her body holds the code and that it works properly. Then Ahremena will begin engineering Pearl's and your DNA, but—" He shrugged. "So far all her tinkering keeps damaging the epigenome. I think she's right that the mother's DNA controls code expression, but in practice she hasn't made it work. If she can't replicate your functional code in my people, you become a useless weapon."

"It worked once." I poked him in the ribs.

"Aiya." He caught my finger and my gaze then pulled my hand to his lips and murmured against my skin. "Eresh." *True*.

"Excuse me, Thrai?" We both turned to find Adam standing in the hall leading from his room. "I'm sorry to interrupt, fra, but I have a message. Pearl thinks it's what you've been looking for."

Ehtishem stood and ordered him to speak: "Framru."

Adam answered in Ohnenrai. "Purge list recorded. Order Number Zo15579921. Action commences oh-one-hundred hours, thrai's quarters."

Ehtishem looked hard at him. "Bisham." The boy obeyed the command to repeat his message. When he'd delivered it twice, Ehtishem asked, "Initiator and receiver?"

"From Aevadasa Vindira to all her dasas, fra." Aevadasa Vindira was Isphahan's right hand.

Ehtishem gestured for Adam to approach. The boy stopped in front of us. The thrai crouched to his eye level. "You're certain about this message? Word for word?"

Adam nodded. "Yes, fra."

Ehtishem retrieved a carved wooden dog from the table beside the couch and turned it over and over. Finally, he gripped Adam's shoulder and relayed his instructions. "Take this message to Councilor Athusha's messenger in the messenger barracks. Do *not* go directly to the Councilor—our enemies will be watching for you. Then pass word to the messengers to go to the Butcher Bay. Are you ready?"

Adam nodded and looked down. Ehtishem said in Ohnenrai, "Unseal Order Z015579921. Thrai Command Authorization, TMZ Cathru-cashmem."

Once the boy had left on his errand, Ehtishem paced the room's perimeter, stopping before the grandfather clock. "Two hours, Rachel."

"Until what?"

"Isphahan's personal guard arrives to finish the job they started twelve Terran years ago."

I stood. "But the Council decision hasn't been rendered."

"My uncle is tired of waiting." He faced me. "That's neither surprising nor the most troubling aspect of that message."

"Well, it troubles *me* a great deal, Ehtishem."

He smiled, though the expression dissolved almost as quickly as it had appeared. "It's the purge list that alarms me. Isphahan is launching a massacre starting here." He pointed at the floor.

"*What?*" I went to him.

"You, Pearl, and as many Terrans as possible are getting off this ship tonight."

I clutched his hand. "How?"

"I've called in favors and twisted arms. The messengers already know. Some of the workers are already gone." He rubbed his chin. "I'd hoped for a little more time, but that was foolish."

"That's why you ordered the messengers to the Butcher Bay." I bit my lip. "But what will happen when they realize we've left? Won't they come looking for you? And what about the Azatem?"

He pulled his hand away to stroke my cheek. "I'm staying aboard."

"No, Ehtishem. You can't."

"I have to. I can avoid Isphahan's assassins easily until the Council decision is recorded. But if the judgment comes down against me, they'll carry out the punishment whether I'm shipboard or dirtside. If I'm down there, all the Terrans will receive that punishment too." He held his hands out, palms upward. "I can't have more innocent blood on these hands, Pairika."

"Pearl and I will stay." I grabbed his fingers. "The judgment will favor you, and then you'll need our DNA."

"I won't risk you."

"We're not leaving."

Ehtishem's expression hardened. "I promised you safety and freedom. Those are not found here, Rachel. Even if I'm not charged, even if my uncle is censured, if you stay with me, you'll be facing death, or worse, from the Azatem. I can't accept that. You have to leave tonight."

"No." I held on even as he tried to tug his hands from mine. "I won't leave you."

He stopped. "Why are you being unreasonable? You asked for your freedom and safety. I'm offering it. Why won't you go?"

"Because I want all of us together. And your people need me."

"You don't care if they survive, and I don't blame you for that. So why?" He pulled on his hands, but I still clung to them. "Let go, Rachel."

"No." I stared at Draxtu Mainyu.

"Why?"

"Shit." I looked up. "Because I love you." Ehtishem stared at me. "I love you, Ehtishem. And the thought of being away from you, of you dying, makes me sick. It makes me want to find a cold, dark corner where I can curl up and die, too." Now I was crying like a goddamn little girl.

Instead of pulling his hands free, he twined his fingers with mine, and pulled me against him. "I love you, too, Rachel." He kissed me, slid his hands to my waist, stepped back, and released me. "That's why I'm sending you to safety."

As his hands slipped from my body, I grabbed his jacket and pressed against him. "Goddamn it, don't ask me to walk away from you again, Stranger. I don't want to be alone, without you. I can't."

"*Rahzhel.*" Ehtishem crushed me to his chest and kissed me hard and deep. But, once more, he broke our kiss. He caught my chin and tilted my face until our eyes met. "You must go, Pairika. Knowing you and Pearl are safe will free me to pull the ships from orbit and lead the Azatem away from Terra."

I looked down. *Damn it.* He was right, and I knew it. I nodded and wiped my cheeks and nose with my stupid, long sleeves. Then I met his gaze. "You're an asshole. You know you can't win without me."

"Maybe. But this big, old son of a bitch has been through too goddamned much to just quit." Ehtishem leaned forward to brush his lips against my forehead. "Ferahi-va. For giving me a reason to fight." He pivoted toward the passway. "You get Audie. I'll inform my guard."

I headed for the stairs but stopped at the first step. "Pearl." Icy panic wrapped my chest. I turned. "Ehtishem, we have to get her. *Now.*"

He faced me again. "She'll meet us in the Butcher Bay." He was the aloof, controlled soldier once more. "Adam will pass on his message. She's not staying in Isphahan's quarters; she's in the messenger barracks. It's an easy matter for the children to slip away."

"Are you sure?"

"Zant. She knows her part in the plan." I hesitated. "Rachel, we won't leave her behind. I promise."

I went straight to my room and slipped my parents' rings onto my fingers then brought Audie downstairs, harnessed and tethered. Mahzel and Huorem stood in the passway. Tinish and Gahlen stood just beyond the open front door. All four carried their guns at ready-rest. Their usual easy banter and relaxed camaraderie had been replaced by the lethal focus of Ohnenrai infantry. Even my dog's manner changed as his ears pricked and his tail arched. Mahzel took his lead and Audie's focus went to his trainer.

I shivered and turned at the distinctive, rising whine of an Ohnenrai weapon charging as Ehtishem descended the stairs. He set the safety on a black shockgun and holstered the pistol at his hip as he strode past me to the interceptor. He twisted off the domed top and slipped it into his jacket, then pulled open a flap on the back of Audie's harness and activated a small device. He removed the dog's tether and turned to me. "Time to go, Rachel."

I hurried to keep up with his long stride as he caught my hand and led me down the hallway toward Sree and Adam's quarters. Audie followed until we halted before a side door marked Aruva Pantam—*Military Corridor*. Ehtishem thumbed on his com and said, "Audie. Aste." The thrai's voice echoed from the device on Audie's harness. The dog sat as ordered. Ehtishem nodded to Huorem and the soldier opened the door.

I looked back at my dog. "Why's he staying?" I clutched Ehtishem's hand. "We can't leave him."

"He's a decoy, Rachel, life signs for the monitors. I'll summon him when we reach the Military Launch Bay." Ehtishem spoke into the com again. "Audie. Paiti." He returned it to his pocket and pulled me into a bright corridor as Mahzel closed the door. Audie now would guard his master's quarters.

"But how will he find us?" Surrounded by the soldiers, I had no choice but to gather my dress and jog along the passage.

"This corridor leads to the shipping and launch bays. I'll unlock the door with the transponder in Audie's harness." Ehtishem looked down at me. "You said you trust me."

I nodded. "Zant." And I did.

The corridor sloped downward, bisected every few hundred feet by retracted floor-to-ceiling pressure doors as thick as my body.

Ehtishem explained his plan as we jogged. "You suggested the livestock transports, and I saw a perfect opportunity. We move troops in those containers and the supply ships run prescribed routes. Yesterday, Isphahan ordered them retrofitted with jumpseats and I knew change was coming. He's been cycling troops up for the last twelve hours. And I've been sending Terrans down."

"You've been sending them home?"

He nodded and glanced at his com. "The next cycle starts in sixty-eight minutes. And the remaining Terran prisoners have to be in those transports, including Pearl and you."

"That soon? What if we miss the cycle?"

"You can't. Isphahan will halt all outgoing traffic once his forces have transferred from Pohru-Mahrko." Ehtishem glanced down at me. "This is the only opportunity to get you off Dathusha."

Then the only sounds were our footfalls and the jingle and creak of military gear until the rapid slap of feet carried to us. Ahead, the corridor formed a "T" and Huorem, on point, held up his hand. We stopped. He and Mahzel sighted their weapons and eased forward. Ehtishem pulled me behind him and lifted his gun from its holster. Tinish and Gahlen, their weapons ready, swept the area behind us.

The footfalls grew louder.

I held my breath.

No one spoke.

Adam rounded the corner and came face-to-face with two

humming shock rifles. "Whoa! Don't shoot!" He squeaked and stopped so suddenly that he fell on his ass.

Mahzel and Huorem resighted their weapons as Ehtishem straightened and holstered his gun. Tinish and Gahlen continued their surveillance as the thrai pulled his messenger up. "You have a message?"

"From Pearl, sir. The zosh ordered Timsai in for questioning. She stopped me on her delivery." Ehtishem nodded and began to turn, but Adam added, "After she told me, two guards pulled her off her run."

The thrai looked at him sharply. "Pulled? Do you mean they redirected her?"

Adam shook his head. "No, sir. She said she was on a run for the zosh, but they said he wanted her aboard Pohru-Mahrko immediately. And that he's done withdrawing the troops. Any personnel not aboard the transports will be left behind on Terra. He's not coming back."

A chill enveloped me. I forced it away, forced myself to remain calm, and met Ehtishem's sure gaze. He wouldn't leave her behind.

"Change of plans." He gestured to his soldiers. They gathered closer, though their weapons didn't return to rest. "Huorem and Mahzel, you'll continue with Rachel to the original destination. She must reach the Butcher Bay without delay. Command will start containment soon, if not already, so use public lanes if you can't stay in the Ar-Pan. The outbound military lanes likely have been switched to inbound by now."

The men nodded.

"Adam, take this." He handed his weapon to the boy. "It's charged and ready. Thumb off the safety here," he pointed to the release, "and trigger it here. This will auto-charge after firing. You will go with Rachel." The boy nodded and was careful to point the weapon downward.

Ehtishem pulled out his com and entered a code, then ordered my dog to come. "Audie. Eti." He pocketed the com. "Tinish, Gahlen, with me. I have other duties for you." He turned to me. "I will bring Pearl and Audie to the Butcher Bay."

I nodded.

Ehtishem feathered a finger from my temple to my jaw, following the twists of a mahle vine, then he stepped back, pivoted, and took the corridor on the right.

As our group went left, the floor rumbled beneath our feet. "What was that?" I asked.

"We're above the fleet hangars," Huorem answered. "Ships are being docked. They're shutting down all outgoing flights so traffic needs to be cleared."

After passing a few more retracted emergency doors, we were stopped by a set of closed ones. My legs and lungs ached. I leaned against the wall trembling, tired. Then I gasped as a klaxon sounded and the lights went out.

Huorem said, "Remain calm." Lights on the front of his and Mahzel's rifles and helmets brightened to white even as red emergency lights strobed above the door. He jogged back along the Ar-Pan to a recessed wall panel. He popped it open and extracted two tube lights, shook them several times, and twisted the end of each. They emitted bright white beams. Huorem returned and gave them to Adam and me.

Mahzel had opened a latched panel beside the doors' palm pad. He was entering a series of codes and muttering about design flaws.

"It's not much further, Mother Rachel," Huorem said. "There's a helix stairwell just beyond the next door. We'll take that down to the shipping bay. From there it's a little over a mile to the Stoaca Varef-shar. We'll get you on a transport, don't worry."

"How much time do we have?" I asked.

He glanced at the chron on his rifle. "Forty-six minutes."

A smaller panel popped opened and Mahzel twisted a recessed knob. The enormous doors separated with a hiss. The soldiers shouldered their weapons and pushed the doors apart.

There were two lightning-bright flashes, two booms, and my protectors dropped like marionettes without masters.

TWENTY-ONE

I SCREAMED and blinked the blinding afterimage from my eyes only to find Sree standing beyond the threshold with a shockgun in each hand. Their muzzles were glowing white-hot and their chargers began pitching higher as they reset.

Everything seemed so slow as Adam raised Ehtishem's weapon. Sree sighted on both of us. She fired on him. His body arched, he stumbled backwards, and hit the wall.

She kept her weapon trained on me as she said, "I don't want to harm you, Mother Rachel, but I cannot allow you to leave. You're too important to the survival of my people."

I looked from the glowing muzzle of her gun, to the two prone soldiers, to Adam. Then I scrambled to the boy's body, not caring if she shot me. The acrid stink of ozone and burned hair stung my sinuses and brought bile up my throat. I swallowed.

"I'll take you to Genetics. Ehtishem's quarters are compromised."

I searched for Adam's pulse and pressed my ear to his chest. Nothing. "Jesus Christ, Sree, you killed him!" I began chest compressions and eyed the gun jutting out from beneath his hip. "Call for med techs."

"That's impossible. I used a shock round."

"Which was set for a three-hundred-pound soldier! Adam doesn't weigh a third of that. You stopped his heart!"

She looked from me to the boy's prone body and shook her head. "You're mistaken."

"I know how to find a goddamn pulse and Adam doesn't have one. Call the med techs!"

I checked for a pulse again while she stood and stared and repeated, "No. That's not what I wanted." Still nothing. His pupils were dilated and fixed. I went back to the compressions, but I had no hope and knew I had to abandon him if I was going to escape with Pearl. Goddamn, I didn't want to leave him. Adam's life shouldn't have ended this way.

Sree stepped toward me then looked up. I did too and saw glowing green eyes in the beam of her gun light. She ordered, "Audie. Aste."

And I ordered, "Take hold!" as he charged past me. I yanked the gun from beneath Adam and cringed as Sree fired a wild shot. Audie leapt, latched onto her upraised arm, and began thrashing her about.

"Apa! Apa!" She commanded him off as she struggled to stay on her feet.

I sighted the gun and thumbed off the safety. "Audie, leave off." He released her. Sree looked at me. I fired. She crumpled to the ground, twitching. Her guns clattered across the floor.

I scrambled back to the dead boy. "Adam, goddamn it, Adam." I hunched over him, closed his eyes, kissed his forehead. "I'm so sorry," I whispered.

Audie whined and nudged me. I hugged him and cried into his soft fur. "Good dog, good dog. Such a good dog." Then the lights came on, and the sound of voices and boots got us up and running.

We found the helix stairwell and descended one, two, six, eight levels. When we finally reached the bottom, I thought my legs would give out, but the sound of soldiers still followed. With a groan, I went through another door and found we were in a wide service corridor. The lights still strobed red. Ships continued to rumble the floor, louder and close enough to rattle my teeth. Another set of doors loomed ahead. Audie sprinted through them and around a corner. I wanted to call him but didn't know how close the soldiers were or how long Sree would be unconscious.

I stumbled and grabbed the wall, panting and shaking. But, as I straightened and pushed away, air whooshed across my face and blew back my dress as the giant doors slammed shut. I stared at them, waiting for what seemed like forever. Waiting, as if Audie could open them with a bark. Waiting, as if Audie could help me out of this jam. "No! Goddamn it!" Pounding the access panel did nothing but hurt my hands and bloody my knuckles.

I jerked around at the rhythmic sound of boots on metal. I dashed back down the corridor to the bisecting hallway. I'd passed a door halfway down. Voices accompanied the thudding feet. I scurried to the door. *Please, God. Please let it fucking open.* I palmed the access panel. There was a click and I pushed through as I heard a man say in Ohnenrai: "It came from down here."

I clutched the light tube to my chest and stared into black. Then I twisted the light on. The beam bounced off metal as I swept it over service equipment—drills and drivers, coiled metal conduit, buckets, tools. I was in a large storage room. Maneuvering around boxes and shelves, I reached another door on the far wall and pressed my ear to it. A ship rumbled by, vibrating the door, the floor, my bones and teeth. When it stopped, I listened.

Nothing.

Holding my breath I opened the door. The dark room beyond held only chairs and tables. A darkened window filled one wall and a long counter took up another. There was a door behind it and one in the opposite wall.

I dashed to the window and peered out and down into the Northwest Shipping Bay. Workers stood in groups as soldiers moved from ship to ship, climbing in, on, and around each one. More soldiers—hundreds, maybe thousands—stood in long ranks receiving orders. I squinted toward the Butcher Bay. The transports sat and the workers lounged. I searched every corner and crevice for brunette curls but saw no sign of Pearl or Ehtishem.

I stiffened at the sound of muffled Ohnenrai and the buzz of a headset.

"Status on the crew lounge, Tavisht?"

"On my way, fra."

I dashed around the counter and through the door, through a small room with desks and chairs, and into a bathing and dressing room. A muted voice past the door behind me. I glanced around and bolted for the door marked Terasca—*Exit*. I came out to a stairwell enclosed by metal grating and covered my mouth to block the stink of hot grease, ozone, and sweat. I'd reached the shipping bay. Finally.

Clutching my dress hem in one hand and the smooth metal rail in the other, I clattered down the stairs to a door. I peered through the grating, praying no one had noticed me. I palmed the door panel, slipped through the doorway, and skittered around the grate into the shadows between the wall and the stairs.

A dirty hand covered my mouth, a muscular arm caught my waist, and someone yanked me into the area beneath the stairwell. "Calm and quiet." His accent was American. "We won't hurt you." People—Terrans—surrounded my captor and me. He dumped me on the dank floor against the wall and dropped a stinking tarp over me.

"But I have to get to the Butcher Bay."

"Don't move," he said. "They're looking for you."

People settled against me. Someone said, "Poker?" Cards snapped and clacked as they were shuffled.

"Hey, what're ya playin'?"

"Seven card stud. You in?"

"What're the stakes?"

"Shifts."

"Yeah, okay."

Feet scraped the floor. "Me, too."

Shit. How long until the transports leave? I concentrated on the slap of cards, teasing, and insults to distract me from the passing time, the stifling air, and the sweat that soaked my dress and stung my eyes. Then I held my breath at the jangle and creak of military gear and Ohnenrai- accented English.

"What are you playing?"

"Poker. Fra."

"Have you seen anyone unfamiliar? A Terran vira with a flower mark on her face?"

Mutters of "nah" and "nope."

"When can we get back to work? We're gonna get flack for not finishing our load quota. Fra."

"I don't know. I'm just a grunt." The workers chuckled. The soldier's gear rattled and his headset buzzed with Ohnenrai orders.

"Tavisht, report."

"Clear at Third Mark, fra."

"Vis. Move down."

While the workers continued their game and joking, I found the tarp's edge and lifted it to suck some fresh air. I didn't care about the metal and grease and body odor anymore. They were better than rebreathing my own damn fear.

After what felt like hours of being sandwiched between men and the wall, the tarp was lifted and I was tugged back into the dark alcove. Slender fingers wrapped around my wrist. I looked into a young woman's face as she asked, "You're the thrai's woman, right?"

"Yes, I—"

A man interrupted. "We'll get you to the Butcher Bay, Rachel, and down to Earth."

I whirled at the familiar baritone. "Lot?"

"Ehtishem took Pearl dirtside directly from Pohru-Mahrko. He said he'd wait for you there." With the whites of his eyes almost glowing against his grease-blackened face, Lot Jones looked like pictures I'd seen of Terran coal miners. The last words we'd exchanged were angry. But now he hugged me, kissed my forehead, and I clung to his coveralls.

"How do you know?" I asked.

"He told us what was happening as we prepped his ship." Lot led me down a short passageway and into a small, cramped room that looked like the crew lounge I'd abandoned.

"How are you here? Are Judith and the boys—" I shut up at the look of agony that twisted his face. "Oh, Lot." I swallowed a lump.

His voice was tight as he spoke. "I earned this punishment when I helped chase you out of Suffer. Judith was furious. She sent me to find you. I doubled back when I saw the patrol heading for Suffer, but I was too late, Rachel. God's House was burning. The soldiers were trying to help—" He swallowed. "We were all too late. Only Adam escaped. Adam, and that...*psychopath*." He cleared his throat. And again. "I promised Ehtishem that we'd get you on a transport." He glanced at a wall chron. "We have twenty minutes."

"But, Lot, why would you help me—us—after everything that's happened?"

The slender girl and a shorter woman pulled me behind a partition and yanked my dress over my head.

Lot answered from the other side of the thin wall. "Because it's the right thing, Rachel. It was the last thing Judith asked me to do. The right thing."

The slender woman handed me stained coveralls and said, "Already, the thrai's helped so many of us."

"And returning you to Earth is our only way to thank Ehtishem. Without his knowledge and willingness to risk himself, we wouldn't have freed so many Terrans."

"I don't understand." I fastened the coveralls. They stank of sweat and grease and shit. I gagged until the girl smeared something minty and mentholated beneath my nose. "What is that?" I asked her.

"We call it fresh air. Better, right?"

I nodded.

Lot continued. "We've been evacuating Terrans to Earth in the livestock containers all day. Your thrai planned and coordinated the whole operation." I stared at the divider as Lot continued. "Ehtishem said Dathusha and Pohru-Mahrko are leaving orbit, so most of the transports have been retrofitted for personnel transfer. As soon as they unlock the bay, we'll start cycling them down to Earth-based stations again. He redirected some to unmanned stations so the remaining Terran floor crew can escape."

The women rubbed a filthy rag over my face, neck, ears, and hands. Special attention was paid to blackening my marked face and a short-billed knit cap was pulled over my peach-fuzz hair. I rolled the pants and sleeves up. It was one-size-fits-all when it came to laborers' wear.

"Don't push your sleeves up too far or your clean skin will blind us," the short woman said.

Lot poked his head around the corner. "They've unlocked. Let's do this while everything's chaotic."

Head down, I followed him.

Lot's casual pace surprised me. "Look bored," he said as we

climbed into a large battered version of the cars I'd ridden throughout the ship. This one traveled a closed track around the shipping bay, moving people and cargo. I slouched down and closed my eyes.

Lot's elbow in my ribs woke me. "Let's go, sleepy." I stumbled after him.

We'd reached the Butcher Bay where row upon row of massive containers stood open. Lot and I threaded past groups of workers who were pushing towers of folded jump seats into the containers. The towers locked into tracks along the top and bottom of the transports and each folded seat had a harness to hold a passenger in place. The Ohnenrai moved hundreds of personnel in a single container.

Lot grabbed a wrench of sorts from a tool rack and handed it to me as we turned and moved between two containers. He stopped a few feet into the space. "If any soldiers ask, I told you to check all the lock-mech nuts." He pointed to the nut between a group of grease-coated gears.

I stuck the wrench between them. "Right. Look busy."

Lot hesitated. "Rachel, I promised Judith I would find you, help you, and believe in you." He swallowed. "I failed you. I failed Joshua. And I failed my family."

I returned his gaze through fresh tears.

He shook his head. "I hurt you—again and again. Every time that *bastard* touched you and I did nothing. Every time you begged me to believe you and I turned my back." He wiped his sleeve over his face, leaving dirty streaks behind. "And I hurt Pearl. I stood by while you struggled, while you gave up food so she could eat, while you helped and healed everyone else, while Cyrus..." He looked down. "And when you found a protector, a Stranger who believed in you, I tried to drive him away."

"Lot—" Tears dripped onto my filthy coveralls.

"I earned this, but you didn't. I'm sorry." I nodded. He cleared his throat and squeezed my arm. "I'll be back. First launch is in fourteen minutes. You'll be on it." He slipped between the containers and disappeared around the corner, his head down and hands jammed into his pockets.

I left the wrench between the gears and rubbed more tears and snot on my sleeve. "This sucks." Lot had lost everyone he loved, and now I might too. I wanted to be with Pearl *and* Ehtishem, but my idiotic lover was choosing to be selfless. I had to convince him to bring us back to Dathusha or stay with us on Terra. Neither of those would be easy sells. Not to Thrai Ehtishem Mahle, the stupid, stubborn jerk.

Something scraped against metal behind me. I turned and came face-to-face with Cyrus as he crept from the shadows beneath the container. "Going somewhere? Not yet, Rachel. This *bastard's* not through with you." Ragged coveralls hung off his shoulders, stinking and stained.

I stood my ground and bit back knee-jerk fear. "Piss off. You've tortured me enough."

Cyrus's lips pulled back from his teeth. He gestured toward the human workers scuttling in and around the bay. "You did this. You brought them down upon us, you bitch."

"Me? *You* called the Gate Patrol. *You* poisoned them. *You* set them on fire. *Not. Me.*" My gaze flicked to the wrench. But the former Elder still had strength and speed. He bore an evil sneer on his serpent-marked face as he yanked the tool free.

"Cyrus." A booming voice made me jump, but I kept my eyes on my enemy. He jerked around and tossed the wrench beneath the transport as the zosh appeared behind him.

I made a dive for the tool and freedom, scrambling into the shadowy undercarriage on all fours. But the Elder was right behind me, cursing and growling. He caught my cuffed pants. I yanked them away. I didn't know where I was going other than away from him and Isphahan.

With a grunt, Cyrus lunged forward and caught my ankle. I hit the floor, twisted onto my back, kicked out. My heel hit his nose. My pursuer cursed. His grip loosened. But not enough. He dragged me into the open, grabbed the front of my coveralls, and yanked me to my feet.

I pulled away from the Elder's grasp as Isphahan said, "Bring the woman here, vira."

Cyrus's bloodied face twisted into a sickening caricature as he looked from his master to me, but his sneer quickly returned.

"Now, vira."

The lifeless Ohnenrai monotone I hated so much brought me relief this time. Until I realized, *Isphahan knew I was here.* A chill invaded my chest and crept across my scalp.

Cyrus's eyes narrowed. The sneer grew, drew his lips back, and furrowed his brow so deeply the serpent shut its mouth. He pointed at me. "Abomination." Spittle foamed at the corners of his mouth as he howled, a rabid, spiteful animal. "You are the Devil's concubine!"

His words cut through me, but clarity filled their path. "Fuck you!" All the fear, pain, and rejection I'd swallowed because of my tormentor's depravity churned, bubbled, and surfaced. "Your face finally matches your soul, you rotten bastard. And I hope you live a long, miserable life down here."

His sneer went slack. But he recovered in a blink. His experience in mental brutality far outweighed mine, and it showed as he dug a new weapon from his arsenal. His eyes tightened. His lips curved into a leer. "Still, I can't blame the Ohnenran for *fucking* you." He turned the word into the most brutal violation. "I wonder that Joshua left you alone so easily. I told him I would be on you the moment he turned his back. He knew that, even before he claimed you."

"Go to hell. Joshua knew you raped me. And I know you killed him."

"You're so naive, woman." He laughed and wiped blood from his nose. "I bet you think your Stranger *loves* you."

He made "loves" sound even worse than "fucking."

"Vira, you have your orders." Isphahan's words dropped between us like a stone.

Cyrus lunged forward, seized my wrist, and dragged me to the front of the transports. We stopped before Isphahan and his soldiers. The former Elder bared his teeth. "I take orders from no one but God, Ohnenran." He turned his back on the zosh and spat in my face. "Whore."

I gasped. Something in me cracked. The dam holding back all my pain and fear crumbled. I yanked a black metal wrench off the tool rack and slammed it into Cyrus's skull, a hammer striking an anvil. The former Elder staggered two steps and collapsed like a tower. His head smacked the metal plating at my feet. Blood oozed from his broken face and gaping mouth. It mingled with oil and water and dripped between the drainage grates.

I stared at his sprawled, broken body as his still-warm spittle slid down my cheek. I dropped the wrench.

Isphahan sniffed and turned to a group of gawking Terrans. "Throw that trash in one of the transports and dump it back where it came from." Two men picked up the Elder's body and carried it into the nearest livestock container. "You can wait in the Nest, Rachel." The zosh turned and strode away, soldiers and advisors at his heels.

A soldier manacled my wrists, and I stumbled after him.

TWENTY-TWO

THE NEST, an offshoot of Ohnenrai Genetics, was where children were conceived, carried, born, and raised until they were ready for career training. From my point of view, it was where the Ohnenrai went to get their rocks off and, if they had the money, buy a surrogate to make their babies—if they could produce any.

Shit. Fuck. Shit. I paced and twisted my hands together until my scabbed knuckles bled. Time was flying. I'd missed the drop for sure. "Pearl." Would Ehtishem leave her? Would he find Lot? "Lot will take care of her. He *will*." I looked down at my bloody hands. "I've gotta get outta here."

I was locked in a room with a bed, a toilet, and a sink—a cell with sweet-scented sheets and erotic artwork. No windows, only narrow vents and a door that ignored my stabs at its control panel. "Open, damn you."

Then it did. I jumped back and stared as it admitted Ahremena. She got right to the point. "You don't belong here, Rachel. You belong to an Elite—a Mahle." The geneticist looked around. "And I can remove you back to the Elite Level right now."

I glared at her. "Why would you do that? You have me right where you want me."

She shook her head. "I don't want you in the Nest. Your genes are too important to waste on the highest bidder. I designed you for Ehtishem. Your genome complements his."

Complements? "Don't you mean 'corrects'?"

"Both." Her gaze stopped on my bloody knuckles. "I know Pearl's lineage, Rachel. I know Cyrus is her father against your consent. Being here must be terrible. It must bring back such horror. You don't need to feel that. You are important to my son. Let me help you."

I knew she was playing all my cards, but the tremors and memories still returned. I clung to the thought of Pearl and found some strength. "What do you want, Ahremena? You aren't here out of pity. Ehtishem and I are nothing more than buckets of genetic stew to you. Stop insulting my intelligence."

Her face, hard and beautiful as a diamond, somehow hardened even more. She nodded. "Good. I will protect you and your child if you agree to influence my son according to my wishes."

"What makes you think I can?"

"Now you're insulting me."

I studied her. *Why does she need to buy my influence? She has Ehtishem's DNA, and mine... Or not.* "You're threatened by Zosh Uahdim too."

She blinked and her mouth twitched—a crack in her veneer, quickly repaired. Her voice certainly didn't betray weakness. "You are even more capable than I imagined. Some of my finest work." She held my gaze, reassessing. "I struggled long and hard to create you and Ehtishem, and Cyrus. Two out of three is an excellent success rate considering the challenges I faced."

I clenched my fists. She'd known Cyrus was psychotic and had left me with him anyway.

"But I cannot stop my brother without Ehtishem's military influence. The thrai is the only one capable of prying control from Isphahan. The Ohnenrai military and populace will side with Ehtishem, but I need you to solidify my power over him."

"Why should I help you? You left me in Suffer with Cyrus, knowing he was nuts."

"Unless Ehtishem stops him, Isphahan will destroy every record, every gene, every molecule of my work. No one will survive, Rachel, not even the Ohnenrai." She turned away. "He already holds the records of all Ohnenrai offspring born from Ehtishem's DNA. They will be destroyed."

"The records?"

"The offspring."

I stared at her. I knew Isphahan wanted the Terrans dead, but I couldn't believe he'd kill his own populace too. "The citizens won't allow it. Find better lies than that, Ahremena."

"The people have no say. It's been ordered and the executioners are moving through the ship as we speak. It will be done quickly and quietly before we break orbit. My brother holds the military. The military holds the people. Freedom for the Ohnenrai is illusory as long as we're trapped aboard this ship." Now she turned. "I know you don't trust me. It's logical not to. But you, your child, and Ehtishem top Isphahan's list."

The purge list. All the soldiers in the bays. I crossed my arms. "Where do you fall on that list?"

"Where indeed?"

I jumped at the voice. Isphahan's massive frame blocked the hall light, plunging us into darkness but not before I saw Ahremena stiffen.

"Sarem Mahlei, my guard will escort you to your quarters," he said.

For once I admired Ahremena's self-control as she strode past her brother and into house arrest, her chin lifted and her eyes cold.

The zosh stepped into the room and clamped his hand around my wrist. "Come along, vira. There's something you must see." He jerked me through the doorway.

I had to run to keep up as he strode the halls. Soldiers and civilians scattered from his path. "I knew Ehtishem wouldn't leave your child behind. He's welcome to her and met little opposition when he fetched her from Pohru-Mahrko. But you were delayed, and he couldn't wait for your arrival before departing for Terra. Too bad," he glanced at me, "for all of you."

His tight grip made my hand tingle. I stumbled, but Isphahan's stride didn't slow. He shoved me into a waiting elevator, planted his hand against the back of my neck, and pinned me against the wall. "I should thank Ehtishem for removing the Terrans from this ship. That was a bonus. The second favor he's done for me."

"Gatu, vana," the elevator asked.

Isphahan leaned close. "It's laughable that he thought I wouldn't notice his maneuvering. Twelve years among your people made him weak." He loomed over me. "His care for your child makes him vulnerable. And I'm more than willing to exploit that weakness, Terran."

"Gatu, vana."

One of the soldiers asked, "Fra?"

He replied, "Pohru-Mahrko."

My head cracked against the view port and I bit my tongue as the zosh threw me into the transport's seat. I tasted blood. "Strap her in," he snapped in Ohnenrai at the four soldiers barring my escape. One of the men obeyed. He didn't meet my gaze, but his hands were gentle.

The zosh glared down at me. "This time, Rachel Pryne, I'll wipe out every last bit of dirty DNA in one glorious blaze, and send the thrai to his grave with your people. *Finally*." He pivoted, dropped into the ship's cockpit, and slipped into the pilot's seat.

Oh, hell no. "Please." I looked from face to emotionless face as the soldier straightened and stepped back in line with his comrades. All four men exchanged glances but avoided my gaze. "Don't let the zosh kill your thrai. Your people need him." I didn't know if they'd heard me over the whine of the transport's firing engines.

"Dathusha Command, give me immediate clearance. Put me through to Pohru-Mahrko." Isphahan's hands moved across the controls tapping screens and hitting buttons, engaging this and damping that. The engines whined higher as the transport lifted and shifted from its docking bay, cleared the entrance, and cut in and around slower ships. Isphahan didn't wait for the lights to strobe purple.

"You're clear, Zosh. Pohru-Mahrko Command, go ahead."

"This is Pohru-Mahrko Command, Zosh. What are your orders, fra?"

"I'm launching for Pohru-Mahrko. I want evac complete by hour fourteen. We drop full orbital bombardment at hour twenty. Inform Dathusha to break orbit by hour twenty-two. I want a wormhole open by hour twenty-three and a course plotted to the Kevrian System. Uahdim Primary out."

"Zant, fra. Pohru-Mahrko Command out."

Full orbital bombardment. "No. No, Isphahan, please! You can't do this!"

He turned and looked up from the cockpit, his expression colder than space. "Yes, I can. In twenty-two hours your planet and everything on it will be dust. You have the privilege of watching. It's spectacular."

"Please! Stop, please." I choked on a lump in my throat.

The ship settled into the arms of a guide and Isphahan climbed from the cockpit. He shoved the soldiers aside and leaned over me, his face so emotionless it looked plastic. I didn't see his hand, but his slap whipped my head to the right. "Stop sniveling."

Blood slid down my throat. I gagged, shook my head, and drew a ragged breath. His strike had cleared horror from my mind and rage had rushed in to fill the opening. Isphahan still leaned over me. I lifted my chin and spat blood in his face.

The soldiers stepped between us.

He caught my bloody spittle as it dripped from his chin then flicked it back in my face. "So there *is* some truth behind your rumored steel spine, woman." He took a cloth from one of the soldiers, wiped his face, and tossed the rag in my lap. "After I'm done with your planet, maybe I'll see what kind of sport you offer."

"I've had better and worse, you bastard."

Isphahan ignored the signal beeping incessantly from the cockpit. "Good sport, indeed. I finally see what Ehtishem finds so attractive."

The sound of his name brought Ehtishem's face and Pearl's to mind. I saw red. "I welcome the chance to cut off your balls, old man. You won't be the first man I've killed."

He turned to answer the guide ship's hail.

Artificial gravity pulled my body down as the airlock doors thudded overhead. An alarm sounded, lights strobed, the ship slipped from Dathusha's belly to float in nothingness. She gently rotated away. Then my body pressed back into the seat as the transport twisted down and shot toward Pohru-Mahrko. My stomach and my hope threatened to stay behind.

If Dathusha was a sleek beauty, Pohru-Mahrko was a blunt and brutal monster. The warship's exterior bristled cannons and weaponry. Her interior was cramped, gray, and sprouted conduits and equipment from every surface.

Isphahan dragged me through her docking bay, into a transport, and threw me at a seat. "I don't want you to miss this, Terran. Time to get rid of my nephew and that dirt clod you call a planet. Two birds with a few big stones." I took the impact with my side and shrank away from his clenched fists. Two soldiers faced me, guns drawn, as their zosh barked orders at the driver.

I hated to think of Pearl following the zosh in this cold, violent environment, so I pushed thoughts of her and Ehtishem away. I didn't have time for worry or pity. I had to stop Isphahan.

"Loyalty means a lot to the Ohnenrai military, Rachel." Ehtishem's words were my only weapon. I looked up at the soldiers. "Thrai Mahle trusts you. Zosh Uahdim murdered the last zosh. Are you going to let him assassinate your thrai too?"

Both men glanced at me. It wasn't much response, but for an Ohnenrai soldier it was a lot, hopefully enough. I chewed my lower lip and said no more. I couldn't push. I couldn't beg. I could only hope I'd touched a nerve.

The transport stopped and the doors opened to a bustling platform. Isphahan manacled my arm. My head snapped back as he jerked me from the seat. He strode past all manner of military personnel. I stumbled along behind him. He ignored their salutes and slapped the lift plate so hard it cracked. The doors opened. He shoved me ahead of him and his guard followed. He faced the internal lift pad. "Command Deck, no stops." He smacked his hand on the surface.

Its red glow flashed green, and then turned a steady purple. "Command Deck. No stops.W elcome back, Zosh Uahdim."

My knees went wobbly as the lift shot up but Isphahan didn't let go of me. The lift slowed, bumped to a stop, and the doors opened onto the Command Deck. A soldier snapped to attention. "Zosh Uahdim on deck," he announced as Isphahan's guard stepped through the doors and we followed.

The zosh shoved me at one of his soldiers. "Make sure she stays put." He turned and took two steps down to a second tier where men and women sat at banks of controls.

"Good of you to bring Rachel, Isphahan. Thank you."

My head jerked up. I lunged forward, but the soldier caught my arm. "Stay here." He spoke for my ears only.

Isphahan eased around to face his nephew. "Well, you surprise me again, Ehtishem." He tapped a seated officer and said, "Open a dual ship-wide channel."

The man nodded and tapped the display before him. "Open, fra. Both ships are receiving."

Ehtishem stood one tier below his uncle. Pearl was beside him. He touched her shoulder and gestured for her to move away. "I'm sure finding I'd survived your assassination attempt was a rude surprise, Dvai. And now I'm here instead of on Terra, so there's no need to destroy the planet. That must be disappointing." Pearl retreated another level and put a control bank between herself and Isphahan.

I blinked back tears. Pearl and Ehtishem were with me, but none of us were safe.

Isphahan clasped his hands behind his back and angled his body away from Ehtishem. "Not as disappointing as discovering your attempted mutiny, Thrai. I hate to think badly of you, but the evidence is clear."

Ehtishem stepped toward Isphahan. "That's a sticky point,

Zosh." He picked up a reader. "I never relinquished strategic military control, and since I'm not dead, asserting my authority isn't mutiny."

"You deserted your post, soldier."

Ehtishem tapped the screen. "I beg to differ. And so do Dasa Borv and Dasa Nahnesh."

A seamless bank of windows turned opaque and became a massive screen that wrapped around the front of the bridge. Moving images flickered and appeared on it. Shadowy faces in green, grainy light showed that the recorder was set for night vision. The soldiers leaned close to the lens and kept their voices low.

"I'm Dasa Borv."

"I'm Dasa Nahnesh. We're filing this record because we'll be dead in a few hours, whether for treason or knowing too much, I'm not sure."

I squinted. The woman, Dasa Nahnesh, looked familiar.

"Hopefully this will be useful," Borv said. "Thrai Ehtishem Mahle isn't dead. We had execution orders directly from Dvai Isphahan Uahdim. But we're loyal soldiers, not assassins."

Silence filled the bridge.

"And we're not traitors," Nahnesh added. "We faked his death and dropped Thrai Mahle on Terra in the Northern Pacific Sector U.S."

"This R.O.O. was filed Terran date 05.18.2020. The thrai knows all of this. And he knows the dvai targeted Zosh Zainabahn Mahle too."

"We don't know how or when this will help. But—" Dasa Nahnesh looked away from the recorder. The image went black.

"I'll testify to the truth of that video and those statements." Everyone turned to see Dasa Nahnesh step through a door at the edge of the Command Deck. I recognized her, finally, as the woman who'd followed and questioned me in the Ohnenrai entertainment district; the woman who'd said I seemed lost.

"You'd better," the zosh said. "Recordings are weak evidence."

"But orders with your signature are not, Isphahan." Ahremena appeared beside Dasa Nahnesh accompanied by the soldier Isphahan had assigned to arrest her. She nodded at Ehtishem and he tapped his reader again.

This time an official order appeared on the screen. "I'll save everyone the trouble of quick reading," Ahremena said. "That directive was filed last night. It identifies all the recipients of Ehtishem's DNA and orders their immediate execution." Sure enough a list of names, identification numbers, and faces appeared on the screen as Ehtishem scrolled down. Isphahan's signature and authorization code graced the bottom of the notice. Ahremena continued, "If you're wondering why your zosh did this, the answer lies with my department. He is a Purist and Ohnenrai Genetics has introduced Terran DNA into our genome."

Isphahan glared at his sister. He turned to the communications officer. "Cut that channel, soldier. That's an order."

"It's the only source for a complete, functional Azatem Code." She looked at me. "If the Terrans—Rachel Pryne and her daughter—are killed, we will have lost that solution. Their DNA holds the key to Ohnenrai survival."

Isphahan turned to his guard. "Arrest Thrai Mahle, Sarem Mahlei, that Terran woman, and Dasa Nahnesh on the grounds of treason." Some of the soldiers glanced at each other. Some of them shifted in their seats. Most ignored him.

Ehtishem put down the reader and took another step toward his uncle. Two stairs and a twelve-foot platform separated the men. Isphahan's gaze settled on me. Ehtishem lunged as his uncle charged me. He dove at the zosh, captured his hips, twisted, and threw his uncle down the stairs. But Isphahan held onto Ehtishem and both men tumbled to the first platform.

Suddenly soldiers were tripping over each other to reach them. Ehtishem and Isphahan were on their feet and combat-ready in a blink. Guns drawn, the soldiers surrounded Isphahan and chorused, "Drop your weapon."

There was a knife in his hand. Blue blood slicked the blade. He opened his fingers and the weapon tumbled to the floor.

"Varet," Ehtishem ordered. A stain appeared beneath the thrai's open jacket, a wound below his left heart. "I signed an order of my own today and received Council approval. You're marked for death, Isphahan Uahdim, for the assassination of Zosh Mahle and the attempt on my life. I claim my right to carry out that sentence."

Isphahan bared his teeth. "Fine. How do you want to take me, nephew?"

"Here. Now." Ehtishem stripped off his jacket. "Timsai?" The stain grew.

"Thrai?"

"You're my second. If anything happens to me you have command until the Vote of Authority determines leadership."

"I understand, fra."

I knew Ehtishem's capabilities. I didn't know his injury. A hand slipped into mine and I looked down. Pearl.

"Don't worry, Momma. Ehtishem will win."

The men circled and tested. They landed kicks, deflected blows. Each sought an opening but found nothing.

Ehtishem bloodied Isphahan's nose with a kick. His uncle shrugged off the blow and caught Ehtishem with a kidney punch. My Stranger doubled over, ducked a blow, and another one. His head at Isphahan's waist, he launched forward, slamming his skull into his uncle's stomach and propelling the older man into a console.

But Isphahan twisted away and hammered Ehtishem's bloodied

side. The thrai dropped his left arm and hip, brought his right arm around, and hooked his fist into his uncle's face, again and again and again.

Isphahan ducked the next blow and lunged low to catch Ehtishem's legs. But the thrai countered, dropping his hips. His legs went out behind him, and he drove his body down atop Isphahan. Both men hit the floor. Ehtishem's arms wrapped beneath his uncle's armpits and locked behind the man's back. In one powerful move, Ehtishem pulled up his knees, twisted Isphahan to his back, and rolled his own torso over his opponent's skull. The force and weight torqued the zosh's neck to an unnatural angle.

Isphahan grunted. There was a *crack* and he lay still.

For a moment, the only sound on the Command Deck was Ehtishem's labored, bubbling breath. We all jerked as a shrill klaxon sounded and the lights turned amber.

"We have wormhole formation, fra."

Ehtishem raised his head. "Ours?"

"No, fra."

Every Ohnenran on the deck exhaled and the hair on my arms rose.

Ehtishem straightened and two soldiers helped him stand. "Time?" He coughed and someone handed him a cloth to wipe away the blood. His lips were already grey.

"Fifteen, fra."

I whirled to the soldier behind me. "Get me a medical kit."

He blinked. "Barethri Rachel?"

"A medical kit. For emergencies. There must be one on the bridge. Get it." Whether it was my tone or his thrai's condition, I didn't know, but the man nodded and crossed the deck.

Ehtishem relayed orders. "Hail Dathusha." He dragged in a rasping breath. "Launch the paradox lock and all sling ships." Another bubbling inhalation. "Confirm coordinates for that hole as soon as you can." He coughed and leaned on the soldiers who helped him to the command seat.

The soldier returned with a kit.

"C'mon." I pulled Pearl with me as I strode across the deck to Ehtishem. But before we reached him, another soldier blocked our path.

"Step back," he said.

Ehtishem gave orders to Dathusha's captain who was now on screen. "We jump when that ship emerges, Ahnoru."

My chin jerked up. "No, you step back. He needs my help."

The soldier glanced at the medical kit. "A med team has been summoned. You're not needed." He grabbed my arm.

Pearl stepped forward. "Let go of my mom, you big jerk."

"Thrai?" Fravaz Ahnoru asked.

"There's no time to open our own exit, Fravaz. We'll use what they give us."

I pulled at the soldier's grip. "I can have a chest tube in and the thrai breathing before your team hits the lift. Now *move*."

"But, fra, that's never been done." The captain's voice tightened.

"No, ma'am," the soldier replied.

Ehtishem glanced away from the screen. "Perets, they're right, you're being a big jerk. Let them help." His breaths came faster, tighter, shallower. He returned to Ahnoru. "Dathusha first. Pohru-Mahrko follows blazing. You better move that fat can, Fravaz." He cut the signal and closed his eyes.

Perets stepped aside.

I reached Ehtishem and pulled up his shirt. "This won't be gentle." He nodded. His chest rose and fell quickly. Blood bubbled from the wound with each labored breath. "Hemothorax, Pearl. See the blood? That means leakage into the pleural space. Thread a needle. We need to relieve the pressure so the lung can reinflate." She handed me an antiseptic cloth. I wiped my hands then reached past her for gauze and cleaned around the wound. "I need a tube and scissors."

"We have surge, fra."

Ehtishem opened his eyes. "Are those slings in place?"

"Last one is locking now, fra."

I lifted his left arm and bent it to rest behind his head. "Keep it there."

He nodded. "Where's the lock?"

"Dathusha reports full ready, Thrai."

"Lock is away, fra."

"Good." He panted between words now. "Zavin, do you... have...Dathusha?"

"Yes, fra. Fravaz Ahnoru just released the con. We're tethered and engaged."

I took the tube from Pearl and spread the wound, but Ehtishem inhaled to respond then coughed. I held the gauze to the wound as each cough gushed blood through the hole in his chest.

He wiped his mouth, finally caught some breath, and continued. "Pilot Lormei, right?"

"Yes, Thrai," an officer answered without turning from her controls.

"Full up and on my mark, Pi-*lot*." The last word pitched up as I pushed my finger into the wound to feel for obstructions. Ehtishem looked down at me. "That. Hurt."

I met his gaze. "Sorry. It's about to get worse." I held my hand out to Pearl. "Needle."

His jaw popped as he shifted it. "Do it now so I can focus."

I ran a single stitch through the top of the wound then pushed the tube into the space between his lung and chest wall. I stitched the wound down to the tube, tied it off, and used the remaining thread to secure the tube. Ehtishem didn't flinch this time, though the chair arm creaked under his grip. "Inhale." He did. The tube misted. Blue blood trickled into the container Pearl had connected to the end. Ehtishem inhaled deeper.

"Better?"

"Zant." He turned to the crew. "Weapons status, Ohmet?"

"Full up, fra, and ready to blaze."

"Wormhole parameters locked, Thrai."

Ehtishem's voice sounded stronger as he said, "Zavin, Lormei, move us up. Sling?"

"Full power, Thrai. Awaiting your mark."

The lifts opened and two med techs stepped onto the bridge.

"Good. Lock?"

"On the nose and tail, fra."

"We have breach, Thrai. On screen."

All eyes turned to the screen where Dathusha maneuvered ahead of Pohru-Mahrko. A small, orange, bullet-shaped ship moved just ahead of the civilian ship. A wide umbrella-shaped grate jutted from the tip of its nose. Then stars and space warped and the leading edge of a monstrous red ship appeared seemingly from nowhere.

I slowly stood.

The behemoth birthed from nothing. And it made massive Dathusha look like a toy. Pearl slipped her hand into mine.

Ehtishem relayed orders, his voice stronger still. "Fire the slings, please. Send in the lock. Zavin, move Dathusha on its tail. Lormei, cuddle up right behind her. Ohmet, shields please and open fire once Dathusha clears the horizon."

A chorus of "Zant, fra" followed his orders even as a brilliant white glow enveloped the mothership we followed. The small orange lead ship blinked out of existence. Next, Dathusha disappeared nose-first as she passed the incoming leviathan.

The moment Dathusha winked out of sight, Pohru-Mahrko unleashed a volley of hellfire, strangely silenced by space and the ship's thick hull. Then the screen flashed bright white, warped, and went blank.

My brain felt like jelly. I clutched the command chair and looked at the floor. *Are we dead?* I shook my head. Then Ehtishem took my hand, and I knew I was still alive.

"What will happen to Earth, Ehtishem?" Pearl's small voice broke the silence.

"They destroy what we create," he answered.

"But all those people." I stared at him. "We can't abandon them."

"We aren't. But we can't face the Azatem without a plan." He returned my gaze. "And we finally have an effective weapon."

Strike when you need to. I clutched his hand. "Me."

"Do you still trust me, Rachel?"

I nodded and pulled Pearl against me. "I do."

GLOSSARY

A brief guide to Ohnenrai pronunciation:

a: (ä) soft as in about, abbreviate, baklava
e: (e) soft and flat as in friend, hen, pent
i: (ē) long "e" as in magazine, figurine, chlorine
o: (ō) long "o" as in mold, open, poke
u: (oo) long "u" as in immune, use, tune
ae: (äe) soft "a" + "eh"
dh: (TH) "d" + hard "th"
sh: (SH) soft "sh" as in sheet, shine, wash
th: (TH) soft "th" as in three, with, thank
x: (aks) hard as in exit, x-ray, ax
y: (y) soft as in yam, yellow, yo-yo

adha: now; so
adhem: to begin; to start; to go
aeva: one
aevadasa: First Lieutenant Commander; ten thousand; a commander of ten sets of ten thousand soldiers

ahn: the

ahzish: snake; serpent; winged Ohnenrai serpent

aiwiyo: water

aiya: an exclamation of annoyance, pain, or surprise

ajam: to come; to follow

amat: us; we

antara: in; within; inside

apa: off; leave off; get off

Aruva Pantam: Military Corridor (restricted to all but the highest-level personnel)

asanghem: orders; instructions

ashaishtem: to feel grief; to be sorry; to regret; regret; grief; sorrow

asmanaca: stone

astasca: the body

aste: to rest; to stay; to continue; to persist

astu: to mean; to define; definition; message

at: and; but; then

avare: thousand

axtica: danger

Azatem: unborn

Barathrishma: womb; The Womb; a park in the center of Dathusha

Barethri: mother; an honorific title reserved for a woman who has conceived naturally and given birth to a living child)

Bisham: to repeat

cathru-cashmem: four-eyed dog (a dog who sees in all directions)

dam: wisdom; stupidity

dasa: ten; a commander of ten sets of one hundred soldiers

Dathusha: genesis; creation

dosh: ten; a commander of ten sets of ten soldiers

Draxtu Mainyu: The Great Hunter (spirit warrior in the form of a white dog)

druj: lies; liar

dva: two

Dvai: Second in command of the Ohnenrai Military and primary commander of the Civilian Defensive Forces, responsible for all civilian defensive and legal matters

erenavi: to grant; to permit; to allow

eti: to come; to arrive

ferahi-va: thank you

fra (fratemo): sir

framru: to speak; to say; to state; speech; language

frayan: to move; move (a command)

Fravaz: captain

frei (Freitamo): ma'am; miss

frena: because; as a result; to cause

gatu: route; way; destination; place

gered: to try; to attempt

ghinvat: an ancient Ohnenrai game played with stones

hantaoj: receiver; person you're calling or speaking with hei: she

hu: a pig-like Ohnenrai animal

idha: now

izhagatu: The Nest (a breeding center aboard Dathusha) jahika: prostitute; slut

jaidhyantai: to need; to want; to request

ka: what

kanikar: to be welcome; to welcome

kar: to do

karana: to end; to stop; to cease; closure

maibyo: my; mine

Maidhya Terasca: Central Cross

meh: me

mem: I

nama: name

namana: home; house

namanyu: guardian; protector

nava: no

nerem: man

nishidet: to sit; to relax

nitemem: cowardly

nyancyo: one who throws down; a destroyer; someone who is dangerously uncontrolled

pa: creates the plural form (Ex: pa'nerem)

Pairika: shooting star; sorceress

paiti: to move; to throw

pa'nerem: men; gentlemen

Pohru-Mahrko: apocalypse

rashnu: justice

ratheshto: soldier; warrior (male or female)

Ratheshtolo: little warrior

sadayeiti: to leave; to depart; to move away from; to give privacy

Sarem: Councilor

spenta-vohyatem: compassion; empathy

sraeshta: fairest; finest; most beautiful

Stoaca Varefshar: Butcher Bay (where slaughtered animals are offloaded, butchered, and prepared for distribution throughout Dathusha)

suxra: A red tea-like beverage with strong stimulant effects tahkaesha: trainer; teacher

tanu: personal; sin; error; mistake

terasca: exit; cross

thrai: Third in command of the Ohnenrai Military and Civilian Defensive Forces, primary commander responsible for all military personnel, activities, and strategy

thrish: three

utha: an expletive; the effluent that leaks from a rotting corpse (Considered very offensive) va: you

vairim: self-control; emotional control

vana: please

vangudha: discretion; care

vanvuisha: conqueror; controller

varet: enough; stop

vayem: we

vira: servant; slave; property

vis: okay; acceptable

visdi: to see; to look

zant: yes

Zosh: Supreme Command General of the Ohnenrai Military and Civilian Defensive Forces

OHNENRAI PHRASES

Ferahi-va. *Thank you.*

Kar-va jaidhyantai aiwiyo? *Do you need water?*

Va kanikar. *You're welcome.*

Mem anagava iristahe. *I'm getting nothing.*

Frena manaya-hei framru-hei ahn eresh. *Because she believes she speaks the truth.*

Va'gaoshrutavan. *Your compad.*

Ushta visdi-va. *Good to see you.*

Anghu framarez pantham, vana. *Clear a path, please.*

Marez'aste, pa'ratheshto. *Ready-rest, soldiers.*

Mem kanikar-va, fra. *Welcome back, sir.*

Ka fradat visdi-va. *What a relief to see you.*

Framru-va nama, vana. *State your name, please.* Nama nava vaeda. *Name not recognized.*

Vaxsh huxta vist. Ahngano vayaxanem vist. Zasta, vana. *Voice accepted. Face accepted. Palm, please.*

Kanikar namana. *Welcome home.*

Sarem Ahremena Uahdimei Mahlei hei jaidhyantai vis. *Councilor Ahremena Uahdimei Mahlei requests entry.*

Mem erenavi vis. *Entry granted.*

Ka kar Ratheshtolo astu? *What does Ratheshtolo mean?*

Mem ashaishtem. *I apologize.*

Gatu, vana. *Destination, please.*

Anghu framarez pantham. Idha. *Clear a path. Now.*

Ma'zaste. *Don't touch.*

Vana framru va hantaoj. *Please name your receiver.*

Mem ashaishtem, nama nava vaeda. *I apologize, name not recognized.*

Va upaman, vana. *Wait, please.*

Mem visdi-va. *Let me see.*

Va nishidet. *Sit.*

Frena va'ngho dam asmanaca. *Because you're stupid as stone.*

Va'jam. *Come.*

Aeva, aev'avare. Dva, aev'avare. Thrish, aev'avare. *One-one thousand. Two-one thousand. Three-one thousand.*

Mareza daitim vaedhem. Vayem nisirinu hayem at fratem daxshtem adha. *Prepare the property records. We'll submit them and make the mark today.*

Mem gered. *I'm trying.*

Sadayeiti amat. *Leave us.*

ALSO BY MONICA ENDERLE PIERCE

Glass and Iron Novels & Stories

Girl Under Glass

The Mother Element

A Sad Jar of Atoms (short)

Rust and Ruin (short)

Militess & Mage Novels & Stories

The Shadow & The Sun

A Castle to Keep

The Bones Beneath (coming in 2019)

To Give Her Heart (short)

The Apocalyptics Series

Famine

Anthologies & Collections

The Dragon Chronicles

Prep For Doom

The Doomsday Chronicles

Once Upon a Time in Gravity City

ABOUT THE AUTHOR

Best-selling author Monica Enderle Pierce and her characters have been kicking the crap out of evil since 2012. She writes epic romantic fantasy and romantic science fiction. Her stories are filled with strong women, smart men, love, adventure, and magic. She has an English literature degree from the University of California, Los Angeles, and she lives in Seattle, Washington, with her husband, their daughter, a neurotic dog, and two crazy tomcats. When she's not sending characters into bed or battle, she's reading minds, seeing through walls, and reveling in the glorious Pacific Northwest rain.

How to reach me:
monicaenderlepierce.com
monicaenderlepierce@gmail.com